TERRIFYING TRANSFORMATIONS

TERRIFYING TRANSFORMATIONS

AN ANTHOLOGY OF VICTORIAN WEREWOLF FICTION,
1838-1896

EDITED AND INTRODUCED BY

Alexis Easley and Shannon Scott

Kansas City:
VALANCOURT BOOKS
2013

Terrifying Transformations
First edition published 2013

ISBN 978-1-934555-80-4

Design and typography by James D. Jenkins
Set in Dante MT

Published by Valancourt Books
Kansas City, Missouri
http://www.valancourtbooks.com

Contents

Introduction

THE werewolf is a creature of transformation. The metamorphosis from human to wolf is an ancient motif that occurs in myth and folktale throughout the world, wherever wolves have existed. The werewolf appears in the *Epic of Gilgamesh*, the *Volsung Saga*, and Ovid's *Metamorphosis*. A popular figure in British and French literature of the Middle Ages, the werewolf became nearly extinct in the literature of the seventeenth and eighteenth centuries. Attempting to explain the werewolf's absence from writing during this period, W. M. S. Russell and Claire Russell claim that the "Age of Reason" had "no use for werewolves in fact or fiction."[1] During the nineteenth century, however, werewolves made a dramatic resurgence, inspiring writers as diverse as Rudyard Kipling, Arthur Conan Doyle, and Bram Stoker to create a distinctly Victorian monster.

The reappearance of the werewolf as a literary figure during the Victorian era corresponded with popular interest in British and European folklore. Jacob and Wilhelm Grimm's *Children's and Household Tales* (1812) was republished and revised throughout the Victorian era, as was *Aesop's Fables*. Increased interest in folklore led to investigations of the werewolf in fable, legend, and medieval history, including Sabine Baring-Gould's influential study, *The Book of Were-wolves* (1865). In this work, Baring-Gould used the superstitions of the past to highlight the enlightened rationality of the present and offered scientific explanations for supernatural phenomena. Yet readers were most likely drawn to the book for its research on folktales and historical cases of lycanthropy. Indeed, it was used as a source text for many authors of werewolf fiction later in the century. The popularity of antiquarian studies such as *The Book of Were-wolves* in part explains why so many Victorian werewolf stories are set during the medieval period or in the mythical past, the "once upon a time" associated with folk traditions.

---

1 Russell and Russell, "The Social Biology of Werewolves," 145.

The Victorian werewolf story was also informed by the birth of a distinctly literary form—the gothic novel—which became a major genre beginning in the late eighteenth century. Gothic novelists such as Horace Walpole and Matthew Lewis crafted tales of mystery and suspense that incorporated monstrous anti-heroes, supernatural plot elements, and medieval settings. While some gothic novels, such as Ann Radcliffe's, concluded by offering rational explanations for supernatural phenomena, they nevertheless had the effect of shocking and enthralling readers. By the mid-Victorian era, the gothic genre was immensely popular, in part due to the expansion of print culture. "In the middle class," Richard Altick notes, "the reading circle was the most familiar and beloved of domestic institutions; and as cheap printed matter became more accessible, hardly a family in Britain was without its little shelf of books and its sheaf of current periodicals, whether church papers or the latest hair-raising episodes."[1] As the number of cheap magazines and serials proliferated, so did the number of gothic short stories and serialized novels. Tales of terror were particularly popular during the Christmas season, when middle-class Victorian families gathered around the hearth and read the latest gothic stories produced by their favorite writers. As the century progressed, these stories were increasingly set in contemporary Britain or its colonies. This further heightened the terror of gothic fiction because it collapsed the distance between the world of fiction and the business of everyday life.

During the Victorian era, the werewolf story, like other gothic genres, was viewed as a form of escapist entertainment. Beginning in the 1820s and '30s, gothic stories were widely available to all classes of society. As Richard Altick points out, penny novels and cheap serials provided an imaginative outlet for working-class readers, "transporting them from their dingy world into the dungeons of sinister castles hidden in German forests, or convents where nuns found recreation in flogging screaming novices."[2] One of the most significant authors of gothic fiction at mid-century was G. W. M. Reynolds, who wrote many lurid serials, including *Wagner, the*

---

1 Altick, *The English Common Reader*, 5.
2 *Ibid.*, 289.

Wehr-Wolf (1846-47). As Louis James has shown, these serials made Reynolds "the most popular writer of his time" whose "readership was probably wider even than that of Dickens."[1] Reynolds wrote content he knew would appeal to a working-class audience, but some critics considered his work pornographic and inflammatory. According to Troy Boone, there was a fear that "readers would imitate their criminal heroes [. . .] whose transgressions enact a fantasy of working-class economic mobility born of criminality."[2]

In response to this concern, many middle-class writers used gothic motifs as a vehicle for imparting bourgeois morality. For example, during the 1880s and '90s, when working-class demonstrations shook London and Manchester, the werewolf became a device for denouncing political unrest. An 1893 cartoon from *Punch*, "The Were-wolf of Anarchy," illustrates how the figure of the werewolf could be used to symbolize middle-class fear of social and political anarchy. Contrary to Victorian popular belief, anarchists in Britain were largely peaceful and focused their energies on promoting individualism and a de-centralized, non-hierarchal social order. Nevertheless, because some anarchists argued for the dissolution of parliament and anarchism was associated with violence on the Continent, the movement prompted a great deal of social anxiety at the fin de siècle. The werewolf was an ideal symbol for embodying this perceived danger to social stability.

The werewolf was a crucial figure in the history of Victorian fiction because it embodied cultural anxieties about social change. During the Victorian era (1837-1901), London quadrupled in size, the British Empire grew to cover one quarter of the earth's surface, and Great Britain became the world's leading industrialized nation. Along with this growth came pressure for increased democratization, as women, religious minorities, the working classes, and subjects of Empire agitated for political representation and social equity. This agitation had the effect of calling into question basic assumptions about the nature of the self. As Chantal Du Coudray has shown, the werewolf was a hybrid creature that embodied "anxieties about working-class degeneracy, aristocratic

---

1 James, "The View from Brick Lane," 95.

2 Boone, *Youth of Darkest England*, 59.

"The Were-wolf of Anarchy," *Punch* 105 (December 23, 1893): 290.

decadence, racial atavism, women's corporeality and sexuality, and the human relationship to the animal world."[1] Conceptions of Englishness, which had long been associated with white male privilege, were challenged by new social identities that were simultaneously threatening and full of exciting possibility.

As a hybrid creature—part human, part wolf—the werewolf embodied cultural anxieties about Darwinist notions of human evolution and biological degeneration. After publication of Charles Darwin's *The Origin of Species* (1859) and *The Descent of Man* (1871) gothic writers became interested in humankind's relation to other animal species, ancestrally and biologically. While the concepts of evolution and natural selection seemed to reinforce Victorian belief in the progress of man, they also suggested humankind's degenerative possibilities. If humans could evolve, might they not devolve as well? By the end of the century, theories of degeneration abounded, and the werewolf became a useful device for expressing anxieties about the "animal within," the atavistic double self that had the potential to destroy British civilization from the inside out. Meanwhile, fears about miscegenation, women's liberation, and reverse colonization inspired new literary "monsters," whose transgressive sexuality and "perverse" methods of reproduction must be kept in check by vigilant male heroes.

At the end of the Victorian era, werewolf stories were primarily focused on defining notions of British national identity. Stories such as Bram Stoker's "Dracula's Guest" depict the misadventures of Englishmen abroad who define their own moral virtuousness in reaction to non-British others. Werewolf fiction of the fin de siècle expresses Victorian xenophobia regarding European foreigners and the racist ideology associated with British imperialism. The werewolf is depicted as an uncivilized "savage" who morally and physically threatens Britons who stray outside British national boundaries. Werewolf stories also express the fear that those who set out to civilize colonial others might "go native," giving up their British allegiances along with their human civility. In Rudyard Kipling's short story, "The Mark of the Beast," the threat against British identity reveals itself not only through foreign contamination and

---

1 Du Coudray, *The Curse of the Werewolf*, 50.

contagion (lycanthropy and leprosy) but also through the *supernatural* consequences of contact with the colonized other. Instead of contracting leprosy after he is bitten, the antagonist devolves into a werewolf, a degeneration that reflects broader Victorian anxieties about the threat of foreign contamination. Although all three Englishmen in Kipling's imperialist romance survive their contact with the colonized other, they do not emerge as the Englishmen they formerly thought themselves to be.

The figure of the werewolf was not only used as a symbol of dangerous foreign otherness but also treachery emanating from within British national boundaries. As Judith Halberstam has pointed out, the xenophobic attitudes associated with gothic texts are often focused on the "monsters at home," those who are British citizens but are nevertheless the "anti-thesis of 'Englishness'" and "symbols of a diseased culture."[1] At the end of the Victorian era, one of these "monsters at home" was the emancipated woman. While the women's movement as an organized effort was well underway beginning in the 1850s, it was not until the 1890s that the "New Woman" emerged as an icon of feminist identity in British literature and culture. The term "New Woman," coined by Sarah Grand in "The New Aspect of the Woman Question" (1894), captures the desire of first-wave feminists for significant social and political change. Women achieved key legal advances during the late-Victorian era, including the Married Women's Property Acts (1870-1908), which gave women the right to own and manage their own property. Even though women did not receive the vote until 1918, they made considerable inroads in education, employment, and divorce rights throughout the Victorian period. Sarah Grand claimed that women of the future—educated, independent New Women—would be "wiser and stronger" due to their increased education and freedom, while not losing any of their "true womanliness."[2]

New Women rode bicycles, smoked cigarettes, attended university, and held emancipated views on sex and marriage. Because these behaviors and attitudes violated the rules of middle-class

---

1 Halberstam, *Skin Shows*, 14-15.
2 Grand, "The New Aspect of the Woman Question," 143-144.

convention, New Women came under fire in the popular press and were often stereotyped as sexually aggressive, dangerous femmes fatales. As Sally Ledger points out, criticism of the New Woman "included claims that she was a threat to the human race, was probably an infanticidal mother and at the very least sexually 'abnormal.'"[1] In gothic fiction, the New Woman sometimes makes an appearance as a werewolf who must be vanquished in order to restore social stability. For example, in Frederick Marryat's "The White Wolf of the Hartz Mountains" (1839) and Gilbert Campbell's "The White Wolf of Kostopchin" (1889), the werewolf is depicted as a beautiful, independent woman who possesses "masculine" strength and intelligence. Yet she is also shown to be a dangerous outsider who preys upon widowers and bachelors, luring them away from their paternal and fraternal responsibilities with the promise of sexual intrigue. Likewise, she consumes children rather than nurturing them into adulthood. The representation of women as werewolves had broader resonances in late nineteenth-century medical discourse, which, as Kelly Hurley has shown, often viewed women as "incomplete human subjects" who were only "partially evolved from the state of animalism."[2] The presumption was that if the Victorian woman's "natural" sexual instinct was not kept in check, she would destroy all civilized ties of blood and affection. As Victorian critic Walter Besant put it, the notion of women's sexual liberation was "outside the social pale" and "destructive of the very basis of society."[3] By vanquishing the female werewolf, writers attempted to quell cultural anxieties about the perceived threat of women's sexual liberation to traditional family structures.

Even though the female werewolf was often represented as a dangerous other, she was nevertheless a compelling, attractive figure in gothic fiction of the fin de siècle. In feminist writer Clemence Housman's "The Were-wolf," for instance, the female werewolf is a powerful, charismatic character who outshines the male hero in both charm and intelligence. Indeed, as Kelly Hurley has argued, "the fin-de-siècle Gothic as a genre [is] marked by both

1 Ledger, *The New Woman*, 10.
2 Hurley, *The Gothic Body*, 119.
3 Besant, "Candour in English Fiction," 9.

attraction towards and aversion from the object of its obsession, occluding that object through mechanisms of textual hysteria and yet compelled by the prospect of abhuman becomings."[1] In some late Victorian stories, the werewolf's dangerous sensuality is interpreted as a necessary counterpoint to the staid conservatism of church and family institutions. In "The Other Side: A Breton Tale" (1893), for example, Eric Stenbock departs from convention by depicting a female werewolf who survives at the end of the story. Focusing more thoroughly than most Victorian writers on the physical appearance of the werewolf, Stenbock endows the creature with both animal and human traits—the head of a golden-haired woman and the body of a wolf. Stenbock's dreamlike narrative includes meditative passages on the moon and other motifs associated with both werewolf lore and fin de siècle aestheticism.

In the hands of aesthete writers such as Eric Stenbock and William Butler Yeats, the werewolf story lost much of its didactic moralism. The aesthetic movement emphasized the appreciation of beauty for its own sake and reinterpreted stock symbols from gothic literary tradition in innovative ways. The werewolf, rather than symbolizing a form of pure evil that must be vanquished, became a more subtle reference point for exploring issues of spirituality, sexuality, and freedom. At the same time, the werewolf came to embody decadence—the exploration of free love, transgressive sexualities, and other anti-bourgeois attitudes inspired by French writers such as Émile Zola and Charles Baudelaire.

While the werewolf was taking on new, more complex symbolic meanings in the 1890s, real-life wolves were becoming nearly extinct. Stories demonizing wolves and werewolves had been used to justify the slaughter of wolves for centuries. By the late Victorian period, with the expansion of scientific discourse came an attempt to understand the wolf not as a demon but as a species that played an important role in British natural history. In "The Extinct British Wolf," published in *Popular Science Review* (1878),

---

1 Hurley, *The Gothic Body*, 155. Hurley defines "abhuman" as a "not-quite-human subject, characterized by its morphic variability, continually in danger of becoming not-itself, becoming other" (3-4). She suggests that "abhumanity" is a site of danger and anxiety at the same time that it is a reference point for imagining exciting definitions of a more fluid, morphic human self.

J. E. Harting expresses regret for the extinction of native British species, writing, "It seems almost incredible that the number of wild animals which have become extinct in the British Islands should equal, if it does not exceed, the number of the still existing forms with which we are familiar."[1] If, on one hand, late Victorian Britain was characterized as a time of expansion and progress, it was nonetheless also imagined as a period of decline in biodiversity. The werewolf thus served as a signifier of what Freud identified as the return of the repressed,[2] not only repressed anxieties about social change but also repressed memories of the distant past, when wolves freely roamed the British landscape.

During the Victorian era, the werewolf came to represent a host of fears about working-class unrest, social change, Darwinism, imperialism, women's liberation, and sexual freedom. Consequently, Victorian werewolves became what Judith Halberstam calls "meaning-machines"—monsters whose bodies "condense as many fear-producing traits as possible."[3] Yet the werewolf also symbolized the period's deepest desire for democratization and freedom from repressive stereotypes and social institutions. The shifting, hybrid nature of the werewolf makes it an ideal focal point for studying the ideological complexities and contradictions of the Victorian period. By examining the Victorian werewolf, we can begin to understand the roots of our own struggle with the "animal within" in twenty-first century literature and film.

A Note about the Text

When editing this anthology, our aim was to assemble a selection of stories that would represent the Victorian period in its entirety, from the 1830s to the fin de siècle. Many of the stories we selected, such as "Lycanthropy in London; or, The Wehr-wolf of Wilton-Crescent" (1855), have never been anthologized, and others, such as Rudyard Kipling's "The Mark of the Beast" (1890), have generally appeared in de-contextualized form in anthologies

---

1 Harting, "The Extinct British Wolf," 53.

2 Freud, *The Uncanny*, 144-147.

3 Halberstam, *Skin Shows*, 21.

of gothic fiction. By organizing these stories chronologically, we hope readers will understand them as products of particular social, cultural, and literary contexts. As an acknowledgment of the importance of this context, we drew our texts directly from the pages of Victorian periodicals. We decided to use the earliest published version of each story as our source text, where possible, even when later revised editions were available. We did so in order to enable readers to understand each story as a text written for a particular journal and audience. We provide historical background and publication information in order to encourage readers to further investigate this Victorian publishing context.

In addition to the selection of fiction in the anthology, we also included an appendix of supplementary materials intended to provide a broader context for understanding the werewolf as a figure in Victorian culture. The emergence of a cheap press led not only to the proliferation of stories but also to an increase in the number of poems and essays featuring the werewolf. In these texts, the werewolf emerges as a figure of folklore as well as a metaphor for criminality, degeneration, and social transgression. These supplementary materials demonstrate the far-reaching impact of the Victorian discourse on werewolves, which spanned diverse genres and incorporated a variety of compelling literary motifs. When preparing the stories and supplementary materials for publication in this anthology, we added content notes where necessary but otherwise kept editorial interventions to a minimum.

For Further Reading

Altick, Richard. *The English Common Reader: A Social History of the Mass Reading Public, 1800-1900*. Chicago: University of Chicago Press, 1963.

Ashley, Leonard R. N. *The Complete Book of Werewolves*. Fort Lee, N.J.: Barricade, 2001.

Besant, Walter. "Candour in English Fiction." *New Review* 2 (January 1890): 6-9.

Boone, Troy. *Youth of Darkest England: Working-Class Children at the Heart of Victorian Empire*. New York: Routledge, 2005.

Botting, Fred. *Gothic*. London: Routledge, 1996.

Cheilik, Michael. "The Werewolf." In *Mythical and Fabulous Creatures: A Source Book and Research Guide*, edited by Malcolm South, 265-289. Westport, Conn.: Greenwood, 1988.

Du Coudray, Chantal Bourgault. *The Curse of the Werewolf: Fantasy, Horror and the Beast Within*. New York: Tauris, 2006.

Freud, Sigmund. *The Uncanny*. Translated by David Mclintock. New York: Penguin, 2003.

Frost, Brian. *The Essential Guide to Werewolf Literature*. Madison: University of Wisconsin Press, 2003.

Grand, Sarah. "The New Aspect of the Woman Question." In *A New Woman Reader: Fiction, Articles, and Drama of the 1890s*, edited by Carolyn Christensen Nelson, 140-146. Peterborough: Broadview, 2001.

Halberstam, Judith. *Skin Shows: Gothic Horror and the Technology of Monsters*. Durham: Duke University Press, 1995.

Harting, J. E. "The Extinct British Wolf." *Popular Science Review* 2 (January 1878): 53-61.

Hogle, Jerrold, ed. *The Cambridge Companion to Gothic Fiction*. Cambridge: Cambridge University Press, 2002.

Hurley, Kelly. *The Gothic Body: Sexuality, Materialism, and Degeneration at the Fin de Siècle*. Cambridge: Cambridge University Press, 1996.

James, Louis. "The View from Brick Lane: Contrasting Perspectives in Working-Class and Middle-Class Fiction of the Early Victorian Period." *The Yearbook of English Studies* 11 (1981): 87-101.

Ledger, Sally. *The New Woman: Fiction and Feminism at the Fin de Siècle*. Manchester: Manchester University Press, 1997.

Otten, Charlotte, ed. *A Lycanthropy Reader: Werewolves in Western Culture*. Syracuse: Syracuse University Press, 1986.

Porter, J. R. and W. M. S. Russell, eds. *Animals in Folklore*. Totowa, N.J.: Brewer, 1978.

Punter, David, ed. *A Companion to the Gothic*. Oxford: Blackwell, 2001.

Russell, W. M. S. and Claire Russell. "The Social Biology of Werewolves." In *Animals in Folklore*, edited by J. R. Porter and W. M. S. Russell, 142-182. Totowa, N.J.: Brewer, 1978.

Sconduto, Leslie. *Metamorphoses of the Werewolf: A Literary*

Study from Antiquity through the Renaissance. Jefferson, N.C.: McFarland, 2008.

Shipping, Tom, ed. *The Shadow-Walkers: Jacob Grimm's Mythology of the Monstrous.* Tempe, Ariz.: ACMRS, 2005.

Acknowledgments

We would like to thank Fernando Sanchez and Professor Martin Warren for their valuable assistance as we developed this manuscript. The Luann Dummer Center for Women and the Faculty Development Center at the University of St. Thomas (UST) provided crucial financial support for this project. We would also like to acknowledge JoAnn Toussaint and Faith Bonitz, of the UST O'Shaughnessy-Frey Library, as well as Meredith Gillies and Jennifer Torkelson, of the University of Minnesota Libraries, for their assistance accessing rare books, periodicals, and images for this anthology.

Ḫugues, the Wer-Wolf

SUTHERLAND MENZIES

Sutherland Menzies was born in 1806 and attended Magdalen College, Cambridge. Soon thereafter he married, and his wife Flora Louise later gave birth to seventeen children, thirteen of whom died before reaching adulthood. Menzies supported his family by working as a private tutor and as a journalist. In 1838, he began writing for the Court and Ladies' Magazine *and in 1839 became its editor, a post he held until 1841. A year later, he served briefly as editor of* St. James's Magazine. *In the 1860s, he was a contributor to* St. James's Magazine *as well as* Fraser's Magazine. *He also wrote popular historical books, including* Royal Favourites *(1865) and* Turkey, Old and New *(1880), both of which were published in three editions. By the 1870s, he was incapacitated due to ill health but nevertheless managed to publish a series of history text-books for schoolchildren (1875-77). Throughout his adult life he suffered not only from illness but also from financial distress, which led to bankruptcy and frequent applications for assistance from the Royal Literary Fund. He died in 1886.*

Menzies published "Hugues, the Wer-Wolf" in 1838 in the Court and Ladies' Magazine, *a domestic magazine for women focused on light reading, fashion, and society. The story was republished as "The Wer-wolf" in* St. James's Magazine *in 1864. In its original publishing context, "Hugues, the Wer-Wolf" was accompanied by a brief essay that chronicled the history of werewolf lore. This essay was intended to document the "very singular superstition" that would then be illustrated in the accompanying tale."[1] Both the essay and the story are footnoted in order to show the depth of Menzies's antiquarian research. The story employs a variety of motifs associated with werewolf lore, including the severing of a werewolf's paw, which was said to reveal the identity of*

---

1 Menzies, "The Wer-wolf," 263.

the lycanthrope in its human form. In late Renaissance witch trials and werewolf lore, a person with a severed limb, when linked to a wolf with a similar injury, was often accused of lycanthropy

Bibliography

Case File of Sutherland Menzies. Royal Literary Fund. British Library Loan 96 RLF 1/1572.

Menzies, Sutherland. "Hugues, the Wer-Wolf." *Court and Ladies' Magazine* 13 (August 1838): 264-274.

———. "The Wer-wolf." *Court and Ladies' Magazine* 13 (August 1838): 259-263.

Summers, Montague. *Victorian Ghost Stories*. London: Simpkin, 1936.

HUGUES, THE WER-WOLF.

A KENTISH LEGEND OF THE MIDDLE AGES.

CHAPTER I.

"Ye hallowed bells whose voices thro' the air
The awful summons of afflictions bear."
Honoria, or the Day of All Souls[1]

ON the confines of that extensive forest-tract formerly spreading over so large a portion of the county of Kent, a remnant of which, to this day, is known as the weald[2] of Kent, and where it stretched its almost impervious covert[3] midway between Ashford

---

[1] A poem by Edward Jerningham published in 1782.

[2] That woody district, at the period to which our tale belongs, was an immense forest, desolate of inhabitants, and only occupied by wild swine and deer; and though it is now filled with towns and villages and well peopled, the woods that remain sufficiently indicate its former extent. "And being at first," says Hasted, "neither peopled nor cultivated, and only filled with herds of deer and droves of swine, belonged wholly to the king, for there is no mention of it but in royal grants and donations. And it may be presumed that when the weald was first made to belong to certain known owners, as well as the rest of the country, it was not then allotted into tenancies, nor manured like the rest of it: but only as men were contented to inhabit it, and by piecemeal to clear it of the wood, and convert it into tillage."—*Hasted's Kent*, vol. 1, p. 134. [Menzies's note.]

[3] Covering.

and Canterbury during the prolonged reign of our second Henry,[1] a family of Norman extraction,[2] by name Hugues (or Wulfric, as they were commonly called by the Saxon inhabitants of that district) had, under protection of the ancient forest laws, furtively erected for themselves a lone and miserable habitation. And amidst those sylvan fastnesses,[3] ostensibly following the occupation of woodcutters, the wretched outcasts, for such, from some cause or other, they evidently were, had for many years maintained a secluded and precarious existence. Whether from the rooted antipathy still actively cherished against all of that usurping nation from which they derived their origin, or from recorded malpractice by their superstitious Anglo-Saxon neighbours, they had long been looked upon as belonging to the accursed race of wer-wolves, and as such, churlishly refused work on the domains of the surrounding franklins[4] or proprietors, so thoroughly was accredited the descent of the original lycanthropic stain transmitted from father to son through several generations. That the Hugues Wulfric reckoned not a single friend among the adjacent homesteads of serf or freedman, was not to be wondered at, possessing as they did so unenviable a reputation; for to them was invariably attributed even the misfortunes which chance alone might seem to have given birth. Did midnight fire consume the grange;—did the time-decayed barn, over-stored with an abundant harvest, tumble into ruins;—were the shocks of wheat lain prostrate over the fields by a tempest;—did the smut[5] destroy the grain;—or the cattle perish, decimated by a murrain;[6]—a child sink under some wasting malady;—or a woman give premature birth to her offspring, it was ever the Hugues Wulfric who were openly accused, eyed askaunt[7] with mingled fear and detestation, the finger of young and old pointing them out with bitter

---

1 Henry II, King of England from 1154 to 1189.
2 After the Norman occupation (1066-1154), many descendants of the French invaders remained in England.
3 Strongholds.
4 Land holders.
5 Fungal disease.
6 Infectious disease.
7 Askance.

execrations—in fine, they were almost as nearly classed *feræ natura* as their fabled prototype, and dealt with accordingly.[1]

Terrible, indeed, were the tales told of them round the glowing hearth at eventide, whilst spinning the flax, or plucking the geese; equally affirmed, too, in broad daylight, whilst driving the cows to pasturage, and most circumstantially discussed on Sundays between mass and vespers, by the gossip groups collected within Ashford parvyse,[2] with most seasonable admixture of anathema[3] and devout crossings. Witchcraft, larceny, murther, and sacrilege, formed prominent features in the bloody and mysterious scenes of which the Hugues Wulfrics were the alleged actors: sometimes they were ascribed to the father, at others to the mother, and even the sister escaped not her share of vilification; fain would they have attributed an atrocious disposition to the unweaned babe, so great, so universal was the horror in which they held that race of Cain! The churchyard at Ashford, and the stone cross, from whence diverged the several roads to London, Canterbury, and Ashford, situated midway between the two latter places, served, so tradi-tion avouched, as nocturnal theatres for the unhallowed deeds of the Wulfrics, who thither prowled by moonlight, it was said, to batten on the freshly-buried dead, or drain the blood of any living wight[4] who might be rash enough to venture among those solitary spots. True it was that the wolves had, during some of the severe winters, emerged from their forest lairs, and, entering the cemetery by a breach in its walls, goaded by famine, had actually disinterred the dead; true was it, also, that the Wolf's Cross, as the hinds commonly designated it, had been stained with gore on one occasion through the fall of a drunken mendicant,[5] who chanced

---

1 King Edgar is said to have been the first who attempted to rid England of these animals; criminals even being pardoned by producing a stated number of these creatures' tongues. Some centuries after, they increased to such a degree as to become again the object of royal attention; and Edward I. appointed persons to extirpate this obnoxious race. It is one of the principal bearings in armoury. Hugh, surnamed *Lupus*, the first Earl of Kent, bore for his crest a wolf's head. [Menzies's note.]

2 Enclosed court in front of a church.

3 Curses.

4 Creature.

5 Beggar.

to fracture his skull against a pointed angle of its basement. But these accidents, as well as a multitude of others, were attributed to the guilty intervention of the Wulfrics, under their fiendish guise of wer-wolves.

These poor people, moreover, took no pains to justify themselves from a prejudice so monstrous: full well apprised of what calumny they were the victims, but alike conscious of their impotence to contradict it, they tacitly suffered its infliction, and fled all contact with those to whom they knew themselves repulsive. Shunning the highways, and never venturing to pass through the town of Ashford in open day, they pursued such labour as might occupy them within doors, or in unfrequented places. They appeared not at Canterbury market, never numbered themselves amongst the pilgrims at Becket's far-famed shrine,[1] or assisted at any sport, merry-making, hay-cutting, or harvest home: the priest had interdicted them from all communion with the church—the ale-bibbers from the hostelry.[2]

The primitive cabin which they inhabited was built of chalk and clay, with a thatch of straw, in which the high winds had made huge rents, and closed up by a rotten door, exhibiting wide gaps, through which the gusts had free ingress. As this wretched abode was situated at considerable distance from any other, if, perchance, any of the neighbouring serfs strayed within its precincts towards nightfall, their credulous fears made them shun near approach so soon as the vapours of the marsh were seen to blend their ghastly wreaths with the twilight; and as that darkling time drew on which explains the diabolical sense of the old saying, "'tween dog and wolf," "'twixt hawk and buzzard," at that hour the will-o'-the-wisps[3] began to glimmer around the dwelling of the Wulfrics, who patriarchally supped—whenever they had a supper—and forthwith betook themselves to their rest.

Sorrow, misery, and the putrid exhalations of the steeped hemp, from which they manufactured a rude and scanty attire, combined eventually to bring sickness and death into the bosom

---

1 Canterbury Cathedral, which once housed a shrine to the medieval martyr St. Thomas Becket.

2 Ale drinkers from the local inn.

3 Entities that lead others astray by means of false appearances.

of this wretched family, who, in their utmost extremity, could neither hope for pity or succour. The father was first attacked, and his corpse was scarce cold, ere the mother rendered up her breath. Thus passed that fated couple to their account, unsolaced by the consolation of the confessor, or the medicaments of the leech. Hugues Wulfric, their eldest son, himself dug their grave, laid their bodies within it swathed with hempen shreds for grave-cloths, and raised a few clods of earth to mark their last resting-place. A hind,[1] who chanced to see him fulfilling this pious duty in the dusk of evening, crossed himself, and fled as fast as his legs would carry him, fully believing that he had assisted at some hellish incantation. When the real event transpired, the neighbouring gossips congratulated one another upon the double mortality, which they looked upon as the tardy chastisement of heaven: they spoke of ringing the bells, and singing masses of thanks for such an action of grace.

It was All Souls' eve, and the wind howled along the bleak hill side, whistling drearily through the naked branches of the forest trees, whose last leaves it had long since stripped; the sun had disappeared; a dense and chilling fog spread through the air like the mourning veil of the widowed, whose day of love hath early fled. No star shone in the still and murky sky. In that lonely hut, through which death had so lately passed, the orphan survivors held their lonely vigil by the fitful blaze emitted by the reeking logs upon their hearth. Several days had elapsed since their lips had been imprinted for the last time upon the cold hands of their parents; several dreary nights had passed since the sad hour in which their eternal farewell had left them desolate on earth.

Poor lone ones! Both, too, in the flower of their youth—how sad, yet how serene did they appear amid their grief! But what sudden and mysterious terror is it that seems to overcome them? It is not, alas! the first time since they were left alone upon earth, that they have found themselves at this hour of the night by their deserted hearth, enlivened of old by the cheerful tales of their mother. Full often had they wept together over her memory, but never yet had their solitude proved so appalling; and, pallid as very

---

1 Field laborer.

spectres, they tremblingly gazed upon one another as the flickering ray from the wood-fire played over their features.

"Brother! heard you not that loud shriek which every echo of the forest repeated? It sounds to me as if the ground were ringing with the tread of some gigantic phantom, and whose breath seems to have shaken the door of our hut. The breath of the dead they say is icy cold. A mortal shivering has come over me."

"And I, too, sister, thought I heard voices as it were at a distance, murmuring strange words. Tremble not thus—am I not beside you?"

"Oh, brother! let us pray the Holy Virgin, to the end that she may restrain the departed from haunting our dwelling."

"But, perhaps, our mother is amongst them: she comes, unshrieved and unshrouded, to visit her forlorn offspring—her well-beloved! For, knowest thou not, sister, 'tis the eve on which the dead forsake their tombs. Let us open the door, that our mother may enter and resume her wonted place by the hearth-stone."

"Oh, brother, how gloomy is all without doors, how damp and cold the gust sweeps by. Hearest thou what groans the dead are uttering round our hut? Oh, close the door, in heaven's name!"

"Take courage, sister, I have thrown upon the fire that holy branch, plucked as it flowered on last Palm Sunday, which thou knowest will drive away all evil spirits, and now our mother can enter alone."

"But how will she look, brother? They say the dead are horrible to gaze upon; that their hair has fallen away; their eyes become hollow; and that, in walking, their bones rattle hideously. Will our mother, then, be thus?"

"No; she will appear with the features we loved to behold; with the affectionate smile that welcomed us home from our perilous labours; with the voice which, in early youth, sought us when, belated, the closing night surprised us far from our dwelling."

The poor girl busied herself awhile in arranging a few platters of scanty fare upon the tottering board which served them for a table; and this last pious offering of filial love, as she deemed it, appeared accomplished only by the greatest and last effort, so enfeebled had her frame become.

"Let our dearly-loved mother enter then," she exclaimed,

sinking exhausted upon the settle. "I have prepared her evening meal, that she may not be angry with me, and all is arranged as she was wont to have it. But what ails thee, my brother, for now thou tremblest as I did awhile agone?"

"See'st thou not, sister, those pale lights which are rising at a distance across the marsh? They are the dead, coming to seat themselves before the repast prepared for them. Hark! list to the funeral tones of the Allhallowtide[1] bells, as they come upon the gale, blended with their hollow voices.—Listen, listen!"

"Brother, this horror grows insupportable. This, I feel, of a verity, will be my last night upon earth! And is there no word of hope to cheer me, mingling with those fearful sounds? Oh, mother! mother!"

"Hush, sister, hush! see'st thou now the ghastly lights which herald the dead, gleaming athwart the horizon? Hearest thou the prolonged tolling of the bell? They come! they come!"

"Eternal repose to their ashes!" exclaimed the bereaved ones, sinking upon their knees, and bowing down their heads in the extremity of terror and lamentation; and as they uttered the words, the door was at the same moment closed with violence, as though it had been slammed to by a vigorous hand. Hugues started to his feet, for the cracking of the timber which supported the roof seemed to announce the fall of the frail tenement; the fire was suddenly extinguished, and a plaintive groan mingled itself with the blast that whistled through the crevices of the door. On raising his sister, Hugues found that she too was no longer to be numbered among the living.

CHAPTER II.

HUGUES, on becoming the head of his family, composed of two sisters younger than himself, saw them likewise descend into the grave in the short space of a fortnight; and when he had laid the last within her parent earth, he hesitated whether he should not

---

1 On this eve formerly the Catholic church performed a most solemn office for the repose of the dead. [Menzies's note.]

extend himself beside them, and share their peaceful slumber. It was not by tears and sobs that grief so profound as his manifested itself, but in a mute and sullen contemplation over the sepulture[1] of his kindred and his own future happiness. During three consecutive nights he wandered, pale and haggard, from his solitary hut, to prostrate himself and kneel by turns upon the funereal turf. For three days food had not passed his lips.

Winter had interrupted the labours of the woods and fields, and Hugues had presented himself in vain among the neighbouring domains to obtain a few days' employment to thresh grain, cut wood, or drive the plough; no one would employ him from fear of drawing upon himself the fatality attached to all bearing the name of Wulfric. He met with brutal denials at all hands, and not only were these accompanied by taunts and menace, but dogs were let loose upon him to rend his limbs: they deprived him even of the alms accorded to beggars by profession; in short, he found himself overwhelmed with injuries and scorn.

Was he, then, to expire of inanition[2] or deliver himself from the tortures of hunger by suicide? He would have embraced that means, as a last and only consolation, had he not been retained earthward to struggle with his dark fate by a feeling of love. Yes, that abject being, forced in very desperation, against his better self, to abhor the human species in the abstract, and to feel a savage joy in waging war against it; that *paria*[3] who scarce longer felt confidence in that heaven which seemed an apathetic witness of his woes; that man so isolated from those social relations which alone compensate us for the toils and troubles of life, without other stay than that afforded by his conscience, with no other fortune in prospect than the bitter existence and miserable death of his departed kin: worn to the bone by privation and sorrow, swelling with rage and resentment, he yet consented to live—to cling to life; for, strange—he loved! But for that heaven-sent ray gleaming across his thorny path, a pilgrimage so lone and wearisome would he have gladly exchanged for the peaceful slumber of the grave.

Hugues Wulfric would have been the finest youth in all that

---

1 Burial.
2 Exhaustion due to insufficient nourishment.
3 Pariah.

part of Kent, were it not that the outrages with which he had so unceasingly to contend, and the privations he was forced to undergo, had effaced the colour from his cheeks, and sunk his eyes deep in their orbits: his brows were habitually contracted, and his glance oblique and fierce. Yet, despite that recklessness and anguish which clouded his features, one, incredulous of his atrocities, could not have failed to admire the savage beauty of his head, cast in nature's noblest mould, crowned with a profusion of waving hair, and set upon shoulders whose robust and harmonious proportions were discoverable through the tattered attire investing them. His carriage was firm and majestic; his motions were not without a species of rustic grace, and the tone of his naturally soft voice accorded admirably with the purity in which he spoke his ancestral language—the Norman-French: in short, he differed so widely from people of his imputed condition, that one is constrained to believe that jealousy or prejudice must originally have been no stranger to the malicious persecution of which he was the object. The women alone ventured first to pity his forlorn condition, and endeavoured to think of him in a more favourable light.

Branda, niece of Willieblud, the flesher[1] of Ashford, had, among other of the town maidens, noticed Hugues with a not unfavouring eye, as she chanced to pass one day on horseback, through a coppice[2] near the outskirts of the town, into which the latter had been led by the eager chase of a wild hog, and which animal, from the nature of the country was, single-handed, exceedingly difficult of capture. The malignant falsehoods of the ancient crones continually buzzed in her ears, in nowise diminished the advantageous opinion she had conceived of this ill-treated and good-looking wer-wolf. She sometimes, indeed, went so far as to turn considerably out of her way, in order to meet and exchange his cordial greeting: for Hugues, recognising the attention of which he had now become the object, had, in his turn, at last summoned up courage to survey more leisurely the pretty Branda; and the result was, that he found her as buxom and pretty a lass as, in his

---

1 Butcher.
2 Small forest or woodlot.

hitherto restricted rambles out of the forest, his timorous gaze had ever encountered. His gratitude increased proportionally; and, at the moment when his domestic losses came one after another to overwhelm him, he was actually on the eve of making Branda, on the first opportunity presenting itself, an avowal of the love he bore her.

It was chill winter—Christmas-tide—the distant toll of the curfew had long ceased, and all the inhabitants of Ashford were safe housed in their tenements for the night. Hugues, solitary, motionless, silent, his forehead grasped between his hands, his gaze dully faced upon the decaying brands that feebly glimmered upon his hearth: he heeded not the cutting north wind, whose sweeping gusts shook the crazy roof, and whistled through the chinks of the door; he started not at the harsh cries of the herons fighting for prey in the marsh, nor at the dismal croaking of the ravens perched over his smoke-vent. He thought of his departed kindred, and imagined that his hour to join them would soon be at hand; for the intense cold congealed the marrow of his bones, and fell hunger gnawed and twisted his entrails. Yet, at intervals, would a recollection of nascent love, of Branda, suddenly appease his else intolerable anguish, and cause a faint smile to gleam across his wan features.

"Oh, blessed Virgin! grant that my sufferings may speedily cease!" murmured he, despairingly. "Oh, would I might be a wer-wolf, as they call me! I could then requite them for all the foul wrong done me. True, I could not nourish myself with their flesh; I would not shed their blood; but I would be able to terrify and torment those who have wrought my parents' and sisters' death— who have persecuted our family even to extermination! Why have I not the power to change my nature into that of a wolf, if, of a verity, my ancestors possessed it, as they avouch? I should at least find carrion to devour,[1] and not die thus horribly. Branda is the sole being in this world who cares for me; and that conviction alone reconciles me to life!"

Hugues gave free current to these gloomy reflections. The

---

1 Horseflesh was an article of food among our Saxon forefathers in England. [Menzies's note.]

smouldering embers now emitted but a feeble and vacillating light, faintly struggling with the surrounding gloom, and Hugues felt the horror of darkness coming strong upon him; frozen with the ague-fit[1] one instant, and troubled the next by the hurried pulsation of his veins, he arose, at last, to seek some fuel, and threw upon the fire a heap of faggot-chips, heath and straw, which soon raised a clear and crackling flame. His stock of wood had become exhausted, and, seeking wherewith to replenish his dying hearth-light, whilst foraging under the rude oven amongst a pile of rubbish placed there by his mother wherewith to bake bread—handles of tools, fractured joint-stools,[2] and cracked platters, he discovered a chest rudely covered with a dressed hide, and which he had never seen before; and seizing upon it as though he had discovered a treasure, broke open the lid, strongly secured by a spring.

This chest, which had evidently remained long unopened, contained the complete disguise of a wer-wolf:—a dyed sheepskin, with gloves in the form of paws, a tail, a mask with an elongated muzzle, and furnished with formidable rows of yellow horse-teeth.

Hugues started backwards, terrified at his discovery—so opportune, that it seemed to him the work of sorcery; then, on recovering from his surprise, he drew forth one by one the several pieces of this strange envelope, which had evidently seen some service, and from long neglect had become somewhat damaged. Then rushed confusedly upon his mind the marvellous recitals made him by his grandfather, as he nursed him upon his knees during earliest childhood; tales, during the narration of which his mother wept silently, as he laughed heartily. In his mind there was a mingled strife of feelings and purposes alike undefinable. He continued his silent examination of this criminal heritage, and by degrees his imagination grew bewildered with vague and extravagant projects.

Hunger and despair conjointly hurried him away: he saw objects no longer save through a bloody prism: he felt his very teeth on edge with an avidity for biting; he experienced an inconceivable desire to run: he set himself to howl as though he had

---

1 Shaking fit.
2 Broken stools that had once been carefully constructed.

practised wer-wolfery all his life, and began thoroughly to invest himself with the guise and attributes of his novel vocation. A more startling change could scarcely have been wrought in him, had that so horribly grotesque metamorphosis really been the effect of enchantment; aided, too, as it was, by the fever which generated a temporary insanity in his frenzied brain.

Scarcely did he thus find himself travestied into a wer-wolf through the influence of his vestment, ere he darted forth from the hut, through the forest and into the open country, white with hoar frost, and across which the bitter north wind swept, howling in a frightful manner, and traversing the meadows, fallows, plains, and marshes, like a shadow. But, at that hour, and during such a season, not a single belated wayfarer was there to encounter Hugues, whom the sharpness of the air, and the excitation of his course, had worked up to the highest pitch of extravagance and audacity: he howled the louder proportionally as his hunger increased.

Suddenly the heavy rumbling of an approaching vehicle arrested his attention; at first with indecision, then with a stupid fixity, he struggled with two suggestions, counselling him at one and the same time to fly and to advance. The carriage, or whatever it might be, continued, rolling towards him; the night was not so obscure but that he was enabled to distinguish the tower of Ashford church at a short distance off, and hard by which stood a pile of unhewn stone, destined either for the execution of some repair, or addition to the saintly edifice, in the shade of which he ran to crouch himself down, and so await the arrival of his prey.

It proved to be the covered cart of Willieblud, the Ashford flesher, who was wont twice a week to carry meat to Canterbury, and travelled by night in order that he might be among the first at market-opening. Of this Hugues was fully aware, and the departure of the flesher naturally suggested to him the inference that his niece must be keeping house by herself, for our lusty flesher had been long a widower. For an instant he hesitated whether he should introduce himself there, so favourable an opportunity thus presenting itself, or whether he should attack the uncle and seize upon his viands. Hunger got the better of love this once, and the monotonous whistle with which the driver was accustomed to urge forward his sorry jade warning him to be in readiness, he howled in a plaintive tone, and, rushing forward, seized the horse by the bit.

"Willieblud, flesher," said he, disguising his voice, and speaking to him in the *lingua Franca* of that period, "I hunger; throw me two pounds of meat if thou would'st have me live."

"St. Willifred[1] have mercy on me!" cried the terrified flesher, "is it thou, Hugues Wulfric, of Wealdmarsh, the born wer-wolf?"

"Thou say'st sooth—it is I," replied Hugues, who had sufficient address to avail himself of the credulous superstition of Willieblud; "I would rather have raw meat than eat of thy flesh, plump as thou art. Throw me, therefore, what I crave, and forget not to be ready with the like portion each time thou settest out for Canterbury market; or, failing thereof, I tear thee limb from limb."

Hugues, to display his attributes of a werwolf before the gaze of the confounded flesher, had mounted himself upon the spokes of the wheel, and placed his forepaw upon the edge of the cart, which he made semblance of snuffing at with his snout. Willieblud, who believed in wer-wolves as devoutly as he did in his patron saint, had no sooner perceived this monstrous paw, than, uttering a fervent invocation to the latter, he seized upon his daintiest joint of meat, let it fall to the ground, and whilst Hugues sprung eagerly down to pick it up, the butcher at the same instant having bestowed a sudden and violent blow upon the flank of his beast, the latter set off at a round gallop without waiting for any reiterated invitation from the lash.

Hugues was so satisfied with a repast which had cost him far less trouble to procure than any he had long remembered, readily promised himself the renewal of an expedient, the execution of which was at once easy and diverting; for though smitten with the charms of the fair-haired Branda, he not the less found a malicious pleasure in augmenting the terror of her uncle Willieblud. The latter, for a long while, revealed not to living being the tale of his terrible encounter and strange compact, which had varied according to circumstances, and he submitted unmurmuringly to the imposts[2] levied each time the wer-wolf presented himself before

---

1 Wilfrid (634-c. 709) was a medieval English bishop and saint.
2 Taxes.

him, without being very nice about either the weight or quality of the meat; he no longer even waited to be asked for it, any thing to avoid the sight of that fiend-like form clinging to the side of his cart, or being brought into such immediate contact with that hideous mis-shapen paw stretched forth, as it were to strangle him, that paw too, which had once been a human hand. He had become dull and thoughtful of late; he set out to market unwillingly, and seemed to dread the hour of departure as it approached, and no longer beguiled the tedium of his nocturnal journey by whistling to his horse, or trolling snatches of ballads, as was his wont formerly; he now invariably returned in a melancholy and restless mood.

Branda, at loss to conceive what had given birth to this new and permanent depression which had taken possession of her uncle's mind, after in vain exhausting conjecture, proceeded to interrogate, importune, and supplicate him by turns, until the unhappy flesher, no longer proof against such continued appeals, at last disburthened himself of the load which he had at heart, by recounting the history of his adventure with the wer-wolf.

Branda listened to the whole of the recital without offering interruption or comment; but, at its close—

"Hugues is no more a wer-wolf than thou or I," exclaimed she, offended that such unjust suspicion should be cherished against one for whom she had long felt more than an interest; "'tis an idle tale, or some juggling device; I fear me thou must needs dream these sorceries, uncle Willieblud, for Hugues of the Wealmarsh, or Wulfric, as the silly fools call him, is worth far more, I trow, than his reputation."

"Girl, it boots not saying me nay, in this matter," replied Willieblud, pertinaciously urging the truth of his story; "the family of Hugues, as everybody knows, were wer-wolves born, and, since they are all of late, by the blessing of heaven, defunct, save one, Hugues now inherits the wolf's paw."

"I tell thee, and will avouch it openly, uncle, that Hugues is of too gentle and seemly a nature to serve Satan, and turn himself into a wild beast, and that will I never believe until I have seen the like."

"Mass,[1] and that thou shalt right speedily, if thou wilt but along with me. In very troth 'tis he, besides, he made confession of his name, and did I not recognise his voice, and am I not ever bethinking me of his knavish paw, which he places me on the shaft while he stays the horse. Girl, he is in league with the foul fiend."

Branda had, to a certain degree, imbibed the superstition in the abstract, equally with her uncle, and, excepting so far as it touched the hitherto, as she believed, traduced[2] being on whom her affections, as if in feminine perversity, had so strangely lighted. Her woman's curiosity, in this instance, less determined her resolution to accompany the flesher on his next journey, than the desire to exculpate her lover, fully believing the strange tale of her kinsman's encounter with, and spoliation by the latter, to be the effect of some illusion, and of which to find him guilty, was the sole fear she experienced on mounting the rude vehicle laden with its ensanguined viands.

It was just midnight when they started from Ashford, the hour alike dear to wer-wolves as to spectres of every denomination. Hugues was punctual at the appointed spot; his howlings, as they drew nigh, though horrible enough, had still something human in them, and disconcerted not a little the doubts of Branda. Willieblud, however, trembled even more than she did, and sought for the wolf's portion; the latter raised himself upon his hind legs, and extended one of his fore paws to receive his pittance, as soon as the cart stopped at the heap of stones.

"Uncle, I shall swoon with affright," exclaimed Branda, clinging closely to the flesher, and tremblingly pulling the coverchief over her eyes: "loose rein and smite thy beast, or evil will surely betide us."

"Thou art not alone, gossip,"[3] cried Hugues, fearful of a snare; "if thou essay'st to play me false, thou art at once undone."

"Harm us not friend Hugues, thou know'st I weigh not my pounds of meat with thee; I shall take care to keep my troth. It is Branda, my niece, who goes with me to-night to buy wares at Canterbury."

---

1 On my oath.
2 Slandered.
3 Friend.

"Branda with thee? By the mass 'tis she indeed, more buxom and rosy too, than ever; come pretty one, descend and tarry awhile, that I may have speech with thee."

"I conjure thee, good Hugues, terrify not so cruelly my poor wench, who is well nigh dead already with fear; suffer us to hold our way, for we have far to go, and the morrow is early market-day."

"Go thy ways then alone, uncle Willieblud, 'tis thy niece I would have speech with, in all courtesy and honour; the which, if thou permittest not readily, and of a good grace, I will rend thee both to death."

All in vain was it that Willieblud exhausted himself in prayers and lamentations in hopes of softening the blood-thirsty wer-wolf, as he believed him to be, refusing as the latter did, every sort of compromise in avoidance of his demand, and at last replying only by horrible threats, which froze the hearts of both. Branda, although especially interested in the debate, neither stirred foot, or opened her mouth, so greatly had terror and surprise over-whelmed her; she kept her eyes fixed upon the wolf, who peered at her likewise through his mask, and felt incapable of offering resistance when she found herself forcibly dragged out of the vehicle, and deposited by an invisible power, as it seemed to her, beside the pile of stones: she swooned without uttering a single scream.

The flesher was no less dumbfounded at the turn which the adventure had taken, and he, too, fell back among his meat as though stricken by a blinding blow; he fancied that the wolf had swept his bushy tail violently across his eyes, and on recovering the use of his senses, found himself alone in the cart, which rolled jolt-ingly at a swift pace towards Canterbury. At first he listened, but in vain, for the wind bringing him either the shrieks of his niece, or the howlings of the wolf; but stop his beast he could not, which, panic-stricken, kept trotting as though bewitched, or felt the spur of some fiend pricking her flanks.

Willieblud, however, reached his journey's end in safety, sold his meat, and returned to Ashford, reckoning full sure upon having to say a *De Profundis*[1] for his niece, whose fate he had not ceased to bemoan during the whole night. But how great was his astonish-ment to find her safe at home, a little pale, from recent fright and

---

[1] Prayer of penitence and sorrow.

want of sleep, but without a scratch; still more was he astonished to hear that the wolf had done her no injury whatsoever, contenting himself, after she had recovered from her swoon, with conducting her back to their dwelling, and acting in every respect like a loyal suitor, rather than a sanguinary[1] wer-wolf. Willieblud knew not what to think of it.

This nocturnal gallantry towards his niece had additionally irritated the burly Saxon against the wer-wolf, and although the fear of reprisals kept him from making a direct and public attack upon Hugues, he ruminated not the less upon taking some sure and secret revenge; but previous to putting his design into execution, it struck him that he could not do better than relate his misadventures to the ancient sacristan[2] and parish grave-digger of St. Michael's, a worthy of profound sagacity in those sort of matters, endowed with a clerk-like erudition, and consulted as an oracle by all the old crones and love-lorn maidens throughout the township of Ashford and its vicinity.

"Slay a wer-wolf thou canst not," was the repeated rejoinder of the wise-acre to the earnest queries of the tormented flesher; "for his hide is proof against spear or arrow, though vulnerable to the edge of a cutting weapon of steel. I counsel thee to deal him a slight flesh wound, or cut him over the paw, in order to know of a surety whether it really be Hugues or no; thou'lt run no danger, save thou strikest him a blow from which blood flows not therefrom, for, so soon as his skin is severed, he taketh flight."

Resolving implicitly to follow the advice of the sacristan, Willieblud that same evening determined to know with what werwolf it was with whom he had to do, and with that view hid his cleaver, newly sharpened for the occasion, under the load in his cart, and resolutely prepared to make use of it as a preparatory step towards proving the identity of Hugues with the audacious spoiler of his meat, and eke his peace. The wolf presented himself as usual, and anxiously enquired after Branda, which stimulated the flesher the more firmly to follow out his design.

"Here, wolf," said Willieblud, stooping down as if to choose

---

1 Bloodthirsty.

2 An officer responsible for church property (e.g., objects associated with religious rituals).

a piece of meat; "I give thee double portion to-night; up with thy paw, take toll, and be mindful of my frank alms."

"Sooth, I will remember me, gossip,"[1] rejoined our wer-wolf; "but when shall the marriage be solemnized for certain, betwixt the fair Branda and myself?"

Hugues believing he had nothing to fear from the flesher, whose meats he so readily appropriated to himself, and of whose fair niece he hoped shortly no less to make lawful possession; both that he really loved, and viewed his union with her as the surest means of placing him within the pale of that sociality from which he had been so unjustly exiled, could he but succeed in making intercession with the holy fathers of the church to remove their interdict. Hugues placed his extended paw upon the edge of the cart; but instead of handing him his joint of beef, or mutton, Willieblud raised his cleaver, and at a single blow lopped off the paw laid there as fittingly for the purpose as though upon a block. The flesher flung down his weapon, and belaboured his beast, the wer-wolf roared aloud with agony, and disappeared amid the dark shades of the forest, in which, aided by the wind, his howling was soon lost.

The next day, on his return, the flesher, chuckling and laughing, deposited a gory cloth upon the table, among the trenchers[2] with which his niece was busied in preparing his noonday meal, and which, on being opened, displayed to her horrified gaze a freshly severed human hand enveloped in wolf-skin. Branda, comprehending what had occurred, shrieked aloud, shed a flood of tears, and then hurriedly throwing her mantle round her, whilst her uncle amused himself by turning and twitching the hand about with a ferocious delight, exclaiming, whilst he staunched the blood which still flowed:

"The sacristan said sooth; the wer-wolf has his meed, I trow,[3] at last, and now I wot[4] of his nature, I fear no more his witchcraft."

Although the day was far advanced, Hugues lay writhing in torture upon his couch, his coverings drenched with blood, as well also, the floor of his habitation; his countenance of a ghastly

---

1 Truthfully, I will remember, friend.
2 Platters.
3 Reward, I trust.
4 Know.

pallor, expressed as much moral, as physical pain; tears gushed from beneath his reddened eyelids, and he listened to every noise without, with an increased inquietude painfully visible upon his distorted features. Footsteps were heard rapidly approaching, the door was hurriedly flung open, and a female threw herself beside his couch, and with mingled sobs and imprecations sought tenderly for his mutilated arm, which, rudely bound round with hempen wrappings, no longer dissembled the absence of its wrist, and from which a crimson stream still trickled. At this piteous spectacle she grew loud in her denunciations against the sanguinary flesher, and sympathetically mingled her lamentations with those of his victim.

These effusions of love and dolour,[1] however, were doomed to sudden interruption; some one knocked at the door. Branda ran to the window that she might recognise who the visitor was that had dared to penetrate the lair of a wer-wolf, and on perceiving who it was, she raised her eyes and hands on high, in token of her extremity of despair, whilst the knocking momentarily grew louder.

"'Tis my uncle," faltered she. "Ah! woes me, how shall I escape hence without his seeing me? Whither hide? Oh, here, here, nigh to thee, Hugues, and we will die together," and she crouched herself into an obscure recess behind his couch. "If Willieblud should raise his cleaver to slay thee, he shall first strike through his kinswoman's body."

Branda hastily concealed herself amidst a pile of hemp, whispering Hugues to summon all his courage, who, however, scarce found strength sufficient to raise himself to a sitting posture, whilst his eyes vainly sought around for some weapon of defence.

"A good morrow to thee, Wulfric!" exclaimed Willieblud, as he entered, holding in his hand a napkin tied in a knot, which he proceeded to place upon the coffer beside the sufferer. "I come to offer thee some work, to bind and stack me a faggot-pile,[2] knowing that thou art no laggard at bill-hook and wattle.[3] Wilt do it?"

"I am sick," replied Hugues, repressing the wrath, which,

---

1 Distress.
2 Woodpile.
3 Not lazy about cutting brush or chopping sticks.

despite of pain, sparkled in his wild glance; "I am not in fitting state to work."

"Sick, gossip; sick, art thou, indeed? Or is it but a sloth fit? Come, what ails thee? Where lieth the evil? Your hand, that I may feel thy pulse."

Hugues reddened, and for an instant hesitated whether he should resist a solicitation, the bent of which he too readily comprehended; but in order to avoid exposing Branda to discovery, he thrust forth his left hand from beneath the coverlid, all imbrued in dried gore.

"Not that hand, Hugues, but the other, the right one. Alack, and well-a-day, hast thou lost thy hand, and I must find it for thee?"

Hugues, whose purpling flush of rage changed quickly to a death-like hue, replied not to this taunt, nor testified by the slightest gesture or movement, that he was preparing to satisfy a request as cruel in its preconception, as the object of it was slenderly cloaked. Willieblud laughed, and ground his teeth in savage glee, maliciously revelling in the tortures he had inflicted upon the sufferer. He seemed already disposed to use violence, rather than allow himself to be baffled in the attainment of the decisive proof he aimed at. Already had he commenced untying the napkin, giving vent all the while to his implacable taunts; one hand alone, displaying itself upon the coverlid, and which Hugues, well nigh senseless with anguish, thought not of withdrawing.

"Why tender me that hand?" continued his unrelenting persecutor, as he imagined himself on the eve of arriving at the conviction he so ardently desired:—"That I should lop it off? quick, quick, Master Wulfric, and do my bidding; I demand to see your right hand."

"Behold it then!" ejaculated a suppressed voice, which belonged to no supernatural being, however it might seem appertaining to such; and Willieblud to his utter confusion and dismay saw a second hand, sound and unmutilated, extend itself towards him as though in silent accusation. He started back; he stammered out a cry for mercy, bent his knees for an instant, and raising himself, palsied with terror, fled from the hut, which he firmly believed under the possession of the foul fiend. He carried not with him the severed hand, which henceforward became a perpetual vision ever present before his eyes, and which all the potent exorcisms of the sacristan, at whose hands he continually sought council and consolation, signally failed to dispel.

"Oh, that hand! To whom then, belongs that accursed hand?" groaned he, continually. "Is it really the fiend's, or that of some wer-wolf? Certain 'tis, that Hugues is innocent, for have I not seen both his hands? But wherefore was one bloody? There's sorcery at bottom of it."

The next morning, early, the first object that struck his sight on entering his stall, was the severed hand that he had left the preceding night upon the coffer in the forest hut; it was stripped of its wolf's-skin covering, and lay among the viands. He dared no longer touch that hand, which now, he verily believed to be enchanted; but in hopes of getting rid of it forever, he had it flung down a well, and it was with no small increase of despair that he found it shortly afterwards again lying upon his block. He buried it in his garden, but still without being able to rid himself of it; it returned livid and loathsome to infect his shop, and augment the remorse which was unceasingly revived by the reproaches of his niece.

At last, flattering himself to escape all further persecution from that fatal hand, it struck him that he would have it carried to the cemetery at Canterbury, and try whether exorcism, and sepulture in holy ground would effectually bar its return to the light of day. This was also done; but, lo! on the following morning he perceived it nailed to his shutter. Disheartened by these dumb, yet awful reproaches, which wholly robbed him of his peace, and impatient to annihilate all trace of an action with which heaven itself seemed to upbraid him, he quitted Ashford one morning without bidding adieu to his niece, and some days after was found drowned in the river Stour. They drew out his swollen and discoloured body, which was discovered floating on the surface among the sedge,[1] and it was only by piecemeal that they succeeded in tearing away from his death-contracted clutch, the phantom hand, which, in his suicidal convulsions he had retained firmly grasped.

A year after this event, Hugues, although minus a hand, and consequently a confirmed wer-wolf, married Branda, sole heiress to the stock and chattels of the late unhappy flesher of Ashford.

---

1 Wetland plants.

The White Wolf of the Hartz Mountains

Frederick Marryat

Frederick Marryat (1792-1848) was born into a wealthy family, yet from an early age longed for a career at sea. After several failed attempts to run away from home, he finally joined the Royal Navy in 1806 and was stationed on the frigate Impérieuse. *He served aboard several other ships and achieved the rank of commander before retiring from the navy in 1830. In the final years of his service, he began writing novels based on his real-life adventures at sea, including* The Naval Officer (1829) *and* The King's Own (1830). *In 1832, he became chief proprietor and editor of the* Metropolitan Magazine, *a position he held until 1836. During this period, he serialized many of his most popular novels in the magazine, including* Peter Simple (1832-34), Jacob Faithful (1834), *and* Mr. Midshipman Easy (1836). *In the following decade he began writing children's fiction and soon achieved fame as the author of* Masterman Ready (1841-42) *and* The Children of the New Forest (1847). *Although most of Marryat's novels are out of print, he was enormously popular and influential in his day. As Joseph Conrad wrote in 1921, "His greatness is undeniable."[1] At the peak of his career, Marryat received over £1,000 per novel, a princely sum at the time. In 1819, Marryat married Catherine Shairp and eventually fathered eleven children, including three daughters, Charlotte, Augusta, and Florence, who later became novelists in their own right.*

Marryat's "White Wolf of the Hartz Mountains" is an excerpt from The Phantom Ship, *a novel published serially in the* New Monthly Magazine and Humourist *from March 1837 to August 1839. It was subsequently published in three volumes by Henry Colburn in 1839.*

---

1 Conrad, *Notes on Life and Letters*, 54.

Bibliography

Burne, Glenn. "Frederick Marryat." In *Writers for Children*, edited by Jane Bingham, 381-387. New York: Scribner's, 1988.

Conrad, Joseph. *Notes on Life and Letters*. Garden City, N.Y.: Doubleday, 1921.

Engel, Elliot, and Margaret F. King. *The Victorian Novel before Victoria: British Fiction during the Reign of William IV, 1830-37*. New York: St. Martin's, 1984.

Hannay, David. *Life of Frederick Marryat*. London: Walter Scott, 1889.

Laughton, J. K. "Frederick Marryat." Revised by Andrew Lambert. *Oxford Dictionary of National Biography*. Oxford: Oxford University Press, 2009. http://www.oxforddnb.com.

Lloyd, Christopher. *Captain Marryat and the Old Navy*. London: Longmans, Green, 1939.

Marryat, Florence. *Life and Letters of Captain Marryat*. 2 vols. London: Bentley, 1872.

Marryat, Frederick. "White Wolf of the Hartz Mountains." *New Monthly Magazine and Humorist* 56 (July 1839): 396-412.

Parascandola, Louis. *"Puzzled Which to Choose": Conflicting Socio-Political Views in the Works of Captain Frederick Marryat*. New York: Peter Lang, 1997.

Pocock, Tom. *Captain Marryat: Seaman, Writer and Adventurer*. London: Chatham, 2000.

Spence, Nigel. "Frederick Marryat." In *British Children's Writers, 1800-1880*. *Dictionary of Literary Biography*, Vol. 163, edited by Meena Khorana. Detroit: Gale, 1996. *Literature Resource Center*, http://gogalegroup.com.

Stokes, Roy. "Frederick Marryat." In *Victorian Novelists before 1885*. *Dictionary of Literary Biography*, Vol. 21, edited by Ira Bruce Nadel and William E. Fredeman. Detroit: Gale, 1983. *Literature Resource Center*, http://gogalegroup.com.

Warner, Olive. *Captain Marryat: A Rediscovery*. London: Constable, 1953.

THE WHITE WOLF OF THE HARTZ MOUNTAINS.

My father was not born, or originally a resident, in the Hartz Mountains;[1] he was the serf of a Hungarian nobleman, of great

---

[1] The Harz Mountains in Northern Germany.

possessions, in Transylvania; but, although a serf, he was not by any means a poor or illiterate man. In fact, he was rich, and his intelligence and respectability were such, that he had been raised by his lord to the stewardship; but, whoever may happen to be born a serf, a serf must he remain, even though he become a wealthy man: such was the condition of my father. My father had been married for about five years; and, by his marriage, had three children—my eldest brother Cæsar, myself (Hermann), and a sister named Marcella. You know, Philip,[1] that Latin is still the language spoken in that country; and that will account for our high-sounding names. My mother was a very beautiful woman, unfortunately more beautiful than virtuous: she was seen and admired by the lord of the soil; my father was sent away upon some mission; and, during his absence, my mother, flattered by the attentions, and won by the assiduities, of this nobleman, yielded to his wishes. It so happened that my father returned very unexpectedly, and discovered the intrigue. The evidence of my mother's shame was positive: he surprised her in the company of her seducer! Carried away by the impetuosity of his feelings, he watched the opportunity of a meeting taking place between them, and murdered both his wife and her seducer. Conscious that, as a serf, not even the provocation which he had received would be allowed as a justification of his conduct, he hastily collected together what money he could lay his hands upon, and, as we were then in the depth of winter, he put his horses to the slugh,[2] and taking his children with him, he set off in the middle of the night, and was far away before the tragical circumstance had transpired. Aware that he would be pursued, and that he had no chance of escape if he remained in any portion of his native country (in which the authorities could lay hold of him), he continued his flight without intermission until he had buried

---

1 Krantz tells this story to Philip Vanderdecken, protagonist of *The Phantom Ship*. The two men become friends when serving as officers at sea. Philip is troubled by the loss of his father, who is doomed to haunt the seas as a spirit on *The Flying Dutchman*. Throughout the novel, Philip attempts to find his father so that he can release him from the curse. After Philip tells Krantz the cause of his secret mission, Krantz reciprocates by recounting the story of his own supernatural family curse.

2 A sleigh or sledge.

himself in the intricacies and seclusion of the Hartz Mountains. Of course, all that I have now told you I learned afterwards. My oldest recollections are knit to a rude, yet comfortable cottage, in which I lived with my father, brother, and sister. It was on the confines of one of those vast forests which cover the northern part of Germany; around it were a few acres of ground, which, during the summer months, my father cultivated, and which, though they yielded a doubtful harvest, were sufficient for our support. In the winter we remained much in doors; for, as my father followed the chase,[1] we were left alone, and the wolves, during that season incessantly prowled about. My father had purchased the cottage, and land about it, of one of the rude foresters, who gain their livelihood partly by hunting, and partly by burning charcoal, for the purpose of smelting the ore from the neighbouring mines; it was distant about two miles from any other habitation. I can call to mind the whole landscape now: the tall pines which rose up on the mountain above us, and the wide expanse of forest beneath, on the topmost boughs and heads of whose trees we looked down from our cottage, as the mountain below us rapidly descended into the distant valley. In summer-time the prospect was beautiful; but during the severe winter, a more desolate scene could not well be imagined.

I said that, in the winter, my father occupied himself with the chase; every day he left us, and often would he lock the door, that we might not leave the cottage. He had no one to assist him, or to take care of us—indeed, it was not easy to find a female servant who would live in such a solitude; but could he have found one, my father would not have received her, for he had imbibed a horror of the sex, as the difference of his conduct towards us, his two boys, and my poor little sister, Marcella, evidently proved. You may suppose we were sadly neglected; indeed, we suffered much, for my father, fearful that we might come to some harm, would not allow us fuel, when he left the cottage; and we were obliged, therefore, to creep under the heaps of bears'-skins, and there to keep ourselves as warm as we could until he returned in the evening, when a blazing fire was our delight. That my father chose

---

1 Went hunting.

this restless sort of life may appear strange, but the fact was that
he could not remain quiet; whether from the remorse for having
committed murder, or from the misery consequent on his change
of situation, or from both combined, he was never happy unless
he was in a state of activity. Children, however, when left much to
themselves, acquire a thoughtfulness not common to their age. So
it was with us; and during the short cold days of winter we would
sit silent, longing for the happy hours when the snow would melt,
and the leaves burst out, and the birds begin their songs, and when
we should again be set at liberty.

Such was our peculiar and savage sort of life until my brother
Cæsar was nine, myself seven, and my sister five years old, when
the circumstances occurred on which is based the extraordinary
narrative which I am about to relate.

One evening my father returned home rather later than usual;
he had been unsuccessful, and, as the weather was very severe, and
many feet of snow were upon the ground, he was not only very
cold, but in a very bad humour. He had brought in wood, and we
were all three of us gladly assisting each other in blowing on the
embers to create the blaze, when he caught poor little Marcella by
the arm and threw her aside; the child fell, struck her mouth, and
bled very much. My brother ran to raise her up. Accustomed to ill-
usage, and afraid of my father, she did not dare to cry, but looked
up in his face very piteously. My father drew his stool nearer to
the hearth, muttered something in abuse of women, and busied
himself with the fire, which both my brother and I had deserted
when our sister was so unkindly treated. A cheerful blaze was soon
the result of his exertions; but we did not, as usual, crowd round
it. Marcella, still bleeding, retired to a corner, and my brother and
I took our seats beside her, while my father hung over the fire
gloomily and alone. Such had been our position for about half an
hour, when the howl of a wolf, close under the window of the
cottage, fell on our ears. My father started up, and seized his gun:
the howl was repeated, he examined the priming,[1] and then hastily
left the cottage, shutting the door after him. We all waited (anxiously listening), for we thought that if he succeeded in shooting

---

[1] Placement of gunpowder in the firearm.

the wolf, he would return in a better humour; and although he was harsh to all of us, and particularly so to our little sister, still we loved our father, and loved to see him cheerful and happy, for what else had we to look up to? And I may here observe, that perhaps there never were three children who were fonder of each other; we did not, like other children, fight and dispute together: and if, by chance, any disagreement did arise between my elder brother and me, little Marcella would run to us, and kissing us both, seal, through her entreaties, the peace between us. Marcella was a lovely, amiable child; I can recall her beautiful features even now—Alas! poor little Marcella.

"She is dead then?" observed Philip.

"Dead! yes, dead!—but how did she die?—But I must not anticipate, Philip; let me tell my story."

We waited for some time, but the report of the gun did not reach us, and my elder brother then said, "Our father has followed the wolf and will not be back for some time. Marcella, let us wash the blood from your mouth, and then we will leave this corner, and go to the fire and warm ourselves."

We did so, and remained there until near midnight, every minute wondering, as it grew later, why our father did not return. We had no idea that he was in any danger, but we thought that he must have chased the wolf for a very long time.

"I will look out and see if father is coming," said my brother Cæsar, going to the door.

"Take care," said Marcella, "the wolves must be about now, and we cannot kill them, brother."

My brother opened the door very cautiously, and but a few inches: he peeped out.—"I see nothing," said he, after a time, and once more he joined us at the fire.

"We have had no supper," said I, for my father usually cooked the meat as soon as he came home; and during his absence we had nothing but the fragments of the preceding day.

"And if our father comes home after his hunt, Cæsar," said Marcella, "he will be pleased to have some supper; let us cook it for him and for ourselves."

Cæsar climbed upon the stool, and reached down some meat—I forget now whether it was venison or bear's meat; but we cut off the usual quantity, and proceeded to dress it, as we used to do under our father's superintendence. We were all busied putting it into the platters before the fire, to await his coming, when we heard the sound of a horn. We listened—there was a noise outside, and a minute afterwards my father entered, ushering in a young female, and a large dark man in a hunter's dress.

Perhaps I had better now relate, what was only known to me many years afterwards. When my father had left the cottage, he perceived a large white wolf about thirty yards from him; as soon as the animal saw my father, it retreated slowly, growling and snarling. My father followed: the animal did not run, but always kept at some distance; and my father did not like to fire, until he was pretty certain that his ball[1] would take effect: thus they went on for some time, the wolf now leaving my father far behind, and then stopping and snarling defiance at him, and then again on his approach, setting off at speed.

Anxious to shoot the animal (for the white wolf is very rare), my father continued the pursuit for several hours, during which he continually ascended the mountain.

You must know, Philip, that there are peculiar spots on those mountains which are supposed, and, as my story will prove, truly supposed, to be inhabited by the evil influences; they are well known to the huntsmen, who invariably avoid them. Now, one of these spots, an open space in the pine forests above us, had been pointed out to my father as dangerous on that account. But, whether he disbelieved these wild stories, or whether, in his eager pursuit of the chase, he disregarded them, I know not; certain, however, it is, that he was decoyed by the white wolf to this open space, when the animal appeared to slacken her speed. My father approached, came close up to her, raised his gun to his shoulder, and was about to fire; when the wolf suddenly disappeared. He thought that the snow on the ground must have dazzled his sight, and he let down his gun to look for the beast—but she was gone; how she could have escaped over the clearance, without his seeing her, was beyond his comprehension. Mortified at the ill success of his chase, he was about to retrace his steps, when he heard the

---

1 Ammunition used in a firearm.

distant sound of a horn. Astonishment at such a sound—at such an hour—in such a wilderness, made him forget for the moment his disappointment, and he remained rivetted to the spot. In a minute the horn was blown a second time, and at no great distance; my father stood still, and listened: a third time it was blown. I forget the term used to express it, but it was the signal which, my father well knew, implied that the party was lost in the woods. In a few minutes more my father beheld a man on horseback, with a female seated on the crupper,[1] enter the cleared space, and ride up to him. At first, my father called to mind the strange stories which he had heard of the supernatural beings who were said to frequent these mountains; but the nearer approach of the parties satisfied him that they were mortals like himself. As soon as they came up to him, the man who guided the horse accosted him.

"Friend Hunter, you are out late, the better fortune for us: we have ridden far, and are in fear of our lives, which are eagerly sought after. These mountains have enabled us to elude our pursuers; but if we find not shelter and refreshment, that will avail us little, as we must perish from hunger and the inclemency of the night. My daughter, who rides behind me, is now more dead than alive—say, can you assist us in our difficulty?"

"My cottage is some few miles distant," replied my father, "but I have little to offer you besides a shelter from the weather; to the little I have you are welcome. May I ask whence you come?"

"Yes, friend, it is no secret now; we have escaped from Transylvania, where my daughter's honour and my life were equally in jeopardy!"

This information was quite enough to raise an interest in my father's heart. He remembered his own escape: he remembered the loss of his wife's honour, and the tragedy by which it was wound up. He immediately, and warmly, offered all the assistance which he could afford them.

"There is no time to be lost, then, good sir," observed the horseman; "my daughter is chilled with the frost, and cannot hold out much longer against the severity of the weather."

"Follow me," replied my father, leading the way towards his home.

---

1 Behind the saddle on the horse's rump.

"I was lured away in pursuit of a large white wolf," observed my father; "it came to the very window of my hut, or I should not have been out at this time of night."

"The creature passed by us just as we came out of the wood," said the female in a silvery tone.

"I was nearly discharging my piece at it," observed the hunter; "but since it did us such good service, I am glad that I allowed it to escape."

In about an hour and a half, during which my father walked at a rapid pace, the party arrived at the cottage, and, as I said before, came in.

"We are in good time, apparently," observed the dark hunter, catching the smell of the roasted meat, as he walked to the fire and surveyed my brother and sister, and myself. "You have young cooks here, Meinheer."[1]—"I am glad that we shall not have to wait," replied my father. "Come, mistress, seat yourself by the fire; you require warmth after your cold ride."—"And where can I put up my horse, Meinheer?" observed the huntsman."—"I will take care of him," replied my father, going out of the cottage door.

The female must, however, be particularly described. She was young, and apparently twenty years of age. She was dressed in a travelling-dress, deeply bordered with white fur, and wore a cap of white ermine on her head. Her features were very beautiful, at least I thought so, and so my father has since declared. Her hair was flaxen, glossy and shining, and bright as a mirror; and her mouth, although somewhat large when it was open, showed the most brilliant teeth I have ever beheld. But there was something about her eyes, bright as they were, which made us children afraid; they were so restless, so furtive; I could not at that time tell why, but I felt as if there was cruelty in her eye; and when she beckoned us to come to her, we approached her with fear and trembling. Still she was beautiful, very beautiful. She spoke kindly to my brother and myself, patted our heads, and caressed us; but Marcella would not come near her; on the contrary, she slunk away, and hid herself in the bed, and would not wait for the supper, which half an hour before she had been so anxious for.

---

1 "My Lord" or "Sir."

My father, having put the horse into a close shed, soon returned, and supper was placed upon the table. When it was over, my father requested that the young lady would take possession of his bed, and he would remain at the fire, and sit up with her father. After some hesitation on her part, this arrangement was agreed to, and I and my brother crept into the other bed with Marcella, for we had as yet always slept together.

But we could not sleep; there was something so unusual, not only in seeing strange people, but in having those people sleep at the cottage, that we were bewildered. As for poor little Marcella, she was quiet, but I perceived that she trembled during the whole night, and sometimes I thought that she was checking a sob. My father had brought out some spirits, which he rarely used, and he and the strange hunter remained drinking and talking before the fire. Our ears were ready to catch the slightest whisper—so much was our curiosity excited.

"You said you came from Transylvania?" observed my father.

"Even so, Meinheer," replied the hunter. "I was a serf to the noble house of ——; my master would insist upon my surrendering up my fair girl to his wishes; it ended in my giving him a few inches of my hunting-knife."

"We are countrymen, and brothers in misfortune," replied my father, taking the huntsman's hand, and pressing it warmly.

"Indeed! Are you, then, from that country?"

"Yes; and I too have fled for my life. But mine is a melancholy tale."

"Your name?" inquired the hunter.

"Krantz."

"What! Krantz of —— I have heard your tale; you need not renew your grief by repeating it now. Welcome, most welcome, Meinheer, and, I may say, my worthy kinsman! I am your second cousin, Wilfred of Barnsdorf," cried the hunter, rising up and embracing my father.

They filled their horn-mugs to the brim, and drank to one another, after the German fashion. The conversation was then carried on in a low tone; all that we could collect from it was, that our new relative and his daughter were to take up their abode in our cottage, at least for the present. In about an hour they both fell back in their chairs, and appeared to sleep.

"Marcella, dear, did you hear?" said my brother in a low tone.

"Yes," replied Marcella, in a whisper; "I heard all. Oh! brother, I cannot bear to look upon that woman—I feel so frightened."

My brother made no reply, and shortly afterwards we were all three fast asleep.

When we awoke the next morning, we found that the hunter's daughter had risen before us. I thought she looked more beautiful than ever. She came up to little Marcella and caressed her; the child burst into tears, and sobbed as if her heart would break.

But, not to detain you with too long a story, the huntsman and his daughter were accommodated in the cottage. My father and he went out hunting daily, leaving Christina with us. She performed all the household duties; was very kind to us children; and, gradually, the dislike even of little Marcella wore away. But a great change took place in my father; he appeared to have conquered his aversion to the sex, and was most attentive to Christina. Often, after her father and we were in bed, would he sit up with her, conversing in a low tone by the fire. I ought to have mentioned, that my father and the huntsman Wilfred slept in another portion of the cottage, and that the bed which he formerly occupied, and which was in the same room as ours, had been given up to the use of Christina. These visitors had been about three weeks at the cottage, when, one night, after we children had been sent to bed, a consultation was held. My father had asked Christina in marriage, and had obtained both her own consent and that of Wilfred; after this a conversation took place, which was, as nearly as I can recollect, as follows:

"You may take my child, Meinheer Krantz, and my blessing with her, and I shall then leave you and seek some other habitation—it matters little where."

"Why not remain here, Wilfred?"

"No, no, I am called elsewhere; let that suffice, and ask no more questions. You have my child."

"I thank you for her, and will duly value her; but there is one difficulty."

"I know what you would say; there is no priest here in this wild country: true; neither is there any law to bind; still must some ceremony pass between you, to satisfy a father. Will you consent to marry her after my fashion? if so, I will marry you directly."

"I will," replied my father.

"Then take her by the hand. Now, Meinheer, swear."

"I swear," repeated my father.

"By all the spirits of the Hartz Mountains—"

"Nay, why not by Heaven?" interrupted my father.

"Because it is not my humour," rejoined Wilfred; "if I prefer that oath, less binding perhaps, than another, surely you will not thwart me."

"Well, be it so then; have your humour. Will you make me swear by that in which I do not believe?"

"Yet many do so, who in outward appearance are Christians," rejoined Wilfred; "say, will you be married, or shall I take my daughter away with me?"

"Proceed," replied my father, impatiently.

"I swear by all the spirits of the Hartz Mountains, by all their power for good or for evil, that I take Christina for my wedded wife; that I will ever protect her, cherish her, and love her; that my hand shall never be raised against her to harm her."

My father repeated the words after Wilfred.

"And if I fail in this my vow, may all the vengeance of the spirits fall upon me and upon my children; may they perish by the vulture, by the wolf, or other beasts of the forest; may their flesh be torn from their limbs, and their bones blanch in the wilderness; all this I swear."

My father hesitated, as he repeated the last words; little Marcella could not restrain herself, and as my father repeated the last sentence, she burst into tears. This sudden interruption appeared to discompose the party, particularly my father; he spoke harshly to the child, who controlled her sobs, burying her face under the bedclothes.

Such was the second marriage of my father. The next morning, the hunter Wilfred mounted his horse, and rode away.

My father resumed his bed, which was in the same room as ours; and things went on much as before the marriage, except that our new mother-in-law[1] did not show any kindness towards us; indeed, during my father's absence, she would often beat us, particularly little Marcella, and her eyes would flash fire, as she looked eagerly upon the fair and lovely child.

One night, my sister awoke me and my brother.

"What is the matter?" said Cæsar.

"She has gone out," whispered Marcella.

"Gone out!"

"Yes, gone out at the door, in her night-clothes," replied the child; "I saw her get out of bed, look at my father to see if he slept, and then she went out at the door."

What could induce her to leave her bed, and all undressed to go out, in such bitter wintry weather, with the snow deep on the ground, was to us incomprehensible; we lay awake, and in about an hour we heard the growl of a wolf, close under the window.

"There is a wolf," said Cæsar; "she will be torn to pieces!"

"Oh no!" cried Marcella.

In a few minutes afterwards our mother-in-law appeared; she was in her night-dress, as Marcella had stated. She let down the latch of the door, so as to make no noise, went to a pail of water, and washed her face and hands, and then slipped into the bed where my father lay.

We all three trembled, we hardly knew why, but we resolved to watch the next night: we did so—and not only on the ensuing night, but on many others, and always at about the same hour, would our mother-in-law rise from her bed, and leave the cottage—and after she was gone, we invariably heard the growl of a wolf under our window, and always saw her, on her return, wash herself before she retired to bed. We observed, also, that she seldom sat down to meals, and that when she did, she appeared to eat with dislike; but when the meat was taken down, to be prepared for dinner, she would often furtively put a raw piece into her mouth.

My brother Cæsar was a courageous boy; he did not like to speak to my father until he knew more. He resolved that he would follow her out, and ascertain what she did. Marcella and I endeavoured to dissuade him from this project; but he would not be

---

1 Stepmother.

controlled, and, the very next night he lay down in his clothes, and as soon as our mother-in-law had left the cottage, he jumped up, took down my father's gun, and followed her.

You may imagine in what a state of suspense Marcella and I remained, during his absence. After a few minutes, we heard the report of a gun. It did not awaken my father; and we lay trembling with anxiety. In a minute afterwards we saw our mother-in-law enter the cottage—her dress was bloody. I put my hand to Marcella's mouth to prevent her crying out, although I was myself in great alarm. Our mother-in-law approached my father's bed, looked to see if he was asleep, and then went to the chimney, and blew up the embers into a blaze.

"Who is there?" said my father, waking up.

"Lie still, dearest," replied my mother-in-law; "it is only me; I have lighted the fire to warm some water; I am not quite well."

My father turned round and was soon asleep; but we watched our mother-in-law. She changed her linen, and threw the garments she had worn into the fire; and we then perceived that her right leg was bleeding profusely, as if from a gun-shot wound. She bandaged it up, and then dressing herself, remained before the fire until the break of day.

Poor little Marcella, her heart beat quick as she pressed me to her side—so indeed did mine. Where was our brother, Cæsar? How did my mother-in-law receive the wound unless from his gun? At last my father rose, and then, for the first time I spoke, saying, "Father, where is my brother, Cæsar?"

"Your brother!" exclaimed he; "why, where can he be?"

"Merciful Heaven! I thought, as I lay very restless last night," observed our mother-in-law, "that I heard somebody open the latch of the door; and, dear me, husband, what has become of your gun?"

My father cast his eyes up above the chimney, and perceived that his gun was missing. For a moment he looked perplexed; then, seizing a broad axe, he went out of the cottage without saying another word.

He did not remain away from us long: in a few minutes he returned, bearing in his arms the mangled body of my poor brother; he laid it down and covered up his face.

My mother-in-law rose up, and looked at the body, while Marcella and I threw ourselves by its side wailing and sobbing bitterly.

"Go to bed again, children," said she sharply. "Husband," continued she, "your boy must have taken the gun down to shoot a wolf, and the animal has been too powerful for him. Poor boy! he has paid dearly for his rashness."

My father made no reply; I wished to speak—to tell all—but Marcella, who perceived my intention, held me by the arm, and looked at me so imploringly, that I desisted.

My father, therefore, was left in his error; but Marcella and I, although we could not comprehend it, were conscious that our mother-in-law was in some way connected with my brother's death.

That day my father went out and dug a grave, and when he laid the body in the earth, he piled up stones over it, so that the wolves should not be able to dig it up. The shock of this catastrophe was to my poor father very severe; for several days he never went to the chase, although at times he would utter bitter anathemas and vengeance against the wolves.

But during this time of mourning on his part, my mother-in-law's nocturnal wanderings continued with the same regularity as before.

At last, my father took down his gun, to repair to the forest; but he soon returned, and appeared much annoyed.

"Would you believe it, Christina, that the wolves—perdition to the whole race—have actually contrived to dig up the body of my poor boy, and now there is nothing left of him but his bones?"

"Indeed!" replied my mother-in-law. Marcella looked at me, and I saw in her intelligent eye all she would have uttered.

"A wolf growls under our window every night, father," said I.

"Ay, indeed!—why did you not tell me, boy?—wake me the next time you hear it."

I saw my mother-in-law turn away; her eyes flashed fire, and she gnashed her teeth.

My father went out again, and covered up with a larger pile of stones the little remnants of my poor brother which the wolves had spared. Such was the first act of the tragedy.

The spring now came on: the snow disappeared, and we were permitted to leave the cottage; but never would I quit, for one moment, my dear little sister, to whom, since the death of my brother, I was more ardently attached than ever; indeed, I was afraid to leave her alone with my mother-in-law, who appeared to have a particular pleasure in ill-treating the child. My father was now employed upon his little farm, and I was able to render him some assistance.

Marcella used to sit by us while we were at work, leaving my mother-in-law alone in the cottage. I ought to observe that, as the spring advanced, so did my mother-in-law decrease her nocturnal rambles, and that we never heard the growl of the wolf under the window after I had spoken of it to my father.

One day, when my father and I were in the field, Marcella being with us, my mother-in-law came out, saying that she was going into the forest to collect some herbs my father wanted, and that Marcella must go to the cottage and watch the dinner. Marcella went, and my mother-in-law soon disappeared in the forest, taking a direction quite contrary to that in which the cottage stood, and leaving my father and I, as it were, between her and Marcella.

About an hour afterwards we were startled by shrieks from the cottage, evidently the shrieks of little Marcella. "Marcella has burnt herself, father!" said I, throwing down my spade. My father threw down his, and we both hastened to the cottage. Before we could gain the door, out darted a large white wolf, which fled with the utmost celerity. My father had no weapon; he rushed into the cottage, and there saw poor little Marcella expiring: her body was dreadfully mangled, and the blood pouring from it had formed a large pool on the cottage floor. My father's first intention had been to seize his gun and pursue, but he was checked by this horrid spectacle; he knelt down by his dying child, and burst into tears: Marcella could just look kindly on us for a few seconds, and then her eyes were closed in death.

My father and I were still hanging over my poor sister's body, when my mother-in-law came in. At the dreadful sight she expressed much concern, but she did not appear to recoil from the sight of blood, as most women do.

"Poor child!" said she, "it must have been that great white wolf which passed me just now, and frightened me so—she's quite dead, Krantz."

"I know it—I know it!" cried my father, in agony.

I thought my father would never recover from the effects of this second tragedy: he mourned bitterly over the body of his sweet child, and for several days would not consign it to its grave, although frequently requested by my mother-in-law to do so. At last he yielded, and dug a grave for her close by that of my poor brother, and took every precaution that the wolves should not violate her remains.

I was now really miserable, as I lay alone in the bed which I had formerly shared with my brother and sister. I could not help thinking that my mother-in-law was implicated in both their deaths, although I could not account for the manner; but I no longer felt afraid of her: my little heart was full of hatred and revenge.

The night after my sister had been buried, as I lay awake, I perceived my mother-in-law get up and go out of the cottage. I waited some time, then dressed myself, and looked out through the door, which I half opened. The moon shone bright, and I could see the spot where my brother and my sister had been buried; and what was my horror, when I perceived my mother-in-law busily removing the stones from Marcella's grave.

She was in her white night-dress, and the moon shone full upon her. She was digging with her hands, and throwing away the stones behind her with all the ferocity of a wild beast. It was some time before I could collect my senses and decide what I should do. At last, I perceived that she had arrived at the body, and raised it up to the side of the grave. I could bear it no longer; I ran to my father and awoke him.

"Father! father!" cried I, "dress yourself, and get your gun."

"What!" cried my father, "the wolves are there, are they?"

He jumped out of bed, threw on his clothes, and in his anxiety did not appear to perceive the absence of his wife. As soon as he was ready, I opened the door, he went out, and I followed him.

Imagine his horror, when (unprepared as he was for such a sight) he beheld, as he advanced towards the grave, not a wolf, but his wife, in her night-dress, on her hands and knees, crouching by the body of my sister, and tearing off large pieces of the flesh, and devouring them with all the avidity of a wolf. She was too busy to be aware of our approach. My father dropped his gun, his hair stood on end; so did mine; he breathed heavily, and then his breath for a time stopped. I picked up the gun and put it into his hand. Suddenly he appeared as if concentrated rage had restored him to double vigour; he levelled his piece, fired, and with a loud shriek, down fell the wretch whom he had fostered in his bosom.

"Merciful Heaven!" cried my father, sinking down upon the earth in a swoon, as soon as he had discharged his gun.

I remained some time by his side before he recovered. "Where am I?" said he, "what has happened?—Oh!—yes, yes! I recollect now. Heaven forgive me!"

He rose and we walked up to the grave; what again was our astonishment and horror to find that instead of the dead body of my mother-in-law, as we expected, there was lying over the remains of my poor sister, a large, white she-wolf.

"The white wolf!" exclaimed my father, "the white wolf which decoyed me into the forest—I see it all now—I have dealt with the spirits of the Hartz Mountains."

For some time my father remained in silence and deep thought. He then carefully lifted up the body of my sister, replaced it in the grave, and covered it over as before, having struck the head of the dead animal with the heel of his boot, and raving like a madman. He walked back to the cottage, shut the door, and threw himself on the bed; I did the same, for I was in a stupor of amazement.

Early in the morning we were both roused by a loud knocking at the door, and in rushed the hunter Wilfred.

"My daughter!—man—my daughter!—where is my daughter?" cried he in a rage.

"Where the wretch, the fiend, should be, I trust," replied my father, starting up and displaying equal choler;[1] "where she should be—in hell!—Leave this cottage, or you may fare worse."

"Ha—ha!" replied the hunter, "would you harm a potent spirit of the Hartz Mountains? Poor mortal, who must needs wed a weir wolf."

"Out, demon! I defy thee and thy power."

---

1 Wrath.

"Yet shall you feel it; remember your oath—your solemn oath—never to raise your hand against her to harm her."

"I made no compact with evil spirits."

"You did; and if you failed in your vow, you were to meet the vengeance of the spirits. Your children were to perish by the vulture, the wolf—"

"Out, out, demon!"

"And their bones blanch in the wilderness. Ha!—ha!"

My father, frantic with rage, seized his axe, and raised it over Wilfred's head to strike.

"All this I swear!" continued the huntsman mockingly.

The axe descended; but it passed through the form of the hunter, and my father lost his balance, and fell heavily on the floor.

"Mortal!" said the hunter, striding over my father's body, "we have power over those only who have committed murder. You have been guilty of a double murder—you shall pay the penalty attached to your marriage vow. Two of your children are gone; the third is yet to follow—and follow them he will, for your oath is registered. Go—it were kindness to kill thee—your punishment is—that you live!"

With these words the spirit disappeared. My father rose from the floor, embraced me tenderly, and knelt down in prayer.

The next morning he quitted the cottage for ever. He took me with him and bent his steps to Holland, where we safely arrived. He had some little money with him; but he had not been many days in Amsterdam before he was seized with a brain fever, and died raving mad. I was put into the asylum, and afterwards was sent to sea before the mast. You now know all my history. The question is, whether I am to pay the penalty of my father's oath? I am myself perfectly convinced that, in some way or another, I shall.[1]

---

[1] In the scene that follows, Krantz is dragged away by a tiger. Philip reflects, "It is his destiny, and it has been fulfilled. His bones will bleach in the wilderness, and the spirit-hunter and his wolfish daughter are revenged." Meanwhile, Philip fulfills his own destiny at the end of the novel by freeing his father of the curse of the phantom ship.

𝔄 Story of a 𝔚eir-𝔚olf

CATHERINE CROWE

Catherine Crowe (1790-1872) was born to John and Mary Stevens on a farm in Borough Green, Kent. Her father eventually gave up farming and became a wine-merchant and proprietor of the well-known Stevens's Hotel, which served famous patrons such as Lord Byron. In 1822, Catherine married Major John Crowe, a war hero of Waterloo, and the couple had a son, John William. Unhappy with her marriage, Crowe separated from her husband in 1838 and relocated to Edinburgh. The money she inherited from her father's business left her financially independent, which enabled her to start a new life as a writer and researcher of the paranormal.

Once established in Edinburgh's literary society, Crowe was known for hosting elegant dinner parties, and she soon formed friendships with other writers, including Harriet Martineau, W. M. Thackeray, and Thomas De Quincey. Crowe's first published work was a verse tragedy, Aristodemus *(1838), and she composed a second play,* The Cruel Kindness, *in 1853. Her debut novel,* The Adventures of Susan Hopley, or, Circumstantial Evidence *(1841) was extremely popular and twice adapted for the stage. In addition, Crowe published* Men and Women, or, Manorial Rights *(1844) and* The Story of Lily Dawson *(1847). Although both novels sold well, they were never as popular as* Susan Hopley, *which was the first novel to feature amateur female sleuths.* Susan Hopley *so inspired Pre-Raphaelite artist Dante Gabriel Rossetti that he composed sketches of characters from the novel.*

Crowe's numerous stories and nonfiction articles appeared in periodicals throughout the Victorian era. She formed professional relationships with several editors, including Robert Chambers, editor of Chambers' Edinburgh Journal, *whom she rebuked for his policy of removing morally questionable material from the journal. Unfortunately, her literary reputation was tarnished in 1854 after she was found walking naked at night in Edinburgh, saying that spirits had made her invisible.*

However, she soon recovered her sanity after a stay in Hanwell Asylum. In an attempt to quell growing rumors, Crowe wrote a letter to the Daily News blaming the incident on a digestive disorder.

Ultimately, Crowe's literary legacy remains with her ghost stories and her explorations of the supernatural. She was extremely, even obsessively, interested in paranormal phenomena, befriending several mediums, attending séances, and hiring phrenologists. In 1845, she translated The Seeress of Provost, by Justinus Kerner, which recounts the German writer's experience with a clairvoyant. In 1848, she published a bestseller, The Night Side of Nature, or, Ghosts and Ghost Seers, featuring accounts of hauntings, apparitions, mesmerism, doppelgängers, and somnambulism. The Night Side of Nature had many fans, including Charles Baudelaire, who quoted favorite passages in the Salon de 1859.

Crowe's interest in the paranormal led to articles such as "Lycanthropy" (1849), which related the case of infamous grave-robber and necrophiliac Francis Bertrand, as well as fiction such as "A Story of a Weir-Wolf" (1846), which is perhaps based on a 1588 case in Auvergne, France where a woman was accused of transforming into a werewolf and later burned at the stake. Henri Boguet, a judge who presided over the most infamous witch trials of the Renaissance period, discussed the case in Discours des Sorciers (1602).[1] "A Story of a Weir-Wolf" appeared in Hogg's Weekly Instructor in 1846.

Bibliography

Clapton, G. T. "Baudelaire and Catherine Crowe." Modern Language Review 25, no. 3 (1930): 286-305.

Crowe, Catherine. "A Story of a Weir-Wolf." Hogg's Weekly Instructor 3 (May 16, 1846): 184-189.

Mitchell, Sally. The Fallen Angel: Chastity, Class and Women's Reading, 1835-1880. Bowling Green, Ohio: Bowling Green University Popular Press, 1981.

Otten, Charlotte, ed. A Lycanthropic Reader: Werewolves in Western Culture. Syracuse: Syracuse University Press, 1986.

Sergeant, Adeline. "Mrs. Crowe." In Women Novelists of Queen Victoria's Reign; A Book of Appreciations, edited by Margaret Oliphant and Elizabeth Lynn Linton, 149-160. London: Hurst and Blackett, 1897.

---

1 See Otten, A Lycanthropy Reader, 80.

Sussex, Lucy. *Women Writers and Detectives in Nineteenth-Century Crime Fiction: The Mothers of the Mystery Genre.* Basingstoke: Palgrave Macmillan, 2010.

Wilkes, Joanne. "Catherine Crowe." *Oxford Dictionary of National Biography.* Oxford: Oxford University Press, 2004. http://www.oxforddnb.com.

———

A STORY OF A WEIR-WOLF.

It was on a fine bright summer's morning, in the year 1596, that two young girls were seen sitting at the door of a pretty cottage, in a small village that lay buried amidst the mountains of Auvergne.[1] The house belonged to Ludovique Thierry, a tolerably prosperous builder; one of the girls was his daughter Manon, and the other his niece, Francoise, the daughter of his brother-in-law, Michael Thilouze, a physician.

The mother of Francoise had been some years dead, and Michael, a strange old man, learned in all the mystical lore of the middle ages, had educated his daughter after his own fancy; teaching her some things useless and futile, but others beautiful and true. He not only instructed her to glean information from books, but he led her into the fields, taught her to name each herb and flower, making her acquainted with their properties; and, directing her attention "to the brave o'erhanging firmament," he had told her all that was known of the golden spheres that were rolling above her head.

But Michael was also an alchemist, and he had for years been wasting his health in nightly vigils over crucibles, and his means in expensive experiments; and now, alas! he was nearly seventy years of age, and his lovely Francoise seventeen, and neither the elixir vitæ nor the philosopher's stone had yet rewarded his labours.[2] It was just at this crisis, when his means were failing and his hopes expiring, that he received a letter from Paris, informing him that

---

1 A region in central France.

2 The "elixir of life" was a substance sought by alchemists as a means of prolonging life. The philosopher's stone was thought to transform base metals into gold and to possess curative and life-prolonging properties.

the grand secret was at length discovered by an Italian, who had lately arrived there. Upon this intelligence, Michael thought the most prudent thing he could do was to waste no more time and money by groping in the dark himself, but to have recourse to the fountain of light at once; so sending Francoise to spend the interval with her cousin Manon, he himself started for Paris to visit the successful philosopher. Although she sincerely loved her father, the change was by no means unpleasant to Francoise. The village of Loques, in which Manon resided, humble as it was, was yet more cheerful than the lonely dwelling of the physician; and the conversation of the young girl more amusing than the dreamy speculations of the old alchemist. Manon, too, was rather a gainer by her cousin's arrival; for as she held her head a little high, on account of her father being the richest man in the village, she was somewhat nice about admitting the neighbouring damsels to her intimacy; and a visitor so unexceptionable as Francoise was by no means unwelcome. Thus both parties were pleased, and the young girls were anticipating a couple of months of pleasant companionship at the moment we have introduced them to our readers, seated at the front of the cottage.

"The heat of the sun is insupportable, Manon," said Francoise; "I really must go in."

"Do," said Manon.

"But won't you come in too?" asked Francoise.

"No, I don't mind the heat," replied the other.

Francoise took up her work and entered the house, but as Manon still remained without, the desire for conversation soon overcame the fear of the heat, and she approached the door again, where, standing partly in the shade, she could continue to discourse. As nobody appeared disposed to brave the heat but Manon, the little street was both empty and silent, so that the sound of a horse's foot crossing the drawbridge, which stood at the entrance of the village, was heard some time before the animal or his rider were in sight. Francoise put out her head to look in the direction of the sound, and, seeing no one, drew it in again; whilst Manon, after casting an almost imperceptible glance the same way, hung hers over her work, as if very intent on what she was doing; but could Francoise have seen her cousin's face, the blush that first overspread it, and the paleness that succeeded, might have awakened a suspicion that Manon was not exposing her complexion to the sun for nothing.

When the horse drew near, the rider was seen to be a gay and handsome cavalier, attired in the perfection of fashion, whilst the rich embroidery of the small cloak that hung gracefully over his left shoulder, sparkling in the sun, testified no less than his distinguished air to his high rank and condition. Francoise, who had never seen anything so bright and beautiful before, was so entirely absorbed in contemplating the pleasing spectacle, that forgetting to be shy or to hide her own pretty face, she continued to gaze on him as he approached with dilated eyes and lips apart, wholly unconscious that the surprise was mutual. It was not till she saw him lift his bonnet[1] from his head, and, with a reverential bow, do homage to her charms, that her eye fell and the blood rushed to her young cheek. Involuntarily, she made a step backwards into the passage; but when the horse and his rider had passed the door, she almost as involuntarily resumed her position, and protruded her head to look after him. He too had turned round on his horse and was "riding with his eyes behind," and the moment he beheld her he lifted his bonnet again, and then rode slowly forward.

"Upon my word, Mam'selle Francoise," said Manon, with flushed cheeks and angry eyes, "this is rather remarkable, I think! I was not aware of your acquaintance with Monsieur de Vardes!"

"With whom?" said Francoise. "Is that Monsieur de Vardes?"

"To be sure it is," replied Manon; "do you pretend to say you did not know it?"

"Indeed, I did not," answered Francoise. "I never saw him in my life before."

"Oh, I dare I say," responded Manon, with an incredulous laugh. "Do you suppose I'm such a fool as to believe you?"

"What nonsense, Manon! How should I know Monsieur de Vardes? But do tell me about him? Does he live at the Chateau?"

"He has been living there lately," replied Manon, sulkily.

"And where did he live before?" inquired Francoise.

"He has been travelling, I believe," said Manon.

This was true. Victor de Vardes had been making the tour

---

1   Helmet or cap.

of Europe, visiting foreign courts, jousting in tournaments, and winning fair ladies' hearts, and was but now returned to inhabit his father's chateau; who, thinking it high time he should be married, had summoned him home for the purpose of paying his addresses to Clemence de Montmorenci, one of the richest heiresses in France.[1]

Victor, who had left home very young, had been what is commonly called *in love* a dozen times, but his heart had in reality never been touched. His loves had been mere boyish fancies, "dead ere they were born," one putting out the fire of another before it had had time to hurt himself or any body else; so that when he heard that he was to marry Clemence de Montmorenci, he felt no aversion to the match, and prepared himself to obey his father's behest without a murmur. On being introduced to the lady, he was by no means struck with her. She appeared amiable, sensible, and gentle; but she was decidedly plain, and dressed ill. Victor felt no disposition whatever to love her; but, on the other hand, he had no dislike to her; and as his heart was unoccupied, he expressed himself perfectly ready to comply with the wishes of his family and hers, by whom this alliance had been arranged from motives of mutual interest and accommodation.

So he commenced his course of love; which consisted in riding daily to the chateau of his intended father-in-law, where, if there was company, and he found amusement, he frequently remained great part of the morning. Now, it happened that his road lay through the village of Loques, where Manon lived, and happening one day to see her at the door, with the gallantry of a gay cavalier, he had saluted her. Manon, who was fully as vain as she was pretty, liked this homage to her beauty so well that she thereafter never neglected an opportunity of throwing herself in the way of enjoying it; and the salutation thus accidentally begun had, from almost daily repetition, ripened into a sort of silent flirtation. The young count smiled, she blushed and half smiled too; and whilst he in reality thought nothing about her, she had brought herself to believe he was actually in love with her, and that it was for her sake he so often appeared riding past her door.

---

1 The Montmorencis were one of France's most illustrious families, taking their name from the family seat at Montmorency in the Île-de-France.

But, on the present occasion, the sight of Francoise's beautiful face had startled the young man out of his good manners. It is difficult to say why a gentleman, who looks upon the features of one pretty girl with indifference, should be "frightened from his propriety" by the sight of another, in whom the world in general see nothing superior; but such is the case, and so it was with Victor. His heart seemed taken by storm; he could not drive the beautiful features from his brain; and although he laughed at himself for being thus enslaved by a low-born beauty, he could not laugh himself out of the impatience he felt to mount his horse and ride back again in the hope of once more beholding her. But this time Manon alone was visible; and although he lingered, and allowed his eyes to wander over the house and glance in at the windows, no vestige of the lovely vision could he descry.

"Perhaps she did not live there—she was probably but a visiter to the other girl?" He would have given the world to ask the question of Manon; but he had never spoken to her, and to commence with such an interrogation was impossible, at least Victor felt it so, for his consciousness already made him shrink from betraying the motives of the inquiry. So he saluted Manon and rode on; but the wandering anxious eyes, the relaxed pace, and the cold salutation, were not lost upon her. Besides, he had returned from the Chateau de Montmorenci before the usual time, and the mortified damsel did not fail to discern the motive of this deviation from his habits.

Manon was such a woman as you might live with well enough as long as you steered clear of her vanity, but once come in collision with that, the strongest passion of her nature, and you aroused a latent venom that was sure to make you smart. Without having ever "vowed eternal friendship," or pretending to any remarkable affection, the girls had been hitherto very good friends. Manon was aware that Francoise was possessed of a great deal of knowledge of which she was utterly destitute; but as she did not value the knowledge, and had not the slightest conception of what it was worth, she was not mortified by the want of it nor envious of the advantage; she did not consider that it was one. But in the matter of beauty the case was different. She had always persuaded herself that she was much the handsomer of the two. She had black shining hair and dark flashing eyes; and she honestly thought the soft blue eyes and auburn hair of her cousin tame and ineffective.

But the too evident *saisissement*[1] of the young count had shown her a rival where she had not suspected one, and her vexation was as great as her surprise. Then she was so puzzled what to do. If she abstained from sitting at the door herself, she should not see Monsieur de Vardes, and if she did sit there her cousin would assuredly do the same. It was extremely perplexing; but Francoise settled the question by seating herself at the door of her own accord. Seeing this, Manon came too to watch her, but she was sulky and snappish, and when Victor not only distinguished Francoise as before, but took an opportunity of alighting from his horse to tighten his girths,[2] just opposite the door, she could scarcely control her passion.

It would be tedious to detail how, for the two months that ensued, this sort of silent courtship was carried on. Suffice it to say, that by the end of Francoise's visit to Loques she was in complete possession of Victor's heart, and he of hers, although they had never spoken a word to each other; and when she was summoned home to Cabanis to meet her father, she was completely divided betwixt the joy of once more seeing the dear old man and the grief of losing, as she supposed, all chance of beholding again the first love of her young heart.

But here her fears deceived her. Victor's passion had by this time overcome his diffidence, and he had contrived to learn all he required to know about her from the blacksmith of the village, one day when his horse very opportunely lost a shoe; and as Cabanis was not a great way from the Chateau de Montmorenci, he took an early opportunity of calling on the old physician, under pretence of needing his advice. At first he did not succeed in seeing Francoise, but perseverance brought him better success; and when they became acquainted, he was as much charmed and surprised by the cultivation of her mind as he had been by the beauty of her person. It was not difficult for Victor to win the heart of the alchemist, for the young man really felt, without having occasion to feign, an interest and curiosity with respect to the occult

---

1 Amazement.

2 Belts or bands used to secure a saddle or pack.

researches so prevalent at that period; and thus, gradually, larger and larger portions of his time were subtracted from the Chateau de Montmorenci to be spent at the physician's. Then, in the green glades of that wide domain which extended many miles around, Victor and Francoise strolled together arm in arm; he vowing eternal affection, and declaring that this rich inheritance of the Montmorenci should never tempt him to forswear his love.

But though thus happy, "the world forgetting," they were not "by the world forgot."[1] From the day of Victor's first salutation to Francoise, Manon had become her implacable enemy. Her pride made her conceal as much as possible the cause of her aversion; and Francoise, who learned from herself that she had no acquaintance with Victor, hardly knew how to attribute her daily increasing coldness to jealousy. But by the time they parted the alienation was complete, and as, after Francoise went home, all communication ceased between them, it was some time before Manon heard of Victor's visits to Cabanis. But this blissful ignorance was not destined to continue. There was a young man in the service of the Montmorenci family called Jacques Renard; he was a great favourite with the marquis, who had undertaken to provide for him, when in his early years he was left destitute by the death of his parents, who were old tenants on the estate. Jacques, now filling the office of private secretary to his patron, was extremely in love with the alchemist's daughter; and Francoise, who had seen too little of the world to have much discrimination, had not wholly discouraged his advances. Her heart, in fact, was quite untouched; but very young girls do not know their own hearts; and when Francoise became acquainted with Victor de Vardes, she first learned what love is, and made the discovery that she entertained no such sentiment for Jacques Renard. The small encouragement she had given him was therefore withdrawn, to the extreme mortification of the disappointed suitor, who naturally suspected a rival, and was extremely curious to learn who that rival could be; nor was it long before he obtained the information he desired.

Though Francoise and her lover cautiously kept far away from that part of the estate which was likely to be frequented by the Montmorenci family, and thus avoided any inconvenient

---

1 A quotation from the poem *Eloisa to Abelard* (1717) by Alexander Pope.

rencounter with them, they could not with equal success elude the watchfulness of the foresters attached to the domain; and some time before the heiress or Manon suspected how Victor was passing his time, these men were well aware of the hours the young people spent together, either in the woods or at the alchemist's house, which was on their borders. Now the chief forester, Pierre Bloui, was a suitor for Manon's hand. He was an excellent huntsman, but being a weak, ignorant, ill-mannered fellow, she had a great contempt for him, and had repeatedly declined his proposals. But Pierre, whose dullness rendered his sensibilities little acute, had never been reduced to despair. He knew that his situation rendered him, in a pecuniary point of view, an excellent match, and that old Thierry, Manon's father, was his friend; so he persevered in his attentions, and seldom came into Loques without paying her a visit. It was from him she first learned what was going on at Cabanis.

"Ay," said Pierre, who had not the slightest suspicion of the jealous feelings he was exciting; "ay, there'll be a precious blow up by and by, when it comes to the ears of the family! What will the Marquis and the old Count de Vardes say, when they find that, instead of making love to Mam'selle Clemence, he spends all his time with Francoise Thilouze!"

"But is not Mam'selle Clemence angry already that he is not more with her?" inquired Manon.

"I don't know," replied Pierre; "but that's what I was thinking of asking Jacques Renard, the first time he comes shooting with me."

"I'm sure I would not put up with it if I were she!" exclaimed Manon, with a toss of the head; "and I think you would do very right to mention it to Jacques Renard. Besides, it can come to no good for Francoise; for of course the count would never think of marrying *her*."

"I don't know that," answered Pierre; "Margot, their maid, told me another story."

"You don't mean that the count is going to marry Francoise Thilouze!" exclaimed Manon, with unfeigned astonishment.

"Margot says he is," answered Pierre.

"Well, then, all I can say is," cried Manon, her face crimsoning with passion—"all I can say is, that they must have bewitched him, between them; she and that old conjuror, my uncle!"

"Well, I should not wonder," said Pierre. "I've often thought old Michael knew more than he should do."

Now, Manon in reality entertained no such idea, but under the influence of the evil passions that were raging within her at the moment, she nodded her head as significantly as if she were thoroughly convinced of the fact—in short, as if she knew more than she chose to say; and thus sent away the weak superstitious Pierre possessed with a notion that he lost no time in communicating to his brother huntsmen; nor was it long before Victor's attentions to Francoise were made known to Jacques Renard, accompanied with certain suggestions, that Michael Thilouze and his daughter were perhaps what the Scotch call, *no canny*;[1] a persuasion that the foresters themselves found little difficulty in admitting.

In the meanwhile, Clemence de Montmorenci had not been unconscious of Victor's daily declining attentions. He had certainly never pressed his suit with great earnestness; but now he did not press it at all. Never was so lax a lover! But as the alliance was one planned by the parents of the young people, not by the election of their own hearts, she contemplated his alienation with more surprise than pain. The elder members of the two families, however, were far from equally indifferent; and when they learned from the irritated, jealous Jacques Renard the cause of the dereliction, their indignation knew no bounds. It was particularly desirable that the estates of Montmorenci and De Vardes should be united, and that the lowly Francoise Thilouze, the daughter of a poor physician, who probably did not know who his grandfather was, should step in to the place designed for the heiress of a hundred quarterings,[2] and mingle her blood with the pure stream that flowed through the veins of the proud De Vardes, was a thing not to be endured. The strongest expostulations and representations were first tried with Victor, but in vain. "He was in love, and pleased with ruin." These failing, other measures must be resorted to; and as in those days, pride of blood, contempt for the rights of the people, ignorance,

---

1 Someone harmful or evil in character, such as a witch.

2 A quartering refers to heraldry. The shield is divided into quarters, bringing together the various coats onto one shield that reflects alliances and marriages in a noble family.

and superstition, were at their climax, there was little scruple as to the means, so that the end was accomplished.

It is highly probable that these great people themselves believed in witchcraft; the learned, as well as the ignorant, believed in it at that period; and so unaccountable a perversion of the senses as Victor's admiration of Francoise naturally appeared to persons who could discern no merit unadorned by rank, would seem to justify the worst suspicions; so that when Jacques hinted the notion prevailing amongst the foresters with respect to old Michael and his daughter, the idea was seized on with avidity. Whether Jacques believed in his own allegation it is difficult to say; most likely not; but it gratified his spite and served his turn; and his little scrupulous nature sought no further. The marquis shook his head ominously, looked very dignified and very grave, said that the thing must be investigated, and desired that the foresters, and those who had the best opportunities for observation, should keep an attentive eye on the alchemist and his daughter, and endeavour to obtain some proof of their malpractices, whilst he considered what was best to be done in such an emergency.

The wishes and opinions of the great have at all times a strange omnipotence; and this influence in 1588 was a great deal more potential than it is now. No sooner was it known that the Marquis de Montmorenci and the Count de Vardes entertained an ill will against Michael and Francoise, than every body became suddenly aware of their delinquency, and proofs of it poured in from all quarters. Amongst other stories, there was one which sprung from nobody knew where—probably from some hasty word, or slight coincidence, which flew like wildfire amongst the people, and caused an immense sensation. It was asserted that the Montmorenci huntsmen had frequently met Victor and Francoise walking together, in remote parts of the domain; but that when they drew near, she suddenly changed herself into a wolf and ran off. It was a favourite trick of witches to transform themselves into wolves, cats, and hares, and weir-wolves were the terror of the rustics; and as just at that period there happened to be one particularly large wolf, that had almost miraculously escaped the forester's guns, she was fixed upon as the representative of the metamorphosed Francoise.

Whilst this storm had been brewing, the old man, absorbed in his studies, which had received a fresh impetus from his late journey to Paris, and the young girl, rapt in the entrancing pleasures of a first love, remained wholly unconscious of the dangers that were gathering around them. Margot, the maid, had indeed not only heard, but had *felt* the effects of the rising prejudice against her employers. When she went to Loques for her weekly marketings, she found herself coldly received by some of her old familiars; whilst by those more friendly, she was seriously advised to separate her fortunes from that of persons addicted to such unholy arts. But Margot, who had nursed Francoise in her infancy, was deaf to their insinuations. She knew what they said was false; and feeling assured that if the young count married her mistress, the calumny would soon die away, she did not choose to disturb the peace of the family, and the smooth current of the courtship, by communicating those disagreeable rumours.

In the mean time, Pierre Bloui, who potently believed "the mischief that himself had made," was extremely eager to play some distinguished part in the drama of witch-finding. He knew that he should obtain the favour of his employers if he could bring about the conviction of Francoise; and he also thought that he should gratify his mistress. The source of her enmity he did not know, nor care to inquire; but enmity he perceived there was; and he concluded that the destruction of the object of it would be an agreeable sacrifice to the offended Manon. Moreover, he had no compunction, for the conscience of his superiors was his conscience; and Jacques Renard had so entirely confirmed his belief in the witch story, that his superstitious terrors, as well as his interests, prompted him to take an active part in the affair. Still he felt some reluctance to shoot the wolf; even could he succeed in so doing, from the thorough conviction that it was in reality not a wolf, but a human being he would be aiming at; but he thought if he could entrap her, it would not only save his own feelings, but answer the purpose much better; and accordingly he placed numerous snares, well baited, in that part of the domain most frequented by the lovers; and expected every day, when he visited them, to find Francoise, either in one shape or the other, fast by the leg. He was for some time disappointed; but at length he found in one of the traps, not the wolf or Francoise, but a wolf's foot. An animal had evidently been caught, and in the violence of its struggles for freedom had left its foot behind it. Pierre carried away the foot and baited his trap again.

About a week had elapsed since the occurrence of this circumstance, when one of the servants of the chateau, having met with a slight accident, went to the apothecary's at Loques, for the purpose of purchasing some medicaments; and there met Margot, who had arrived from Cabanis for the same purpose. Mam'selle Francoise, it appeared, had so seriously hurt one of her hands, that her father had been under the necessity of amputating it. As all gossip about the Thilouze family was just then very acceptable at home, the man did not fail to relate what he had heard; and the news, ere long, reached the ears of Pierre Bloui.

It would have been difficult to decide whether horror or triumph prevailed in the countenance of the astonished huntsman at this communication. His face first flushed with joy, and then became pale with affright. It was thus all true! The thing was clear, and he the man destined to produce the proof! It *had* been Francoise that was caught in the trap; and she had released herself at the expense of one of her hands, which, divided from herself, was no longer under the power of her incantations; and had therefore retained the form she had given it, when she resumed her own.

Here was a discovery! Pierre Bloui actually felt himself so overwhelmed by its magnitude, that he was obliged to swallow a glass of cogniac to restore his equilibrium, before he could present himself before Jacques Renard to detail this stupendous mystery and exhibit the wolf's foot.

How much Jacques Renard, or the marquis, when he heard it, believed of this strange story, can never be known. Certain it is, however, that within a few hours after this communication had been made to them, the *commissaire du quartier*,[1] followed by a mob from Loques, arrived at Cabanis, and straightway carried away Michael Thilouze and his daughter, on a charge of witchcraft. The influence of their powerful enemies hurried on the judicial

---

1 Commissioner of a quarter or district.

process, by courtesy called a trial, where the advantages were all on one side, and the disadvantages all on the other, and poor, terrified, and unaided, the physician and his daughter were, with little delay, found guilty, and condemned to die at the stake. In vain they pleaded their innocence; the wolf's foot was produced in court, and, combined with the circumstance that Francoise Thilouze had really lost her left hand, was considered evidence incontrovertible.

But where was her lover the while? Alas, he was in Paris, where, shortly before these late events, his father had on some pretext sent him; the real object being to remove him from the neighbourhood of Cabanis.

Now, when Manon saw the fruits of her folly and spite, she became extremely sorry for what she had done, for she knew very well that it was with herself the report had originated. But though powerful to harm, she was weak to save. When she found that her uncle and cousin were to lose their lives and die a dreadful death on account of the idle words dropped from her own foolish tongue, her remorse became agonising. But what could she do? Where look for assistance? Nowhere, unless in Victor de Vardes, and he was far away. She had no jealousy now; glad, glad would she have been, to be preparing to witness her cousin's wedding instead of her execution! But those were not the days of fleet posts—if they had been, Manon would have doubtless known how to write. As it was, she could neither write a letter to the count, nor have sent it when written. And yet, in Victor lay her only hope. In this strait she summoned Pierre Bloui, and asked him if he would go to Paris for her, and inform the young count of the impending misfortune. But it was not easy to persuade Pierre to so rash an enterprise. He was afraid of bringing himself into trouble with the Montmorencis. But Manon's heart was in the cause. She represented to him, that if he lost one employer he would get another, for that the young count would assuredly become his best friend; and when she found that this was not enough to win him to her purpose, she bravely resolved to sacrifice herself to save her friends.

"If you will hasten to Paris," she said, "stopping neither night nor day, and tell Monsieur de Vardes of the danger my uncle and cousin are in, when you come back I will marry you."

The bribe succeeded, and Pierre consented to go, owning that he was the more willing to do so, because he had privately changed his own opinion with respect to the guilt of the accused parties. "For," said he, "I saw the wolf last night under the chestnut trees, and as she was very lame, I could have shot her, but I feared my lord and lady would be displeased."

"Then, how can you be foolish enough to think it's my cousin," said Manon, "when you know she is in prison?"

"That's what I said to Jacques Renard," replied Pierre; "but he bade me not meddle with what did not concern me."

In fine, love and conscience triumphed over fear and servility, and as soon as the sun set behind the hills, Pierre Bloui started for Paris.

How eagerly now did Manon reckon the days and hours that were to elapse before Victor could arrive. She had so imperfect an idea of the distance to be traversed, that after the third day she began hourly to expect him; but sun after sun rose and set, and no Victor appeared; and in the meantime, before the very windows of the house she dwelt in, she beheld preparations making day by day for the fatal ceremony. From early morn to dewy eve, the voices of the workmen, the hammering of the scaffolding, and the hum of the curious and excited spectators, who watched its progress, resounded in the ears of the unhappy Manon; for a witch-burning was a sort of *auto da fe*,[1] like the burning of a heretic, and was anticipated as a grand spectacle, alike pleasing to gods and men, especially in the little town of Loques, where exciting scenes of any kind were very rare.

Thus time crept on, and still no signs of rescue; whilst the anguish and remorse of the repentant sinner became unbearable.

Now, Manon was not only a girl of strong passions but of a fearless spirit. Indeed the latter was somewhat the offspring of the former; for when her feelings were excited, not only justice and charity, as we have seen, were apt to be forgotten, but personal danger and feminine fears were equally overlooked in the tempest

---

1 During an *auto da fe* (act of faith), the charges brought against those accused of crimes such as heresy, witchcraft, or other seeming offenses during the Spanish Inquisition would be read out loud and the sentences determined. There would often be a procession to the city plaza, followed by a mass.

that assailed her. On the present occasion, her better feelings were in full activity. Her whole nature was aroused, self was not thought of, and to save the lives she had endangered by her folly, she would have gladly laid down her own. "For why live," thought she, "if my uncle and cousin die? I can never be happy again; besides, I must keep my promise and marry Pierre Bloui; and I had better lose my life in trying to expiate my fault than live to be miserable."

Manon had a brother called Alexis, who was now at the wars;[1] often and often, in this great strait, she had wished him at home; for she knew that he would have undertaken the mission to Paris for her, and so have saved her the sacrifice she had made in order to win Pierre to her purpose. Now, when Alexis lived at home, and the feuds between the king and the grand seigneurs[2] had brought the battle to the very doors of the peasants of Auvergne, Manon had many a time braved danger in order to bring this much loved brother refreshments on his night watch; and he had, moreover, as an accomplishment which might be some time needed for her own defence, taught her to carry a gun and shoot at a mark. In those days of civil broil and bloodshed, country maidens were not infrequently adept in such exercises. This acquirement she now determined to make available; and when the eve of the day appointed for the execution arrived without any tidings from Paris, she prepared to put her plan in practice. This was no other than to shoot the wolf herself, and, by producing it, to prove the falsity of the accusation. For this purpose, she provided herself with a young pig, which she slung in a sack over her shoulder, and with her brother's gun on the other, and disguised in his habiliments,[3] when the shadows of twilight fell upon the earth, the brave girl went forth into the forest on her bold enterprise alone.

She knew that the moon would rise ere she reached her destination, and on this she reckoned for success. With a beating heart she traversed the broad glades, and crept through the narrow paths that intersected the wide woods till she reached the chestnut avenue where Pierre said he had seen the lame wolf. She was

---

1 This may refer to the civil wars in France between Protestants and Roman Catholics that occurred as the Protestant Reformation spread in Europe.
2 Feudal lords.
3 Clothing.

aware that old or disabled animals, who are rendered unfit to hunt their prey, will be attracted a long distance by the scent of food; so having hung her sack with the pig in it to the lower branch of a tree, she herself ascended another close to it, and then presenting the muzzle of her gun straight in the direction of the bag, she sat still as a statue; and there, for the present, we must leave her, whilst we take a peep into the prison of Loques, and see how the unfortunate victims of malice and superstition are supporting their captivity and prospect of approaching death.

Poor Michael Thilouze and his daughter had had a rude awakening from the joyous dreams in which they had both been wrapt. The old man's journey to Paris had led to what he believed would prove the most glorious results. It was true that report had as usual exaggerated the success of his fellow-labourer there. The Italian Alascor had not actually found the philosopher's stone—but he was on the eve of finding it—one single obstacle stood in his way, and had for a considerable time arrested his progress; and as he was an old man, worn out by anxious thought and unremitting labour, who could scarcely hope to enjoy his own discovery, he consented to disclose to Michael not only all he knew, but also what was the insurmountable difficulty that had delayed his triumph. This precious stone, he had ascertained, which was not only to ensure to the fortunate possessor illimitable wealth, but perennial youth, could not be procured without the aid of a virgin, innocent, perfect, and pure; and, moreover, capable of inviolably keeping the secret which must necessarily be imparted to her.

"Now," said the Italian, "virgins are to be had in plenty; but the second condition I find it impossible to fulfill; for they invariably confide what I tell them to some friend or lover; and thus the whole process becomes vitiated, and I am arrested on the very threshold of success."

Great was the joy of Michael on hearing this; for he well knew that Francoise, his pure, innocent, beautiful Francoise, *could* keep a secret; he had often had occasion to prove her fidelity; so bidding the Italian keep himself alive but for a little space, when he, in gratitude for what he had taught him, would return with the long sought for treasure, and restore him to health, wealth, and vigorous youth, the glad old man hurried back to Cabanis, and "set himself about it like the sea."

It was in performing the operation required of her that Francoise had so injured her hand that amputation had become unavoidable; and great as had been the joy of Michael was now his grief. Not only had his beloved daughter lost her hand, but the hopes he had built on her co-operation were for ever annihilated; maimed and dismembered, she was no longer eligible to assist in the sublime process. But how much greater was his despair, when he learned the suspicions to which this strange coincidence had subjected her, and beheld the innocent, and till now happy girl, led by his side to a dungeon. For himself he cared nothing; for her everything. He was old and disappointed, and to die was little to him—but his Francoise, his young and beautiful Francoise, cut off in her bloom of years, and by so cruel and ignominious a death! And here they were in prison alone, helpless and forsaken! Absorbed in his studies, the poor physician had lived a solitary life; and his daughter, holding a rank a little above the peasantry and below the gentry, had had no companion but Manon, and she was now her bitterest foe; this at least they were told.

How sadly and slowly, and yet how much too fleetly, passed the days that were to intervene betwixt the sentence and the execution. And where was Victor? Where were his vows of love and eternal faith? Ah, all forgotten. So thought Francoise, who, ignorant of his absence from the Chateau de Vardes, supposed him well acquainted with her distress.

Thus believing themselves abandoned by the world, the poor father and daughter, in tears, and prayers, and attempts at mutual consolation, spent this sad interval, till at length the morning dawned that was to witness the accomplishment of their dreadful fate. During the preceding night old Michael had never closed his eyes; but Francoise had fallen asleep shortly before sunrise, and was dreaming that it was her wedding day; and that, followed by the cheers of the villagers, Victor, the still beloved Victor, was leading her to the altar. The cheers awoke her, and with the smile of joy still upon her lips, she turned her face to her father. He was stretched upon the floor overcome by a burst of uncontrollable anguish at the sounds that had aroused her from her slumbers;

for the sounds were real. The voices of the populace, crowding in from the adjacent country and villages to witness the spectacle, had pierced the thick walls of the prison and reached the ears and the hearts of the captives. Whilst the old man threw himself at her feet, and, pouring blessings on her fair young head, besought her pardon, Francoise almost forgot her own misery in his; and when the assistants came to lead them forth to execution, she not only exhorted him to patience, but supported with her arm the feeble frame that, wasted by age and grief, could furnish but little fuel for the flames that awaited them.

Nobody would have imagined that in this thinly peopled neighbourhood so many persons could have been brought together as were assembled in the market-place of Loques to witness the deaths of Michael Thilouze and his daughter. A scaffolding had been erected all round the square for the spectators—that designed for the gentry being adorned with tapestry and garlands of flowers. There sat, amongst others, the families of Montmorenci and De Vardes—all except the Lady Clemence, whose heart recoiled from beholding the death of her rival; although, no more enlightened than her age, she did not doubt the justice of the sentence that had condemned her. In the centre of the area was a pile of faggots, and near it stood the assistant executioners and several members of the church—priests and friars in their robes of black and grey.

The prisoners, accompanied by a procession which was headed by the judge and terminated by the chief executioner of the law, were first marched round the square several times, in order that the whole of the assembly might be gratified with the sight of them; and then being placed in front of the pile, the bishop of the district, who attended in his full canonicals, commenced a mass for the souls of the unhappy persons about to depart this life under such painful circumstances, after which he pronounced a somewhat lengthy oration on the enormity of their crime, ending with an exhortation to confession and repentance.

These, which constituted the whole of the preliminary ceremonies, being concluded, and the judge having read the sentence, to the effect, that, being found guilty of abominable and devilish magic arts, Michael and Francoise Thilouze were condemned to be burnt, especially for that the said Francoise, by her own arts, and those of her father, had bewitched the Count Victor de Vardes, and had sundry times visibly transformed herself into the shape of a wolf, and being caught in a trap, had thereby lost her hand, &c., the prisoners were delivered to the executioner, who prepared to bind them previously to their being placed on the pile. Then Michael fell upon his knees, and crying aloud to the multitude, besought them to spare his daughter, and to let him die alone; and the hearts of some amongst the people were moved. But from that part of the area where the nobility were seated, there issued a voice of authority, bidding the executioner proceed; so the old man and the young girl were placed upon the pile, and the assistants, with torches in their hands, drew near to set it alight, when a murmur arose from afar, then a hum of voices, a movement in the assembled crowd, which began to sway to and fro like the swing of vast waters. Then there was a cry of "Make way! make way! open a path! let her advance!" and the crowd divided, and a path was opened, and there came forward, slowly and with difficulty, pale, dishevelled, with clothes torn and stained with blood, Manon Thierry, dragging behind her a dead wolf. The crowd closed in as she advanced, and when she reached the centre of the arena, there was straightway a dead silence. She stood for a moment looking around, and when she saw where the persons in authority sat, she fell upon her knees and essayed to speak; but her voice was choked by emotion, no word escaped her lips; she could only point to the wolf, and plead for mercy by her looks; where her present anguish of soul, and the danger and terror she had lately encountered, were legibly engraved.

The appeal was understood, and gradually the voices of the people rose again—there was a reaction. They who had been so eager for the spectacle, were now ready to supplicate for the victims—the young girl's heroism had conquered their sympathies. "Pardon! pardon!" was the cry, and a hope awoke in the hearts of the captives. But the interest of the Montmorencis was too strong for that of the populace—the nobility stood by their order, and stern voices commanded silence, and that the ceremony should proceed; and once more the assistants brandished their torches and advanced to the pile; and then Manon, exhausted with grief, terror, and loss of blood, fell upon her face to the ground.

But now, again, there is a sound from afar, and all voices are hushed, and all ears are strained—it is the echo of a horse's foot galloping over the drawbridge; it approaches; and again, like the surface of a stormy sea, the dense crowd is in motion; and then a path is opened, and a horse, covered with foam, is seen advancing, and thousands of voices burst forth into "Viva! Viva!" The air rings with acclamations. The rider was Victor de Vardes, bearing in his hand the king's order for arrest of execution.

Pierre Bloui had faithfully performed his embassy; and the brave Henry IV,[1] moved by the prayers and representations of the ardent lover, had hastily furnished him with a mandate commanding respite till further investigation.

Kings were all-powerful in those days; and it was no sooner known that Henry was favourable to the lovers, than the harmlessness of Michael and his daughter was generally acknowledged; the production of the wolf wanting a foot being now considered as satisfactory a proof of their innocence, as the production of the foot wanting the wolf had formerly been of their guilt.

Strange human passions, subject to such excesses and to such revulsions! Michael Thilouze and his daughter happily escaped; and under the king's countenance and protection, the young couple were married; but we need not remind such of our readers as are learned in the annals of witchcraft, how many unfortunate persons have died at the stake for crimes imputed to them, on no better evidence than this.

As for the heiress of Montmorenci, she bore her loss with considerable philosophy. She would have married the young Count de Vardes without repugnance, but he had been too cold a lover to touch her heart or occasion regret; but poor Manon was the sacrifice for her own error. What manner of contest she had had with the wolf was never known, for she never sufficiently recovered from the state of exhaustion in which she had fallen to the earth, to be able to describe what had passed. Alone she had vanquished the savage animal, alone dragged it through the forest and the village, to the market square, where every human being able to stir, for miles round, was assembled; so that all other places

---

1 Henry IV was king of France from 1589 to 1610.

were wholly deserted. The wolf had been shot, but not mortally; its death had evidently been accelerated by other wounds. Manon herself was much torn and lacerated; and on the spot where the creature had apparently been slain, was found her gun, a knife, and a pool of blood, in which lay several fragments of her dress. Though unable to give any connected account of her own perilous adventure, she was conscious of the happy result of her generous devotion; and before she died received the heartfelt forgiveness and earnest thanks of her uncle and cousin, the former of whom soon followed her to the grave. Despairing now of ever succeeding in his darling object, what was the world to him! He loved his daughter tenderly, but he was possessed with an idea, which it had been the aim and hope of his life to work out. She was safe and happy, and needed him no more; and the hope being dead, life seemed to ooze out with it.

By the loss of that maiden's hand, who can tell what we have missed! For doubtless it is the difficulty of fulfilling the last condition named by the Italian, which has been the real impediment in the way of all philosophers who have been engaged in alchemical pursuits; and we may reasonably hope, that when women shall have learned to hold their tongues, the philosopher's stone will be discovered, and poverty and wrinkles thereafter cease to deform the earth.

For long years after these strange events, over the portcullis[1] of the old chateau of the De Vardes, till it fell into utter ruin, might be discerned the figure of a wolf, carved in stone, wanting one of its fore-feet; and underneath it the following inscription—"*In perpetuam rei memoriam.*"[2]

---

1 A grating of iron bars suspended in the gateway of a building that is lowered to prevent passage.
2 In everlasting remembrance.

Wagner, the Wehr-Wolf

G. W. M. Reynolds

George William MacArthur Reynolds (1814-1879) was born in Sandwich, Kent, to wealthy parents, George and Caroline Kent, both of whom died by the time he was a teenager. Although his guardian enrolled him in the Royal Military College, Reynolds rebelled and left England for France with his younger brother Edward in tow. In France, Reynolds worked in a Paris bookstore, composed his first novel, The Youthful Imposter *(1835), and wed Susannah Pierson at the British embassy. When Reynolds returned to England with his family in 1835, he was bankrupt. Unfortunately, this was only the beginning of Reynolds's financial woes, for he would declare bankruptcy again in 1840 and 1848.*

Reynolds was a prolific writer, publishing novels, short stories, and nonfiction articles, some of which were original, some plagiarized. Reynolds's Pickwick Abroad *(1837-38) shamelessly borrowed from Charles Dickens's* Pickwick Papers *(1836-37), as did his* Master Timothy's Bookcase *(1841-42), which was based on Dickens's* Master Humphrey's Clock *(1839). In 1844, Reynolds published* The Mysteries of London, *modeled on* Les Mystères de Paris *by Eugène Sue. Reynolds's* Mysteries *was wildly successful, selling over a million copies within a decade. Reynolds would go on to write over twenty serialized novels, including* Wagner, the Wehr-Wolf *(1846-47),* The Coral Island *(1848-49), and* The Rye House Plot *(1853-54). His oeuvre included historical and gothic fiction, along with tales of adventure that frequently featured violence, gore, and licentious female characters. Reynolds's fiction primarily targeted a lower- and middle-class readership and was enormously popular.*

Reynolds was also a journalist. He worked as an editor for the Monthly Magazine *before being fired for plagiarism. Later, as co-founder and editor of the* London Journal, *Reynolds increased circulation by featuring sensational fiction accompanied by equally sensational wood-cuts; however, Reynolds soon had a falling out with the owner, George Stiff, which led him to found his own publication,* Reynolds's Miscellany, *in 1846.* Reynolds's Miscellany *remained in circulation until 1869 when it merged with* Bow Bells.

Serialization of Wagner, the Wehr-Wolf *began in the first issue of* Reynolds's Miscellany *on November 6, 1846, and concluded on July 24, 1847. It was a great year for "penny bloods" since* Varney the Vampyre; or, The Feast of Blood *and* The String of Pearls, *featuring Sweeney Todd, both written by James Malcolm Rymer, appeared simultaneously with* Wagner *in contemporary periodicals. With its monstrous transformations, exotic locales, and voluptuous women,* Wagner *boasted a wide readership and included provocative illustrations by Henry Anelay. At the beginning of* Wagner, *set in 1516,* Wagner, *a lonely, impoverished old man, makes a deal with John Faust, based on the legendary figure who sells his soul to the devil in exchange for power. In return for restored youth, intelligence, social graces, and wealth,* Wagner *must agree to transform into a werewolf on the last day of each month. At the end of the novel,* Wagner *is released from his deal with the devil and returns to his frail form before dying.*

Bibliography

Boone, Troy. *Youth of Darkest England: Working-Class Children at the Heart of the Victorian Empire.* New York: Routledge, 2005.

Collins, Dick. Introduction to *Wagner the Werewolf,* by G. W. M. Reynolds, ix-xvii. Hertfordshire: Wordsworth Editions, 2006.

Humphreys, Anne, and Louis James, eds. *G. W. M. Reynolds: Nineteenth-Century Fiction, Politics, and the Press.* Aldershot: Ashgate, 2008.

James, Louis. "George William MacArthur Reynolds." *Oxford Dictionary of National Biography.* Oxford: Oxford University Press, 2004. http://www.oxforddnb.com.

Reynolds, G. W. M. *Wagner, The Wehr-Wolf.* 1846-47. Edited by E. F. Bleiler. New York: Dover, 1975.

WAGNER, THE WEHR-WOLF.

CHAPTER XII.[1]

'Twas the hour of sunset.

The eastern horizon, with its gloomy and sombre twilight, offered a strange contrast to the glorious glowing hues of vermilion, and purple, and gold, that blended in long streaks athwart the western sky.

For even the winter sunset of Italy is accompanied with resplendent tints—as if an Emperor, decked with a refulgent[2] diadem, were repairing to his imperial couch.

The declining rays of the orb of light bathed in molten gold the pinnacles, steeples, and lofty palaces of proud Florence, and toyed with the limpid waves of the Arno,[3] on whose banks innumerable villas and casinos already sent forth delicious strains of music, broken only by the mirth of joyous revellers.

And by degrees, as the sun went down, the palaces of the superb city began to shed light from their lattices set in rich sculptured masonry; and here and there where festivity prevailed, grand illuminations sprung up with magical quickness,—the reflection from each separate galaxy rendering it bright as day,—far—far around.

Vocal and instrumental melody floated through the still air, and the perfume of exotics, decorating the halls of the Florentine nobles, poured from the widely-opened portals, and rendered that air delicious.

For Florence was gay that evening—the last day of each month being the one which the wealthy lords and high-born ladies set apart for the reception of their friends.

The sun sank behind the western hills; and even the hothouse

---

1 Wagner appears in Florence as a noble aristocrat. This chapter describes the price for his deal with John Faust—transformation into a werewolf.

2 Shining or reflecting brilliant light.

3 A river in Tuscany.

flowers closed up their buds—as if they were eye-lids weighed down by slumber, and not to awake again until the morning should arouse them again to welcome the return of their lover—that glorious sun!

Darkness seemed to dilate upon the sky like an image in the midst of a mirage, expanding into superhuman dimensions,—then rapidly losing its shapeliness, and covering the vault above densely and confusedly.

But by degrees, countless stars began to stud the colourless canopy of heaven, like gems of orient splendor; for the last—last flickering ray of the twilight in the west had expired in the increasing obscurity.

But, hark! what is that wild and fearful cry?

In the midst of a wood of evergreens on the banks of the Arno, a man—young, handsome, and splendidly attired—has thrown himself upon the ground, where he writhes like a stricken serpent.

He is the prey of a demoniac excitement: an appalling consternation is on him—madness is in his brain—his mind is on fire.

Lightnings appear to gleam from his eyes—as if his soul were dismayed, and withering within his breast.

"Oh! no—no!" he cries with a piercing shriek, as if wrestling madly—furiously—but vainly against some unseen fiend that holds him in his grasp.

And the wood echoes to that terrible wail: and the startled bird flies fluttering from its bough.

But, lo! what awful change is taking place in the form of that doomed being? His handsome countenance elongates into one of savage and brute-like shape;—the rich garments which he wears become a rough, shaggy, and wiry skin;—his body loses its human contours—his arms and limbs take another form; and, with a frantic howl of misery, to which the woods give horribly faithful reverberations, and with a rush like a hurling wind, the wretch starts wildly away—no longer a man, but a monstrous wolf!

On—on he goes: the wood is cleared—the open country is gained. Tree—hedge—and isolated cottage appear but dim points in the landscape—a moment seen, the next left behind; the very hills appear to leap after each other.

A cemetery stands in the monster's way, but he turns not

aside:—through the sacred enclosure, on—on he goes. There are situate many tombs, stretching up the slope of a gentle acclivity, from the dark soil of which the white monuments stand forth with white and ghastly gleaming, and on the summit of the hill is the church of St. Benedict the Blessed.[1]

From the summit of the ivy-grown tower the very rooks, in the midst of their cawing, are scared away by the furious rush and the wild howl with which the Wehr-Wolf thunders over the hallowed ground.

At the same instant a train of monks appear round the angle of the church—for there is a funeral at that hour; and their torches flaring with the breeze that is now springing up, cast an awful and almost magical light on the dark gray walls of the edifice,—the strange effect being enhanced by the prismatic reflection of the lurid blaze from the stained glass of the oriel window.

The solemn spectacle seemed to madden the Wehr-Wolf. His speed increased—he dashed through the funeral train—appalling cries of terror and alarm burst from the lips of the holy fathers, and the solemn procession was thrown into confusion. The coffin-bearers dropped their burden—and the corpse rolled out upon the ground—its decomposing countenance seeming horrible by the glare of the torchlight.

The monk who walked nearest the head of the coffin was thrown down by the violence with which the ferocious monster cleared its passage; and the venerable father—on whose brow sat the snow of eighty winters—fell with his head against a monument, and his brains were dashed out.

On—on fled the Wehr-Wolf—over mead and hill, through valley and dale. The very wind seemed to make way: he clove the air—he appeared to skim the ground—to fly.

Through the romantic glades and rural scenes of Etruria[2] the monster sped—sounds, resembling shrieking howls, bursting ever and anon from his foaming mouth—his red eyes glaring in the dusk of the evening like ominous meteors—and his whole aspect so full

---

1 St. Benedict of Nursia (480-547) founded the Benedictine monastery at Monte Cassino.

2 A region in central Italy comprising Tuscany and Umbria.

"HE DASHED THROUGH THE FUNERAL TRAIN." (See p. 23.)

Henry Anelay, illustration from *Wagner, The Wehr-Wolf*, by G. W. M. Reynolds

of appalling ferocity, that never was seen so monstrous—so terrific a spectacle!

A village is gained—he turns not aside—but dashes madly through the little street formed by the huts and cottages of the Tuscan vine-dressers.

A little child is in his path—a sweet, blooming, ruddy, noble boy, with violet-coloured eyes and flaxen hair,—disporting merrily at a short distance from his parents who are seated at the threshold of their dwelling.

Suddenly a strange and ominous rush—an unknown trampling of rapid feet falls upon their ears: then with a savage cry, a monster sweeps past.

"My child! my child!" screams the affrighted mother; and simultaneously the shrill cry of an infant in the sudden agony of death carries desolation to the ear!

'Tis done—'twas but the work of a moment—the wolf has swept by—the quick rustling of his feet is no longer heard in the village. But those sounds are succeeded by awful wails and heart-rending lamentations; for the child—the blooming, violet-eyed, flaxen-haired boy—the darling of his poor but tender parents, is weltering in his blood!

On—on speeds the destroyer, urged by an infernal influence which maddens the more intensely because its victim strives vainly to struggle against it:—on—on, over the beaten road—over the fallow field—over the cottager's garden—over the grounds of the rich one's rural villa.

And now, to add to the horrors of the scene, a pack of dogs have started in pursuit of the wolf,—dashing—crushing—hur-rying—pushing—pressing upon one another in all the anxious ardour of the chase.

The silence and shade of the open country, in the mild star-light, seem eloquently to proclaim the peace and happiness of a rural life:—but now that silence is broken by the mingled howling of the wolf and the deep baying of the hounds,—and that shade is crossed and darkened by the forms of the animals as they scour so fleetly—oh! with such whirlwind speed along.

But that Wehr-Wolf bears a charmed life; for though the hounds overtake him—fall upon him—and attack him with all the courage of their nature,—yet does he hurl them from him—toss them aside—spurn them away—and at length free himself from their pursuit altogether!

And now the moon rises with unclouded splendour, like a maiden looking from her lattice screened with purple curtains; and still the monster hurries madly on with unrelaxing speed.

For hours has he pursued his way thus madly;—and, on a sudden, as he passes the outskirts of a sleeping town, the church bell is struck by the watcher's hand to proclaim midnight. Over the town—over the neighboring fields—through the far-off forest, clanged that iron tongue: and the Wehr-Wolf sped all the faster— as if he were with ominous flapping, like the wings of a fabulous Simoorg.[1]

But in the midst of the appalling spasmodic convulsions—with direful writhings on the soil, and with cries of bitter anguish, the Wehr-Wolf gradually threw off his monster-shape; and at the very moment when the first sunbeam penetrated the wood and glinted on his face, he rose a handsome—young—and perfect man once more!

FROM CHAPTER XXXIX.[2]

IT was the last day of the month; and the hour of sunset was fast approaching.

Great was the sensation that prevailed throughout the city of Florence.

Rumour had industriously spread, and with equal assiduity exaggerated, the particulars of Fernand Wagner's trial—and the belief that a man on whom the horrible destiny of a Wehr-Wolf had been entailed, was about to suffer the extreme penalty of the law, was generally prevalent.

The great square of the ducal palace, where the scaffold was erected, was crowded with the Florentine populace; and the windows were literally alive with human faces.

Various were the emotions and feelings which influenced that mass of spectators. The credulous and superstitious—forming more than nine-tenths of the whole multitude—shook their heads, and commented amongst themselves in subdued whispers, on the profane rashness of the Chief Judge who dared to doubt the existence of such a being as a Wehr-Wolf. The few who shared the scepticism of the judge, applauded that high functionary for his courage in venturing so bold a stroke in order to destroy what he and they deemed an idle superstition.

---

1 A simurgh is a bird from Persian mythology that possessed the power of speech.
2 Wagner is arrested and placed in prison for a crime he did not commit, namely the murder of his niece, Agnes. He is found guilty after a trial and sentenced to death. However, the real murderer of Agnes is, in fact, Wagner's lover, Nisida.

But the great mass were dominated by a profound and indeed most painful sensation of awe: curiosity induced them to remain, though their misgivings prompted them to fly from the spot which had been fixed upon for the execution. The flowers of Florentine loveliness—and never in any age did the Republic boast of so much female beauty—were present; but bright eyes flashed forth uneasy glances, and snowy bosoms beat with alarms, and fair hands trembled in the lovers' pressure.

In the midst of the square was raised a high platform covered with black cloth, and presenting an appearance so ominous and sinister that it was but little calculated to revive the spirits of the timid. On this scaffold was a huge block; and near the block stood the headsman, carelessly leaning on his ax, the steel of which was polished and bright as silver.

A few minutes before the hour of sunset, the Chief Judge, the Procurator Fiscal, the two Assistant-Judges, and the lieutenant of sbirri,[1] attended by a turnkey and several subordinate police-officers, were repairing in procession along the corridor leading to the doomed prisoner's cell.

The Chief Judge alone was dignified in manner; and he alone wore a demeanour denoting resolution, and at the same time self-possession. Those who accompanied him were, without a single exception, a prey to the most lively fear; and it was evident that had they dared to absent themselves, they would not have been present on this occasion.

At length the door of the prisoner's cell was reached: and there the procession paused.

"The moment is now at hand," said the Chief Judge, "when a monstrous and ridiculous superstition—imported into our country from that cradle and nurse of preposterous legends, Germany—shall be annihilated forever. This knave who is about to suffer has doubtless propagated the report of his lupine destiny in order to inspire terror and thus prosecute his career of crime and infamy with the greater security from chances of molestation. For this end he painted the picture which appalled so many of you in the Judgment Hall, but which, believe me, my friends,

---

1 Italian police.

he did not always believe destined to retain its sable covering. Well did he know that the curiosity of a servant or of a friend would obtain a peep beneath the mystic veil; and he calculated that the terror with which he sought to invest himself would be enhanced by the rumours and representations spread abroad by those who had thus penetrated into his feigned secrets. But let us not waste that time which now verges towards a crisis whereby doubt shall be dispelled and a ridiculous superstition destroyed forever."

At this moment a loud—a piercing—and an agonizing cry burst from the interior of the cell.

"The knave has overheard me, and would fain strike terror to your hearts!" exclaimed the Chief Judge: then, in a still louder tone, he commanded the turnkey to open the door of the dungeon.

But when the man approached, so strange—so awful—so appalling were the sounds which came from the interior of the cell, that he threw down the key in dismay, and rushed from the dreaded vicinity.

"My lord, I implore you to pause!" said the Procurator Fiscal, trembling from head to foot.

"Would you have me render myself ridiculous in the eyes of all Florence?" demanded the Chief Judge sternly.

Yet, so strange were now the noises which came from the interior of the dungeon—so piercing the cries of agony—so violent the rustling and tossing on the stone floor, that for the first time this bold functionary entertained a partial misgiving, as if he had indeed gone too far.

But to retreat was impossible: and, with desperate resolution, the Chief Judge picked up the key, and thrust it into the lock.

His assistants, the Procurator Fiscal, and the sbirri, drew back with instinctive horror, as the bolts groaned in the iron work which held them: the chain fell with a dismal, clanking sound; and as the door was opened, a horrible monster burst forth from the dungeon with a terrific howl.

Yells and cries of despair reverberated through the long corridor: and those sounds were for an instant broken by that of the falling of a heavy body.

'Twas the Chief Judge—hurled down and dashed violently

against the rough, uneven masonry, by the mad careering of the Wehr-Wolf as the monster burst from his cell.

On—on he sped, with the velocity of lightning, along the corridor—giving vent to howls of the most horrifying description.

Fainting with terror, the Assistant-Judges, the Procurator Fiscal, and the sbirri, were for a few moments so overcome by the appalling scene they had just witnessed, that they thought not of raising the Chief Judge, who lay motionless on the pavement. But at length some of the police-officers so far recovered themselves as to be able to devote attention to that high functionary:—it was however too late—his skull was fractured by the violence with which he had been dashed against the wall—and his brains were scattered on the pavement.

Those who now bent over his disfigured corpse exchanged looks of unutterable horror.

In the meantime, the Wehr-Wolf had cleared the corridor—rapid as an arrow shot from the bow—he sprang bounding up a flight of steep stone stairs as if the elastic air bore him on—and rushing through an open door, burst suddenly upon the crowd that was so anxiously waiting to behold the procession issue thence!

Terrific was the yell that the multitude sent forth—a yell formed of a thousand combining voices,—so long—so loud—so wildly agonizing, that never had the welkin[1] rung with so appalling an ebullition of human misery before!

Madly rushed the wolf amidst the people—dashing them aside—overturning them—hurling them down—bursting through the mass too dense to clear a passage of its own accord—and making the scene of horror more horrible still by mingling his hideous howlings with the cries—the shrieks—the screams that escaped from a thousand tongues.

No pen can describe the awful scene of confusion and death which now took place. Swayed by no panic fear, but influenced by terrors of dreadful reality, the people exerted all their force to escape from that spot; and thus the struggling—crushing—pushing—crowding—fighting—and all the oscillations of a multitude set in motion by the direst alarms, were succeeded by the

---

1 Heavens.

most fatal results. Women were thrown down and trampled to death—strong men were scarcely able to maintain their footing—females were literally suffocated in the pressure of the crowd—and mothers with young children in their arms excited no sympathy.

Never was the selfishness of human nature more strikingly displayed than on this occasion: no one bestowed a thought upon his neighbour—the chivalrous Florentine citizen dashed aside the weak and helpless female who barred his way, with as little remorse as if she were not a being of flesh and blood—and even husbands forgot their wives, lovers abandoned their mistresses, and parents waited not an instant to succour their daughters.

Oh! it was a terrible thing to contemplate—that dense mass, oscillating furiously like the waves of the sea—sending up to heaven such appalling sounds of misery,—rushing furiously towards the avenues of egress,—falling back, baffled and crushed, in the struggle where only the very strongest prevailed,—labouring to escape from death, and fighting for life,—fluctuating, and rushing, and wailing in maddening excitement, like a raging ocean,—oh! all this wrought a direful sublimity, with those cries of agony and that riot of desperation!

And all this while the wolf pursued its furious career, amid the mortal violence of a people thrown into horrible disorder, pursued its way with savage howls, glaring eyes, and foaming mouth—the only living being there that was infuriate and not alarmed—battling for escape, and yet unhurt!

As a whirlpool suddenly assails the gallant ship—makes her agitate and rock fearfully for a few moments, and then swallows her up altogether,—so was the scaffold in the midst of the square shaken to its very basis for a little space, and then hurled down—disappearing altogether amidst the living vortex.

In the balconies and at the windows overlooking the square the awful excitement spread like wild-fire; and a real panic prevailed amongst those who were at least beyond the reach of danger. But horror paralyzed the power of sober reflection; and the hideous spectacle of volumes of human beings battling—and roaring—and rushing—and yelling in terrific frenzy, produced a kindred effect, and spread the wild delirium amongst the spectators at those balconies and those windows.

At length, in the square below, the crowds began to pour forth from the gates,—for the Wehr-Wolf had by this time cleared himself a passage, and escaped from the midst of that living ocean so fearfully agitated by the storms of fear.

But even when the means of egress were thus obtained, the most frightful disorder prevailed—the people rolling in heaps upon heaps,—while infuriate and agile men ran on the tops of the compact masses, and leapt in their delirium as if with barbarous intent.

On—on sped the Wehr-Wolf, dashing like a whirlwind through the streets leading to the open country—the white flakes of foam flying from his mouth like spray from the prow of a vessel,—and every fibre of his frame vibrating as if in agony.

And oh! what dismay—what terror did that monster spread in the thoroughfares through which he passed; how wildly,— how madly flew the men and women from his path—how piteously screamed the children at the house-doors in the poor neighbourhoods!

But as if sated with the destruction already wrought in the great square of the palace, the wolf dealt death no more in the precincts of the city:—as if lashed on by invisible demons, his aim—or his instinct was to escape.

The streets are threaded—the suburbs of the city are passed— the open country is gained; and now along the bank of the Arno rushes the monster—by the margin of that pure stream to whose enchanting vale the soft twilight lends a more delicious charm.

On the verge of a grove, with its full budding branches all impatient for the Spring, a lover and his mistress were murmuring fond language to each other. In the soft twilight blushed the maiden, less in bashfulness than in her own soul's emotion,—her countenance displaying all the magic beauty not only of feature but of feeling; and she raised her large blue eyes in the dewy light of a sweet enthusiasm to the skies, as the handsome youth by her side pressed her fair hand and said, "We must now part until tomorrow, darling of my soul! How calmly has this day, with all its life and brightness, passed away into the vast tomb of eternity! It is gone without leaving a regret on our minds,—gone, too, without clouds in the heavens or mists upon the earth—most beautiful even at the moment of its parting! To-morrow, beloved one, will unite us again in your parents' cot, and renewed happiness———"

The youth stopped—and the maiden clung to him in speechless terror: for an ominous sound, as of a rushing animal—and then a terrific howl, burst upon their ears.

No time had they for flight—not a moment even to collect their scattered thoughts.

The infuriate wolf came bounding over the green sward:[1] the youth uttered a wild and fearful cry—a scream of agony burst from the lips of the maiden as she was dashed from her lover's arms—and in another moment the monster had swept by.

But what misery—what desolation had his passage wrought! Though unhurt by his glistening fangs—though unwounded by his sharp claws,—yet the maiden—an instant before so enchanting in her beauty, so happy in her love—lay stretched on the cold turf, the cords of life snapped suddenly by that transition from perfect bliss to the most appalling terror!

And still the wolf rushed madly—wildly on.

FROM CHAPTER LXXIV.[2]

THE key grated in the lock of the mysterious cabinet—the door was opened—the young Countess of Riverola uttered a dreadful scream, while her husband gave vent to an ejaculation of horror and wild amazement:—for appalling was the spectacle which burst upon their view.

Nor were that scream and that ejaculation the only expressions of fearfully excited emotions which the opening of the closet called forth:—for, at the same instant, a cry of mingled wonder and joy burst from the lips of Fernand Wagner; and, forgetting that he was betraying the presence of Nisida, as well as his own—

---

1 Grassy turf.

2 Wagner is freed from his curse after witnessing the opening of a mysterious cabinet, which holds a secret withheld by the deceased Count of Riverola. The spectacle is witnessed by Flora; her husband, Francisco, the new Count of Riverola; and Francisco's sister, Nisida, who is also Wagner's former lover.

forgetting all and everything save the prophecy of the Rosicrucian[1] chief and the spectacle now before him—he sprang from behind the curtain—rushed towards the open cabinet—and, falling on his knees, exclaimed triumphantly, "I am saved! I am saved!"

For, behold! in that closet, two bleached and perfect skeletons were suspended to a beam;—and a voice whispered in Wagner's ear, that the spell of the Demon was now broken forever,—while his inmost soul seemed to sing the canticle[2] of a blessed salvation!

Yes: there—in that cabinet—suspended side by side—were the two skeletons,—horrible—hideous to gaze upon!

It is scarcely possible to convey to the reader an adequate idea of the wild emotions—the conflicting thoughts—and the clashing sentiments, which the dread revelation of that ghastly spectacle suddenly excited in the hearts of the four persons now assembled together—stirring up and agitating terribly all their acutest feelings, as the hurricane, abruptly bursting forth, takes up the withered leaves and scattered straws, and whirls them round and round as if they were in the eddies of the Maelstroom.[3]

Here was Flora clinging to her husband in speechless horror,—there was Wagner on his knees before the open cabinet: here was Francisco gazing in astonishment on his sister,—and there was Nisida herself, wrapt up in the stupefaction of bewilderment at the conduct of her lover!

But, oh! wondrous—amazing—and almost incredible sight!—what change comes over the person of Fernand Wagner?

There—even there, as he kneels,—and now—even now, as his looks remain bent upon the ghastly skeletons which seem to grin with their fleshless mouths, and to look forth with their eyeless sockets,—yes—even there and even now—is an awful and a frightful change taking place in him whom Nisida loves so well:—for his limbs rapidly lose their vigour, and his form its uprightness—his eyes, bright and gifted with the sight of an eagle, grow dim and failing—the hair disappears from the crown of his head, leaving it completely bald—his brow and his cheeks shrivel up into countless

---

1 A member of an organization dedicated the study of ancient religions and philosophy.
2 Song or chant.
3 Whirlpool.

wrinkles—his beard becomes long, flowing, and white as threads of silver—his mouth falls in, brilliant teeth sustaining the lips no more—and with the hollow moan of an old, old man, whose years are verging fast towards a century, the dying Wagner sinks upon the floor!

"Merciful God!" exclaimed Nisida, in a paroxysm of dreadful anguish, mingled with amazement and alarm; then, as if overwhelmed by the blow which the sudden fate of her lover inflicted upon her, she likewise sank down, her heart-strings crackling with burning grief.

* * *

Francisco immediately took his handkerchief, and threw it over the countenance of Fernand Wagner's corpse,—that countenance which still appeared to wear the bland and heavenly smile of a soul filled with sure and certain hope of eternal salvation!

Lycanthropy in London;

OR, THE WEHR-WOLF OF WILTON-CRESCENT

DUDLEY COSTELLO

Dudley Costello (1803-1865) was born in Sussex to a family with Irish roots. In his youth, Costello attended Sandhurst, where he trained for a military career. He received his commission in 1821 and was later stationed in Nova Scotia and Bermuda. In 1828, he retired from active service in the army and rejoined his mother and sister in Paris. There he began a career as an illustrator and copyist before accepting a position as foreign correspondent to the Morning Herald. *He returned to Great Britain in 1833 but spent a great deal of time in France throughout his life. A transnational perspective is consequently reflected in much of his journalistic work. In 1846, Costello accepted a position as foreign correspondent to the* Daily News, *and he worked as sub-editor of the* Examiner *from 1845 to 1865.*

Costello contributed articles and fiction to a variety of other publications, including the New Monthly Magazine, Gentleman's Magazine, *and* Ainsworth's Magazine. *At the same time, he became acquainted with Charles Dickens when contributing to* Bentley's Miscellany, *which Dickens edited from 1837 to 1839. Later, he contributed to two other periodicals edited by Dickens:* Household Words *and* All the Year Round. *While contributing prolifically to the periodical press, Costello also wrote book-length works, including a popular travel narrative,* A Tour through the Valley of the Meuse *(1845), and the novel* Faint Heart Never Won a Fair Lady *(1859). He also published a collection of ghost stories and essays,* Holidays with Hobgoblins, *and* Talk of Strange Things *(1861), illustrated by George Cruikshank.*

"Lycanthropy in London; or, The Wehr-Wolf of Wilton-Crescent" was published in Bentley's Miscellany *in 1855. It was subsequently reprinted in two American periodicals,* Littel's Living Age *and the* Western

Literary Messenger. *By 1855, Costello had been a longtime contributor to* Bentley's Miscellany, *an association which began in 1837 and ended in 1865, the year of his death. During his years at* Bentley's, *Costello was known for his comic fiction focused on the foibles of everyday life. As editors of* Bentley's Miscellany *put it, "that he saw things from a comic point of view, and that nothing escaped his observation which was likely to tell in narrative, he has shown for many years in this Magazine, which he has enlivened with his clever and brilliant sketches of French life, as well as lightly touching on peculiarities of English manners and habits."*[1]

Dudley Costello died at age 62 just a few months after the death of his beloved wife, Mary, to whom he had been happily married for twenty-two years.

Bibliography

Boase, G. C., and M. Clare Loughlin-Chow. "Dudley Costello." *Oxford Dictionary of National Biography.* Oxford: Oxford University Press, 2004. http://www.oxforddnb.com.

Costello, Dudley. "Lycanthropy in London; or, The Wehr-Wolf of Wilton-Crescent." *Bentley's Miscellany* 38 (1855): 361-379.

"Dudley Costello." *Bentley's Miscellany* 58 (1865): 543-550.

"Dudley Costello." In *The Dictionary of National Biography,* Vol. 22, edited by Leslie Stephen, 276-277. London: Smith, Elder, 1887.

"Dudley Costello." *Examiner* (October 7, 1865): 637.

King, Andrew. "Dudley Costello and Louisa Costello." *Dictionary of Nineteenth-Century Journalism. Nineteenth-Century Index.* Proquest, 2009. www.nineteenthcenturyindex.com.

Lohrli, Anne. *Household Words.* Toronto: University of Toronto Press, 1973.

LYCANTHROPY IN LONDON; OR, THE WEHR-WOLF OF WILTON-CRESCENT.

I.

MODERN honeymoons—as I lately had occasion to observe—are of very short duration. In repeating the remark, however, I do not

---

[1] "Dudley Costello," 544.

mean to impugn the faith or affection of either man or woman, but simply to state a fact with reference to the time which is now generally devoted to the "month"—as it is called—of sweetness, and which rarely exceeds a week or ten days—nay, is often very much less.

Of this class, at all events, was the honeymoon of Mr. and Mrs. Beaufort Fitz-Poodle, who were married about the end of last October, and did not set out on a continental tour or migrate farther than Reigate,[1] where they only remained three days, and then returned to town to take possession of their new house in Wilton-crescent.

The locality of their future residence had been the subject of much amicable discussion between Mr. and Mrs. Beaufort Fitz-Poodle, while they were lovers only. The lady liked this quarter because it was fashionable, because she had friends there, and because, if she had any leaning *from* the Established Church[2] (which she denied as strenuously as if she wore a mitre[3]), it was rather in favour of the sect known as "The Decorative Christians."[4] The gentleman also acknowledged his predilection for Belgravia[5] "on account," he said—and his words were remembered—"of its being almost in the country, while it was, in point of fact, in the very middle of town." When so much unanimity existed, all that remained was to find a suitable house, and this anybody may have in London at the very shortest notice, provided there be no objection to pay for the accommodation. Now Mr. Beaufort Fitz-Poodle had plenty of money, and—singularly enough—was liberal in the use of it, so the question of rent, with all its concomitants, was soon disposed of, and Wilton-crescent rejoiced in another important addition to its respectability.

There are some people who take the greatest delight in furnishing their houses themselves, and leave nothing but the supply to upholsterers. Mrs. Fitz-Poodle was a lady whose tendencies

___

Surrey that is located about 60 miles south of London.

of England.

reference to high-church Anglicanism, which favored formal

neighborhood in London.

inclined that way—I have said something to this effect already—and it was in a great degree owing to her desire to indulge her taste for decoration that the wedding tour was so greatly abbreviated. Had Mr. Fitz-Poodle's wishes been alone consulted, I believe he would have postponed their return until the leaves were quite off the trees, for—as he made no scruple of saying—he was passionately fond of the country; but, whatever were his own inclinations, like a good husband—as I think he was, notwithstanding what others have said—he sacrificed them to his wife's fantasy, and abandoned the downs of Reigate for the level of Belgravia, apparently without a sigh.

Mrs. Fitz-Poodle was speedily in her element, amid damask curtains, Aubusson carpets, tapestried *portières*,[1] carved chairs (including a *Prie-Dieu*[2] of exquisite workmanship, for her *boudoir*) buhl cabinets, marqueterie tables, encaustic tiles, India matting and all the requisite paraphernalia for the ornamentation convenience of her *ménage*.[4] Being thus engaged, the duln November was unheeded, her only regret arising from th culty of obtaining more than two hours of positive daylig of the twenty-four for the proper selection of patterr were the long evenings a bore, though nobody was what she bought during the day supplied her with p' pation in examining and arranging at night.

With Mr. Fitz-Poodle the case was not exac' was pleased, as most men are, to see his house he had no great genius for domestic embelli he revel—as it were—in Panklibanons[5] and the only real good in life was household fv ance with his wife's wishes, he accompar night at least, in her daily drives abour of luxury and *virtù*,[7] but at the expirar

---

1 Curtains hanging over an entryway.
2 Kneeling stool with a desk used for pr
3 These objects are elaborately design
4 Household.
5 A commercial showroom of dec
6 A large warehouse where carri
7 Love of art.

1 A town in
2 The Church
3 Bishop's hat.
4 A humorous
ritual.
5 A fashionable r

mean to impugn the faith or affection of either man or woman, but simply to state a fact with reference to the time which is now generally devoted to the "month"—as it is called—of sweetness, and which rarely exceeds a week or ten days—nay, is often very much less.

Of this class, at all events, was the honeymoon of Mr. and Mrs. Beaufort Fitz-Poodle, who were married about the end of last October, and did not set out on a continental tour or migrate farther than Reigate,[1] where they only remained three days, and then returned to town to take possession of their new house in Wilton-crescent.

The locality of their future residence had been the subject of much amicable discussion between Mr. and Mrs. Beaufort Fitz-Poodle, while they were lovers only. The lady liked this quarter because it was fashionable, because she had friends there, and because, if she had any leaning *from* the Established Church[2] (which she denied as strenuously as if she wore a mitre[3]), it was rather in favour of the sect known as "The Decorative Christians."[4] The gentleman also acknowledged his predilection for Belgravia[5] "on account," he said—and his words were remembered—"of its being almost in the country, while it was, in point of fact, in the very middle of town." When so much unanimity existed, all that remained was to find a suitable house, and this anybody may have in London at the very shortest notice, provided there be no objection to pay for the accommodation. Now Mr. Beaufort Fitz-Poodle had plenty of money, and—singularly enough—was liberal in the use of it, so the question of rent, with all its concomitants, was soon disposed of, and Wilton-crescent rejoiced in another important addition to its respectability.

There are some people who take the greatest delight in furnishing their houses themselves, and leave nothing but the supply to the upholsterers. Mrs. Fitz-Poodle was a lady whose tendencies

---

1 A town in Surrey that is located about 60 miles south of London.

2 The Church of England.

3 Bishop's hat.

4 A humorous reference to high-church Anglicanism, which favored formal ritual.

5 A fashionable neighborhood in London.

inclined that way—I have said something to this effect already—and it was in a great degree owing to her desire to indulge her taste for decoration that the wedding tour was so greatly abbreviated. Had Mr. Fitz-Poodle's wishes been alone consulted, I believe he would have postponed their return until the leaves were quite off the trees, for—as he made no scruple of saying—he was passionately fond of the country; but, whatever were his own inclinations, like a good husband—as I think he was, notwithstanding what others have said—he sacrificed them to his wife's fantasy, and abandoned the downs of Reigate for the level of Belgravia, apparently without a sigh.

Mrs. Fitz-Poodle was speedily in her element, amid damask curtains, Aubusson carpets, tapestried *portières*,[1] carved chairs (including a *Prie-Dieu*[2] of exquisite workmanship, for her *boudoir*), buhl cabinets, marqueterie tables, encaustic tiles, India mattings,[3] and all the requisite paraphernalia for the ornamentation and convenience of her *ménage*.[4] Being thus engaged, the dulness of November was unheeded, her only regret arising from the difficulty of obtaining more than two hours of positive daylight in each of the twenty-four for the proper selection of patterns. Neither were the long evenings a bore, though nobody was in town, for what she bought during the day supplied her with plenty of occupation in examining and arranging at night.

With Mr. Fitz-Poodle the case was not exactly the same. He was pleased, as most men are, to see his house well furnished, but he had no great genius for domestic embellishment, neither did he revel—as it were—in Panklibanons[5] and Pantechnicons,[6] as if the only real good in life was household furniture. Still, in compliance with his wife's wishes, he accompanied her, for a whole fortnight at least, in her daily drives about town in search of objects of luxury and *virtù*,[7] but at the expiration of that time he began to

---

1 Curtains hanging over an entryway.
2 Kneeling stool with a desk used for private prayer.
3 These objects are elaborately designed, exotic furniture pieces.
4 Household.
5 A commercial showroom of decorative iron works.
6 A large warehouse where carriages, furniture, and other goods were sold.
7 Love of art.

tire of this kind of *chasse*,[1] and would willingly have exchanged it for more legitimate sport at the cover's side.[2] But it was too soon to announce that desire: he must give up his hunting and shooting this year—that he knew—but before the next season came round—thus he mused, after dinner, while Mrs. Fitz-Poodle was testing by a bright light the comparative brilliancy of striped satins and figured silks—he would have a snug box[3] in a good sporting country, and take a little of what *he* called pleasure at that time of the year. The partner of his bosom would also, he thought, have had enough of her present occupation long before then, so with this prospect in view he submitted to the existing privation. As he did not, however, intend to pass the whole of the interval in upholstery warehouses and china-shops, he cast about for some plausible device to release him from a constant attendance which—I must confess the truth—in spite of his wife's great personal attractions, began to be a little irksome.

Having alluded to the beauty of Mrs. Fitz-Poodle, I may as well pause in my story for a moment to describe it. In the gallery of the Luxembourg in Paris, there is, or was a few years ago, a small picture of Sainte Geneviève,[4] seated on a mound in a flowery meadow, with her distaff in her hand, guarding a flock of sheep. She is represented as exquisitely fair, with eyes of that clear but decided blue which you see on the corolla of the Myosotis,[5] and with long-flowing hair, between flaxen and brown, on which a ray of sunshine seems to linger. Her features are small and faultless in expression—that is to say, if placidity be what you like best in the female countenance; and supposing the features to be the index of the mind, it is as well to marry a woman with that expression. You may be beaten off your guard more suddenly, be more madly enthralled—if you choose to suppose so—by a dark-haired brunette with damask cheek and flashing eyes, but the probability is that, at the end of three months, you will not be quite so much

---

1 Hunt.

2 Near the foxhole where hunters gather.

3 Hideaway.

4 Saint Geneviève (c. 422-500) was the patron saint of Paris who was believed to have saved the city from the Huns.

5 Forget-me-not flowers.

your own master as if you had wedded a *blonde*. I say "the probability," because, after all, calculations based on physiognomy alone are not absolute certainties, and I have known two or three fair ones who had wills of their own, and did not refrain from exercising them. To return, however, to the Sainte Geneviève of the Luxembourg. She was as like Mrs. Fitz-Poodle as one lily resembles another, with this advantage in favour of the mortal, that she was not ideal. On the other hand, to avoid the charge of exaggeration, I will say that the canonised wife of Clovis[1] had, in a moral point of view, a slight advantage over Mrs. Beaufort Fitz-Poodle, who, though very near it, was not *quite* a saint. I presume it was on account of the likeness he fancied he saw between the two, that when Mr. Beaufort Fitz-Poodle was in Paris last spring, being already engaged, he had a copy made of the Luxembourg picture which he afterwards gave to his bride, who, the first thing she did when she went to Wilton-crescent, hung it up in her *boudoir*.

It is of little consequence, provided a man be not depressingly hideous, whether he is handsome or plain; some of the cleverest fellows of the present day are about the ugliest, and I need not go further than the House of Commons—than the Treasury bench,[2] in particular—to prove what I say; although if I were in want of something more than mere cleverness it is certainly not there I should go to seek for it. Male beauty then, being quite a secondary consideration in comparison with mental charms, it is only because I want a companion-portrait to that of Mrs. Beaufort Fitz-Poodle that I trace the lineaments of her spouse. Indeed, if I had been confined to those whom the world calls "good-looking," this second sketch would not have been attempted, for *he* had no claim to the distinction. It is very possible, even under these circumstances, that I might have fitted him also with a Dromio[3] in the shape of a saint, but perhaps the selection would have been invidious.[4] I shall, therefore, simply say that he was a tall, spare, long-limbed, wiry kind of man, with hard, angular features, a sharp nose, what is called "a

---

1 Clotilda, a Catholic saint known for her beauty.
2 A bench in the House of Commons occupied by the Prime Minister and other government dignitaries.
3 A double.
4 Offensive.

mouth full of teeth," small searching eyes obliquely set in his head, harsh, sandy eyebrows, strong iron-grey hair which no persuasion (or tongs) could induce to curl, and that the only personal foppery[1] in which he indulged was the cultivation of a considerable quantity of yellowish beard and whiskers, which met under his chin. I can scarcely think it was vanity—though it might have been—which made him sit to Mayall[2] for a daguerreotype, but he paid that excellent artist a visit a few days before his marriage, and we need not say that the resemblance was second nature. It is probable that, had it been less like and rather more flattering, Mrs. Fitz-Poodle would have been better pleased with the portrait. However, she accepted the present very philosophically, and seldom opened the case to look at it. "It was of no use doing so," she said, "when the other was always there."

Always! If it had been so! However, I will not anticipate.

I have adverted already to the period of the year when the furnishing excitement of Mrs. Fitz-Poodle was in full flow, and the delight of her husband in being compelled to witness it rather on the ebb. Dreams, although we disbelieve in them as portents—we wise ones—have still some influence over our waking thoughts. If the vision of the night has been cheerful, serenity sits on our brow next day; if gloomy, we are not, perhaps, such very pleasant companions as usual. If conscience depends upon digestion, as many imagine, dreams may have something to do with temper. The complex machine called Man is not so well put together as to be always in perfect order. I will, therefore, ascribe to a dream,— in which looking-glasses, chairs and tables, sofa-pillows, footstools, doormats, window-blinds, wardrobes, washing-stands, and upholsterers' men played very conspicuous, but very confused and contradictory parts beneath the *pia mater*[3] of Mr. Fitz-Poodle one night,—the sense of unwillingness which he felt on the following morning—it was, to the best of my belief, on the 20th of November—to accompany his wife to Messrs. Jehoshaphat Brothers in Bond-street, to choose a small gold-and-white cabinet, there being some there, "such loves of things," just arrived from

---

1 Male costume that is elaborate and affected.
2 John Mayall (1813-1901), a famous studio photographer.
3 The brain.

Paris. There might have been some other reason—it is so ungracious to expose all a person's motives—but, at any rate, I shall imagine it was a dream that made him say, when the prototype of Sainte Geneviève had just finished her description of the cabinets, which she had only just had a glimpse of, "I am very much afraid, my love, that I can't go with you to-day."

"Not go with me, Beaufort!" exclaimed the Belgravian Saint. "Why, what have you got to do?"

"To do?" asked Beaufort, using iteration in his turn, in the absence of a more direct reply, which was not quite ready.

"Yes. What prevents you from going?"

"Why, the fact is,"—this was said with hesitation, the dream, I dare say, still bothering him—"the fact is, I have another engagement."

"You did not mention it last night when I first spoke to you about the cabinet."

"I did not recollect it then; but happening to see the day of the month, over the chimney-piece there, I was reminded that this was the first meeting of our council for the season, when there is always a good deal to do."

"Council? what council?"

"The council of my society."

"I did not know you belonged to any society. I thought those things were always given up when gentlemen married!"

"Not the scientific ones, Eliza," said Beaufort, smiling. "The Botanical, for instance, is quite a ladies' society; so is mine."

"And which *is* yours?"

"Oh, the Zoological." Here he became more animated. "I shall take a double subscription this year, for we expect a good many rare animals, and you can oblige more friends on the Sunday afternoon. The meeting to-day will be interesting—the first of the season always is—we generally get letters from our agents at a distance respecting fresh purchases. We expect a *Mydaus meliceps*, that is, a Java polecat; by-the-by, it is one of the most vulgar-looking animals in existence; then we are to have a *Galago Moholi*, one of the *Lemuridæ*, from the Limpopo river in South Africa;—a *Wombat* from Port Jackson;—and a *Dumba*, or four-horned sheep, from Nepaul, which I am exceedingly anxious to see."

"It does not appear to me," observed the saintly Geneviève's likeness, with something in her tone not quite so heavenly as the expression of her celestial eyes—when tranquil—"it does not appear to me, Beaufort, that your expectations are raised particularly high. Vulgar-looking polecats and bats and sheep seem to me not so *very* attractive."

"I can assure you, Eliza, you are mistaken. That polecat now is a perfect *desideratum*.[1] The Wombat—it is not a bat, my love, nothing of the sort, but a *Marsupian*, its scientific name is *Phascolomys*— well, the Wombat is a very desirable animal—we have not had one these twenty years. And as for the *Dumba*, if we get that, we shall be very fortunate. Every breed of sheep is a subject of interest, not only to the man of science, but to the agriculturist, the manufacturer, and the general consumer. We can't introduce varieties enough. I am amazingly fond of all kinds of sheep, and whenever we live in the country I shall certainly kill my own mutton."

"Very well, Beaufort. I had no idea of disparaging your collection, only the things you named seemed common enough to me. But then I am not *at all* scientific—and, indeed, until now, I didn't know that *you* were."

"Neither am I, Eliza. I just know a little. Enough to interest me in the subject. Nothing more."

"*I* like *beautiful* animals," said the lady, "though, perhaps, I can't call them all by their right names——"

"By-the-by," interrupted her husband, desirous of giving a turn to the conversation, "I have had a note from Wimbush about a pair of carriage-horses; he tells me that *they* are just what I think you will like: magnificent steppers, just the same colour, height, and action, a perfect match. I must look in there, too. If they answer the description he gives, I shall not stand out about the price."

It was Mrs. Fitz-Poodle's turn now to smile, and she did so very sweetly, looking more like Sainte Geneviève than ever: the "magnificent steppers" had reconciled her to the solitary drive. But, before she went out, she wrote a letter to her cousin, Adela Cunninghame, whom she shortly expected from Devonshire, on a visit; and, as that young lady was in her perfect confidence, she mentioned—incidentally—that Mr. Fitz-Poodle was gone to

1 Object of desire.

attend a meeting of the Zoological Council, and that she was, "for the first time since her wedding-day—*alone!*"

II.

In marriage, as in miracles, *ce n'est que le premier pas qui coûte.*[1] Having once broken the ice about engagements that must be kept, Mr. Fitz-Poodle found no difficulty in discovering what they were, or, at all events, in announcing their existence. Not that he was in the slightest degree tired of the constant society of his beautiful wife, but, he argued, when she is so entirely absorbed in things that I don't care about, it can't make much difference to her whether I am always at her side or not. The Zoological Society had proved so very good a card that he made it his regular *cheval de bataille;*[2] when once they began it seemed as if the meetings in Hanover-square were continually taking place, and if Mr. Fitz-Poodle attended all he named, and worked on the council as assiduously as he said he did, it must clearly have been only want of capacity that prevented him from rivalling the scientific fame of Professor Owen.[3] You must observe, that I am far from saying he did *not* attend; only I agree with his wife in thinking that it was—to say the least of it—rather extraordinary he should suddenly manifest so strong an inclination for a pursuit of which he had never even spoken before they were married.

If the lady brooded over this thought rather oftener than wisdom would have counselled—for her husband did not make her a propitiatory *cadeau* every time he kept an "engagement"—it is possible its more frequent recurrence to her mind was owing to the intimacy of her correspondence with Adela Cunninghame, who, in the true spirit of feminine friendship, threw out a number of suggestive ideas which did not much improve the original aspect of the question.

As we shall presently make the acquaintance of that charming *"jeune personne,"* it may not be amiss to say something about her beforehand.

---

1 It is only the first step that is difficult.
2 Hobby horse or favorite excuse.
3 Sir Richard Owen (1804-1892), comparative anatomist and paleontologist.

Adela Cunninghame and Eliza Coryton had been brought up in Devonshire together, at the house of Adela's mother, the parents of Eliza having died while she was still an infant, leaving her a very sufficient fortune. Like Hermia and Helena,[1] they had "grown together," and if their occupations were not precisely the same as those of the Athenian maidens, if the Devonshire damsels did not "sit on one cushion," creating "both one flower, both on one sampler," it was merely because samplers have become obsolete, and modern young ladies occupy themselves in a different way. In other respects the parallel held better, their studies and amusements being for the most part alike. In one thing, however, they differed. Adela was fonder of reading than her cousin, and the books she preferred were those which most excited her imagination. She eagerly devoured every work that fell in her way of which the theme was supernatural, and a large library, in which there were many rare and curious volumes (the late Mr. Cunninghame, her father, having been an unsparing collector), afforded her, when she could steal there unknown to her mother, who was a very matter-of-fact sort of person, a great deal of delightful, because prohibited, entertainment. To a certain extent, Eliza shared in Adela's discoveries. The more energetic and passionate nature of Adela gave her considerable influence over the yielding character of Eliza, who, without equal courage to speculate as wildly, was equally prone to superstition, and the consequence was, that when Adela abandoned her mind to any new or singular idea, she impressed it sooner or later on that of her cousin. For instance, in the matter of religious worship, it was Adela who first inspired Eliza with admiration for the candlesticks and credence-tables[2] of the Decorative Christians, and had the former changed her religion entirely, instead of stopping half-way, there is no doubt that the latter would have followed her example. If Adela had resolved on being a nun, the same day would have seen Eliza take the veil.

Circumstances, however, separated the cousins at rather a critical moment, family affairs obliging Miss Coryton to take up

---

1 Characters in Shakespeare's *A Midsummer Night's Dream*.
2 Table located near the altar in a Catholic church.

her residence for a time with a paternal uncle in London, and it was during the period of their arrangement that Mr. Beaufort Fitz-Poodle—(he had taken the latter name for an estate, as you or I would do to-morrow)—fell in love with her, and she put on a Brussels lace veil instead of a conventual[1] one. An illness had prevented Adela from being present at her cousin's marriage, but she was recovering fast at the time I first alluded to her, and about the middle of December was able to come to town, "her own room"—as Eliza wrote to say—being quite ready to receive her.

The meeting between the cousins was most affectionate, for they had been separated more than a twelvemonth, and though letters had passed between them at least twice a week, there were still thousands of those things to say that are never put down on paper. As it so happened that Mr. Fitz-Poodle was absent from home when Miss Cunninghame arrived in Wilton-crescent, the interval until it was time to dress for dinner was fully occupied in the discussion of confidential matters. Eliza's marriage was, of course, the principal theme for Adela's questioning: when she first saw him, whether he fell in love at first sight, how it came to pass altogether, what he really *was* like, whether she thought she should be *perfectly* happy, and so forth, repetitions all of them, and all previously answered; but asked and replied to now with all the effect of novelty. *Les affaires de ménage* came next on the *tapis*,[2] and Mrs. Fitz-Poodle promised herself much pleasure in showing her cousin all the domestic arrangements she had made, not that they were by any means complete, "for," observed Eliza, "you have no idea, until you begin, what an immense deal of time it takes to fit up a house properly; and you know, Adela, I have it all to do myself, for Beaufort, as I think I told you, does not go with me now to the different shops and places so regularly as he did at first."

"I remember perfectly well, Eliza," replied Miss Cunninghame; "he attends scientific meetings and things of that sort. However, men's tastes are sometimes very different from ours; they have occupations, too, which we take no interest in; so, before I pronounce any opinion on this subject, I shall judge from my own

---

1 Veil worn by nuns in a convent.
2 On the agenda.

observation. I have been studying Lavater[1] a great deal more
than ever, and I don't think I can be deceived now by any one's
physiognomy."

This little grievance apart, Eliza confessed that she had nothing
in the world to complain of; on the contrary, Beaufort did everything he could to make her happy: he was very generous, refused
her nothing she expressed a wish for, and was always contriving
some agreeable surprise. "It was only yesterday morning," she
said, "that I was admiring a beautiful little Dresden china clock,
which I thought Mrs. Jehoshaphat asked too much money for—
though I meant to have had it, and went in the course of the day
to tell her so, but when I got there it was gone—a gentleman, she
said, had come in, paid the price she put upon it, and taken it away
in a common cab; well, I was a good deal disappointed and could
almost have cried, it was such a darling little dear, and, what do
you think, when I came home, the first thing I saw on my dressing-
table was the identical clock. Beaufort had never uttered a syllable
about what he meant to do, but went at once and bought it."

"That," observed Adela, "is, I admit, a very fine trait of character; but, after all, it may be only the result of a particular
idiosyncrasy."

"Ah, but I can tell you of something that proves he is not
always following his own inclination, but acting contrary to it. It
is a curious fact that Beaufort does not appear to be fond of dogs,
although he is, I believe, a great sportsman. They are useful to him
in the field, and that, I fancy, is all he cares about them. In the house
I am sure he can't endure them, for he as much as said so one day.
Well, I was reading an odd advertisement in the *Times* the other
morning, just after he had bought the pair of carriage-horses I told
you of. It was about some Dalmatian dogs, which the advertiser
said were 'as beautifully spotted as leopards, gracefully formed,
with the spring or action of little tigers, as playful as lambs, and
most sagacious,' adding, rather absurdly, that they were 'an ornament for ladies or gentlemen.' I was amused by the description,
and just said I supposed the way the ornament should be worn

---

1 Johann Kaspar Lavater (1741-1801), a promoter of the science of physiognomy,
i.e., the idea that human personality can be assessed through analysis of physical
appearance.

was behind the carriage. Beaufort said nothing, only smiled in a peculiar way he has, but he wrote into Yorkshire, where the dogs were to be obtained, and three days afterwards, when the coach-man brought the carriage round, there was the prettiest Dalmatian you ever saw in your life, with my name on his collar!"

I think most people will agree with me that these things—not-withstanding Miss Cunninghame's philosophical conjecture—showed Beaufort Fitz-Poodle to be a very good-natured fellow, and fully bore out the general character given him by his wife. Judgment, however, had yet to be passed upon him by a more criti-cal arbiter.

III.

IF a warm, perhaps some might have called it an eager, welcome awaited Adela Cunninghame, that circumstance was not likely to operate unfavourably against the person who offered it, for in ninety-nine cases out of a hundred, attentions paid to ourselves outweigh all other considerations. But the hundredth case, in this instance, was that which concerned Mr. Fitz-Poodle. Miss Cunninghame was not at all insensible to the kindness of his dem-onstrations, and had she not relied upon her fatal skill in physiog-nomy, all would have gone as her cousin, or her cousin's husband, desired. But that Helvetian[1] prig, Lavater, had so inoculated her with the infallibility of his rules, that a moral dissection would have failed to overthrow her impressions, which were always rapidly, and you may, therefore, guess how fairly made. With such physi-ognomists a single obnoxious feature very often mars the effect of all the rest. Now Mr. Fitz-Poodle had nothing in his face that you could admire, and several points were decidedly objectionable. His sharp nose, his small eyes, his sandy eyebrows, his large teeth, his wiry hair, and his yellow whiskers, were severally objects of dislike to Miss Cunninghame—particularly those last named—and, taken in combination, she thought them detestable. It was her custom, after setting down every departure from her standard of beauty at its very lowest moral value, to compare the individual whom

---

1 Swiss.

she scrutinised to one or other of the inferior animals. The comparison she made on this occasion was not flattering to the party concerned.

"Very like a wolf!" was her silent remark. "I must observe his habits."

People who have a fixed idea always contrive to make everything square with it. Mr. Fitz-Poodle was blest with a very good appetite;—that told against him. He ate fast, or, as she phrased it, voraciously; another *item, per contra*.[1] Then, she noticed, he had a decided predilection for mutton; he preferred *côtelettes en papillotte* to *ris de veau, rognons au vin de champagne* to *rissoles*, and declared, as he carved a haunch of Southdown, that he thought it immeasurably superior to venison.[2] Now you or I might have avowed similar preferences in the hearing of Miss Adela Cunninghame, and yet her conclusions would have been wholly different, because, having made up her mind in the first instance that Mr. Fitz-Poodle resembled a wolf, she was only alive to illustrations that tended to support her theory. After dinner it was the same: instead of sitting quietly round the fire, he was restless, and, according to her view of the matter, "prowled" about the drawing-rooms, though, poor fellow, it was only in his anxiety to show her a number of pretty *objets* belonging to her cousin that lay on different tables. Then, again, when Eliza played and sang "While gazing on the moon's light," he struck up the most discordant noise that ever was heard, not by way of *refrain, that* Adela was convinced of, but from an impulse of uncontrollable antagonism to the lunar orb, from which she drew another inference. At last, when he sat quiet in an easy-chair, his *lair* she mentally called it, she watched his face as he silently looked with a pleased expression at his pretty wife, and detected in his twinkling eyes and the upturned corners of his wide mouth a resemblance "really painful to think of."

"How do you like Adela?" asked Mrs. Fitz-Poodle of her husband when they went up-stairs.

"A very handsome girl," was his reply, "though with rather a strange, dreamy expression in those large eyes of hers."

---

1 Further evidence against him.
2 He preferred cutlets fried in butter to calf's sweetbread and kidneys in champagne to minced meat fritters.

"But what do you think of her in other respects?"

"Really I can hardly tell: she spoke so little that I can form no estimate of her powers of mind. To judge only by her silence, I should say she was very reserved; but then, on the other hand, she seems to listen so attentively, to watch—as it were—for everything that falls from one's lips, that I am inclined to think she could speak if she chose; whether to the purpose or beside it must be determined hereafter."

"Ah!" said Mrs. Fitz-Poodle, smiling, "I thought Adela would puzzle you! Now, I'll let you into a little secret. She has been studying *you* all the evening. She is a wonderful physiognomist: her skill in detecting character is something quite extraordinary."

"Well, I gave her a long sitting this evening, for every time I looked at her I observed her eyes were fixed upon me. The likeness ought to be a good one; I hope it will be flattering."

"You may depend upon this, Beaufort: it will be perfectly true. I never knew Adela make a mistake of this kind in her life. I rely most implicitly on her judgment."

"An additional reason, dearest, for me to desire her favourable opinion."

"Oh, I did not mean that, Beaufort. Nothing, you know, can shake my faith in you!"

As "the bird in the cage" pursued Yorick[1] till the image assumed its most expressive form, so it happened with Adela Cunninghame when she reached her own room and was left alone. The little *lupine* traits with which she had begun to invest the disposition of Mr. Fitz-Poodle, wore larger and more decisive proportions the longer she dwelt upon them. I have said that her course of reading had been desultory, and directed almost entirely by her inclination towards the marvellous. Old French editions of such authors as Bodin, Cornelius Agrippa, Wierius, Vincent and Fincel,[2] were

---

1 Reverend Yorick, the narrator of Laurence Sterne's unfinished novel, *A Sentimental Journey through France and Italy* (1768). In the novel, Yorick becomes obsessed with a bird in a cage.

2 French philosopher Jean Bodin (1530-1596) wrote about persecutions for witchcraft, including lycanthropy, in *De la démonomanie des sorciers*. Heinrich Cornelius Agrippa von Nettesheim (1486-1535) composed a study on magic, *De occulta philosophia*. Physician Johann Wierius (1515-1588) wrote *De præstigiis*

amongst the volumes in the late Mr. Cunninghame's curiously-assorted library, and so completely was Adela imbued with the spirit in which those worthies wrote, that there was little related by them which she did not receive for truth. Everything in nature, she argued to herself, returns in one round, at longer or shorter intervals; what once has been, may, assuredly, be again; certain epidemical diseases which, to all appearance, have been extinct for centuries, suddenly return in their old destructive shape, none can tell why or how. If this be the case in the physical, why not in the moral world? The mind of man is no less subject to disease than the body: the same bad desires that actuated people centuries ago may spring up again, and with those desires the means of carrying them into effect. That there were, not more than forty years since, such beings as Vampires, Adela *knew* (from the Notes to the *Giaour*),[1] and if *they* existed, what was to prevent other beings equally fearful from existing also? Had she not read in Wierius the famous process which took place at Besançon in the year 1571, before the Inquisitor Borin, when Pierre Burgot and Michel Verdun[2] confessed themselves to be *loups-garoux*,[3] acknowledging that they had danced before the Evil One, each with a green-wax candle in his hand, had been anointed with a certain salve, and were straightway transformed into wolves and endowed with incredible swiftness? Did not Peter Marmot[4] say that he had *frequently witnessed* the changes of men into wolves in Savoy? Was there not at Padua, a place famous at all times for magic as well as classical learning, a *well-known* lycanthropist who, being pursued by men on horseback while in his transformed shape, was caught and had his paws cut off, and when he recovered his natural form did he not crawl about the streets of Padua a mutilated cripple, without either hands or feet? Adela's memory teemed with similar

---

dæmonum. Vincent of Beauvais (1190-1264) wrote *Speculum Maius* or "The Great Mirror." Philosopher Job Fincelius (d. 1582), touched on the werewolf myth in *De mirabilibus*.

1 *The Giaour* is a Orientalist poem by Lord Byron first published in 1813.

2 This narrative is recounted in Johann Wierius's guide to demonology, *De præstigiis dæmonum* (1563).

3 Werewolves.

4 Probably Pierre Marnor, author of a treatise on sorcery, quoted in Jean Bodin's *De la démonomanie des sorciers* (1580).

instances, all *proved* by the most competent witnesses, many of whom were the parties themselves. Such being the *fact*—and she trembled to think of it—what was to hinder people, if they were so minded, from becoming wehr-wolves in the nineteenth century as well as in the fifteenth? We had gone back lately to many of the customs of our ancestors, and this practice was just as likely to be revived as any other. Did not almost every man you met in society own that he was completely *blasé*, that he wanted a new excitement, something to happen to him that had never occurred before—and why should not Mr. Fitz-Poodle be one of these men? Her cousin's peace of mind, so she went on—not very logically—to argue, was at stake in the matter, and she resolved to leave no stone unturned until her suspicions were either confirmed or altogether disproved.

I have already adverted to the arbitrary influence of past events over our dreams: sometimes the subject most occupies them that has been latest in our waking thoughts—sometimes our imaginations are at work, in sleep, upon things for years forgotten. In Adela's case, the idea that Mr. Beaufort Poodle might be a wehr-wolf became, in the visions of the night, an absolute certainty. He appeared to her then with all his fell nature fully developed: she saw him in wolfish guise with a long swirling tail, careering after the sheep in the Green Park, hunting down his victims, swinging them over his shoulder, leaping the iron railings, defying the gatekeeper in the most violent language (as wolves—in dreams—are in the habit of doing), and galloping into the drawing-room at Wilton-crescent, where, casting his prey on the carpet, he mangled it in the most furious manner, howling all the while a hideous song, the words of which she recognised as German; anon he paused, and, addressing his wife, who did not seem at all disturbed by the scene, requested her, in the gentlest accents, to play while he danced a polka with Miss Cunninghame; and under some inexplicable fascination she found herself clasped round the waist by one gory paw, while the other waved in the air the fragments of what he called—and she literally laughed in her dream at his words—a *gigot au naturel*;[1] suddenly the Dalmatian dog rushed into the room

---

1 Boiled lamb.

barking violently, but the sounds he uttered resembled the tones of a church-bell—Mr. Fitz-Poodle relinquished his grasp, turned fiercely on the dog which continued to bark, and—Adela awoke, the *pendule* on the chimneypiece striking twelve. She slept again, and again she dreamt of her host, "more or less of a wolf," as she said to herself, all the night through.

With a mind predisposed to certain conclusions before she went to bed, and haunted in her sleep by the same notions, outrageously exaggerated, it was no wonder when she went down to breakfast that her cousin told her she was not looking well, and that Mr. Fitz-Poodle feared she had passed a bad night. He shook hands with her cordially as he spoke, but the squeeze he gave was very faintly returned; indeed, it was all she could do to suppress a shudder at his touch; she controlled her emotion, however, and sat down. During breakfast, on hospitable designs intent, he pressed her to taste a variety of nice things with which the table was covered, but the recollection of "that *gigot*" had completely taken away her appetite; neither did she seem more disposed to talk than to eat, and Mr. Fitz-Poodle began to think he had some uphill work before him. However, he good-naturedly persevered in the endeavour to entertain his guest until the *Times* was brought in, and then, like every other husband and host in the kingdom, he gave his mind to public affairs, and the ladies withdrew to discuss and arrange theirs.

The same question which Mrs. Fitz-Poodle had put to her husband the night before, she now asked of her cousin. What did she think of *him*?

"I would rather," answered Adela—"I would much rather not give any opinion."

This was exactly the way to make Mrs. Fitz-Poodle still more anxious to obtain it.

"You need not be afraid, Adela, of saying how much you admire him. I shall not be the least jealous!"

"I should imagine not," returned Miss Cunninghame, very gravely.

"Good gracious, Adela! what do you mean?" exclaimed her cousin, almost ready to cry.

"Simply that I have not fallen in love with your husband."

"Ah, but I am sure you mean something else. What is it you *don't* like him for?"

"I never said I did not like him."

"No, but you looked as if you thought so. And now I recollect, you did not speak to him all breakfast-time, except just to say 'Yes' or 'No.' Oh, Adela, *do* tell me!"

"Eliza," said Miss Cunninghame in a mysterious tone, "listen to me quietly. I don't pretend to be infallible; none of us are so; but I am not, as you are aware, without penetration. I hope and trust that Mr. Fitz-Poodle may be all your fancy pictures him, but appearances, I grieve to remark, are greatly against him. I am desirous, however, of studying him still closer before I deliver my verdict, and on that account I should prefer not to say anything at present."

"Oh, this is worse than if you said he was ever so bad. Is there anybody else, do you think, that he—was he ever engaged to—oh, pray what is it, Adela?" And Mrs. Fitz-Poodle, unable to restrain her feelings any longer, fairly burst into tears.

"You must not cry, Eliza," said Miss Cunninghame, soothingly; "it may not, after all, be what my fears imagine."

"I ho-o-o-pe n-n-o-ot," sobbed Mrs. Fitz-Poodle; though what her cousin really feared she had not the least idea.

"Now, answer me one or two questions, dear!"

"Ye-e-e-s,—if—I—ca-a-n."

"Do you remember the day of the month when he went out by himself that first time?"

"Oh ye-e-s. It was the twe-e-en-tieth of No-vember."

"You have the Gregorian calendar,[1] I think! Is that it on the prie-dieu? Give it me, dear. The 8th, I know, is the 'Holy Relics,'—the 11th, 'St. Martin,'—what is the 20th?—Let me see." She ran her finger down the column, glanced at the saint's day, and closed the book. "This is, indeed, remarkable," she said. "The 20th is the day of *St. Loup.*"[2]

"What is there remarkable in that?" asked Eliza, innocently.

"Poor dear!" said Adela, in an under tone; "it may be as well not to tell her just yet."

---

1 A conventional calendar.

2 Probably Saint Lupus, a fifth-century Catholic saint.

"And where did he say he was going to?"

"To a meeting of the Council of the Zoological Society."

"Zoological, indeed! Well?"

"What, Adela, have you any doubt about his having attended the council?"

"None in the world, dear. My firm impression is that he *did* go."

"Oh, I'm so glad! Then you don't think he went to see— anybody—that is to say any *former*—acquaintance?"

"Um! Not in the way you mean. It's not at all unlikely he met with some old friends that day. How long was he away?"

"I can't exactly say, for I was out myself all the afternoon. Probably four or five hours."

"He came home before you?"

"Oh yes; I found him in the library."

"Did he seem tired—exhausted?"

"I think he said he was rather tired. I know he told me they had had a good deal to do at the meeting."

"Um! What sort of a day was it?"

"Very gloomy and dark. I know I had a great deal of trouble in choosing the silk for those very curtains. They were obliged to light the gas at Tiwlls',[1] and I said that would never do for green, so I put off buying the curtains and went to look at some cabinets at Mrs. Jehoshaphat's."

"Were his boots and—and—his—*other* things muddy—as if they had been splashed?"

"I don't remember—I did not look; but I dare say they were, for he observed that the streets were uncommonly dirty, and *that* had helped to tire him."

"The streets? You are sure he didn't say the 'fields'?"

"Dear me, no! What should take him into the fields on a dark, foggy November day?"

"Well, if not the fields, he might have come home across the Park. However, *of course* he'd *say* the streets. Now tell me, Eliza, what did he do at dinner?"

"How do you mean?"

"Did he eat with his usual appetite?"

---

1 A fabric shop.

"Yes, I think so. No! now I recollect, he didn't. He sent away his soup without tasting it. He said it was smoked;—if it was, I never discovered it. I'm not sure whether he had fish or not, but I perfectly remember he wouldn't take any ham and chicken. As to sweet things, he never touches them."

"Was he gay, or the reverse?"

"At first he seemed jaded and out of spirits—I fancied because he had not gone with me. But he ordered some champagne, and then he rallied amazingly; indeed, he made himself particularly agreeable."

"What did he talk about?"

"Oh, everything. About the weather and the war, the storm in the Black Sea, the battle of Inkerman[1]—all the things that were going on, you know—about the country and the hunting-season——"

"Ah! Is he very fond of hunting?"

"I believe he is. Then, I remember, he wanted me to go down to Brighton—he said it was just the right time of the year."

"What for?"

"Oh, for the place, to be sure."

"You didn't go, I think?"

"No, I said I could *not* spare the time."

"And he seemed disappointed?"

"Well, I don't know. He is fond of Brighton. He likes galloping across the Downs. He says there's nothing like it."

"What! he actually confesses so much?"

"I don't understand you, Adela. I see nothing remarkable to confess in that. I like a good canter myself. You remember how we used to ride about Dartmoor. Beaufort talks about buying a cottage somewhere there for the summer. He says I must select the spot, as I know the country. I have told him a good deal about Dartmoor."

"And he wants to try the mutton there as well as at Brighton, I suppose?"

"What a strange idea! I only talked to him of the wild scenery. But I am glad you have given the conversation a turn, for I can't tell why you have been asking all these questions."

---

1 A Crimean War battle waged between the allied armies of Britain and France against the Russian army on November 5, 1854.

"A turn, Eliza," said Miss Cunninghame, solemnly. "No! it's *not* a turn. I am coming more to the point.—How do you amuse yourselves generally of an evening?"

"Oh, sometimes I play, and Beaufort listens; then I take my work, and he reads to me."

"What does he read?"

"Novels and biography, or, if we have nothing new from Mudie's,[1] he takes down a volume of natural history."

"Natural history—um! A coincidence."

"And poetry, too. Is that a coincidence?"

"It depends on circumstances. Whose poetry does he prefer?"

"Byron's generally; so do I. Beaufort reads very well. He has such a fine voice. We are going through the 'Tales.' The last he read was 'Mazeppa.'[2] I declare I was quite terrified with that fearful account of the flight of the steed through the forest, with the wolves so close behind."

"Quite natural, was it not?" said Adela, in a sepulchral voice.

"Quite."

"Do you ever consider the meaning of that picture?" abruptly asked Miss Cunninghame, pointing to the Sainte Geneviève.

"The meaning of it, Adela? Beaufort had it copied in Paris because he thought the saint's face was so like mine."

"Was that all? And those——victims!"

"Victims! Good gracious! Where?"

"Those lambs and their sainted shepherdess. A type! a type! Oh, Eliza, take care!"

"Take care of what? Of whom?"

"Of your husband!"

"You frighten me again. Your manner is so strange. Why should I take care of Beaufort?"

"Must I tell you the dreadful secret? Be it so! Bend down your head. Let no one else hear my words. I strongly suspect that Mr. Fitz-Poodle—nearer—nearer—that Mr. Fitz-Poodle is nothing more nor less than——"

A tap at the door interrupted the communication which Miss Cunninghame was about to make.

---

1 A private library that distributed books and periodicals to subscribers via post.
2 Lord Byron's long narrative poem, *Mazeppa* (1819).

"Who's there?" asked Mrs. Fitz-Poodle.

"It's only me, m'm—Frost," replied a female voice.

"My maid," said Mrs. Fitz-Poodle to Adela. "What do you want?"

"If you please, m'm, it's a letter for Miss Cunninghame, and master——"

"Let her come in," said Adela, in answer to an inquiring look from her cousin.

Frost entered, presented the letter, which Adela hastily tore open, and went on:

"——And master wishes most particularly to speak to you, m'm, for a few minutes, when you are disengaged."

"Will you excuse me, Adela?" said Mrs. Fitz-Poodle; but Miss Cunninghame was so absorbed by her letter that she did not hear the question till it was repeated.

"I beg your pardon, Eliza. Oh, yes! Go—by all means!"

IV.

When Mrs. Fitz-Poodle descended to the library she found her husband walking to and fro, apparently in some agitation.

"What is the matter, Beaufort?" she eagerly asked.

"I have had some disagreeable news, Eliza. A relation of mine, young Arthur Mervyn, of the 20th Dragoons, has got into a serious scrape, and I am afraid it will go hard with him unless something can be done immediately."

"Pray tell me, how?"

"Arthur," said Mr. Fitz-Poodle, "is a very good fellow in the main, but he is one of those young men whom you ladies call 'romantic' and 'impulsive'—that is to say, he is apt to do the first thing that comes into his head without at all considering the consequences. In this instance he has been quarrelling with his commanding officer, and has had the imprudence to send him a challenge. Any other man but Colonel Walton would have put Mervyn under arrest and brought him to a court-martial at once, and as sure as fate he would have lost his commission. Walton, however, happens to be an old friend of mine—in fact, is under considerable obligations to me—and writes me word that, although the provocation he received was great, and the offence—in a military sense—a very flagrant one, utterly subversive, you know, of all discipline, he has only privately confined Mervyn to his room for the present, in the hope that he will make him an apology."

"Which, of course, he will do," said Mrs. Fitz-Poodle.

"Ah, that's the misfortune of his character," returned her husband. "Arthur is very proud, and never likes to acknowledge himself in the wrong. But I fancy he must give in this time, or his prospects will be ruined for life."

"What was the quarrel about?"

"It arose out of the great cause of quarrel amongst men—young men in particular. While Arthur was on detachment, a few months ago, he thought proper to fall violently in love with some country beauty, a girl of excellent family, Walton says, but with scarcely any fortune. It seems they were engaged—Mervyn never told *me* a word about the matter—but as he is only a lieutenant, and depends entirely upon what his father allows him, all thoughts of marriage were out of the question until he got his troop. Somehow or other the affair got wind in the regiment—young men, you know, don't always keep their own counsel—and reached the commanding officer's ears. Well, under ordinary circumstances, this was no business of the colonel's, but when Walton found that Arthur was always asking for short leave, and got a hint, besides, of the use he made of it—I need not tell *you* what that was—he began to fear that in one of his impulsive moods the young lieutenant might bring back a wife to headquarters, and as he knew that such a step would mortally offend old Mr. Mervyn, who is a great disciplinarian in his family, he point blank refused Arthur's last application for leave of absence, and told him, moreover, the reason why. Arthur did not take this intimation in good part: he said Colonel Walton might refuse him leave if he chose, but he had no right to interfere with his private concerns, and that, as he had made up his mind on the subject, he should go without his permission. Walton mildly but firmly warned him against such a step, observing, good-humouredly, however, that he was still too much of a boy to be trusted. This remark, which was perfectly true, greatly irritated Arthur: he went to his barracks and wrote a most furious letter to Colonel Walton, calling him a tyrant and I don't know what else, and winding up by demanding the satisfaction which was due from one gentleman to another. Walton in reply, as I have already mentioned, sent word to Arthur to keep his room till he was in a more temperate mood, intimating that he should then expect to hear from him in a different strain. This is the state of affairs at present. Walton has waited three days, but as the foolish fellow has shown no signs of amendment, he begins to have some apprehension lest Arthur should carry his threat into execution and go off in quest of his *inamorata*,[1] in which case the whole story must be told, and it will be all up with the young *entêté*. Knowing, however, that I have more influence over Mervyn than most people, Walton has asked me to run down to Canterbury and see if I can't bring him to reason. I am sorry to be called away just as your cousin has arrived, but it can't be helped, and I hope I shall be able to get back by to-morrow night, or the next day at latest. There is no occasion to let anyone know why I leave town—I mean, you need not tell Miss Cunninghame even, as it might be awkward for Arthur in case he should come to the house while she is staying here."

"I shall tell nobody the reason, and Adela is not at all inquisitive. You never saw her before, did you?"

"What a question, Eliza! Of course I never did. Why do you ask?"

"Only,—only,—because I had a sort of—of fancy that she knew something about *you*."

"I don't see how that is possible, unless she happens to be gifted with second sight. What did she say of me then?"

"Oh, we were talking about you, and Adela asked me what your pursuits were, and whether you were fond of sporting, and what we did in the evening when we were alone,—and then—she—she advised me to—to take care of you."

"Ha! ha! ha! Is that all, Eliza? I hope you *will* take care of me. I'm sure I shall always take care of *you*. But we didn't want your cousin to remind us *so soon* of our marriage vow. She is a little too apprehensive. But I suppose it is because she is so fond of you, so I shall not quarrel with her on that account. Now, dearest, I must be off. The cab is at the door, I see, and Lucas is putting in my carpet-bag. Make any excuse you like to Adela, and say I was obliged to go in a great hurry. One kiss,—another,—one more,—good-bye."

---

1 Sweetheart.

And thus, unconsciously imitating the Corsair when he left Medora,[1] Mr. Fitz-Poodle departed on his friendly mission.

The offhand frankness of her husband's manner, and the natural construction he put upon Miss Cunninghame's words, completely reassured Mrs. Fitz-Poodle, and banished from her mind an uneasy thought which had begun to lurk there. As soon as the cab drove off she returned to her *boudoir*, but Adela was no longer there. She then went to her cousin's room, and, after knocking twice, the door was unlocked by Adela herself, who was very pale, and appeared as if she had been crying.

"Good gracious, Adela!" she exclaimed, "has anything happened to make you uncomfortable? How is my aunt?"

"Oh, very well, dear, I believe. I have heard nothing to the contrary."

"I thought—perhaps," said Mrs. Fitz-Poodle, slightly hesitating, "that—as you had—received a letter—and looked so—so ill— that something might have happened."

"So there has, Eliza! I am agonised with apprehension—all your poor cousin's hopes and expectations are at this moment trembling on the verge of a precipice—the destroying sword now hangs but by a single thread! Those are his very words!"

"Whose words, Adela ? You distract me! What evil is impending? What is it you dread?"

"I had intended to have reserved this secret for a calmer, happier moment—but fate is stronger than human will. It will astonish you, Eliza, when I announce the fact, unbreathed as yet to any ear, that I am—AN AFFIANCED ONE! Yes, Eliza, three months ago I pledged my maiden troth!"

"Goodness! And is this the cause of your present sorrow? Where is your——the gentleman?"

"Where? I know not! In a dungeon, perhaps! Fatally expiating his cr——no, *not* a crime—at the worst but an offence caused by his love for me."

"Dear me! has he k-k-killed anybody, Adela?"

"*Not yet*, Eliza!"

---

1 An allusion to a scene in Canto I of Lord Byron's poem, *The Corsair* (1814), in which the main character, Conrad (a pirate or corsair), leaves his beloved Medora in order to fight the Pasha.

"But if he is in prison, dear, he can't get at any one to kill, unless it is the gaoler who brings him his black bread and pitcher of water daily—that's what they do, I believe;—but then he must have done something to get put there. What was it? Oh, do tell me!"

"Read that missive!" said Adela. "I did not say he was actually incarcerated, though it may be so!"

Mrs. Fitz-Poodle removed a very damp cambric handkerchief from a crumpled letter that was lying on the bed, and having smoothed out the creases, read as follows:

"Idol of my heart! Little did I think this hand would ever pen aught but tidings of joy to thee! Yet destiny has willed it otherwise. Evil even now is hovering with outstretched wings above the head of your devoted one. All our hopes and expectations are at this moment——" (Perhaps, as this paragraph has been already mentioned, there is no occasion for repeating the "precipice" and the "destroying sword!") "I had arranged for another brief hour of happiness with thee, my Adela (by the express-train at 8.30 A.M. on the 13th), but tyrannous authority interposed its ban and marred the smiling scene. Maddened by disappointment, I said something, I know not what, words of menacing import, nay—more—I put them on paper, and defied my persecutor to the *outrance*.[1] With cynical coldness he refused to raise the gauntlet I had thrown down, and prated of paternal behests. I was of unyielding spirit—thanks to my love for thee—and, though unfettered, I am now—*a captive!* Surrounded as I am by his myrmidons, I dare not venture to say more at present, but at the first unwatched moment I will write again. At the worst, I can but hurl defiance in his teeth again, and fly to those arms which are the haven of Adela's fond and faithful shipwrecked lover."

"You see, Eliza, what a fearful strait he is in!" observed Miss Cunninghame—as I must still call her.

"Upon my word," said Mrs. Fitz-Poodle, "I don't see anything very clearly. I can't make out what it's all about. He seems to have been threatening to knock somebody down, and then—I should say—jumped overboard, and—perhaps—swam ashore, and was taken up for a smuggler!"

"Your penetration," said Adela, scornfully, "does you infinite

---

1 Extreme.

credit. A smuggler, indeed! Henceforth I shall confine my sorrows to my own bosom."

"I'm sure I didn't mean to offend you, Adela," returned Mrs. Fitz-Poodle, meekly; "but really I couldn't understand the letter."

"Enough," said Miss Cunninghame; "we will speak of it no more. All I request is that you will not name the subject to Mr. Fitz-Poodle."

"I came to tell you, Adela—only when I saw you had been crying I forgot it—that Beaufort has been suddenly obliged to go out of town. I hope you will have better news—whatever it relates to—before he comes back."

"Gone out of town!" muttered Miss Cunninghame, in a tone too low for her cousin to hear what she said; "can instinct have forewarned him of my prescience? Or, perchance, an access of fearful appetite!"

"What do you say, dear? I thought I heard the word 'appetite!' Luncheon, I dare say, is quite ready. Shall we go down? Come, kiss me, Adela. You know I never could bear not to be friends with you. There, that's a dear! I dare say it will be all right."

To do Miss Cunninghame justice I must say that she *did* kiss her cousin most affectionately. Though *exaltée*[1] to the last degree, and, as we have seen, apt to indulge in the most absurd fancies, she always acted, as she thought, "for the best," in which endeavour, when common sense and discretion happen to be absent, people frequently reverse their intentions. She was right, however, about one thing. Mrs. Fitz-Poodle, with all her affection, was not a counsellor for such a case as that of Adela Cunninghame; indeed, unless this young lady had unbosomed herself a little more plainly, I don't know whose advice could have done her any good. But it was not in her nature "to descend," as she said, "to common-place details"—and, therefore, she resolved to wait till another post should bring her better tidings—or worse.

Having come to this conclusion, she very wisely accepted her cousin's invitation to dry her tears and go down to luncheon; and whether philosophy or hunger prevailed, or whether some inspiration kept up her spirits, I know not, but she certainly did behave

---

1 Excited or elated.

at that meal as if she were not "an affianced one," with a lover in most mysterious difficulties.

Shall I follow the cousins throughout the occupations of the day—accompany them to Mrs. Jehoshaphat's, and the fifty other charming shops that were Mrs. Fitz-Poodle's delight—break in upon their *tête-à-tête*[1] at dinner—take a stall beside them at Albert Smith's[2] fifteen hundredth representation (given, I believe, on that night)—and then tell you that Miss Biddy Fudge was quite right when she said that a laugh would revive her under the pressure of romantic woe, and that Adela Cunninghame followed her example? Imagine these things, and imagine what Time, the old coralline,[3] is always at work about—for ever constructing new edifices, for ever effacing the past; no respecter is he of either joy or sorrow; his lightest touch produces change.

*   *   *   *   *   *

Quarrel with him as we may, no one in Mr. Fitz-Poodle's household would be likely to object to the change which he wrought there in little more than twenty-four hours from the time of that gentleman's abrupt departure for Canterbury. It was just six o'clock in the evening of the following day, and Mrs. Fitz-Poodle and her cousin—having once more visited half the shops in London—were sitting in the library by firelight, waiting for letters by the day-mail. Adela, whose thoughts insensibly assumed a gloomier complexion as the moment of expectation drew near, had fallen into the train by which she first startled Mrs. Fitz-Poodle, and was narrating, as an induction, no doubt, to something even less pleasant, the delectable history of Gilles Garnier,[4] the notorious loup-garou who was executed for lycanthropy at Dôle, in the year 1574, when the "visitors' bell" was rung violently, a noise of footsteps in

---

1 In private conversation.

2 Smith (1816-1860) was a writer and mountaineer whose lecture, "Mr. Albert Smith's Ascent of Mont Blanc," was a popular sensation in London during the 1850s. It closed in 1858 after its 200th performance.

3 Coral-like in its many branches and formations.

4 In 1573 Gilles Garnier confessed to transforming into a wolf in order to kill and eat children. He was burned at Dôle for his crimes. A review of his case appears in Henri Boguet's *Discours exécrable des sorciers* (1602).

the hall followed almost immediately, the library-door flew open, and more than one person entered the apartment. It was too dark to distinguish faces, but Mrs. Fitz-Poodle had no difficulty in recognising her husband's voice:

"Where are you, Eliza? Oh, here! I hope we're in time for dinner. I've brought an unexpected guest. It's all right, dearest—too long a story to tell just now—let me introduce my friend—don't make a mistake in the dark and salute the wrong person, Arthur—ha! ha! ha!—Mrs. Fitz-Poodle, this is my cousin, Mr. Mervyn, of the 20th Dragoons—Miss Cunninghame, I think this gentleman is known to you already!"

As a spasmodic novel-writer[1] would say: "A faint shriek was heard, and the next moment Adela would have fallen to the ground if Arthur Mervyn had not rushed forward and caught her fainting form in his arms."

Preston salts,[2] eau-de-Cologne, and—and a few tender whispers, rendered the *tableau* of revival quite perfect. It is scarcely necessary to say that Mr. Fitz-Poodle promised "to make things pleasant" to Arthur Mervyn and Adela Cunninghame, or that he kept his word.

*   *   *   *   *   *

When Adela Cunninghame retired to rest that night, her last words were:

"That I should have taken that dear, kind, good Fitz-Poodle for a wehr-wolf. Thank Heaven, I never told Eliza!"

---

1 An emotional, melodramatic work of fiction intended to excite the nerves.
2 Smelling salts.

The Gray Wolf

GEORGE MACDONALD

George MacDonald (1824-1905) was born in Aberdeenshire, Scotland, the second son of Helen and George MacDonald. As a child, he attended Blackfriars Street Church, which adhered to a strict brand of Calvinist Protestantism. Although MacDonald would study to become a minister at Highbury Theological College and receive his own pastorate at Trinity Congressional Chapel in Arundel, Sussex, his Protestantism was far more liberal than that of his youthful training. In fact, MacDonald's sermons often relied on poetry and interpretation as much as the Bible, which offended some of his parishioners. In 1853, when his annual stipend was significantly reduced, MacDonald was forced to resign his pastorate. His integration of poetry and new scientific developments, along with his questioning of Church doctrine, influenced much of his writing, including his fantasy stories.

Unable to find further employment as a pastor, MacDonald moved to Manchester where he began contributing to the Christian Spectator. In 1851, he married Louisa Powell, and the couple soon began their abundant family, ultimately consisting of six sons and five daughters. As his family grew, MacDonald continued writing, alternating between religious poetry, nonfiction, and fantasy fiction, particularly fairy tales for children. MacDonald produced much of his work during what is now referred to as the golden age of Victorian fantasy, publishing alongside writers such as Lewis Carroll and Charles Kingsley. In 1867, MacDonald published Dealings with the Fairies, which included the timeless classics "The Light Princess" and "The Golden Key." As a writer for children, MacDonald created sophisticated characters and plots that required thought and introspection on the meaning of life. MacDonald's adult fiction was similarly complex. His semi-autobiographical novel, Robert Falconer (1868), incorporated spirituality, reason, and science, the themes that most intrigued and motivated him as a Christian writer.

The 1870s proved a prolific decade for MacDonald with the serialization of At the Back of the North Wind (1871) in Good Words for the Young, a periodical he co-edited. He also published The Princess and the Goblin (1872), The Wise Woman (1875), and The Princess and Curdie (1882). The last tale featured a wolf-like girl, Lina, who was eventually able to shed her bestial nature. However, not all of MacDonald's female werewolves were so fortunate. In "The History of Photogen and Nycteris" (1879), a witch named Watho transforms into a wolf in order to attack the lovers. When she is killed by an arrow, her body shapeshifts back into that of a woman. MacDonald's last major novel, Lilith (1895), also dealt with themes such as the choice between good and evil, redemption, and immortality.

"The Gray Wolf" was published in Works of Fancy and Imagination (1871), a ten-volume set of his collected prose and poems. MacDonald's fairy tales, infused with magical and spiritual elements, inspired both Victorian and twentieth-century fantasy writers, including C. S. Lewis, J. R. R. Tolkien, and Maurice Sendak.

Bibliography

Cowan, Yuri. "Allegory and Aestheticism in the Fantasies of George MacDonald." North Wind: Journal of George MacDonald Studies 25 (2006): 39-57.

Fink, Larry. "Natural History—The Heavenly Sort: MacDonald's Integration of Faith and Reason, Religion and Science." In "A Noble Unrest": Contemporary Essays on the Work of George MacDonald, edited by Jean Webb, 59-66. Newcastle upon Tyne: Cambridge Scholars, 2007.

Hein, Rolland. George MacDonald: Victorian Mythmaker. Nashville: Star Song, 1993.

MacDonald, George. "The Gray Wolf." In Works of Fancy and Imagination, vol. 10, 229-244. London: Strahan, 1871.

McGillis, Roderick, ed. George MacDonald: Literary Heritage and Heirs. Wayne, Penn.: Zossima, 2008.

McLaren, Scott. "Saving the Monsters? Images of Redemption in the Gothic Tales of George MacDonald." Christianity and Literature 55, no. 2 (2006): 245-269.

Phillips, Michael R. George MacDonald: Scotland's Beloved Storyteller. Minneapolis: Bethany House, 1987.

Sadler, Glenn Edward. "George MacDonald." Oxford Dictionary of National Biography. Oxford: Oxford University Press, 2004. http://www.oxforddnb.com.

THE GRAY WOLF.

ONE evening-twilight in spring, a young English student, who had wandered northwards as far as the outlying fragments of Scotland called the Orkney and Shetland Islands, found himself on a small island of the latter group, caught in a storm of wind and hail, which had come on suddenly.[1] It was in vain to look about for any shelter; for not only did the storm entirely obscure the landscape, but there was nothing around him save a desert moss.

At length, however, as he walked on for mere walking's sake, he found himself on the verge of a cliff, and saw, over the brow of it, a few feet below him, a ledge of rock, where he might find some shelter from the blast, which blew from behind. Letting himself down by his hands, he alighted upon something that crunched beneath his tread, and found the bones of many small animals scattered about in front of a little cave in the rock, offering the refuge he sought. He went in, and sat upon a stone. The storm increased in violence, and as the darkness grew he became uneasy, for he did not relish the thought of spending the night in the cave. He had parted from his companions on the opposite side of the island, and it added to his uneasiness that they must be full of apprehension about him. At last there came a lull in the storm, and the same instant he heard a footfall, stealthy and light as that of a wild beast, upon the bones at the mouth of the cave. He started up in some fear, though the least thought might have satisfied him that there could be no very dangerous animals upon the island. Before he had time to think, however, the face of a woman appeared in the opening. Eagerly the wanderer spoke. She started at the sound of his voice. He could not see her well, because she was turned towards the darkness of the cave.

"Will you tell me how to find my way across the moor to Shielness?" he asked.

---

1 The Orkney and Shetland Islands are north of the Scottish mainland and consist of about one hundred islands, less than twenty of which are inhabited.

"You cannot find it to-night," she answered, in a sweet tone, and with a smile that bewitched him, revealing the whitest of teeth.

"What am I to do, then?" he asked.

"My mother will give you shelter, but that is all she has to offer."

"And that is far more than I expected a minute ago," he replied. "I shall be most grateful."

She turned in silence and left the cave. The youth followed.

She was barefooted, and her pretty brown feet went catlike over the sharp stones, as she led the way down a rocky path to the shore. Her garments were scanty and torn, and her hair blew tangled in the wind. She seemed about five and twenty, lithe and small. Her long fingers kept clutching and pulling nervously at her skirts as she went. Her face was very gray in complexion, and very worn, but delicately formed, and smooth-skinned. Her thin nostrils were tremulous as eyelids, and her lips, whose curves were faultless, had no colour to give sign of indwelling blood. What her eyes were like he could not see, for she had never lifted the delicate films of her eyelids.

At the foot of the cliff they came upon a little hut leaning against it, and having for its inner apartment a natural hollow within it. Smoke was spreading over the face of the rock, and the grateful odour of food gave hope to the hungry student. His guide opened the door of the cottage; he followed her in, and saw a woman bending over a fire in the middle of the floor. On the fire lay a large fish broiling. The daughter spoke a few words, and the mother turned and welcomed the stranger. She had an old and very wrinkled, but honest face, and looked troubled. She dusted the only chair in the cottage, and placed it for him by the side of the fire, opposite the one window, whence he saw a little patch of yellow sand over which the spent waves spread themselves out listlessly. Under this window there was a bench, upon which the daughter threw herself in an unusual posture, resting her chin upon her hand. A moment after the youth caught the first glimpse of her blue eyes. They were fixed upon him with a strange look of greed, amounting to craving, but as if aware that they belied or betrayed her, she dropped them instantly. The moment she veiled them, her face, notwithstanding its colourless complexion, was almost beautiful.

When the fish was ready, the old woman wiped the deal[1] table, steadied it upon the uneven floor, and covered it with a piece of fine table-linen. She then laid the fish on a wooden platter, and invited the guest to help himself. Seeing no other provision, he pulled from his pocket a hunting knife, and divided a portion from the fish, offering it to the mother first.

"Come, my lamb," said the old woman; and the daughter approached the table. But her nostrils and mouth quivered with disgust.

The next moment she turned and hurried from the hut.

"She doesn't like fish," said the old woman, "and I haven't anything else to give her."

"She does not seem in good health," he rejoined.

The woman answered only with a sigh, and they ate their fish with the help of a little rye bread. As they finished their supper, the youth heard the sound as of the pattering of a dog's feet upon the sand close to the door; but ere he had time to look out of the window, the door opened and the young woman entered. She looked better, perhaps from having just washed her face. She drew a stool to the corner of the fire opposite him. But as she sat down, to his bewilderment, and even horror, the student spied a single drop of blood on her white skin within her torn dress. The woman brought out a jar of whisky, put a rusty old kettle on the fire, and took her place in front of it. As soon as the water boiled, she proceeded to make some toddy[2] in a wooden bowl.

Meantime the youth could not take his eyes off the young woman, so that at length he found himself fascinated, or rather bewitched. She kept her eyes for the most part veiled with the loveliest eyelids fringed with darkest lashes, and he gazed entranced; for the red glow of the little oil-lamp covered all the strangeness of her complexion. But as soon as he met a stolen glance out of those eyes unveiled, his soul shuddered within him. Lovely face and craving eyes alternated fascination and repulsion.

---

1 Made from planks of pine or fir.
2 A beverage composed of hot water, sugar, and whiskey.

The mother placed the bowl in his hands. He drank sparingly, and passed it to the girl. She lifted it to her lips, and as she tasted— only tasted it—looked at him. He thought the drink must have been drugged and have affected his brain. Her hair smoothed itself back, and drew her forehead backwards with it; while the lower part of her face projected towards the bowl, revealing, ere she sipped, her dazzling teeth in strange prominence. But the same moment the vision vanished; she returned the vessel to her mother, and rising, hurried out of the cottage.

Then the old woman pointed to a bed of heather in one corner with a murmured apology; and the student, wearied both with the fatigues of the day and the strangeness of the night, threw himself upon it, wrapped in his cloak. The moment he lay down, the storm began afresh, and the wind blew so keenly through the crannies of the hut, that it was only by drawing his cloak over his head that he could protect himself from its currents. Unable to sleep, he lay listening to the uproar which grew in violence, till the spray was dashing against the window. At length the door opened, and the young woman came in, made up the fire, drew the bench before it, and lay down in the same strange posture, with her chin propped on her hand and elbow, and her face turned towards the youth. He moved a little; she dropped her head, and lay on her face, with her arms crossed beneath her forehead. The mother had disappeared.

Drowsiness crept over him. A movement of the bench roused him, and he fancied he saw some four-footed creature as tall as a large dog trot quietly out of the door. He was sure he felt a rush of cold wind. Gazing fixedly through the darkness, he thought he saw the eyes of the damsel encountering his, but a glow from the falling together of the remnants of the fire, revealed clearly enough that the bench was vacant. Wondering what could have made her go out in such a storm, he fell fast asleep.

In the middle of the night he felt a pain in his shoulder, came broad awake, and saw the gleaming eyes and grinning teeth of some animal close to his face. Its claws were in his shoulder, and its mouth in the act of seeking his throat. Before it had fixed its fangs, however, he had its throat in one hand, and sought his knife with the other. A terrible struggle followed; but regardless of the tearing claws, he found and opened his knife. He had made one futile stab, and was drawing it for a surer, when, with a spring of the whole body, and one wildly-contorted effort, the creature twisted its neck from his hold, and with something betwixt a scream and a howl, darted from him. Again he heard the door open; again the wind blew in upon him, and it continued blowing; a sheet of spray dashed across the floor, and over his face. He sprung from his couch and bounded to the door.

It was a wild night—dark, but for the flash of whiteness from the waves as they broke within a few yards of the cottage; the wind was raving, and the rain pouring down the air. A gruesome sound as of mingled weeping and howling came from somewhere in the dark. He turned again into the hut and closed the door, but could find no way of securing it.

The lamp was nearly out, and he could not be certain whether the form of the young woman was upon the bench or not. Overcoming a strong repugnance, he approached it, and put out his hands—there was nothing there. He sat down and waited for the daylight: he dared not sleep any more.

When the day dawned at length, he went out yet again, and looked around. The morning was dim and gusty and gray. The wind had fallen, but the waves were tossing wildly. He wandered up and down the little strand, longing for more light.

At length he heard a movement in the cottage. By and by the voice of the old woman called to him from the door.

"You're up early, sir. I doubt you didn't sleep well."

"Not very well," he answered. "But where is your daughter?"

"She's not awake yet," said the mother. "I'm afraid I have but a poor breakfast for you. But you'll take a dram[1] and a bit of fish. It's all I've got."

Unwilling to hurt her, though hardly in good appetite, he sat down at the table. While they were eating, the daughter came in, but turned her face away and went to the further end of the hut. When she came forward after a minute or two, the youth saw that her hair was drenched, and her face whiter than before. She looked ill and faint, and when she raised her eyes, all their fierceness had

---

1 A small glass of alcohol.

vanished, and sadness had taken its place. Her neck was now covered with a cotton handkerchief. She was modestly attentive to him, and no longer shunned his gaze. He was gradually yielding to the temptation of braving another night in the hut, and seeing what would follow, when the old woman spoke.

"The weather will be broken all day, sir," she said. "You had better be going, or your friends will leave without you."

Ere he could answer, he saw such a beseeching glance on the face of the girl, that he hesitated, confused. Glancing at the mother, he saw the flash of wrath in her face. She rose and approached her daughter, with her hand lifted to strike her. The young woman stooped her head with a cry. He darted round the table to interpose between them. But the mother had caught hold of her; the handkerchief had fallen from her neck; and the youth saw five blue bruises on her lovely throat—the marks of the four fingers and the thumb of a left hand. With a cry of horror he darted from the house, but as he reached the door he turned. His hostess was lying motionless on the floor, and a huge gray wolf came bounding after him.

There was no weapon at hand; and if there had been, his inborn chivalry would never have allowed him to harm a woman even under the guise of a wolf. Instinctively, he set himself firm, leaning a little forward, with half outstretched arms, and hands curved ready to clutch again at the throat upon which he had left those pitiful marks. But the creature as she sprung eluded his grasp, and just as he expected to feel her fangs, he found a woman weeping on his bosom, with her arms around his neck. The next instant, the gray wolf broke from him, and bounded howling up the cliff. Recovering himself as he best might, the youth followed, for it was the only way to the moor above, across which he must now make his way to find his companions.

All at once he heard the sound of a crunching of bones—not as if a creature was eating them, but as if they were ground by the teeth of rage and disappointment; looking up, he saw close above him the mouth of the little cavern in which he had taken refuge the day before. Summoning all his resolution, he passed it slowly and softly. From within came the sounds of a mingled moaning and growling.

Having reached the top, he ran at full speed for some distance across the moor before venturing to look behind him. When at length he did so, he saw, against the sky, the girl standing on the edge of the cliff, wringing her hands. One solitary wail crossed the space between. She made no attempt to follow him, and he reached the opposite shore in safety.

The Were-wolf of the Grendelwold

F. Scarlett Potter

Frederick Scarlett Potter (1834-1915) was born in Stoke, Gloucestershire, and later studied art at the Royal Academy, where he was awarded a medal in 1863. While pursuing a career as a sculptor and illustrator, he wrote prolifically. He published over fifty children's books, including Erling: or, The Days of St. Olaf (1876), Cousin Flo (1877), *and* Princess Myra and Her Adventures among the Fairy-Folk (1880). *He also wrote two volumes of poetry,* The Volsung Tale (1868) *and* Song-Mead: with Other Narratives in Verse (1876). *In addition, Potter published his work in popular periodicals, including* Time, *the* London Reader, Gentleman's Magazine, *and* Cornhill Magazine. *Potter remained a bachelor throughout his life, living first with his family and then with his sister Elizabeth. In his later years, he lived in Halford, Warwickshire, where he became a local historian and folklorist, publishing* Notes on the History, Antiquities, and Customs of Halford *in 1912.*

"The Were-wolf of the Grendelwold" was published in the June 17, 1882 issue of the London Reader of Literature, Science, Art, and General Information, *a popular illustrated family magazine edited by George Stiff.*

Bibliography

Kirk, John Foster. *A Supplement to Allibone's Critical Dictionary of English Literature and British and American Authors.* 2 vols. 1891. Reprint, Detroit: Gale, 1965.

Potter, Frederick Scarlett. "The Were-wolf of the Grendelwold." *London Reader* 39 (June 17, 1882): 154-156.

Reilly, Catherine. *Mid-Victorian Poetry: 1860-1879: An Annotated Bibliography.* London: Mansell, 2000.

Watson, George, ed. *The New Cambridge Bibliography of English Literature.* Vol. 3, 1800-1900. Cambridge: Cambridge University Press, 1969.

THE WERE-WOLF OF THE GRENDELWOLD.

CHAPTER I.

"This young man runs like a wolf."

THE motives which induced me to become a resident in the Grendelwold[1] can matter little to the reader—suffice it to say that for a time I was a dweller there. I was a lonely man, with no ties or duties to call me elsewhere, and that secluded district pleased me. To me, the little joys and sorrows and loves and quarrels of the simple rustics were as a pastoral drama, of which I was an unconcerned spectator.

Most interesting among the actors in that drama, as well as most charming of the maidens of the valley, was Theresa. When I first came, she was but an opening rosebud. She at once attracted my attention. Around her there could not fail to gather a complication of rustic lovers, and rivalries and jealousies which would furnish me with abundant matter on which to philosophize.

She had already her admirers—and of these it seemed to me that Carl had most chance of success. He was her near neighbour; they had played together as children, and though there were bolder, stronger, and more handsome lads in the valley, he was in no way ill-favoured or to be despised. I watched him closely, and felt kindly towards the youth. His face spoke of honesty and truth. I saw that he loved her, and I wished him every success. My chief fear for him was lest he should prove too modest and retiring, and that he might thus be elbowed from his place by some bolder rival.

But, for a while, all went smoothly. I had begun to picture to myself the future of this young couple. They understood each other, and in their courtship there could be no more stirring incidents than the mildest of lovers' quarrels, to be in due time happily

---

1 "Grendel" echoes the name of a monster in the Old English epic poem *Beowulf.* A "wold" is a forest. Potter may be thinking of Grindelwald, a village in the Alps, in Switzerland.

made up. Then the betrothal, the marriage festival, and a calm wedded life in that peaceful spot such as for ages past had been led by their ancestors. I looked for a pastoral. Alas! the curtain was to rise on a tragedy!

The first disturbing influence was the appearance of Fritz. Well do I remember the day on which he was first seen. It was on the fête of our patron saint, an occasion upon which, after their religious duties had been finished at the church, our whole population gave themselves up to sports and merry-making.

The games had already begun when I first saw the stranger. He was a young man not easily to be overlooked. I noted him whilst still at a distance. None others were present so largely grown or so gaily dressed as he. His clothes were, indeed, of the same fashion as those of our own peasants, but they were of richer material, and bespoke the greater wealth of their wearer.

I asked of more than one of the bystanders who this stranger might be. None seemed to know with any certainty. Some said: "He comes from beyond the Grendel Forest." Others only pointed or nodded towards the dark line of wood which fringed the slope above the village, and into which few of them had cared to penetrate far.

But, just then, the wrestling was about to begin. Among the first, Carl had engaged with a companion of his own age and strength. I was well pleased to see that he was vigorous and active, and that after a well-matched struggle he succeeded in throwing his opponent. I saw him cast a glance of triumph towards where Theresa was standing, among the lookers-on. I thought, too, that I saw an answering smile of pleasure on the happy face of the maiden.

But Carl's triumph was not for long. He was at once challenged by the stranger, Fritz, and quickly overthrown. Several others of our youths in succession measured themselves against the conqueror, but each and all received the fall at his hands. He remained the hero of the sport.

"It was not by greater skill that he overthrew us," I heard one of the vanquished saying to a comrade, later in the day, "but he dragged me down with the force of a wild beast."

The wrestling over, the young men prepared for a trial of speed.

Fritz stripped with the others; and now, for the first time, I was able to see him more closely.

At a distance, I had not only admired his tall and powerful frame, but I had imagined that he must be singularly handsome. I had credited him with regular features and a mass of jet black hair. Now, however, I saw that for one so young, the hair and beard were singularly mixed with grey, and that though his face, or at least the upper part of it, was well formed, it was occasionally lighted by an expression which in some way reminded me of that of an angry dog, and this was no doubt aided by his teeth, which were remarkably long and white, and which glittered whenever he smiled or spoke.

The race began. I felt jealous for the honour of our villagers, and flattered myself that in running, at least, Fritz would find many superiors. For a while, appearances favoured my opinion— all the others were ahead of him, and foremost was the light-footed Carl. Yet the stranger kept doggedly on. I noticed that his style of running differed from that of the other youths. He moved at a kind of trot. I felt that I ought to find some comparison for it, but my memory did not serve me.

I spoke to an old peasant who stood near.

"The master-wrestler," I said, "would have done well not to have attempted the foot-race. He has no chance."

The old man shook his head.

"Do not be too sure," he answered. "Did you ever see the wolves tracking a deer? Their speed cannot compare with the stag's at first, yet, after a time, they outstrip him. This young man runs like a wolf."

Yes, Fritz ran like a wolf! That was the comparison which I had in vain tried to find.

Gradually the others slackened speed, but not so Fritz. That trot of his never relaxed. One by one, he passed and left all his rivals behind, except Carl alone. My young favourite was active and ran well. He smarted under his late defeat, and strained every muscle to hold his own.

The goal was now near at hand. I stood close to the course, and could see how eagerly the stranger was striving to win. His eyes were fixed on Carl with a look which to me seemed to convey

more of hatred than kindly rivalry; and when he came opposite to
him, as he did near the end, I observed that he made a side-motion
towards him with his head, and showed his white teeth as a dog
might do when he snarls at his fellow. From that moment Carl lost
heart; Fritz shot forward, and came in victor.

CHAPTER II.

"Like a bird before a snake."

I soon found that though I had conceived a prejudice against the
stranger, our villagers generally were inclined to look upon him
with favour. Success makes many friends. Fritz had those personal
advantages of size and strength which our rustic belles could best
appreciate, and the evidences of superior wealth which he bore
about him gave him importance in the eyes of our men.

As champion of the sports, it was the privilege of the new-
comer to choose from among all the maidens present a partner
with whom to open the dance. I had before observed his eyes
straying in the direction of Theresa. I was not surprised when they
now rested upon her.

She at once acceded to his request, without even giving a
glance to poor Carl, and throughout the dance I noticed that her
gaze invariably followed the motions of her partner, and that in
every point she appeared implicitly to obey his wishes. I could not
understand this. Was it possible that this gay gallant had so easily
won her fancy, and so soon caused her to forget her faithful friend?

All watched them with admiration, for a more striking couple
had never danced on our greensward; but I turned my eyes on
poor Carl, where, forsaken and humiliated, he stood in the background. I could see the cloud on his brow, and I felt thankful that
his was a timid nature, and one not likely to be roused to deeds of
violence.

The fête was over. Days passed by. Fritz went and came, but
much of his time seemed to be spent in our village. He was in
general favour among the young men, for he scattered his silver

with a liberal hand, and none questioned but that his home beyond the forest must be something far better than our simple cottages.

There could be little doubt as to the motive of his frequent visits. It was near the house of Theresa's parents that he was oftenest to be seen. All held that he was wooing her, and that his wealth caused his suit to be received with favour by the maiden's father.

Theresa herself seemed to shun Carl now, whilst she did not avoid the stranger. It was noticed, too, that when he was present a glance from him was sufficient to make her do or say as he willed. All argued from this that he had won her heart; yet to me it seemed that when he appeared her looks showed more of fear than of joy. The maiden and her ways perplexed me.

I often spoke with Carl, and did my best to comfort him; his comrades were rude peasants incapable of sympathizing with mere sorrow of the heart. To them his forlorn condition was a mere subject for jest. Thus it was that he grew to regard me as his best friend.

Days passed, and one morning it was rumoured that Theresa had fled. At daybreak she had been seen proceeding with the stranger in the direction of the forest. None seemed surprised at it. He was her superior in position, and might, therefore, prefer to carry off his bride secretly. All agreed that she was a fortunate maiden.

When I met with Carl that day I was startled to see how great a change a few hours of trouble had made in him. His distress was so great that I almost feared for his reason. To console him, I bade him be thankful that he had escaped a union with one so light and fickle as his lost love. But he exclaimed, vehemently:

"No, no! Theresa is neither light nor fickle. She loves me still, and has never loved this man. She is bewitched! Under that evil eye of his she is like a bird before a snake. Oh, Theresa, Theresa! What will become of you?" And twisting from me he hurried away towards the forest.

I had gone to bed that night and fallen soundly asleep, when I was aroused by a handful of earth being thrown against my casement. I sprang up and looked out. The moon was full, and I could clearly see Carl standing below and looking far more wild and agitated than when he had left me. Beside him were his two fine hounds, Max and Leo. In his hand he held up something which, in that uncertain light, I could not well make out.

"Come down!" he cried. "You must come with me at once!"

I hastily threw on my clothes, and that I might not disturb the other occupants of the cottage, of which I was but a temporary inmate, I opened the window and lowered myself from it to the ground. The height was trifling.

Carl seized my hand.

"You are my friend," he exclaimed, "and I need one! You must come with me!"

There was so much excitement in his manner that I almost feared my dread of the morning had been realized, and that his trouble had deranged his brain. I answered, somewhat doubtfully:

"I will go," I said, "if I can do any good. But where would you have me go?"

"Into the forest," he answered, "and at once. There is no time to be lost."

"Into the Grendel-Forest!" I exclaimed.

I know well with what superstitious dread the peasants regarded its gloomy recesses, even in broad day; and now, at midnight, could he think of entering it?

"Yes, yes; into the forest. Do you see this?"

And he again held up the object in his hand. I could see it now. It was nothing more than a torn piece of some gaily-coloured fabric.

"Well, and what of that?" I asked.

"What of this! Do you see? It is from a woman's dress—*her* dress. Leo brought it in his mouth out of the wood."

"Is that all? The lovers must have passed through the wood, and this may have caught on a thorn. This is no reason for such a wild-goose chase. Wait till morning, and then if it is necessary the whole village will turn out to search."

"I will not wait," he answered, passionately. "It *may* be too late now. In the morning it *must* be too late. If you will not come, I go alone. No one else will venture with me into the Grendel-Forest at midnight," and he crossed himself.

Excited as he was, there was no sign of madness in his words.

"Lead on!" I said. "I will go with you."

He hurried towards the woods, and I followed. Presently, he turned sharply round and exclaimed:

"Why did I forget it? You are unarmed?"

"Yes. You gave me no time to think of weapons. Shall we go back and find some?"

"No, no. See here," and he touched the axe which was stuck in his belt. "I have this. You shall have my knife," and, drawing out a long, sharp knife, he handed it to me.

CHAPTER III.

"He comes! He comes, comrade!"

WE were now far away from the village, and among the broken upland pastures which skirted the forest. The dark masses of the wood contrasted strangely with the bright moonlight around us, and looked more black and forbidding than usual. I knew well with what superstitious terrors the people regarded these woods, but Carl hurried onwards.

The dogs pressed on in front of us. We passed into some sort of opening between the trees, though it could scarcely be called a path. We were soon in almost pitchy darkness. Scarcely a ray of moonlight could pierce through the thick boughs, and I often stumbled in the uneven way.

Presently a low growl from one of the dogs, some distance in front, reached our ears. Carl clutched his axe nervously, and muttered:

"The scent grows warm, comrade! Come on, come on!"

"What is it?" I asked. "What do they find?"

"Hush!" was the only reply; and again we moved rapidly forward in silence.

But now, from as it seemed the very heart of the forest, there reached us a loud and piercing cry—the howl, as it appeared to me, of some savage brute.

"Do you hear him?" whispered Carl, in an excited voice. "Come on!"

"Are you mad?" I answered; "that cry, startling though it was, was only that of a wild beast."

"Only! I tell you it is himself! We will find him. Follow me!" and his rapid walk became almost a run.

At some distance through the black arch in front of us, we could now see a space of moonlight. We must be nearing an opening in the wood. Yet all around us was still as dark as ever. At our present pace it was impossible to move with much caution. I had already made several false steps. I now placed my foot on some loose object, which, suddenly turning beneath it, threw me violently to the ground.

I rose with difficulty, and then found that my ankle had been so sharply twisted that I was unable to stand, much more to walk. Carl heard my fall, and turned back. I told him what had happened.

A groan escaped his lips, and he stood for a few minutes as if not knowing what course to take. But just then a new sound reached us. It was not now the howl of a beast, but the shriek of a human voice. It sounded to me like that of a woman.

"Heaven help me!" cried Carl, as he heard it. "It is my destiny. I must go alone. Farewell! and, if I do not come back, farewell forever!"

He grasped my hand, and hurried swiftly along the path and out into the open moonlight.

I had again sunk to the ground, and my hand was resting on the object which had caused my fall. It was smooth and rounded. I had taken it for a stone, but now, as my fingers moved over it, they met with strange and regular indentations, and a cry of horror broke from my lips as I became aware that it was a human skull! In spite of the agonizing pain which the effort cost me, I dragged myself from the loathsome thing towards the open moonlight, and when I had reached it supported myself by leaning against the trunk of a tree.

I now found that the open space was of considerable extent. From where I stood the ground sloped gently downwards to a little brook, along whose course were a few bushes. Beyond this the meadow again sloped gently upwards, till, on another slight eminence, like that in which I stood, it was again bounded by the dark wall of woodland.

By the time I had reached my standing-place Carl had already passed the rivulet, and I could see his retreating figure as he strode up the opposite slope. His dogs, scarcely to be seen in the dim light, appeared to be ranging in front of him, and now and then I could hear them give vent to an uneasy growl. How bravely he was pressing on to that danger of which he was so fully conscious!—and I had once thought him timid! I chafed at the thought that I was unable to help him in his peril. I could only watch and listen.

Carl and his dogs disappeared in the distant wood. All was still, and I watched and listened in vain. How long this may have lasted, I cannot tell: it seemed to me to be hours. After a time, however, the silence was broken by a faint shriek, such as I had heard before. But it was not, as before, a solitary one. Others succeeded it. Then, ere long, came the deep baying of the hounds from the same direction, and soon after I heard sounds as of a desperate struggle, amid which I could recognize the tones of Carl's voice.

All these noises came from far away, but on the midnight air at that still spot they were clearly to be distinguished. What could be the meaning of them? In my helplessness, I listened and waited anxiously. After a time, they died away, and all was again still.

I did not keep my eyes fixed upon the opposite slope in vain. After a while I was aware of an approaching figure. I could see no dogs, and the uncertain gait of the coming man was far different from the determined stride with which Carl had gone forth; yet I soon concluded that it must be my friend.

And Carl it was! As he drew nearer, I saw that he bore marks of having been in some desperate encounter. He had no axe now, and his right arm hung powerless by his side. The left, also, seemed so much lacerated as to be almost useless. His clothes were torn and bloody. Now and then he cast a hurried glance backwards, as though he expected pursuit.

"Carl! Carl!" I cried. "I am here, friend! What has happened?"

"What has happened?" he exclaimed, in a hoarse tone. "I was too late! too late! Too late to save, and too weak to avenge! Oh, Theresa! Theresa!"

"Tell me all. Where have you been? With whom have you been fighting?"

"I have been to *him!* The dogs made a good fight; but Leo was throttled before I came up. Max, too, will be dead before this; but he held on bravely when I was disabled, or I should not have come back to you."

"Thank heaven, Carl, that you have escaped with life!"

"Escaped!" he cried; "I have not escaped. I have no wish to escape. I have no more wish for life. I only want to meet him again with some chance of success. I have come back that you may help me."

"Alas, Carl! maimed as I am, I fear that I can do little; but I am ready to share any danger with you."

With his left hand, which was wet with his own blood, he pressed mine, and drew me back under the shadow of the tree. I again entreated him to give me some coherent account of what he had seen; but he only groaned and shuddered.

Yet I noticed that he never for an instant withdrew his eyes from the opposite slope. Soon they appeared to be riveted on some object which was to me invisible.

"He comes! he comes, comrade!" the young man whispered in a low, hollow tone. "Do you see him?"

"I see nothing."

He pointed, and I followed the direction of his finger. No wonder that I had before failed to see this object of his fears. I had looked for some human being. I now found that what he was watching so intently was some animal. It was ranging swiftly to and fro across the open space, much as a pointer might do when beating[1] a field, to make sure of scenting a covey.[2] So the creature moved backwards and forwards; yet at every beat it drew sensibly nearer to where we were hidden.

"It is only a dog," I said. "It is Max. He has escaped, and is searching for us."

"It is indeed searching for us," answered Carl, with a shudder. "But it is no dog. It is *he!* He is coming! Heaven help us! Oh! if I had but my axe and the use of my arm again! Where is the knife, comrade?"

I had been feeling for it before he spoke. The uncertainty of

---

1 Searching.

2 A brood of partridges or other game birds.

the coming danger lent it additional horror; but the knife would at least enable me to make a desperate resistance. I felt eagerly for it; but in vain! I must have dropped it in my fall.

I whispered as much to Carl.

"Then," he groaned, "there is no hope for us. We have only to die. But such a death!"

CHAPTER IV.

"You will not see me again alive!"

NEARER and nearer the creature came. It was now sweeping backwards and forwards in its silent beats on our side of the rivulet. Plainly, it was hunting Carl down, and making sure that its victim had not doubled back. Forwards and backwards, backwards and forwards, it passed; and never did I endure moments of more horrible or sickening suspense than whilst awaiting the coming of the beast, whatever it may be, alike unable to defend myself or to fly.

Nearer and nearer it came, and now I could distinguish its shape more clearly. It seemed to me far beyond the common size—but that might be a delusion of the uncertain moonlight or of my over-excited senses—yet it was only a wolf, a solitary wolf!

"Take courage!" I whispered to Carl. "It is nothing but a single wolf. We are two. It will not dare attack us."

"Not dare!" he answered. "Do you know what that wolf is? It is himself! It is Fritz!"

Yes, I felt it. The old superstition was no myth. Fritz was a werewolf. The very build and motions of the stranger athlete were to be traced in the beast.

A few beats more would bring him upon us, but they gave me time to recover my self-possession.

"Carl," I said, "you have still the use of your legs. You must escape. Leave me to deal with him alone."

"To deal with him," answered Carl, quite calmly, "means only to die; and that must not be, friend. This is my quarrel. You would not have been here but for me. Stay where you are. It is me, not you, that he seeks; and if he finds me you may escape. I must meet him. It is better so. I have no wish to live, after what I have seen to-night. Farewell! and may heaven bless you for your goodness to me! You will not see me again alive!"

I put out a hand to detain him, but he was gone. He had darted out into the moonlight, and, crossing the track of the creature, was hurrying back in that direction from which he had come. He was trying to lead the beast as far as possible from me. Brave and generous Carl, how much had I formerly under-rated your character!

He succeeded in his design. Pursuer and pursued passed from my sight. Time for cool thought was again allowed me. The knife must be at the place where I had fallen. Dark as it was, it was not impossible that I might still find it. Throwing myself upon the ground, I dragged myself on hands and knees towards the spot.

Alas! Before I could gain it a cry reached my ears which told me that I should see my friend Carl no more in life.

In the thick darkness of the wood, it was no easy matter to find the precise place; and more than once, as I groped about, my hands came in contact with what were doubtless human bones, companions probably to the skull which had caused my fall. But these brought me no horror now. Everything depended upon my search. To my joy, I grasped it at last!

But that joy was of brief duration. Almost at the same instant I heard a rustling behind me, and before I could throw myself into any posture of defence I was borne down beneath the monstrous brute that had stolen on me unawares.

At the moment I was as if paralyzed, and when sensation returned it brought only a dull and indistinct knowledge that I was being dragged swiftly onwards, but whither, I neither knew nor cared. Then all was blank again.

But after a while there came a fuller gleam of consciousness. I was no longer in motion. I felt that for the moment I was released from the grip of my enemy. I had even energy enough to cast my eyes round to see that I was in a place where unspeakable horror surrounded me, and that a savage brute face was glaring into mine, with the glittering teeth and the expression which I so well remembered as belonging to Fritz. That the knife was safe in my grasp was my one thought. In another moment I was dealing fierce blows with it; and again all grew darkness around me.

It must have been long ere I recovered from my fainting fit. When I did so my eyes met the light of day, and many voices were talking near me. I knew them for those of my peasant neighbours. I learnt afterwards that the village had become alarmed at the absence of Carl and myself; we had been tracked to the wood, and the whole population had turned out to search for us.

When I looked around I saw that two rude stretchers had been made of branches, and upon these were laid two covered objects whose outlines suggested human bodies. I knew well what they were. I could not easily forget the sight which had met my vision when I had first been dragged to the dreadful place. It was good that they should be closely shrouded. It would be well that no human eyes should ever look upon these forms again—forms that had so recently been the handsome Carl and the pretty Theresa.

A third stretcher was in preparation and a third body lay near me. I could scarcely credit my eyes as they rested on it. It was no wolf, but Fritz, the man as I had known him. The old wolf-like expression was fixed upon his face; the restless eyes were set now and dim, but from the open mouth the long white teeth glittered as of old. He still wore his gay clothes, but they were stained with blood now; and in his breast, in the same places where my knife had pierced to the heart of the savage beast, there were deep and ugly gashes. Not far away lay the carcases of the two brave dogs.

I was taken to the village, and before long was well enough to tell my tale. I need hardly say that it was received by the officials with utter incredulity. I was thrown in prison on the charge of murder.

It was well for me that the so-called superstitions of the peasant witnesses were in my favour. They believed me. By their means it was that I escaped, and barely escaped, with my life. Since then I have never dared to retrace my steps towards the Grendelwold; nor whilst life lasts will anything again induce me to revisit the scenes connected in my memory with the horrors of that dreadful night.

The White Wolf of Kostopchin

Gilbert Campbell

Sir Gilbert Edward Campbell (1838-1899) was born in Romsey, Hampshire, to an aristocratic Irish family originally from Carrick Buoy, Donegal. He attended Harrow (1852-54) and entered military service shortly thereafter, eventually serving as an officer in the Sepoy Rebellion of 1857. In 1870, he married Esther Selina Baynham, and the couple had one son, Claude Robert, born in 1871. Most likely due to financial difficulties, Campbell began working as a translator, producing cheap editions of the works of detective writer Emile Gaboriau and other French authors. He also wrote a number of "shilling shockers," such as Stung by a Saint *(1890), and was a frequent contributor of stories to Christmas anthologies, including* The Mystery of Mandeville Square, *which was published in* Beeton's Christmas Annual *in 1888. Campbell served as editor of* Lambert's Monthly *from 1890 to 1891 and published a handful of sensation novels, including* The Vanishing Diamond *(1890) and* A Ruby Beyond Price *(1891). In 1889, he published a collection of short stories,* Wild and Weird: Tales of Imagination and Mystery.*

It was also in 1889 that Campbell became involved in the management of a fraudulent literary agency, which offered fake diplomas, promises of publication, and editorial assistantships in exchange for cash payments. The agency was particularly successful in fleecing amateur writers, who paid for their manuscripts to be read and published only to find weeks later that the agency had closed shop and its managers were nowhere to be found. The fraud was finally exposed in 1892, and Gilbert Campbell and his collaborators were sentenced to serve time with hard labor. Campbell was given a particularly harsh sentence of eighteen months because the court objected to the ways in which he used his aristocratic title to inspire consumer trust in his criminal scheme. After his release from prison in 1894, Campbell published Through an Indian Mirror: Sensational

Stories of Anglo-Indian Society. *By 1899 he was missing and presumed dead when his son Claude assumed the baronetcy.*

"The White Wolf of Kostopchin" was first published in Wild and Weird, Tales of Imagination and Mystery: Russian, English and Italian. *In his preface to the volume, Campbell notes that the stories are "taken from the folklore of the various countries to which they relate."*[1]

Bibliography

"The Alleged Literary Frauds." *Publisher's Circular* 1369 (Sept. 24, 1892): 322-323.

Campbell, Gilbert. *Wild and Weird: Tales of Imagination and Mystery*. London: Ward, Lock, 1889.

Durrell, Harold Clarke. "Sir Gilbert Edward Campbell." *The New England Historical and Genealogical Register* 84 (1930): 317-318.

"The Literary Frauds Case." *Albany Law Journal*, Nov. 12, 1892, 399.

Mair, Robert H., ed. "Sir Gilbert Edward Campbell." In *Debrett's Illustrated Baronetage and Knightage*, 75. London: Dean, 1879.

"Sir Gilbert Campbell, Bart." *Truth*, Oct. 22, 1891, 831-833.

Wilson, Neil. *Shadows in the Attic: A Guide to British Supernatural Fiction, 1820-1950*. London: British Library, 2000.

THE WHITE WOLF OF KOSTOPCHIN.

CHAPTER I.

A WIDE sandy expanse of country, flat and uninteresting in appearance, with a great staring whitewashed house standing in the midst of wide fields of cultivated land; whilst far away were the low sand-hills and pine-forests to be met with in the district of Lithuania, in Russian Poland. Not far from the great white house was the village in which the serfs[2] dwelt, with the large bakehouse and the public bath which are invariably to be found in all Russian villages, however humble. The fields were negligently cultivated,

---

1 Gilbert Campbell, Introduction to *Wild and Weird: Tales of Imagination and Mystery*, v.

2 A peasant working in forced servitude on an aristocratic estate.

the hedges broken down and the fences in bad repair, shattered agricultural implements had been carelessly flung aside in remote corners, and the whole estate showed the want of the superintending eye of an energetic master. The great white house was no better looked after, the garden was an utter wilderness, great patches of plaster had fallen from the walls, and many of the Venetian shutters were almost off the hinges. Over all was the dark lowering sky of a Russian autumn, and there were no signs of life to be seen, save a few peasants lounging idly towards the *vodki* shop,[1] and a gaunt half-starved cat creeping stealthily abroad in quest of a meal.

The estate, which was known by the name of Kostopchin, was the property of Paul Sergevitch, a gentleman of means, and the most discontented man in Russian Poland. Like most wealthy Muscovites, he had travelled much, and had spent the gold, which had been amassed by serf labour, like water, in all the dissolute revelries of the capitals of Europe. Paul's figure was as well known in the boudoirs of the *demi mondaines*[2] as his face was familiar at the public gaming-tables. He appeared to have no thought for the future, but only to live in the excitement of the mad career of dissipation which he was pursuing. His means, enormous as they were, were all forestalled, and he was continually sending to his intendant[3] for fresh supplies of money. His fortune would not have long held out against the constant inroads that were being made upon it, when an unexpected circumstance took place which stopped his career like a flash of lightning. This was a fatal duel, in which a young man of great promise, the son of the prime minister of the country in which he then resided, fell by his hand. Representations were made to the Czar, and Paul Sergevitch was recalled, and, after receiving a severe reprimand, was ordered to return to his estates in Lithuania. Horribly discontented, yet not daring to disobey the Imperial mandate, Paul buried himself at Kostopchin, a place he had not visited since his boyhood. At first he endeavored to interest himself in the workings of the vast estate; but agriculture had no charm for him, and the only result was that he quarreled with and dismissed his German intendant,

---

1 Vodka bar.

2 Courtesans.

3 Household manager.

replacing him by an old serf, Michal Vassilitch, who had been his father's valet. Then he took to wandering about the country, gun in hand, and upon his return home would sit moodily drinking brandy and smoking innumerable cigarettes, as he cursed his lord and master, the emperor, for consigning him to such a course of dullness and *ennui*.[1] For a couple of years he led this aimless life, and at last, hardly knowing the reason for so doing, he married the daughter of a neighbouring landed proprietor. The marriage was a most unhappy one; the girl had really never cared for Paul, but had married him in obedience to her father's mandates, and the man, whose temper was always brutal and violent, treated her, after a brief interval of contemptuous indifference, with savage cruelty. After three years the unhappy woman expired, leaving behind her two children—a boy, Alexis, and a girl, Katrina. Paul treated his wife's death with the most perfect indifference; but he did not put any one in her place. He was very fond of the little Katrina, but did not take much notice of the boy, and resumed his lonely wanderings about the country with dog and gun. Five years had passed since the death of his wife. Alexis was a fine, healthy boy of seven, whilst Katrina was some eighteen months younger. Paul was lighting one of his eternal cigarettes at the door of his house, when the little girl came running up to him.

"You bad, wicked papa," said she. "How is it that you have never brought me the pretty gray squirrels that you promised I should have the next time you went to the forest?"

"Because I have never yet been able to find any, my treasure," returned her father, taking up the child in his arms and half smothering her with kisses. "Because I have not found them yet, my golden queen; but I am bound to find Ivanovitch, the poacher, smoking about the woods, and if he can't show me where they are, no one can."

"Ah, little father," broke in Old Michal, using the term of address with which a Russian of humble position usually accosts his superior; "Ah, little father, take care; you will go to those woods once too often."

"Do you think I am afraid of Ivanovitch?" returned his master,

---

1 Melancholy idleness.

with a coarse laugh. "Why, he and I are the best of friends; at any rate, if he robs me, he does so openly, and keeps other poachers away from my woods."

"It is not of Ivanovitch that I am thinking," answered the old man. "But oh! Gospodin,[1] do not go into these dark solitudes; there are terrible tales told about them, of witches that dance in the moonlight, of strange, shadowy forms that are seen amongst the trunks of the tall pines, and of whispered voices that tempt the listeners to eternal perdition."

Again the rude laugh of the lord of the manor rang out, as Paul observed, "If you go on addling your brain, old man, with these nearly half-forgotten legends, I shall have to look out for a new intendant."

"But I was not thinking of these fearful creatures only," returned Michal, crossing himself piously. "It was against the wolves that I meant to warn you."

"Oh, father, dear, I am frightened now," whimpered little Katrina, hiding her head on her father's shoulder. "Wolves are such cruel, wicked things."

"See there, graybearded dotard,"[2] cried Paul, furiously, "you have terrified this sweet angel by your farrago[3] of lies; besides, who ever heard of wolves so early as this. You are dreaming, Michal Vassilitch, or have taken your morning dram of vodki too strong."

"As I hope for future happiness," answered the old man, solemnly, "as I came through the marsh last night from Kosma the herdsman's cottage—you know, my lord, that he has been bitten by a viper, and is seriously ill—as I came through the marsh, I repeat, I saw something like sparks of fire in the clump of alders on the right-hand side. I was anxious to know what they could be, and cautiously moved a little nearer, recommending my soul to the protection of Saint Vladamir.[4] I had not gone a couple of paces when a wild howl came that chilled the very marrow in my bones, and a pack of some ten or a dozen wolves, gaunt and famished as you see them, my lord, in the winter, rushed out. At their head was

1 Sir.
2 Fool.
3 Confused mixture.
4 Vladimir I of Kiev (958-1015), Russian saint.

a white she-wolf, as big as any of the male ones, with gleaming tusks and a pair of yellow eyes that blazed with lurid fire. I had round my neck a crucifix that had been given me by the priest of Streletza, and the savage beasts knew this and broke away across the marsh, sending up the mud and water in showers in the air; but the white she-wolf, little father, circled round me three times, as though endeavouring to find some place from which to attack me. Three times she did this, and then, with a snap of her teeth and a howl of impotent malice, she galloped away some fifty yards and sat down, watching my every movement with her fiery eyes. I did not delay any longer in so dangerous a spot, as you may well imagine, Gospodin, but walked hurriedly home, crossing myself at every step; but, as I am a living man, that white devil followed me the whole distance, keeping fifty paces in the rear, and every now and then licking her lips with a sound that made my flesh creep. When I got to the last fence before you come to the house I raised up my voice and shouted for the dogs, and soon I heard the deep bay of Troska and Branscöe as they came bounding towards me. The white devil heard it, too, and, giving a high bound into the air, she uttered a loud howl of disappointment, and trotted back leisurely towards the marsh."

"But why did you not set the dogs after her?" asked Paul, interested, in spite of himself, at the old man's narrative. "In the open Troska and Branscöe would run down any wolf that ever set foot to the ground in Lithuania."

"I tried to do so, little father," answered the old man, solemnly; "but directly they got up to the spot where the beast had executed her last devilish gambol,[1] they put their tails between their legs and ran back to the house as fast as their legs could carry them."

"Strange," muttered Paul, thoughtfully, "that is, if it is truth and not vodki that is speaking."

"My lord," returned the old man, reproachfully, "man and boy, I have served you and my lord your father for fifty years, and no one can say that they ever saw Michal Vassilitch the worse for liquor."

"No one doubts that you are a sly old thief, Michal," returned

---

1 Playful sport.

his master, with his coarse, jarring laugh; "but for all that, your long stories of having been followed by white wolves won't prevent me from going to the forest to-day. A couple of good buckshot cartridges will break any spell, though I don't think that the she-wolf, if she existed anywhere than in your own imagination, has anything to do with magic. Don't be frightened, Katrina, my pet; you shall have a fine white wolf's skin to put your feet on, if what this old fool says is right."

"Michal is not a fool," pouted the child, "and it is very wicked of you to call him so. I don't want any nasty wolf-skins, I want the grey squirrels."

"And you shall have them, my precious," returned her father, setting her down upon the ground. "Be a good girl, and I will not be long away."

"Father," said the little Alexis, suddenly, "let me go with you. I should like to see you kill a wolf, and then I should know how to do so, when I am older and taller."

"Pshaw," returned his father, irritably. "Boys are always in the way. Take the lad away, Michal; don't you see that he is worrying his sweet little sister."

"No, no, he does not worry me at all," answered the impetuous little lady, as she flew to her brother and covered him with kisses. "Michal, you shan't take him away, do you hear?"

"There, there, leave the children together," returned Paul, as he shouldered his gun, and kissing the tips of his fingers to Katrina, stepped away rapidly in the direction of the dark pine woods. Paul walked on, humming the fragment of an air that he had heard in a very different place many years ago. A strange feeling of elation crept over him, very different to the false excitement which his solitary drinking bouts were wont to produce. A change seemed to have come over his whole life, the skies looked brighter, the *spiculæ*[1] of the pine-trees of a more vivid green, and the landscape seemed to have lost that dull cloud of depression which had for years appeared to hang over it. And beneath all this exaltation of the mind, beneath all this unlooked-for promise of a more happy future, lurked a heavy, inexplicable feeling of a power to come,

---

1 Sharp points.

a something without form or shape, and yet the more terrible because it was shrouded by that thick veil which conceals from the eyes of the soul the strange fantastic designs of the dwellers beyond the line of earthly influences.

There were no signs of the poacher, and wearied with searching for him, Paul made the woods re-echo with his name. The great dog Troska, who had followed his master, looked up wistfully into his face, and at a second repetition of the name "Ivanovitch," uttered a long plaintive howl, and then, looking round at Paul as though entreating him to follow, moved slowly ahead towards a denser portion of the forest. A little mystified at the hound's unusual proceedings, Paul followed, keeping his gun ready to fire at the least sign of danger. He thought that he knew the forest well, but the dog led the way to a portion which he never remembered to have visited before. He had got away from the pine trees now, and had entered a dense thicket formed of stunted oaks and hollies. The great dog only kept a yard or so ahead; his lips were drawn back, showing the strong white fangs, the hair upon his neck and back was bristling, and his tail firmly pressed between his hind legs. Evidently the animal was in a state of the most extreme terror, and yet it proceeded bravely forward. Struggling through the dense thicket, Paul suddenly found himself in an open space of some ten or twenty yards in diameter. At one end of it was a slimy pool, into the waters of which several strange-looking reptiles glided as the man and dog made their appearance. Almost in the centre of the opening was a shattered stone cross, and at its base lay a dark heap, close to which Troska stopped, and again raising his head, uttered a long melancholy howl. For an instant or two, Paul gazed hesitatingly at the shapeless heap that lay beneath the cross, and then, mustering up all his courage, he stepped forwards and bent anxiously over it. One glance was enough, for he recognized the body of Ivanovitch the poacher, hideously mangled. With a cry of surprise, he turned over the body, and shuddered as he gazed upon the terrible injuries that had been inflicted. The unfortunate man had evidently been attacked by some savage beast, for there were marks of teeth upon the throat, and the jugular vein had been almost torn out. The breast of the corpse had been torn open, evidently by long sharp claws, and there was a gaping orifice upon the left side, round which the blood had formed in a thick coagulated patch. The only animals to be found in the forests of Russia capable of inflicting such wounds are the bear or the wolf, and the question as to the class of the assailant was easily settled by a glance at the dank ground, which showed the prints of a wolf so entirely different from the plantegrade[1] traces of the bear.

"Savage brutes," muttered Paul. "So, after all, there may have been some truth in Michal's story, and the old idiot may for once in his life have spoken the truth. Well, it is no concern of mine, and if a fellow chooses to wander about the woods at night to kill my game, instead of remaining in his own hovel, he must take his chance. The strange thing is that the brutes have not eaten him, though they have mauled him so terribly."

He turned away as he spoke, intending to return home and send out some of the serfs to bring in the body of the unhappy man, when his eye was caught by a small white object hanging from a bramble bush near the pond. He made towards the spot, and taking up the object, examined it curiously. It was a tuft of coarse white hair, evidently belonging to some animal.

"A wolf's hair, or I am much mistaken," muttered Paul, pressing the hair between his fingers, and then applying it to his nose. "And from its colour, I should think that it belonged to the white lady who so terribly alarmed old Michal on the occasion of his night walk through the marsh."

Paul found it no easy task to retrace his steps towards those parts of the forest with which he was acquainted, and Troska seemed unable to render him the slightest assistance, but followed moodily behind. Many times Paul found his way blocked by impenetrable thicket or dangerous quagmire, and during his many wanderings he had the ever-present sensation that there was a something close to him, an invisible something, a noiseless something; but for all that, a presence which moved as he advanced, and halted as he stopped in vain to listen. The certainty that an impalpable thing of some shape or other was close at hand grew so strong, that as the short autumn day began to close, and darker shadows to fall between the trunks of the lofty trees, it made him hurry on at his

---

1 Flat-footed.

utmost speed. At length, when he had grown almost mad with terror, he suddenly came upon a path he knew, and with a feeling of intense relief, he stepped briskly forward in the direction of Kostopchin. As he left the forest and came into the open country, a faint wail seemed to ring through the darkness; but Paul's nerves had been so much shaken that he did not know whether this was an actual fact or only the offspring of his own excited fancy. As he crossed the neglected lawn that lay in front of the house, old Michal came rushing out of the house with terror convulsing every feature.

"Oh, my lord, my lord!" gasped he, "is not this too terrible?"

"Nothing has happened to my Katrina?" cried the father, a sudden sickly feeling of terror passing through his heart.

"No, no, the little lady is quite safe, thanks to the Blessed Virgin and Saint Alexander of Nevskoi,"[1] returned Michal; "but oh, my lord, poor Marta, the herd's[2] daughter——"

"Well, what of the slut?" demanded Paul, for now that his momentary fear for the safety of his daughter had passed away, he had but little sympathy to spare for so insignificant a creature as a serf girl.

"I told you that Kosma was dying," answered Michal. "Well, Marta went across the marsh this afternoon to fetch the priest, but alas! she never came back."

"What detained her, then?" asked his master.

"One of the neighbors, going in to see how Kosma was getting on, found the poor old man dead; his face was terribly contorted, and he was half in the bed, and half out, as though he had striven to reach the door. The men ran to the village to give the alarm, and as the men returned to the herdsman's hut, they found the body of Marta in a thicket by the clump of alders on the marsh."

"Her body, she was dead then?" asked Paul.

"Dead, my lord, killed by wolves," answered the old man. "And oh, my lord, it is too horrible, her breast was horribly lacerated, and her heart had been taken out and eaten, for it was nowhere to be found."

---

1 Alexander Nevsky (1120-1163) was a prince and warlord who was canonized as a saint in the Russian Orthodox Church in 1547.

2 Herdsman's.

Paul started, for the horrible mutilation of the body of Ivanovitch the poacher occurred to his recollection.

"And, my lord," continued the old man, "this is not all, on a bush close by was this tuft of hair," and, as he spoke, he took it from a piece of paper in which it was wrapped to his master.

Paul took it, and recognized a similar tuft of hair to that which he had seen upon the bramble bush beside the shattered cross.

"Surely, my lord," continued Michal, not heeding his master's look of surprise, "you will have out men and dogs to hunt down this terrible creature, or, better still, send for the priest and holy water, for I have my doubts whether the creature belongs to this earth."

Paul shuddered, and, after a short pause, he told Michal of the ghastly end of Ivanovitch the poacher.

The old man listened with the utmost excitement, crossing himself repeatedly, and muttering invocations to the Blessed Virgin and the saints every instant, but his master would no longer listen to him, and, ordering him to place brandy on the table, sat drinking moodily until daylight.

The next day a fresh horror awaited the inhabitants of Kostopchin. An old man, a confirmed drunkard, had staggered out of the vodki shop with the intention of returning home; three hours later he was found at a turn of the road, horribly scratched and mutilated, with the same gaping orifice in the left side of the breast, from which the heart had been forcibly torn out.

Three several times in the course of the week the same ghastly tragedy occurred—a little child, an able-bodied labourer, and an old woman, were all found with the same terrible marks of mutilation upon them, and in every case the same tuft of white hair was found in the immediate vicinity of the bodies. A frightful panic ensued, and an excited crowd of serfs surrounded the house at Kostopchin, calling upon their master, Paul Sergevitch, to save them from the fiend that had been let loose upon them, and shouting out various remedies, which they insisted upon being carried into effect at once.

Paul felt a strange disinclination to adopt any active measures. A certain feeling which he could not account for urged him to remain quiescent,[1] but the Russian serf when suffering under an excess of superstitious terror is a dangerous person to deal with, and, with extreme reluctance, Paul Sergevitch issued instructions for a thorough search through the estate, and a general *battue* of the pine woods.[2]

CHAPTER II.

THE army of beaters convened by Michal was ready with the first dawn of sunrise, and formed a strange and almost grotesque-looking assemblage, armed with rusty old firelocks, heavy bludgeons, and scythes fastened on to the end of long poles.

Paul, with his double-barrelled gun thrown across his shoulder and a keen hunting-knife thrust into his belt, marched at the head of the serfs, accompanied by the two great hounds, Troska and Branscöe. Every nook and corner of the hedgerows were examined, and the little outlying clumps were thoroughly searched, but without success, and at last a circle was formed round the larger portion of the forest, and with loud shouts, blowing of horns, and beating of copper cooking utensils, the crowd of eager serfs pushed their way through the brushwood. Frightened birds flew up, whirring through the pine branches; hares and rabbits darted from their hiding-places behind tufts and hummocks of grass, and skurried away in the utmost terror. Occasionally a roe deer rushed through the thicket, or a wild boar burst through the thin lines of beaters, but no signs of wolves were to be seen. The circle grew narrower and yet more narrow, when all at once a wild shriek and a confused murmur of voices echoed through the pine trees. All rushed to the spot, and a young lad was discovered weltering[3] in his blood and terribly mutilated, though life still lingered in the mangled frame. A few drops of vodki were poured down his throat, and he managed to gasp out that the white wolf had sprung upon him suddenly, and, throwing him to the ground, had commenced tearing at the flesh over his heart. He would inevitably have been

---

1 Quiet and passive.
2 Beating of the bushes.
3 Writhing.

killed, had not the animal quitted him, alarmed by the approach of the other beaters.

"The beast ran into that thicket," gasped the boy, and then once more relapsed into a state of insensibility.

But the words of the wounded boy had been eagerly passed round, and a hundred different propositions were made.

"Set fire to the thicket," exclaimed one.

"Fire a volley into it," suggested another.

"A bold dash in, and trample the beast's life out," shouted a third.

The first proposal was agreed to, and a hundred eager hands collected dried sticks and leaves, and then a light was kindled. Just as the fire was about to be applied, a soft, sweet voice issued from the centre of the thicket.

"Do not set fire to the forest, my dear friends; give me time to come out. Is it not enough for me to have been frightened to death by that awful creature?"

All started back in amazement, and Paul felt a strange, sudden thrill pass through his heart as those soft musical accents fell upon his ear.

There was a light rustling in the brushwood, and then a vision suddenly appeared, which filled the souls of the beholders with surprise. As the bushes divided, a fair woman, wrapped in a mantle of soft white fur, with a fantastically-shaped travelling cap of green velvet upon her head, stood before them. She was exquisitely fair, and her long Titian[1] red hair hung in dishevelled masses over her shoulders.

"My good man," began she, with a certain tinge of aristocratic hauteur in her voice, "is your master here?"

As moved by a spring, Paul stepped forward and mechanically raised his cap.

"I am Paul Sergevitch," said he, "and these woods are on my estate of Kostopchin. A fearful wolf has been committing a series of terrible devastations upon my people, and we have been endeavouring to hunt it down. A boy whom he has just wounded says

---

1 Like the red hair depicted in the paintings of Titian (Tiziano Vecelli), a Venetian painter, c.1488-1576.

that he ran into the thicket from which you have just emerged, to the surprise of us all."

"I know," answered the lady, fixing her clear, steel-blue eyes keenly upon Paul's face. "The terrible beast rushed past me, and dived into a large cavity in the earth in the very centre of the thicket. It was a huge white wolf, and I greatly feared that it would devour me."

"Ho, my men," cried Paul, "take spade and mattock,[1] and dig out the monster, for she has come to the end of her tether at last. Madam, I do not know what chance has conducted you to this wild solitude, but the hospitality of Kostopchin is at your disposal, and I will, with your permission, conduct you there as soon as this scourge of the countryside has been dispatched."

He offered his hand with some remains of his former courtesy, but started back with an expression of horror on his face.

"Blood," cried he; "why, madam, your hand and fingers are stained with blood."

A faint colour rose to the lady's cheek, but it died away in an instant as she answered, with a faint smile—

"The dreadful creature was all covered with blood, and I suppose I must have stained my hands against the bushes through which it had passed, when I parted them in order to escape from the fiery death with which you threatened me."

There was a ring of suppressed irony in her voice, and Paul felt his eyes drop before the glance of those cold steel-blue eyes. Meanwhile, urged to the utmost exertion by their fears, the serfs plied spade and mattock with the utmost vigour. The cavity was speedily enlarged, but, when a depth of eight feet had been attained, it was found to terminate in a little burrow not large enough to admit a rabbit, much less a creature of the white wolf's size. There were none of the tufts of white hair which had hitherto been always found beside the bodies of the victims, nor did that peculiar rank odour which always indicates the presence of wild animals hang about the spot.

The superstitious Muscovites crossed themselves, and scrambled out of the hole with grotesque alacrity. The mysterious

---

1 Pick-like tool.

disappearance of the monster which had committed such frightful ravages had cast a chill over the hearts of the ignorant peasants, and, unheeding the shouts of their master, they left the forest, which seemed to be overcast with the gloom of some impending calamity.

"Forgive the ignorance of these boors, madam," said Paul, when he found himself alone with the strange lady, "and permit me to escort you to my poor house, for you must have need of rest and refreshment, and——"

Here Paul checked himself abruptly, and a dark flush of embarrassment passed over his face.

"And," said the lady, with the same faint smile, "and you are dying with curiosity to know how I suddenly made my appearance from a thicket in your forest. You say that you are the lord of Kostopchin, then you are Paul Sergevitch, and should surely know how the ruler of Holy Russia takes upon himself to interfere with the doings of his children?"

"You know me, then?" exclaimed Paul, in some surprise.

"Yes, I have lived in foreign lands, as you have, and have heard your name often. Did you not break the bank at Blankburg? Did you not carry off Isola Menuti, the dancer, from a host of competitors; and, as a last instance of my knowledge, shall I recall to your memory a certain morning, on a sandy shore, with two men facing each other pistol in hand, the one young, fair, and boyish-looking, hardly twenty-two years of age, the other——"

"Hush!" exclaimed Paul, hoarsely; "you evidently know me, but who in the fiend's name are you?"

"Simply a woman who once moved in society and read the papers, and who is now a hunted fugitive."

"A fugitive!" returned Paul, hotly; "who dare to persecute you?"

The lady moved a little closer to him, and then whispered in his ear—

"The police!"

"The police!" repeated Paul, stepping back a pace or two. "The police!"

"Yes, Paul Sergevitch, the police," returned the lady, "that body at the mention of which it is said the very Emperor trembles as he sits in his gilded chambers in the Winter Palace.[1] Yes, I have had the imprudence to speak my mind too freely, and—well, you know what women have to dread who fall into the hands of the police in Holy Russia. To avoid such infamous degradations I fled, accompanied by a faithful domestic. I fled in hopes of gaining the frontier, but a few versts[2] from here a body of mounted police rode up. My poor old servant had the impudence to resist, and was shot dead. Half wild with terror I fled into the forest, and wandered about until I heard the noise your serfs made in beating the woods. I thought it was the police, who had organized a search for me, and I crept into the thicket for the purpose of concealment. The rest you know. And now, Paul Sergevitch, tell me whether you dare give shelter to a proscribed fugitive such as I am?"

"Madam," returned Paul, gazing into the clear-cut features before him, glowing with the animation of the recital, "Kostopchin is ever open to misfortune—and beauty," added he, with a bow.

"Ah!" cried the lady, with a laugh in which there was something sinister; "I expect that misfortune would knock at your door for a long time, if it was unaccompanied by beauty. However, I thank you, and will accept your hospitality, but if evil come upon you, remember that I am not to be blamed."

"You will be safe enough at Kostopchin," returned Paul. "The police won't trouble their heads about me; they know that since the Emperor drove me to lead this hideous existence politics have no charm for me, and that the brandy-bottle is the only charm of my existence."

"Dear me," answered the lady, eyeing him uneasily, "a morbid drunkard, are you? Well, as I am half perished with cold, suppose you take me to Kostopchin; you will be conferring a favour on me, and will get back all the sooner to your favourite brandy."

She placed her hand upon Paul's arm as she spoke, and mechanically he led the way to the great solitary white house. The few servants betrayed no astonishment at the appearance of the lady, for some of the serfs on their way back to the village had spread the report of the sudden appearance of the mysterious stranger;

---

1 Residence of Russian czars, located in St. Petersburg.
2 Russian unit of distance equivalent to two-thirds of a mile.

besides, they were not accustomed to question the acts of their somewhat arbitrary master.

Alexis and Katrina had gone to bed, and Paul and his guest sat down to a hastily-improvised meal.

"I am no great eater," remarked the lady, as she played with the food before her; and Paul noticed with surprise that scarcely a morsel passed her lips, though she more than once filled and emptied a goblet of the champagne which had been opened in honour of her arrival.

"So it seems," remarked he; "and I do not wonder, for the food in this benighted hole is not what either you or I have been accustomed to."

"Oh, it does well enough," returned the lady, carelessly. "And now, if you have such a thing as a woman in the establishment, you can let her show me to my room, for I am nearly dead for want of sleep."

Paul struck a handbell that stood on the table beside him, and the stranger rose from her seat, and with a brief "Good night," was moving towards the door, when the old man Michal suddenly made his appearance on the threshold. The aged intendant started backwards as though to avoid a heavy blow, and his fingers at once sought for the crucifix which he wore suspended round his neck, and on whose protection he relied to shield him from the powers of darkness.

"Blessed Virgin!" he exclaimed. "Holy Saint Radislas,[1] protect me, where have I seen her before?"

The lady took no notice of the old man's evident terror, but passed away down the echoing corridor.

The old man now timidly approached his master, who, after swallowing a glass of brandy, had drawn his chair up to the stove, and was gazing moodily at its polished surface.

"My lord," said Michal, venturing to touch his master's shoulder, "is that the lady that you found in the forest?"

"Yes," returned Paul, a smile breaking out over his face. "She is very beautiful, is she not?"

---

[1] Most likely a mistaken reference to Count Radislas, who was converted to Christianity during a battle with Saint Wenceslas (c. 907-935).

"Beautiful!" repeated Michal, crossing himself, "she may have beauty, but it is that of a demon. Where have I seen her before?— where have I seen those shining teeth and those cold eyes? She is not like anyone here and I have never been ten versts from Kostopchin in my life. I am utterly bewildered. Ah, I have it, the dying herdsman—save the mark! Gospodin, have a care. I tell you that the strange lady is the image of the white wolf."

"You old fool," returned his master, savagely, "let me ever hear you repeat such nonsense again, and I will have you skinned alive. The lady is high-born, and of good family, beware how you insult her. Nay, I give you further commands: see that during her sojourn here she is treated with the utmost respect. And communicate this to all the servants. Mind, no more tales about the vision that your addled brain conjured up of wolves in the marsh, and above all do not let me hear that you have been alarming my dear little Katrina with your senseless babble."

The old man bowed humbly, and, after a short pause, remarked—

"The lad that was injured at the hunt to-day is dead, my lord."

"Oh, dead is he, poor wretch!" returned Paul, to whom the death of a serf lad was not a matter of overweening importance. "But look here, Michal, remember that if any inquiries are made about the lady, that no one knows anything about her; that, in fact, no one has seen her at all."

"Your lordship shall be obeyed," answered the old man; and then, seeing that his master had relapsed into his former moody reverie, he left the room, crossing himself at every step he took.

Late into the night Paul sat up thinking over the occurrences of the day. He had told Michal that his guest was of noble family, but in reality he knew nothing more of her than she had condescended to tell him.

"Why, I don't even know her name," muttered he; "and yet somehow or other it seems as if a new feature of my life was opening before me. However, I have made one step in advance by getting her here, and if she talks about leaving, why all that I have to do is threaten her with the police."

After his usual custom he smoked cigarette after cigarette, and poured out copious tumblers of brandy. The attendant serf replenished the stove from a small den which opened into the corridor, and after a time Paul slumbered heavily in his arm-chair. He was aroused by a light touch upon his shoulder, and, starting up, saw the stranger of the forest standing by his side.

"This is indeed kind of you," said she, with her usual mocking smile. "You felt that I should be strange here, and you got up early to see to the horses, or can it really be, those ends of cigarettes, that empty bottle of brandy? Paul Sergevitch, you have not been to bed at all."

Paul muttered a few indistinct words in reply, and then, ringing the bell furiously, ordered the servant to clear away the *débris* of last night's orgy, and lay the table for breakfast; then, with a hasty apology, he left the room to make a fresh toilet, and in about half an hour returned with his appearance sensibly improved by his ablutions[1] and change of dress.

"I dare say," remarked the lady, as they were seated at the morning meal, for which she manifested the same indifference that she had for the dinner of the previous evening, "that you would like to know my name and who I am. Well, I don't mind telling you my name. It is Ravina, but as to my family and who I am, it will perhaps be best for you to remain in ignorance. A matter of policy, my dear Paul Sergevitch, a mere matter of policy, you see. I leave you to judge from my manners and appearance whether I am of sufficiently good form to be invited to the honour of your table——"

"None more worthy," broke in Paul, whose bemuddled brain was fast succumbing to the charms of his guest; "and surely that is a question upon which I may be deemed a competent judge."

"I do not know about that," returned Ravina, "for from all accounts the company that you used was not of the most select character."

"No, but hear me," began Paul, seizing her hand and endeavoring to carry it to his lips. But as he did so an unpleasant chill passed over him, for those slender fingers were icy cold.

"Do not be foolish," said Ravina, drawing away her hand, after she had permitted it to rest for an instant in Paul's grasp; "do you not hear someone coming?"

---

1 Bathing.

As she spoke the sound of tiny pattering feet was heard in the corridor, then the door was flung violently open, and with a shrill cry of delight, Katrina rushed into the room, followed more slowly by her brother Alexis.

"And are these your children?" asked Ravina, as Paul took up the little girl and placed her fondly upon his knee, whilst the boy stood a few paces from the door gazing with eyes of wonder upon the strange woman, for whose appearance he was utterly unable to account. "Come here, my little man," continued she; "I suppose that you are the heir of Kostopchin, though you do not resemble your father much."

"He takes after his mother, I think," returned Paul, carelessly; "and how has my darling Katrina been?" he added, addressing his daughter.

"Quite well, papa dear," answered the child, "but where is the fine white wolf-skin that you promised me?"

"Your father did not find her," answered Ravina, with a little laugh; "the white wolf was not so easy to catch as he fancied."

Alexis had moved a few steps nearer to the lady, and was listening with grave attention to every word she uttered.

"Are white wolves so difficult to kill, then?" asked he.

"It seems so, my little man," returned the lady, "since your father and all the serfs of Kostopchin were unable to do so," answered Ravina.

"I have got a pistol, that good old Michal has taught me to fire, and I am sure I could kill her if ever I got a sight of her," observed Alexis, boldly.

"There is a brave boy," returned Ravina, with one of her shrill laughs; "and now, won't you come and sit on my knee, for I am very fond of little boys?"

"No, I don't like you," answered Alexis, after a moment's consideration, "for Michal says——"

"Go to your room, you insolent young brat," broke in his father, in a voice of thunder. "You spend so much of your time with Michal and the serfs that you have learned all their boorish habits."

Two tiny tears rolled down the boy's cheeks as in obedience to his father's orders he turned about and quitted the room, whilst

Ravina darted a strange look of dislike after him. As soon, however, as the door had closed, the fair woman addressed Katrina.

"Well, perhaps you will not be so unkind to me as your brother," said she. "Come to me," and as she spoke she held out her arms.

The little girl came to her without hesitation, and began to smooth the silken tresses which were coiled and wreathed around Ravina's head.

"Pretty, pretty," she murmured, "beautiful lady."

"You see, Paul Sergevitch, that your little daughter has taken to me at once," remarked Ravina.

"She takes after her father, who was always noted for his good taste," returned Paul, with a bow; "but take care, madam, or the little puss will have your necklace off."

The child indeed had succeeded in unclasping the glittering ornament, and was now inspecting it in high glee.

"That is a curious ornament," said Paul, stepping up to the child and taking the circlet from her hand.

It was indeed a quaintly-fashioned ornament, consisting as it did of a number of what were apparently curved pieces of sharp-pointed horn set in gold, and depending[1] from a snake of the same precious metal.

"Why, these are claws," continued he, as he looked at them more carefully.

"Yes, wolves' claws," answered Ravina, taking the necklet from the child and reclasping it round her neck. "It is a family relic which I have always worn."

Katrina at first seemed inclined to cry at her new plaything being taken from her, but by caresses and endearments Ravina soon contrived to lull her once more into a good temper.

"My daughter has certainly taken to you in a most wonderful manner," remarked Paul, with a pleased smile. "You have quite obtained possession of her heart."

"Not yet, whatever I may do later on," answered the woman, with her strange cold smile, as she pressed the child closer towards her and shot a glance at Paul which made him quiver with an emotion that he had never felt before. Presently, however, the child

---

1 Hanging.

grew tired of her new acquaintance, and sliding down from her knee, crept from the room in search of her brother Alexis.

Paul and Ravina remained silent for a few instants, and then the woman broke the silence.

"All that remains for me now, Paul Sergevitch, is to trespass on your hospitality, and to ask you to lend me some disguise, and assist me to gain the nearest post town, which, I think, is Vitroski."

"And why should you wish to leave this at all," demanded Paul, a deep flush rising to his cheek. "You are perfectly safe in my house, and if you attempt to pursue your journey there is every chance of your being recognized and captured."

"Why do I wish to leave this house?" answered Ravina, rising to her feet and casting a look of surprise upon her interrogator. "Can you ask such a question? How is it possible for me to remain here?"

"It is perfectly impossible for you to leave, of that I am quite certain," answered the man, doggedly. "All I know is, that if you leave Kostopchin, you will inevitably fall into the hands of the police."

"And Paul Sergevitch will tell them where they can find me?" questioned Ravina, with an ironical inflection in the tone of her voice.

"I never said so," returned Paul.

"Perhaps not," answered the woman, quickly, "but I am not slow in reading thoughts, they are sometimes plainer to read than words. You are saying to yourself, 'Kostopchin is but a dull hole after all; chance has thrown into my hands a woman whose beauty pleases me; she is utterly friendless; and is in fear of the pursuits of the police; why should I not bend her to my will?' That is what you have been thinking, is it not so, Paul Sergevitch?"

"I never thought, that is——" stammered the man.

"No, you never thought that I could read you so plainly," pursued the woman, pitilessly, "but it is the truth that I have told you, and sooner than remain an inmate of your house, I would leave it, even if all the police of Russia stood ready to arrest me on its very threshold."

"Stay, Ravina," exclaimed Paul, as the woman made a step towards the door, "I do not say whether your reading of my thoughts is right or wrong, but before you leave, listen to me. I do not speak to you in the usual strain of a pleading lover, you, who know my past, would laugh at me should I do so; but I tell you plainly that from the first moment that I set eyes upon you, a strange new feeling has risen up in my heart, not the cold thing that society calls love, but a burning resistless flood which flows down like molten lava from the volcano's crater. Stay, Ravina, stay, I implore you, for if you go from here you will take my heart with you."

"You may be speaking more truthfully than you think," returned the fair woman, as, turning back, she came close up to Paul, and placing both her hands upon his shoulders, shot a glance of lurid fire from her eyes. "Still, you have but given me a selfish reason for my staying, only your own self-gratification. Give me one that more nearly affects myself."

Ravina's touch sent a tremor through Paul's whole frame which caused every nerve and sinew to vibrate. Gaze as boldly as he might into those steel-blue eyes, he could not sustain their intensity.

"Be my wife, Ravina," faltered he. "Be my wife. You are safe enough from all pursuit here, and if that does not suit you I can easily convert my estate into a large sum of money, and we can fly to other lands, where you can have nothing to fear from the Russian police."

"And does Paul Sergevitch actually mean to offer his hand to a woman whose name he does not even know, and of whose feelings towards him he is entirely ignorant," asked the woman, with her customary mocking laugh.

"What do I care for name or birth," returned he, hotly. "I have enough for both, and as for love, my passion would soon kindle some sparks of it in your breast, cold and frozen as it may now be."

"Let me think a little," said Ravina, and throwing herself into an armchair she buried her face in her hands and seemed plunged in deep reflection, whilst Paul paced impatiently up and down the room like a prisoner awaiting the verdict that would restore him to life or doom him to a shameful death.

At length Ravina removed her hands from her face and spoke.

"Listen," said she, "I have thought over your proposal seriously, and upon certain conditions, I will consent to become your wife."

"They are granted in advance," broke in Paul, eagerly.

"Make no bargains blindfold," answered she, "but listen. At the present moment I have no inclination for you, but on the other hand I feel no repugnance for you. I will remain here for a month, and during that time I shall remain in a suite of apartments which you will have prepared for me. Every evening I will visit you here, and upon your making yourself agreeable my ultimate decision will depend."

"And suppose that decision should be an unfavourable one?" asked Paul.

"Then," answered Ravina, with a ringing laugh, "I shall, as you say, leave this and take your heart with me."

"These are hard conditions," remarked Paul. "Why not shorten the time of probation?"

"My conditions are unalterable," answered Ravina, with a little stamp of her foot. "Do you agree to them or not?"

"I have no alternative," answered he, sullenly; "but remember that I am to see you every evening."

"For two hours," said the woman, "so you must try and make yourself as agreeable as you can in that time; and now, if you will give orders regarding my rooms, I will settle myself in them with as little delay as possible."

Paul obeyed her, and in a couple of hours three handsome chambers were got ready for their fair occupant in a distant part of the great rambling house.

CHAPTER III.

THE AWAKENING OF THE WOLF.

THE days slipped slowly and wearily away, but Ravina showed no signs of relenting. Every evening, according to her bond, she spent two hours with Paul and made herself most agreeable, listening to his far-fetched compliments and asseverations[1] of love and tenderness either with a cold smile or with one of her mocking laughs.

---

1 Declarations.

She refused to allow Paul to visit her in her own apartments, and the only intruder she permitted there, save the servants, was little Katrina, who had taken a strange fancy to the fair woman. Alexis, on the contrary, avoided her as much as he possibly could, and the pair hardly ever met. Paul, to while away the time, wandered about the farm and the village, the inhabitants of which had recovered from their panic as the white wolf appeared to have entirely desisted from her murderous attacks upon belated peasants. The shades of evening had closed in as Paul was one day returning from his customary round, rejoiced with the idea that the hour for Ravina's visit was drawing near, when he was startled by a gentle touch upon the shoulder, and turning round, saw the old man Michal standing just behind him. The intendant's face was perfectly livid, his eyes gleamed with the lustre of terror, and his fingers kept convulsively clasping and unclasping.

"My lord," exclaimed he, in faltering accents; "Oh, my lord, listen to me, for I have terrible news to narrate to you."

"What is the matter?" asked Paul, more impressed than he would have liked to confess by the old man's evident terror.

"The wolf, the white wolf. I have seen it again," whispered Michal.

"You are dreaming," retorted his master, angrily. "You have got the creature on the brain, and have mistaken a white calf or one of the dogs for it."

"I am not mistaken," answered the old man, firmly. "And oh, my lord, do not go into the house, for she is there."

"She—who—what do you mean?" cried Paul.

"The white wolf, my lord. I saw her go in. You know the strange lady's apartments are on the ground floor on the west side of the house. I saw the monster cantering across the lawn, and, as if it knew its way perfectly well, make for the centre window of the reception room; it yielded to a touch of the forepaw, and the beast sprang through. Oh, my lord, do not go in, I tell you that it will never harm the strange woman. Ah! let me——"

But Paul cast off the detaining arm with a force that made the old man reel and fall, and then, catching up an axe, dashed into the house, calling upon the servants to follow him to the strange lady's rooms. He tried the handle, but the door was securely fastened, and then, in all the frenzy of terror, he attacked the panels with heavy blows of his axe. For a few seconds no sound was heard save the ring of metal and the shivering of panels, but then the clear tones of Ravina were heard asking the reason for this outrageous disturbance.

"The wolf, the white wolf," shouted half a dozen voices.

"Stand back and I will open the door," answered the fair woman. "You must be mad, for there is no wolf here."

The door flew open and the crowd rushed tumultuously in; every nook and corner was searched, but no signs of the intruder could be discovered, and with many shame-faced glances Paul and his servants were about to return, when the voice of Ravina arrested their steps.

"Paul Sergevitch," said she, coldly. "Explain the meaning of this daring intrusion on my privacy."

She looked very beautiful as she stood before them; her right arm extended and her bosom heaved violently, but this was doubtless caused by her anger at the unlooked-for invasion.

Paul briefly repeated what he had heard from the old serf, and Ravina's scorn was intense.

"And so," cried she, fiercely, "it is to the crotchets[1] of this old dotard that I am indebted for this. Paul, if you ever hope to succeed in winning me, forbid that man to enter the house again."

Paul would have sacrificed all his serfs for a whim of the haughty beauty, and Michal was deprived of the office of intendant and exiled to a cabin in the village, with orders never to show his face again near the house. The separation from the children almost broke the old man's heart, but he ventured on no remonstrance and meekly obeyed the mandate which drove him away from all he loved and cherished.

Meanwhile, curious rumours began to be circulated regarding the strange proceedings of the lady who occupied the suite of apartments which had formerly belonged to the wife of the owner of Kostopchin. The servants declared that the food sent up, though hacked about and cut up, was never tasted, but that the raw meat in the larder was frequently missing. Strange sounds were often

---

1 Flights of imagination.

heard to issue from the rooms as the panic-stricken serfs hurried past the corridor upon which the doors opened, and dwellers in the house were frequently disturbed by the howlings of wolves, the footprints of which were distinctly visible the next morning, and, curiously enough, invariably in the gardens facing the west side of the house in which the lady dwelt. Little Alexis, who found no encouragement to sit with his father, was naturally thrown a great deal amongst the serfs, and heard the subject discussed with many exaggerations. Weird old tales of folklore were often narrated as the servants discussed their evening meal, and the boy's hair would bristle as he listened to the wild and fanciful narratives of wolves, witches, and white ladies with which the superstitious serfs filled his ears. One of his most treasured possessions was an old brass-mounted cavalry pistol, a present from Michal; this he had learned to load, and by using both hands to the cumbrous weapon could contrive to fire it off, as many an ill-starred sparrow could attest. With his mind constantly dwelling upon the terrible tales he had so greedily listened to, this pistol became his daily companion, whether he was wandering about the long echoing corridors of the house or wandering through the neglected shrubberies of the garden. For a fortnight matters went on in this manner, Paul becoming more and more infatuated by the charms of his strange guest, and she every now and then letting drop occasional crumbs of hope which led the unhappy man further and further upon the dangerous course that he was pursuing. A mad, soul-absorbing passion for the fair woman and the deep draughts of brandy with which he consoled himself during her hours of absence were telling upon the brain of the master of Kostopchin, and except during the brief space of Ravina's visit, he would relapse into moods of silent sullenness from which he would occasionally break out into furious bursts of passion for no assignable cause. A shadow seemed to be closing over the House of Kostopchin; it became the abode of grim whispers and undeveloped fears; the men and maidservants went about their work glancing nervously over their shoulders, as though they were apprehensive that some hideous thing was following at their heels.

After three days of exile, poor old Michal could endure the state of suspense regarding the safety of Alexis and Katrina no longer, and, casting aside his superstitious fears, he took to wandering by night about the exterior of the great white house, and peering curiously into such windows as had been left unshuttered. At first he was in continual dread of meeting the terrible white wolf; but his love for the children and his confidence in the crucifix he wore prevailed, and he continued his nocturnal wanderings about Kostopchin and its environs. He kept near the western front of the house, urged on to do so from some vague feeling which he could in nowise account for. One evening as he was making his accustomed tour of inspection, the wail of a child struck upon his ear. He bent down his head and eagerly listened; again he heard the same faint sounds, and in them he fancied he recognized the accents of his dear little Katrina. Hurrying up to one of the ground-floor windows, from which a dim light streamed, he pressed his face against the pane, and looked steadily in. A horrible sight presented itself to his gaze. By the faint light of a shaded lamp, he saw Katrina stretched upon the ground; but her wailing had now ceased, for a shawl had been tied across her little mouth. Over her was bending a hideous shape, which seemed to be clothed in some white and shaggy covering. Katrina lay perfectly motionless, and the hands of the figure were engaged in hastily removing the garments from the child's breast. The task was soon effected; then there was a bright gleam of steel, and the head of the thing bent closely down to the child's bosom.

With a yell of apprehension, the old man dashed in the window frame, and, drawing the cross from his breast, sprang boldly into the room. The creature sprang to its feet, and the white fur cloak falling from its head and shoulders disclosed the pallid features of Ravina, a short, broad knife in her hand, and her lips discoloured with blood.

"Vile sorceress!" cried Michal, dashing forward and raising Katrina in his arms. "What hellish work are you about?"

Ravina's eyes gleamed fiercely upon the old man, who had interfered between her and her prey. She raised her dagger, and was about to spring in upon him, when she caught sight of the cross in his extended hand. With a low cry, she dropped the knife, and, staggering back a few paces, wailed out, "I could not help it; I liked the child well enough, but I was so hungry."

Michal paid but little heed to her words, for he was busily engaged in examining the fainting child, whose head was resting helplessly on his shoulder. There was a wound over the left breast, from which the blood was flowing; but the injury appeared slight, and not likely to prove fatal. As soon as he had satisfied himself on this point, he turned to the woman, who was crouching before the cross as a wild beast shrinks before the whip of the tamer.

"I am going to remove the child," said he, slowly. "Dare you to mention a word of what I have done or whither she has gone, and I will rouse the village. Do you know what will happen then? Why, every peasant in the place will hurry here with a lighted brand[1] in his hand to consume this accursed house and the unnatural dwellers in it. Keep silence, and I leave you to your unhallowed work. I will no longer seek to preserve Paul Sergevitch, who has given himself over to the powers of darkness by taking a demon to his bosom."

Ravina listened to him as if she scarcely comprehended him; but, as the old man retreated to the window with his helpless burden, she followed him step by step; and as he turned to cast one glance at the shattered window, he saw the woman's pale face and bloodstained lips glued against an unbroken pane, with a wild look of unsatiated appetite in her eyes.

Next morning the house of Kostopchin was filled with terror and surprise, for Katrina, the idol of her father's heart, had disappeared, and no signs of her could be discovered. Every effort was made, the woods and fields in the neighborhood were thoroughly searched; but it was at last concluded that robbers had carried off the child for the sake of the ransom that they might be able to extract from the father. This seemed the more likely as one of the windows in the fair stranger's room bore marks of violence, and she declared that, being alarmed by the sound of crashing glass, she had risen and confronted a man who was endeavouring to enter her apartment, but who, on perceiving her, turned and fled away with the utmost precipitation.

Paul Sergevitch did not display so much anxiety as might have been expected from him, considering the devotion which he had

---

1 Torch.

ever evinced for the lost Katrina, for his whole soul was wrapped up in one mad, absorbing passion for the fair woman who had so strangely crossed his life. He certainly directed the search, and gave all the necessary orders; but he did so in a listless and half-hearted manner, and hastened back to Kostopchin as speedily as he could, as though fearing to be absent for any length of time from the casket in which his new treasure was enshrined. Not so Alexis; he was almost frantic at the loss of his sister, and accompanied the searchers daily until his little legs grew weary, and he had to be carried on the shoulders of a sturdy *moujik*.[1] His treasured brass-mounted pistol was now more than ever his constant companion; and when he met the fair woman who had cast a spell upon his father, his face would flush, and he would grind his teeth in impotent rage.

The day upon which all search ceased, Ravina glided into the room where she knew that she would find Paul awaiting her. She was fully an hour before her usual time, and the lord of Kostopchin started to his feet in surprise.

"You are surprised to see me," said she; "but I have only come to pay you a visit for a few minutes. I am convinced that you love me, and could I but relieve a few of the objections that my heart continues to raise, I might be yours."

"Tell me what these scruples are," cried Paul, springing towards her, and seizing her hands in his; "and be sure that I will find means to overcome them."

Even in the midst of all the glow and fervour of anticipated triumph, he could not avoid noticing how icily cold were the fingers that rested in his palm, and how utterly passionless was the pressure with which she slightly returned his enraptured clasp.

"Listen," said she, as she withdrew her hand; "I will take two more hours for consideration. By that time the whole of the house of Kostopchin will be cradled in slumber, then meet me at the old sundial near the yew tree at the bottom of the garden, and I will give you my reply. Nay, not a word," she added, as he seemed about to remonstrate, "for I tell you that I think it will be a favorable one."

---

1 Russian peasant.

"But why not come back here?" urged he; "there is a hard frost to-night, and——"

"Are you so cold a lover," broke in Ravina, with her accustomed laugh, "to dread the changes of the weather? But not another word; I have spoken."

She glided from the room, but uttered a low cry of rage. She almost fell over Alexis in the corridor.

"Why is that brat not in his bed?" cried she, angrily; "he gave me quite a turn."

"Go to your room, boy," exclaimed his father, harshly, and with a malignant glance at his enemy the child slunk away.

Paul Sergevitch paced up and down the room for the two hours that he had to pass before the hour of meeting. His heart was very heavy, and a vague feeling of disquietude began to creep over him. Twenty times he made up his mind not to keep his appointment, and as often the fascinations of the fair woman compelled him to rescind his resolution. He remembered that he had from childhood disliked that spot by the yew tree, and had always looked upon it as a dreary, uncanny place; and he even now disliked the idea of finding himself here after dark, even with such fair companionship as he had been promised. Counting the minutes, he paced backwards and forwards, as though moved by some concealed machinery. Now and again he glanced at the clock, and at last its deep metallic sound, as it struck the quarter, warned him that he had but little time to lose, if he intended to keep his appointment. Throwing on a heavily-furred coat and pulling a travelling cap down over his ears, he opened a side door and sallied out[1] into the grounds. The moon was at its full, and shone coldly down upon the leafless trees, which looked white and ghost-like in its beams. The paths and unkept lawns were now covered with hoar frost, and a keen wind every now and then swept by, which, in spite of his wraps, chilled Paul's blood in his veins. The dark shape of the yew tree soon rose up before him, and in another moment he stood beside its dusky bows. The old grey sundial stood only a few paces off, and by its side was standing a slender figure, wrapped in a white, fleecy-looking cloak. It was perfectly motionless, and

---

1 Set out.

again a terror of undefined dread passed through every nerve and muscle of Paul Sergevitch's body.

"Ravina!" said he, in faltering accents. "Ravina!"

"Did you take me for a ghost?" answered the fair woman, with her shrill laugh; "no, no, I have not come to that yet. Well, Paul Sergevitch, I have come to give you my answer; are you anxious about it?"

"How can you ask me such a question?" returned he; "do you not know that my whole soul has been aglow with anticipations of what your reply might be. Do not keep me any longer in suspense. Is it yes, or no?"

"Paul Sergevitch," answered the young woman, coming up to him and laying her hands upon his shoulders, and fixing her eyes upon his with that strange weird expression before which he always quailed; "do you really love me, Paul Sergevitch?" asked she.

"Love you!" repeated the lord of Kostopchin; "have I not told you a thousand times how much my whole soul flows out towards you, how I only live and breathe in your presence, and how death at your feet would be more welcome than life without you."

"People often talk of death, and yet little know how near it is to them," answered the fair lady, a grim smile appearing upon her face; "but say, do you give me your whole heart?"

"All I have is yours, Ravina," returned Paul, "name, wealth, and the devoted love of a lifetime."

"But your heart," persisted she; "it is your heart that I want: tell me, Paul, that it is mine and mine only."

"Yes, my heart is yours, dearest Ravina," answered Paul, endeavouring to embrace the fair form in his impassioned grasp; but she glided from him, and then with a quick bound sprang upon him and glared in his face with a look that was absolutely appalling. Her eyes gleamed with a lurid fire, her lips were drawn back, showing her sharp, white teeth, whilst her breath came in sharp, quick gasps.

"I am hungry," she murmured, "oh, so hungry; but now, Paul Sergevitch, your heart is mine."

Her movement was so sudden and unexpected that he stumbled and fell heavily to the ground, the fair woman clinging to him and falling upon his breast. It was then that the full horror of his position came upon Paul Sergevitch, and he saw his fate clearly before him, but a terrible numbness prevented him from using his hands to free himself from the hideous embrace which was paralyzing all his muscles. The face that was glaring into his seemed to be undergoing some fearful change, and the features to be losing their semblance of humanity. With a sudden, quick movement, she tore open his garments, and in another moment she had perforated his left breast with a ghastly wound, and, plunging in her delicate hands, tore out his heart and bit at it ravenously. Intent upon her hideous banquet she heeded not the convulsive struggles which agitated the dying form of the lord of Kostopchin. She was too much occupied to notice a diminutive form approaching, sheltering itself behind every tree and bush until it had arrived within ten paces of the scene of the terrible tragedy. Then the moonbeams glistened upon the long shining barrel of a pistol, which a boy was levelling with both hands at the murderess. Then quick and sharp rang out the report, and with a wild shriek, in which there was something beast-like, Ravina leaped from the body of the dead man and staggered away to a thick clump of bushes some ten paces distant. The boy Alexis had heard the appointment that had been made, and dogged his father's footsteps to the trysting-place. After firing the fatal shot his courage deserted him, and he fled backwards to the house, uttering loud shrieks for help. The startled servants were soon in the presence of their slaughtered master, but aid was of no avail, for the lord of Kostopchin had passed away. With fear and trembling the superstitious peasants searched the clump of bushes, and started back in horror as they perceived a huge white wolf, lying stark and dead, with a half-devoured human heart clasped between its forepaws.

* * * * * *

No signs of the fair lady, who had occupied the apartments in the western side of the house were ever again seen. She had passed away from Kostopchin like an ugly dream, and as the *moujiks* of the village sat around their stoves at night they whispered strange stories regarding the fair woman of the forest and the white wolf of Kostopchin. By order of the Czar a surtee[1] was placed in charge of the estate of Kostopchin, and Alexis was ordered to be sent to a military school until he should be old enough to join the army. The meeting between the boy and his sister, whom the faithful Michal, when all danger was at an end, had produced from his hiding-place, was most affecting; but it was not until Katrina had been for some time resident at the house of a distant relative at Vitepsk, that she ceased to wake at night and cry out in terror as she again dreamed that she was in the clutches of the white wolf.

---

1 Security guard.

A Pastoral Horror

Arthur Conan Doyle

Sir Arthur Conan Doyle (1859-1930) was born in Edinburgh, Scotland, the third of nine children of Charles and Mary Doyle. Charles Doyle, a gifted artist employed as a draughtsman, suffered from alcoholism and epilepsy, which frequently left Mary struggling financially as the sole stable parent in a growing Catholic household. Due to the family's economic difficulties, Conan Doyle's uncles offered to fund his education at Stonyhurst, a Roman Catholic boarding school run by a Jesuit order. Conan Doyle spent the next seven years matriculating at Stonyhurst in a strict, academically rigorous environment.

After graduating in 1875, Conan Doyle spent a year at Stella Matutina, a secondary school run by the same Jesuit order in Feldkirch, Austria. In his letters home to his mother, Conan Doyle vividly described the beauty of the Alps, which he hiked through while singing Tyrolese songs and consuming large quantities of beer with his fellow students. At Stella Matutina, Conan Doyle expanded his interest in German language and history and learned to play the bombardon (a tuba-like instrument) in the school marching band. In his spare time, he read Edgar Allan Poe voraciously and studied for the examinations to enter medical school.

In 1876, Conan Doyle began his studies in medicine at Edinburgh University where he met Professor Joseph Bell, who would later inspire the character Sherlock Holmes. A year before officially receiving his M.B., Conan Doyle served as a ship's surgeon on a whaler bound for Greenland. During his early years as a writer, Conan Doyle opened a medical practice in Southsea, Portsmouth. For Conan Doyle, the professions were complementary since medical case studies led to stories such as "A Study in Scarlet," which marked the first appearance of Sherlock Holmes. From 1888 to 1927, Conan Doyle composed sixty stories featuring Sherlock Holmes, whom he killed in "The Final Problem" (1893) and resurrected, to the pleasure of numerous fans, in The Hound of the Baskervilles

(1902). *Although Conan Doyle would rather have had his other work, particularly his historical novels* Micah Clarke (1889) *and* The White Company (1891), *admired as much as his detective fiction,* Sherlock Holmes *proved to be his bread and butter.*

In January 1891, Conan Doyle set out once again for Austria, this time with his wife, Louisa, whom he married in 1885, and their daughter, Mary. By late March he was back in London setting up an office on Wimpole Street as an oculist. Without any patients in sight, Conan Doyle once again focused on his writing, and after a serious bout of influenza, made the decision to dedicate himself to writing. Yet he did serve as a doctor at the Longman Hospital in 1900 during the South African War. In fact, Conan Doyle's support for the controversial war led to his receiving a knighthood in 1902.

In 1906, Louisa, who had suffered during much of their marriage from tuberculosis, succumbed to the disease, despite trips to Switzerland and Africa meant to extend her life. A year later, Conan Doyle married Jean Blyth Leckie and began a second family. Although happy with his new union, Conan Doyle was devastated when his first son, Kingsley, died of influenza and injuries in WWI. Already a convert to spiritualism, Conan Doyle became increasingly dedicated to the movement, publishing several spiritualist texts, including The Wanderings of a Spiritualist (1921) *and* The History of Spiritualism (1926); *he also owned a spiritualist bookshop in Westminster.*

Conan Doyle's youthful experiences in Feldkirch no doubt spurred the writing of "A Pastoral Horror," *which is set amongst the Alps he so admired. The story was first published in* People, *a weekly literary magazine.*

Bibliography

Doyle, Sir Arthur Conan. "A Pastoral Horror." *People*, Dec. 21, 1890, 21a-21e.

Edwards, Owen Dudley. "Sir Arthur Conan Doyle." *Oxford Dictionary of National Biography*. Oxford: Oxford University Press, 2004. http://www.oxforddnb.com.

Frank, Lawrence. *Victorian Detective Fiction and the Nature of Evidence: The Scientific Investigations of Poe, Dickens, and Doyle*. Basingstoke: Palgrave Macmillan, 2003.

Lellenberg, Jon, Daniel Stashower, and Charles Foley, eds. *Arthur Conan Doyle: A Life in Letters*. New York: Penguin, 2007.

Lycett, Andrew. *The Man Who Created Sherlock Holmes: The Life and Times of Sir Arthur Conan Doyle*. New York: Free Press, 2007.

Stashower, Daniel. *Teller of Tales: The Life of Arthur Conan Doyle*. New York: Holt, 1999.

––––––––––

A PASTORAL HORROR.

FAR above the level of the Lake of Constance, nestling in a little corner of the Tyrolese Alps, lies the quiet town of Feldkirch. It is remarkable for nothing save for the presence of a large and well-conducted Jesuit school and for the extreme beauty of its situation. There is no more lovely spot in the whole of Vorarlberg. From the hills which rise behind the town, the great lake glimmers some fifteen miles off, like a broad sea of quick-silver. Down below in the plains, the Rhine and the Danube prattle along, flowing swiftly and merrily, with none of the dignity which they assume as they grow from brooks into rivers. Five great countries or principalities,—Switzerland, Austria, Baden, Wurtemburg, and Bavaria—are visible from the plateau of Feldkirch.

Feldkirch is the centre of a large tract of hilly and pastoral country. The main road runs through the centre of town, and then on as far as Anspach, where it divides into two branches, one of which is larger than the other. This more important one runs through the valleys across Austrian Tyrol into Tyrol proper, going as far, I believe, as the capital of Innsbruck. The lesser road runs for eight or ten miles amid wild and rugged glens to the village of Laden, where it breaks up into a network of sheep-tracks. In this quiet spot, I, John Hudson, spent nearly two years of my life from the June of '65 to the March of '67, and it was during that time that those events occurred which for some weeks brought the retired hamlet into an unholy prominence, and caused its name for the first, and probably for the last time, to be a familiar word to the European press. The short account of these incidents which appeared in the English papers was, however, inaccurate and misleading, besides which the rapid advance of the Prussians, culminating in the battle of Sadowa, attracted public attention away from what might have moved it deeply in less troublous times.[1] It seems to me that the facts may be detailed now, and be new to the great majority of readers, especially as I was myself intimately connected with the drama, and am in position to give many particulars which have never before been made public.

And first a few words as to my own presence in this out of the way spot. When the great City firm of Spragge, Wilkinson, and Spragge failed, and paid their creditors rather less than eighteen-pence in the pound, a number of humble individuals were ruined, including myself. There was, however, some legal objection which held out a chance of my being made an exception to the other creditors, and being paid in full. While the case was being fought out I was left with a very small sum for my subsistence.

I determined, therefore, to take up my residence abroad in the interim, since I could live more economically there, and be spared the mortification of meeting those who had known me in my more prosperous days. A friend of mine had described Laden to me some years before as being the most isolated place which he had ever come across in all his experience, and as isolation and cheap living are usually synonymous, I bethought me of his words. Besides, I was in a cynical humour with my fellow-man, and desired to see as little of him as possible for some time to come. Obeying, then, the guidance of poverty and of misanthropy, I made my way to Laden, where my arrival created the utmost excitement among the simple inhabitants. The manners and customs of the red-bearded Englander, his long walks, his check suit, and the reasons which had led him to abandon his fatherland, were all fruitful sources of gossip to the topers[2] who frequented the Grüner Mann[3] and the Schwartzer Bar—the two alehouses of the village.

I found myself very happy at Laden. The surroundings were magnificent, and twenty years of Brixton[4] had sharpened my admiration for nature as an olive improves the flavor of wine. In

---

1 The Battle of Sadowa, also called the Battle of Königgrätz, occurred on July 3, 1866, during the Seven Weeks' War between Prussia and Austria, and resulted in a Prussian victory.
2 Heavy drinkers.
3 The Green Man.
4 A gritty neighborhood in Lambeth, London.

my youth I had been a fair German scholar, and I found myself able, before I had been many months abroad, to converse even on scientific and abstruse subjects with the new curé of the parish.

This priest was a great godsend to me, for he was a most learned man and a brilliant conversationalist. Father Verhagen— for that was his name—though little more than forty years of age, had made his reputation as an author by a brilliant monograph upon the early Popes—a work which eminent critics have compared favourably with Von Ranke's.[1] I shrewdly suspect that it was owing to some rather unorthodox views advanced in his book that Verhagen was relegated to the obscurity of Laden. His opinions upon every subject were ultra-Liberal, and in his fiery youth he had been ready to vindicate them, as was proved by a deep scar across his chin, received from a dragoon's sabre in the abortive insurrection at Berlin.[2] Altogether the man was an interesting one, and though he was by nature somewhat cold and reserved, we soon established an acquaintanceship.

The atmosphere of morality in Laden was a very rarefied one. The position of Intendant[3] Wums and his satellites had for many years been a sinecure.[4] Non-attendance at church upon a Sunday or feast-day was about the deepest and darkest crime which the most advanced of the villagers had attained to. Occasionally some hulking Fritz or Andreas would come lurching home at ten o'clock at night, slightly under the influence of Bavarian beer, and might even abuse the wife of his bosom if she ventured to remonstrate, but such cases were rare, and when they occurred the Ladeners looked at the culprit for some time in a half admiring, half horrified manner, as one who had committed a gaudy sin and so asserted his individuality.

It was in this peaceful village that a series of crimes suddenly broke out which astonished all Europe, and for atrocity and for

---

1 Leopold von Ranke (1796-1886) was a renowned German historian.
2 Possibly a reference to the German Revolutions of 1848, which expressed working-class and middle-class demands for increased political freedom and better working conditions.
3 Police superintendant.
4 A position which has no work attached to it, but from which one may draw a salary.

the mystery which surrounded them surpassed anything of which I have ever heard or read. I shall endeavour to give a succinct account of these events in the order of their sequence, in which I am much helped by the fact that it was my custom all my life to keep a journal—to the pages of which I now refer.

It was, then, I find upon the 19th of May in the spring of 1866, that my old landlady, Frau Zimmer, rushed wildly into the room as I was sipping my morning cup of chocolate and informed me that a murder had been committed in the village. At first I could hardly believe the news, but as she persisted in her statement, and was evidently terribly frightened, I put on my hat and went out to find the truth. When I came into the main street of the village I saw several men hurrying along in the front of me, and following them I came up on an excited group in front of the little stadthaus or town hall—a barn-like edifice which was used for all manner of public gatherings. They were collected round the body of one Maul, who had formerly been a steward upon one of the steamers running between Lindau and Fredericshaven, on the Lake of Constance. He was a harmless, inoffensive little man, generally popular in the village, and, as far as was known, without an enemy in the world. Maul lay upon his face, with his fingers dug into the earth, no doubt in his last convulsive struggles, and his hair all matted together with blood, which had streamed down over the collar of his coat. The body had been discovered nearly two hours, but no one appeared to know what to do or whither to convey it. My arrival, however, together with that of the curé, who came almost simultaneously, infused some vigour into the crowd. Under our direction the corpse was carried up the steps, and laid on the floor of the town hall, where, having made sure that life was extinct, we proceeded to examine the injuries, in conjunction with Lieutenant Wurms, of the police. Maul's face was perfectly placid, showing that he had had no thought of danger until the fatal blow was struck. His watch and purse had not been taken. Upon washing the clotted blood from the back of his head a singular triangular wound was found, which had smashed the bone and penetrated deeply into the brain. It had evidently been inflicted by a heavy blow from a sharp-pointed pyramidal instrument. I believe that it was Father Verhagen, the curé, who suggested the probability of the weapon in question having been a short mattock or small pickaxe, such as are to be found in every Alpine cottage. The Intendant, with praiseworthy promptness, at once obtained one and striking a turnip, produced just such a curious gap as was to be seen in poor Maul's head. We felt that we had come upon the first link of a chain which might guide us to the assassin. It was not long before we seemed to grasp the whole clue.

A sort of inquest was held upon the body that same afternoon, at which Pfiffer, the maire,[1] presided, the curé, the Intendant, Freckler, of the post office, and myself forming ourselves into a sort of committee of investigation. Any villager who could throw a light upon the case or give an account of the movements of the murdered man upon the previous evening was invited to attend. There was a fair muster of witnesses, and we soon gathered a connected series of facts. At half-past eight o'clock, Maul had entered the Grüner Mann public-house, and had called for a flagon of beer. At that time there were sitting in the tap-room Waghorn, the butcher of the village, and an Italian pedlar named Cellini, who used to come three times a year to Laden with cheap jewelry and other wares. Immediately after his entrance the landlord had seated himself with his customers, and the four had spent the evening together, the common villagers not being admitted beyond the bar. It seemed from the evidence of the landlord and of Waghorn, both of whom were most respectable and trustworthy men, that shortly after nine o'clock a dispute arose between the deceased and the pedlar. Hot words had been exchanged, and the Italian had eventually left the room, saying that he would not stay any longer to hear his country decried. Maul remained for nearly an hour, and being somewhat elated at having caused his adversary's retreat, he drank rather more than was usual with him. One witness had met him walking toward his home, about ten o'clock, and deposed to his having been slightly the worse for drink. Another had met him just a minute or so before he reached the spot in front of the stadthaus where the deed was done. This man's evidence was most important. He swore confidently that while passing the town hall, and before meeting Maul, he had seen

---

1 Mayor.

a figure standing in the shadow of the building, adding that the person appeared to him, as far as he could make him out, to be not unlike the Italian.

Up to this point we had then established two facts—that the Italian had left the Grüner Mann before Maul, with words of anger on his lips; the second, that some unknown individual had been seen lying in wait on the road which the ex-steward would have to traverse. A third, and most important, was reached when the woman with whom the Italian lodged deposed that he had not returned the night before until half-past ten, an unusually late hour for Laden. How had he employed the time, then, from shortly after nine, when he left the public-house, until half-past ten, when he returned to his rooms? Things were beginning to look very black, indeed, against the pedlar.

It could not be denied, however, that there were points in the man's favour, and that the case against him consisted entirely of circumstantial evidence. In the first place, there was no sign of a mattock or any other instrument which could have been used for such a purpose among the Italian's goods; nor was it easy to understand how he could come by any such a weapon, since he did not go home between the time of the quarrel and his final return. Again, as the curé pointed out, since Cellini was a comparative stranger in the village, it was very unlikely that he would know which road Maul would take in order to reach his home. This objection was weakened, however by the evidence of the dead man's servant, who deposed that the pedlar had been hawking his wares in front of their house the day before, and might very possibly have seen the owner at one of the windows. As to the prisoner himself, his attitude at first had been one of defiance, and even of amusement; but when he began to realise the weight of evidence against him, his manner became cringing, and he wrung his hands piteously, loudly proclaiming his innocence. His defence was that after leaving the inn, he had taken a long walk down the Anspach-road in order to cool down his excitement, and that this was the cause of his late return. As to the murder of Maul, he knew no more about it than the babe unborn.

I have dwelt at some length upon the circumstances of this case, because there are points in connection with it which makes it peculiarly interesting. I intend now to fall back upon my diary, which was very fully kept during this period, and indeed during my whole residence abroad. It will save me trouble to quote from it, and it will be a voucher for the accuracy of facts.

May 20th.—Nothing thought of and nothing talked of but the recent tragedy. A hunt has been made among the woods and along the brook in the hope of finding the weapon of the assassin. The more I think of it, the more convinced I am that Cellini is the man. The fact of the money being untouched proves that the crime was committed from motives of revenge, and who would bear such spite towards poor innocent Maul except the vindictive hot-blooded Italian whom he had just offended. I dined with Pfiffer in the evening, and he entirely agreed with me in my view of the case.

May 21st.—Still no word as far as I can hear which throws any light upon the murder. Poor Maul was buried at twelve o'clock in the neat little village churchyard. The curé read the service with great feeling, and his audience, consisting of the whole population of the village, were much moved, interrupting him frequently by sobs and ejaculations of grief. After the painful ceremony was over I had a short walk with our good priest. His naturally excitable nature has been considerably stirred by recent events. His hand trembles and his face is pale.

"My friend," said he, taking me by the hand as we walked together, "you know something of medicine." (I had been two years at Guy's).[1] "I have been far from well of late."

"It is this sad affair which has upset you," I said.

"No," he answered, "I have felt it coming on for some time, but it has been worse of late. I have a pain which shoots from here to there," he put his hand to his temples. "If I were struck by lightning, the sudden shock it causes me could not be more great. At times when I close my eyes flashes of light pass before them, and my ears are forever singing. Often I know not what I do. My fear is lest I faint some time when performing my holy offices."

"You are overworking yourself," I said, "you must have rest and strengthening tonics. Are you writing just now? And how much do you do each day?"

---

1 Guy's Hospital is a medical school and hospital in Southwark, London.

"Eight hours," he answered. "Sometimes ten, sometimes even twelve, when the pains in my head do not interrupt me."

"You must reduce it to four," I said authoritatively. "You must also take regular exercise. I shall send you some quinine[1] which I have in my trunk, and you can take as much as would cover a gulden[2] in a glass of milk every morning and night."

He departed, vowing that he would follow my directions.

I hear from the maire that four policemen are to be sent from Anspach to remove Cellini to a safer gaol.

May 22nd.—To say that I was startled would give but a faint idea of my mental state. I am confounded, amazed, horrified beyond all expression. Another and a more dreadful crime has been committed during the night. Freckler has been found dead in his house—the very Freckler who had sat with me on the committee of investigation the day before. I write these notes after a long and anxious day's work, during which I have been endeavouring to assist the officers of the law. The villagers are so paralysed with fear at this fresh evidence of an assassin in their midst that there would be a general panic but for our exertions. It appears that Freckler, who was a man of peculiar habits, lived alone in an isolated dwelling. Some curiosity was aroused this morning by the fact that he had not gone to his work, and that there was no sign of movement about the house. A crowd assembled, and the doors were eventually forced open. The unfortunate Freckler was found in the bedroom upstairs, lying with his head in the fireplace. He had met his death by an exactly similar wound to that which had proved fatal to Maul, save that in this instance the injury was in front. His hands were clenched, and there was an indescribable look of horror, and, as it seemed to me, of surprise upon his features. There were marks of muddy footsteps upon the stairs, which must have been caused by the murderer in his ascent, as his victim had put on his slippers before retiring to his bedroom. These prints, however, were too much blurred to enable us to get a trustworthy outline of the foot. They were only to be found upon every third step, showing with what fiendish swiftness this human

---

1 A drug used to treat malaria that was historically used as a tonic.
2 A gold coin.

tiger had rushed upstairs in search of his victim. There was a considerable sum of money in the house, but not one farthing had been touched, nor had any of the drawers in the bedroom been opened.

As the dismal news became known the whole population of the village assembled in a great crowd in front of the house—rather, I think, from the gregariousness of terror than from mere curiosity. Every man looked with suspicion upon his neighbour. Most were silent, and when they spoke it was in whispers, as if they feared to raise their voices. None of these people were allowed to enter the house, and we, the more enlightened members of the community, made a strict examination of the premises. There was absolutely nothing, however, to give the slightest clue as to the assassin. Beyond the fact that he must be an active man, judging from the manner in which he ascended the stairs, we have gained nothing from this second tragedy. Intendant Wurms pointed out, indeed, that the dead man's rigid right arm was stretched out as if in greeting, and that, therefore it was probable that this late visitor was someone with whom Freckler was well acquainted. This, however, was, to a large extent, conjecture. If anything could have added to the horror created by the dreadful occurrence, it was the fact that the crime must have been committed at the early hour of half-past eight in the evening—that being the time registered by a small cuckoo clock, which had been carried away by Freckler in his fall.

No one, apparently, heard any suspicious sounds or saw any one enter or leave the house. It was done rapidly, quietly, and completely, though many people must have been about at the time. Poor Pfiffer and our good curé are terribly cut up by the awful occurrence, and, indeed, I feel very much depressed myself now that all the excitement is over and the reaction set in. There are very few of the villagers about this evening, but from every side is heard the sound of hammering—the peasants fitting bolts and bars upon the doors and windows of their houses. Very many of them have been entirely unprovided with anything of the sort, nor were they ever required until now. Frau Zimmer has manufactured a huge fastening which would be ludicrous if we were in a humour for laughter.

I hear to-night that Cellini has been released, as, of course, there is no possible pretext for detaining him now; also that word has been sent to all the villages near for any police that can be spared.

My nerves have been so shaken that I remained awake the greater part of the night, reading Gordon's translation of Tacitus by candlelight. I have got my navy revolver and cleaned it, so as to be ready for all eventualities.

May 23rd.—The police force has been recruited by three more men from Anspach and two from Thalstadt at the other side of the hills. Intendant Wurms has established an efficient system of patrols, so that we may consider ourselves reasonably safe. Today has cast no light upon the murders. The general opinion in the village seems to be that they have been done by some stranger who lies concealed among the woods. They argue that they have all known each other since childhood, and that there is no one of their number who would be capable of such actions. Some of the more daring of them have made a hunt among the pine forests to-day, but without success.

May 24th.—Events crowd on apace. We seem hardly to have recovered from one horror when something else occurs to excite the popular imagination. Fortunately, this time it is not a fresh tragedy, although the news is serious enough.

The murderer has been seen, and that upon the public road, which proves that his thirst for blood has not been quenched yet, and also that our reinforcements of police are not enough to guarantee security. I have just come back from hearing Andreas Murch narrate his experience, though he is still in such a state of trepidation that his story is somewhat incoherent. He was belated among the hills, it seems, owing to mist. It was nearly eleven o'clock before he struck the main road about a couple of miles from the village. He confesses that he felt by no means comfortable at finding himself out so late after the recent occurrences. However, as the fog had cleared away and the moon was shining brightly, he trudged sturdily along. Just about a quarter of a mile from the village the road takes a very sharp bend. Andreas had got as far as this when he suddenly heard in the still night the sound of footsteps approaching rapidly round this curve. Overcome with fear, he threw himself into the ditch which skirts the road, and lay there motionless in the shadow, peering over the side. The steps came nearer and nearer, and then a tall dark figure came round the corner at a swinging pace, and passing the spot where the moon glimmered upon the white face of the frightened peasant, halted in the road about twenty yards further on, and began probing about among the reeds on the roadside with an instrument which Andreas Murch recognised with horror as being a long mattock. After searching about in this way for a minute or so, as if he suspected that someone was concealed there, for he must have heard the sound of footsteps, he stood still leaning upon his weapon. Murch describes him as a tall, thin man, dressed in clothes of a darkish colour. The lower part of his face was swathed in a wrapper of some sort, and the little which was visible appeared to be of a ghastly pallor. Murch could not see enough of his features to identify him, but thinks that it was no one whom he had ever seen in his life before. After standing for some little time, the man with the mattock had walked swiftly away into the darkness, in the direction in which he imagined the fugitive had gone. Andreas, as may be supposed, lost little time in getting safely into the village, where he alarmed the police. Three of them, armed with carbines, started down the road, but saw no signs of the miscreant. There is, of course, a possibility that Murch's story is exaggerated and that his imagination has been sharpened by fear. Still, the whole incident cannot be trumped up, and this awful demon who haunts us is evidently still active.

There is an ill-conditioned fellow named Hiedler, who lives in a hut on the side of the Spiegelberg, and supports himself by chamois[1] hunting and by acting as guide to the few tourists who find their way here. Popular suspicion has fastened on this man, for no better reason than that he is tall, thin, and known to be rough and brutal. His chalet has been searched to-day, but nothing of importance found. He has, however, been arrested and confined in the same room which Cellini used to occupy.

At this point there is a gap of a week in my diary, during which

---

1 A goat-like animal native to the mountains of Europe and the Middle East.

time there was an entire cessation of the constant alarms which have harassed us lately. Some explained it by supposing that the terrible unknown had moved on to some fresh and less guarded scene of operations. Others imagine that we have secured the right man in the shape of the vagabond Hiedler. Be the cause what it may, peace and contentment reign once more in the village, and a short seven days have sufficed to clear away the cloud of care from men's brows, though the police are still on the alert. The season for rifle shooting is beginning, and as Laden has, like every other Tyrolese village, butts of its own, there is a continual pop, pop, all day. These peasants are dead shots up to about four hundred yards. No troops in the world could subdue them among their native mountains.

My friend Verhagen, the curé, and Pfiffer, the maire, used to go down in the afternoon to see the shooting with me. The former says that the quinine has done him much good and that his appetite is improved. We all agree that it is good policy to encourage the amusements of the people so that they may forget all about this wretched business. Waghorn, the butcher, won the prize offered by the maire. He made five bulls, and what we should call a magpie out of six shots at 100 yards.[1] This is English prize-medal form.

June 2nd.—Who could have imagined that a day which opened so fairly could have so dark an ending? The early carrier brought me a letter by which I learned that Spragge and Co. have agreed to pay my claim in full, although it may be some months before the money is forthcoming. This will make a difference of nearly £400 a year to me—a matter of moment when a man is in his seven-and-fortieth year.

And now for the grand events of the hour. My interview with the vampire[2] who haunts us, and his attempt upon Frau Bischoff, the landlady of the Grüner Mann—to say nothing of the narrow escape of our good curé. There seems to be something almost

---

1 Waghorn shot five bull's-eyes and a magpie, or a shot that struck the outermost division of the target.

2 Although the narrator uses the word "vampire" to refer to the serial murderer, his description of the culprit's "fiendish swiftness" as well as his "wild-beast eyes and a nose which was whitened by being pressed against the glass" suggest a werewolf.

supernatural in the malignity of this unknown fiend, and the impunity with which he continues his murderous course. The real reason of it lies in the badly lit state of the place—or rather the entire absence of light—and also in the fact that thick woods stretch right down to the houses on every side, so that escape is made easy. In spite of this, however, he had two very narrow escapes to-night—one from my pistol, and one from the officers of the law. I shall not sleep much, so I may spend half an hour in jotting down these strange doings in my diary. I am no coward, but life in Laden is becoming too much for my nerves. I believe the matter will end in the emigration of the whole population.

To come to my story, then. I felt lonely and depressed this evening, in spite of the good news of the morning. About nine o'clock, just as night began to fall, I determined to stroll over and call upon the curé, thinking that a little intellectual chat might cheer me up. I slipped my revolver into my pocket, therefore— a precaution which I never neglected—and went out, very much against the advice of good Frau Zimmer. I think I mentioned some months ago in my diary that the curé's house is some little way out of the village upon the brow of a small hill. When I arrived there I found that he had gone out—which, indeed, I might have anticipated, for he had complained lately of restlessness at night, and I had recommended him to take a little exercise in the evening. His housekeeper made me very welcome, however, and, having lit the lamp, left me in the study with some books to amuse me until her master's return.

I suppose I must have sat for nearly half an hour glancing over an odd volume of Klopstock's[1] poems, when some sudden instinct caused me to raise my head and look up. I have been in some strange situations in my life, but never have I felt anything to be compared to the thrill which shot through me at that moment. The recollection of it now, hours after the event, makes me shudder. There, framed in one of the panes of the window, was a human face glaring in, from the darkness, into the lighted room—the face of a man so concealed by a cravat and slouch hat that the only impression I retain of it was a pair of wild-beast eyes and a nose

---

1 German poet Friedrich Gottlieb Klopstock (1724-1803).

which was whitened by being pressed against the glass. It did not need Andreas Murch's description to tell me that at last I was face to face with the man with the mattock. There was murder in those wild eyes. For a second I was so unstrung as to be powerless; the next I cocked my revolver and fired straight at the sinister face. I was a moment too late. As I pressed the trigger I saw it vanish, but the pane through which it had looked was shattered to pieces. I rushed to the window, and then out through the front door, but everything was silent. There was no trace of my visitor. His intention, no doubt, was to attack the curé, for there was nothing to prevent his coming through the folding window had he not found an armed man inside.

As I stood in the cool night air with the curé's frightened housekeeper beside me, I suddenly heard a great hubbub down in the village. By this time, alas! such sounds were so common in Laden that there was no doubting what it forboded. Some fresh misfortune had occurred there. Tonight seemed destined to be a night of horror. My presence might be of use in the village, so I set off there, taking with me the trembling woman, who positively refused to remain behind. There was a crowd round the Grüner Mann public-house, and a dozen excited voices were explaining the circumstances to the curé, who had arrived just before us. It was as I had thought, though happily without the result which I had feared. Frau Bischoff, the wife of the proprietor of the inn, had, it seems, gone some twenty minutes before a few yards from her door to draw some water, and had been at once attacked by a tall disguised man, who had cut at her with some weapon. Fortunately he had slipped, so that she was able to seize him by the wrist and prevent his repeating his attempt, while she screamed for help. There were several people about at the time, who came running towards them, on which the stranger wrested himself free, and dashed off into the woods with two of our police after him. There is little hope of their overtaking or tracing him, however, in such a dark labyrinth. Frau Bischoff had made a bold attempt to hold the assassin, and declares that her nails made deep furrows in his right wrist. This, however, must be mere conjecture, as there was very little light at the time. She knows no more of the man's features than I do. Fortunately she is entirely unhurt. The curé was horrified when I informed him of the incident at his own house. He was returning from his walk, it appears, when hearing cries in the village, he had hurried down to it. I have not told anyone else of my own adventure, for the people are quite excited enough already.

As I said before, unless this mysterious and bloodthirsty villain is captured, the place will become deserted. Flesh and blood cannot stand such a strain. He is either some murderous misanthrope who has declared a vendetta against the whole human race, or else he is an escaped maniac. Clearly after the unsuccessful attempt upon Frau Bischoff he had made at once for the curé's house, bent upon slaking his thirst for blood, and thinking that its lonely situation gave hope of success. I wish I had fired at him through the pocket of my coat. The moment he saw the glitter of the weapon he was off.

June 3rd.—Everybody in the village this morning has learned about the attempt upon the curé last night. There was quite a crowd at his house to congratulate him on his escape, and when I appeared they raised a cheer and hailed me as the "tapferer Englander."[1] It seems that his narrow shave must have given the ruffian a great start, for a thick woollen muffler was found lying on the pathway leading down to the village, and later in the day the fatal mattock was discovered close to the same place. The scoundrel evidently threw those things down and then took to his heels. It is possible that he may prove to have been frightened away from the neighbourhood altogether. Let us trust so!

June 4th.—A quiet day, which is as remarkable a thing in our annals as an exciting one elsewhere. Wurms has made strict inquiry, but cannot trace the muffler and mattock to any inhabitant. A description of them has been printed, and copies sent to Anspach and neighbouring villages for circulation among the peasants, who may be able to throw some light upon the matter. A thanksgiving service is to be held in the church on Sunday for the double escape of the pastor and Martha Bischoff. Pfiffer tells me that Herr von Weissendorff, one of the most energetic detectives in Vienna, is on his way to Laden. I see, too, by the English papers

---

1 Brave Englishman.

sent me, that people at home are interested in the tragedies here, although the accounts which have reached them are garbled and untrustworthy.

How well I can recall the Sunday morning following upon the events which I have described, such a morning as it is hard to find outside the Tyrol! The sky was blue and cloudless, the gentle breeze wafted the balsamic odour of the pine woods through the open windows, and away upon the hills the distant tinkling of the cow bells fell pleasantly upon the ear, until the musical rise and fall which summoned the villagers to prayer drowned their feebler melody. It was hard to believe, looking down that peaceful little street with its quaint top-heavy wooden houses and old-fashioned church, that a cloud of crime hung over it which had horrified Europe. I sat at my window watching the peasants passing with their picturesquely dressed wives and daughters on their way to church. With the kindly reverence of Catholic countries, I saw them cross themselves as they went by the house of Freckler and the spot where Maul had met his fate. When the bell had ceased to toll and the whole population had assembled in the church, I walked up there also, for it has always been my custom to join in religious exercises of any people among whom I may find myself.

When I arrived at the church I found that the service had already begun. I took my place in the gallery which contained the village organ, from which I had a good view of the congregation. In the front seat of all was stationed Frau Bischoff, whose miraculous escape the service was intended to celebrate, and beside her on one side was her worthy spouse, while the maire occupied the other. There was a hush through the church as the curé turned from the altar and ascended the pulpit. I have seldom heard a more magnificent sermon. Father Verhagen was always an eloquent preacher, but on that occasion he surpassed himself. He chose for his text:—"In the midst of life we are in death,"[1] and impressed so vividly upon our minds the thin veil which divides us from eternity, and how unexpectedly it may be rent, that he held his audience spell-bound and horrified. He spoke next with tender pathos of the friends who had been snatched so suddenly and so dreadfully

---

1 From *The Book of Common Prayer* (1549).

from among us, until his words were almost drowned by the sobs of the women, and, suddenly turning, he compared their peaceful existence in a happier land to the dark fate of the gloomy-minded criminal, steeped in blood and with nothing to hope for either in this world or the next—a man solitary among his fellows, with no woman to love him, no child to prattle at his knee, and an endless torture in his own thoughts. So skilfully and so powerfully did he speak that as he finished I am sure that pity for this merciless demon was the prevailing emotion in every heart.

The service was over, and the priest, with his two acolytes before him, was leaving the altar, when he turned, as was his custom, to give his blessing to the congregation. I shall never forget his appearance. The summer sunshine shining slantwise through the single small stained glass window which adorned the little church threw a yellow lustre upon his sharp intellectual features with their dark haggard lines, while a vivid crimson spot reflected from a ruby-coloured mantle in the window quivered over his uplifted right hand. There was a hush as the villagers bent their heads to receive their pastor's blessing—a hush broken by a wild exclamation of surprise from a woman who staggered to her feet in the front pew and gesticulated frantically as she pointed at Father Verhagen's uplifted arm. No need for Frau Bischoff to explain the cause of that sudden cry, for there—there in full sight of his parishioners, were lines of livid scars upon the curé's white wrist—scars which could be left by nothing on earth but a desperate woman's nails. And what woman save her who had clung so fiercely to the murderer two days before!

That in all this terrible business poor Verhagen was the man most to be pitied I have no manner of doubt. In a town in which there was good medical advice to be had, the approach of the homicidal mania, which had undoubtedly proceeded from overwork and brain worry, and which assumed such a terrible form, would have been detected in time and he would have been spared the awful compunction with which he must have been seized in the lucid intervals between his fits—if, indeed, he had any lucid intervals. How could I diagnose with my smattering of science the existence of such a terrible and insidious form of insanity, especially from the vague symptoms of which he informed me.

It is easy now, looking back, to think of many little circumstances which might have put us on the right scent; but what a simple thing is retrospective wisdom! I should be sad indeed if I thought that I had anything with which to reproach myself.

We were never able to discover where he had obtained the weapon with which he had committed his crime, nor how he managed to secrete it in the interval. My experiences proved that it had been his custom to go and come through his study window without disturbing his housekeeper. On the occasion of the attempt on Frau Bischoff he had made a dash for home, and then, finding to his astonishment that his room was occupied, his only resource was to fling away his weapon and muffler, and to mix with the crowd in the village. Being both a strong and an active man, with a good knowledge of the footpaths through the woods, he had never found any difficulty in escaping all observation.

Immediately after his apprehension, Verhagen's disease took an acute form, and he was carried off to the lunatic asylum at Feldkirch. I have heard that some months afterwards he made a determined attempt upon the life of one of his keepers, and afterwards committed suicide. I cannot be positive of this, however, for I heard it quite accidentally during a conversation in a railway carriage.

As for myself, I left Laden within a few months, having received a pleasing intimation from my solicitors that my claim had been paid in full. In spite of my tragic experience there, I had many a pleasing recollection of the little Tyrolese village, and in two subsequent visits I renewed my acquaintance with the maire, the Intendant, and all my old friends, on which occasion, over long pipes and flagons of beer, we have taken a grim pleasure in talking with bated breath of that terrible month in the quiet Vorarlberg hamlet.

The Mark of the Beast

RUDYARD KIPLING

Rudyard Kipling (1865-1936) was born in Bombay (Mumbai), India, the son of John Lockwood Kipling, famed illustrator and professor of architectural sculpture at Sir Jamsetjee Jeejeebhoy School of Art. At the age of six, Rudyard and his younger sister, Alice, were sent to stay at Southsea with Mrs. Holloway, who ran a home specializing in the care of children whose English parents were abroad in India. The young siblings stayed with Mrs. Holloway for five and a half harrowing years, an experience that Kipling recounted as being rife with emotional and physical abuse. Kipling later attended the United Services College in north Devon—a school that primarily prepared young men for military careers.

In 1882, he left England to start his career as a journalist in India, working as a sub-editor for the Civil and Military Gazette *in Lahore (present day Pakistan). Kipling considered it good business to learn the languages of India and, since he was already educated in Hindustani from his early years in Bombay, he began taking lessons in Urdu. During his days at the CMG, he covered local news, including festivals, military trials, and visits by dignitaries. In Lahore, Kipling composed what would later become some of his most famous short fiction, such as "The Phantom Rickshaw" and "The Strange Ride of Morrowbie Jukes." Suffering from chronic insomnia, Kipling would often leave Bikaner House and spend his nights wandering the streets of Lahore, observing and participating in the night life, while simultaneously accumulating material for his literary work. For the rest of his time in India, he used opium and morphine medicinally to relieve incessant anxiety and insomnia. In 1887, he was transferred to work at the* Pioneer *in Allahabad, the sister periodical to the CMG, where he was primarily employed to write fiction.*

During the summers, Kipling often worked as a correspondent in Simla, the summer capital of British India. In 1888, he published Plain Tales of the Hills, *a collection that culled material from his Simla* *experiences. In 1889, Kipling returned to England to pursue his ambitions as a writer. English audiences embraced Kipling's perception of colonial India, as told in his stories, essays, and poems, leading to enormous popular success. After a return trip to Lahore in 1891, and the death of his friend, Wolcott Balestier, Kipling married Balestier's sister, Caroline, and settled in Vermont to live near her family. In Vermont, Kipling pub-*lished The Jungle Book (1894), The Second Jungle Book (1895), *and* Captains Courageous (1897). *After the death of his daughter from pneumonia, Kipling and his family left Vermont for England.*

Although England would be their new home, Kipling took his family to visit South Africa in 1898 and decided to have a winter home in Cape Town, a decision that coincided with the beginning of the South African War. Kipling was involved in South African politics until he left perma-nently in 1908, deeply disappointed with the Liberal victory in Britain. During World War I, Kipling dedicated himself to the war effort and lost his only son, John, in the Battle of Loos. After the war, Kipling was not as prolific a writer, although he continued to work on his autobiography until his death on January 18, 1936. Kipling received the Nobel Prize for literature in 1907.

"The Mark of the Beast" was first published in the Pioneer, *where Kipling was employed as a fiction writer. Before its publication in 1890, artist Vereker Hamilton shopped the manuscript around London, but the story was summarily rejected by editors. It later appeared in Kipling's collection* Life's Handicap (1891), *which sold well and received much acclaim.*

Bibliography

Allen, Charles. *Kipling Sahib: India and the Making of Rudyard Kipling.* New York: Pegasus, 2009.

Battles, Paul. "'The Mark of the Beast': Rudyard Kipling's Apocalyptic Vision of Empire." *Studies in Short Fiction* 33 (1996): 333-344.

Edmond, Rod. "'Without the Camp': Leprosy and Nineteenth-Century Writing." *Victorian Literature and Culture* 29, no. 2 (2001): 507-518.

Kipling, Rudyard. "The Mark of the Beast." *Life's Handicap: Being Stories of Mine Own People,* 208-224. New York: Macmillan, 1891.

Montefiore, Jan. *Rudyard Kipling.* Devon: Northcote House, 2007.

Morey, Peter. "Gothic and Supernatural: Allegories at Work and Play in Kipling's Indian Fiction." In *Victorian Gothic: Literary and Cultural*

Manifestations in the Nineteenth Century, edited by Ruth Robbins and Julian Wolfreys, 201-217. Basingstoke: Palgrave Macmillan, 2000.

Moynihan, Maureen. "The Laughter of Horror: Judgment of the Righteous or Tool of the Devil?" *The Domination of Fear*, edited by Mikko Canini, 173-190. Amsterdam: Rodopi, 2010.

Pinney, Thomas. "Rudyard Kipling." *Oxford Dictionary of National Biography*. Oxford: Oxford University Press, 2004. http://www.oxforddnb.com.

THE MARK OF THE BEAST.[1]

Your Gods and my Gods—do you or I know which are the stronger?
Native Proverb.

EAST of Suez,[2] some hold, the direct control of Providence ceases; Man being there handed over to the power of the Gods and Devils of Asia, and the Church of England Providence only exercising an occasional and modified supervision in the case of Englishmen.

This theory accounts for some of the more unnecessary horrors of life in India: it may be stretched to explain my story.

My friend Strickland of the Police,[3] who knows as much of natives of India as is good for any man, can bear witness to the facts of the case. Dumoise, our doctor, also saw what Strickland and I saw. The inference which he drew from the evidence was entirely incorrect. He is dead now; he died in a rather curious manner, which has been elsewhere described.

When Fleete came to India he owned a little money and some land in the Himalayas, near a place called Dharmsala.[4] Both properties had been left him by an uncle, and he came out to finance them. He was a big, heavy, genial, and inoffensive man. His knowledge of natives was, of course, limited, and he complained of the difficulties of the language.

He rode in from his place in the hills to spend New Year in the

---

1 See Revelations 16:2.
2 The Suez Canal.
3 British military police in India.
4 A city in northern India.

station, and he stayed with Strickland. On New Year's Eve there was a big dinner at the club, and the night was excusably wet.[1] When men foregather from the uttermost ends of the Empire, they have a right to be riotous. The Frontier had sent down a contingent o' Catch-'em-Alive-O's[2] who had not seen twenty white faces for a year, and were used to ride fifteen miles to dinner at the next Fort at the risk of a Khyberee bullet[3] where their drinks should lie. They profited by their new security, for they tried to play pool with a curled-up hedgehog found in the garden, and one of them carried the marker round the room in his teeth. Half a dozen planters had come in from the south and were talking "horse" to the Biggest Liar in Asia, who was trying to cap all their stories at once. Everybody was there, and there was a general closing up of ranks and taking stock of our losses in dead or disabled that had fallen during the past year. It was a very wet night, and I remember that we sang "Auld Lang Syne" with our feet in the Polo Championship Cup, and our heads among the stars, and swore that we were all dear friends. Then some of us went away and annexed Burma, and some tried to open up the Soudan and were opened up by Fuzzies[4] in that cruel scrub outside Suakim,[5] and some found stars and medals, and some were married, which was bad, and some did other things which were worse, and the others of us stayed in our chains and strove to make money on insufficient experiences.

Fleete began the night with sherry and bitters, drank champagne steadily up to dessert, then raw, rasping Capri with all the strength of whisky, took Benedictine with his coffee, four or five whiskies and sodas to improve his pool strokes, beer and bones at

---

1 Drunken.

2 Slang term for a British regiment.

3 Kipling may be alluding to the dangers of the Khyber Pass, which runs through Afghanistan, India, and Pakistan. The British used the pass to invade Afghanistan from India during the Afghan wars.

4 Britain annexed Myanmar (Burma) after the third Anglo-Burmese war in 1885. Britain also invaded Sudan, defeating the Mahdist army at the Battle of Omdurman in 1898. The slang term "fuzzies" or "fuzzy-wuzzy" was used by British soldiers to describe the Beja tribe that sided with the Madhis in their fight against the British.

5 Site of a Beja massacre of Egyptians in 1884.

half-past two, winding up with old brandy.[1] Consequently, when he came out, at half-past three in the morning, into fourteen degrees of frost, he was very angry with his horse for coughing, and tried to leapfrog into the saddle. The horse broke away and went to his stables; so Strickland and I formed a Guard of Dishonour to take Fleete home.

Our road lay through the bazaar, close to a little temple of Hanuman, the Monkey-god, who is a leading divinity worthy of respect.[2] All gods have good points, just as have all priests. Personally, I attach much importance to Hanuman, and am kind to his people—the great grey apes of the hills. One never knows when one may want a friend.

There was a light in the temple, and as we passed, we could hear voices of men chanting hymns. In a native temple, the priests rise at all hours of the night to do honor to their god. Before we could stop him, Fleete dashed up the steps, patted two priests on the back, and was gravely grinding the ashes of his cigar-butt into the forehead of the red, stone image of Hanuman. Strickland tried to drag him out, but he sat down and said solemnly:

"Shee that? 'Mark of the B—beasht! *I* made it. Ishn't it fine?"

In half a minute the temple was alive and noisy, and Strickland, who knew what came of polluting gods, said that things might occur. He, by virtue of his official position, long residence in the country, and weakness for going among the natives, was known to the priests and he felt unhappy. Fleete sat on the ground and refused to move. He said that "good old Hanuman" made a very soft pillow.

Then, without any warning, a Silver Man came out of a recess behind the image of the god. He was perfectly naked in that bitter, bitter cold, and his body shone like frosted silver, for he was what the Bible calls "a leper as white as snow."[3] Also he had no face,

---

1 Bitters are a type of liquor infused with digestive aids. Capri refers to any wine produced in Capri, Italy. Benedictine is a type of liqueur infused with herbs that is produced in France.

2 In Hindu mythology, Hanuman is a monkey with supernatural powers who leads an army of monkeys to retrieve Sita, the wife of Rama, from the demon Ravana.

3 See 2 Kings 5:27.

because he was a leper of some years' standing, and his disease was heavy upon him. We two stooped to haul Fleete up, and the temple was filling and filling with folk who seemed to spring from the earth, when the Silver Man ran in under our arms, making a noise exactly like the mewing of an otter, caught Fleete round the body and dropped his head on Fleete's breast before we could wrench him away. Then he retired to a corner and sat mewing while the crowd blocked all the doors.

The priests were very angry until the Silver Man touched Fleete. That nuzzling seemed to sober them.

At the end of a few minutes' silence one of the priests came to Strickland and said, in perfect English, "Take your friend away. He has done with Hanuman but Hanuman has not done with him." The crowd gave room and we carried Fleete into the road.

Strickland was very angry. He said that we might all three have been knifed, and that Fleete should thank his stars that he had escaped without injury.

Fleete thanked no one. He said that he wanted to go to bed. He was gorgeously drunk.

We moved on, Strickland silent and wrathful, until Fleete was taken with violent shivering fits and sweating. He said that the smells of the bazaar were overpowering, and he wondered why slaughter-houses were permitted so near English residences. "Can't you smell the blood?" said Fleete.

We put him to bed at last, just as the dawn was breaking, and Strickland invited me to have another whisky and soda. While we were drinking he talked of the trouble in the temple, and admitted that it baffled him completely. Strickland hates being mystified by natives, because his business in life is to overmatch them with their own weapons. He has not yet succeeded in doing this, but in fifteen or twenty years he will have made some small progress.

"They should have mauled us," he said, "instead of mewing at us. I wonder what they meant. I don't like it one little bit."

I said that the Managing Committee of the temple would in all probability bring a criminal action against us for insulting their religion. There was a section of the Indian Penal Code[1] which exactly

---

1 Section 295 of the Indian Penal Code prohibited defiling places of worship.

met Fleete's offense. Strickland said he only hoped and prayed that they would do this. Before I left I looked into Fleete's room, and saw him lying on his right side, scratching his left breast. Then I went to bed cold, depressed, and unhappy, at seven o'clock in the morning.

At one o'clock I rode over to Strickland's house to inquire after Fleete's head. I imagined that it would be a sore one. Fleete was breakfasting and seemed unwell. His temper was gone, for he was abusing the cook for not supplying him with an underdone chop. A man who can eat raw meat after a wet night is a curiosity. I told Fleete this and he laughed.

"You breed queer mosquitoes in these parts," he said. "I've been bitten to pieces, but only in one place."

"Let's have a look at the bite," said Strickland. "It may have gone down since this morning."

While the chops were being cooked, Fleete opened his shirt and showed us, just over his left breast, a mark, the perfect double of the black rosettes—the five or six irregular blotches arranged in a circle—on a leopard's hide. Strickland looked and said, "It was only pink this morning. It's grown black now."

Fleete ran to a glass.[1]

"By Jove!" he said, "this is nasty. What is it?"

We could not answer. Here the chops came in, all red and juicy, and Fleete bolted[2] three in a most offensive manner. He ate on his right grinders only, and threw his head over his right shoulder as he snapped the meat. When he had finished, it struck him that he had been behaving strangely, for he said apologetically, "I don't think I ever felt so hungry in my life. I've bolted like an ostrich."

After breakfast Strickland said to me, "Don't go. Stay here, and stay for the night."

Seeing that my house was not three miles from Strickland's, this request was absurd. But Strickland insisted, and was going to say something when Fleete interrupted by declaring in a shame-faced way that he felt hungry again. Strickland sent a man to my house to fetch over my bedding and a horse, and we three went

---

1 Mirror.
2 Quickly ate.

down to Strickland's stables to pass the hours until it was time to go out for a ride. The man who has a weakness for horses never wearies of inspecting them; and when two men are killing time in this way they gather knowledge and lies the one from the other.

There were five horses in the stables, and I shall never forget the scene as we tried to look them over. They seemed to have gone mad. They reared and screamed and nearly tore up their pickets; they sweated and shivered and lathered and were distraught with fear. Strickland's horses used to know him as well as his dogs; which made the matter more curious. We left the stable for fear of the brutes throwing themselves in their panic. Then Strickland turned back and called me. The horses were still frightened, but they let us "gentle" and make much of them, and put their heads in our bosoms.

"They aren't afraid of *us*," said Strickland. "D'you know, I'd give three months' pay if *Outrage* here could talk."

But *Outrage* was dumb, and could only cuddle up to his master and blow out his nostrils, as is the custom of horses when they wish to explain things but can't. Fleete came up when we were in the stalls, and as soon as the horses saw him, their fright broke out afresh. It was all that we could do to escape from the place unkicked. Strickland said, "They don't seem to love you, Fleete."

"Nonsense," said Fleete; "my mare will follow me like a dog." He went to her; she was in a loose-box;[1] but as he slipped the bars she plunged, knocked him down, and broke away into the garden. I laughed, but Strickland was not amused. He took his moustache in both fists and pulled at it till it nearly came out. Fleete, instead of going off to chase his property, yawned, saying that he felt sleepy. He went to the house to lie down, which was a foolish way of spending New Year's Day.

Strickland sat with me in the stables and asked if I had noticed anything peculiar in Fleete's manner. I said that he ate his food like a beast; but that this might have been the result of living alone in the hills out of the reach of society as refined and elevating as ours for instance. Strickland was not amused. I do not think that he listened to me, for his next sentence referred to the mark on Fleete's

---

1 A compartment in a stable.

breast, and I said that it might have been caused by blister-flies,[1] or that it was possibly a birth-mark newly born and now visible for the first time. We both agreed that it was unpleasant to look at, and Strickland found occasion to say that I was a fool.

"I can't tell you what I think now," said he, "because you would call me a madman; but you must stay with me for the next few days, if you can. I want you to watch Fleete, but don't tell me what you think till I have made up my mind."

"But I am dining out to-night," I said.

"So am I," said Strickland, "and so is Fleete. At least if he doesn't change his mind."

We walked about the garden smoking, but saying nothing—because we were friends, and talking spoils good tobacco—till our pipes were out. Then we went to wake up Fleete. He was wide awake and fidgeting about his room.

"I say, I want some more chops," he said. "Can I get them?"

We laughed and said, "Go and change. The ponies will be round in a minute."

"All right," said Fleete. "I'll go when I get the chops—underdone ones, mind."

He seemed to be quite in earnest. It was four o'clock, and we had had breakfast at one; still, for a long time, he demanded those underdone chops. Then he changed into riding clothes and went out into the verandah. His pony—the mare had not been caught—would not let him come near. All three horses were unmanageable—mad with fear—and finally Fleete said that he would stay at home and get something to eat. Strickland and I rode out wondering. As we passed the temple of Hanuman, the Silver Man came out and mewed at us.

"He is not one of the regular priests of the temple," said Strickland. "I think I should peculiarly like to lay my hands on him."[2]

There was no spring in our gallop on the racecourse that evening. The horses were stale, and moved as though they had been ridden out.

---

1 Blister beetles secrete a substance called cantharidin that causes blisters.

2 See Mark 1:40-42.

"The fright after breakfast has been too much for them," said Strickland.

That was the only remark he made through the remainder of the ride. Once or twice I think he swore to himself, but that did not count.

We came back in the dark at seven o'clock, and saw that there were no lights in the bungalow. "Careless ruffians my servants are!" said Strickland.

My horse reared at something on the carriage drive, and Fleete stood up under its nose.

"What are you doing, grovelling about the garden?" said Strickland.

But both horses bolted and nearly threw us. We dismounted by the stables and returned to Fleete, who was on his hands and knees under the orange-bushes.

"What the devil's wrong with you?" said Strickland.

"Nothing, nothing in the world," said Fleete, speaking very quickly and thickly. "I've been gardening—botanising you know. The smell of the earth is delightful. I think I'm going for a walk—a long walk—all night."

Then I saw that there was something excessively out of order somewhere, and I said to Strickland, "I am not dining out."

"Bless you!" said Strickland. "Here, Fleete, get up. You'll catch fever there. Come in to dinner and let's have the lamps lit. We'll all dine at home."

Fleete stood up unwillingly, and said, "No lamps—no lamps. It's much nicer here. Let's dine outside and have some more chops—lots of 'em and underdone—bloody ones with gristle."

Now a December evening in Northern India is bitterly cold, and Fleete's suggestion was that of a maniac.

"Come in," said Strickland sternly. "Come in at once."

Fleete came, and when the lamps were brought, we saw that he was literally plastered with dirt from head to foot. He must have been rolling in the garden. He shrank from the light and went to his room. His eyes were horrible to look at. There was a green light behind them, not in them, if you understand, and the man's lower lip hung down.

Strickland said, "There is going to be trouble—big trouble—to-night. Don't you change your riding things."

We waited and waited for Fleete's reappearance, and ordered dinner in the meantime. We could hear him moving about his own room, but there was no light there. Presently from the room came the long-drawn howl of a wolf.

People write and talk lightly of blood running cold and hair standing up and things of that kind. Both sensations are too horrible to be trifled with. My heart stopped as though a knife had been driven through it, and Strickland turned white as the tablecloth.

The howl was repeated, and was answered by another howl far across the fields.

That set the gilded roof on the horror. Strickland dashed into Fleete's room. I followed, and we saw Fleete getting out of the window. He made beast-noises in the back of his throat. He could not answer us when we shouted at him. He spat.

I don't quite remember what followed, but I think that Strickland must have stunned him with the long boot-jack[1] or else I should never have been able to sit on his chest. Fleete could not speak, he could only snarl, and his snarls were those of a wolf, not of a man. The human spirit must have been giving way all day and have died out with the twilight. We were dealing with a beast that had once been Fleete.

The affair was beyond any human and rational experience. I tried to say "Hydrophobia,"[2] but the word wouldn't come, because I knew that I was lying.

We bound this beast with leather thongs of the punkah-rope,[3] and tied its thumbs and big toes together, and gagged it with a shoe-horn, which makes a very efficient gag if you know how to arrange it. Then we carried it into the dining-room, and sent a man to Dumoise, the doctor, telling him to come over at once. After we had dispatched the messenger and were drawing breath, Strickland said, "It's no good. This isn't any doctor's work." I, also, knew that he spoke the truth.

The beast's head was free, and it threw it about from side to

---

1 Device used to remove a riding boot.
2 Rabies.
3 Cord used to operate a large fan made of canvas or palmyra leaves.

side. Any one entering the room would have believed that we were curing a wolf's pelt. That was the most loathsome accessory of all.

Strickland sat with his chin in the heel of his fist, watching the beast as it wriggled on the ground, but saying nothing. The shirt had been torn open in the scuffle and showed the black rosette mark on the left breast. It stood out like a blister.

In the silence of the watching we heard something without mewing like a she-otter. We both rose to our feet, and, I answer for myself, not Strickland, felt sick—actually and physically sick. We told each other, as did the men in *Pinafore*,[1] that it was the cat.

Dumoise arrived, and I never saw a little man so unprofessionally shocked. He said that it was a heart-rending case of hydrophobia, and that nothing could be done. At least any palliative measures would only prolong the agony. The beast was foaming at the mouth. Fleete, as we told Dumoise, had been bitten by dogs once or twice. Any man who keeps half a dozen terriers must expect a nip now and again. Dumoise could offer no help. He could only certify that Fleete was dying of hydrophobia. The beast was then howling, for it had managed to spit out the shoe-horn. Dumoise said that he would be ready to certify to the cause of death, and that the end was certain. He was a good little man, and he offered to remain with us; but Strickland refused the kindness. He did not wish to poison Dumoise's New Year. He would only ask him not to give the real cause of Fleete's death to the public.

So Dumoise left, deeply agitated; and as soon as the noise of the cart-wheels had died away, Strickland told me, in a whisper, his suspicions. They were so wildly improbable that he dared not say them out loud; and I, who entertained all Strickland's beliefs, was so ashamed of owning to them that I pretended to disbelieve.

"Even if the Silver Man had bewitched Fleete for polluting the image of Hanuman, the punishment could not have fallen so quickly."

As I was whispering this the cry outside the house rose again, and the beast fell into a fresh paroxysm of struggling till we were afraid that the thongs that held it would give way.

---

1 An allusion to the sound of a whip, or cat-o-nine tails, which is mistaken for a cat in W. S. Gilbert and Arthur Sullivan's *H. M. S. Pinafore* (1878).

"Watch!" said Strickland. "If this happens six times I shall take the law into my own hands. I order you to help me."

He went into his room and came out in a few minutes with the barrels of an old shotgun, a piece of fishing-line, some thick cord, and his heavy wooden bedstead. I reported that the convulsions had followed the cry by two seconds in each case, and the beast seemed perceptibly weaker.

Strickland muttered, "But he can't take away the life! He can't take away the life!"

I said, though I knew that I was arguing against myself, "It may be a cat. It must be a cat. If the Silver Man is responsible, why does he dare to come here?"

Strickland arranged the wood on the hearth, put the gun-barrels into the glow of the fire, spread the twine on the table and broke a walking stick in two. There was one yard of fishing line, gut, lapped with wire, such as is used for *mahseer*[1]-fishing, and he tied the two ends together in a loop.

Then he said, "How can we catch him? He must be taken alive and unhurt."

I said that we must trust in Providence, and go out softly with polo-sticks into the shrubbery at the front of the house. The man or animal that made the cry was evidently moving round the house as regularly as a night-watchman. We could wait in the bushes till he came by and knock him over.

Strickland accepted this suggestion, and we slipped out from a bathroom window into the front verandah and then across the carriage drive into the bushes.

In the moonlight we could see the leper coming round the corner of the house. He was perfectly naked, and from time to time he mewed and stopped to dance with his shadow. It was an unattractive sight, and thinking of poor Fleete, brought to such degradation by so foul a creature, I put away all my doubts and resolved to help Strickland from the heated gun-barrels to the loop of twine—from the loins to the head and back again—with all tortures that might be needful.

The leper halted in the front porch for a moment and we

---

1 Large Indian freshwater fish of the carp family.

jumped out on him with the sticks. He was wonderfully strong, and we were afraid that he might escape or be fatally injured before we caught him. We had an idea that lepers were frail creatures, but this proved to be incorrect. Strickland knocked his legs from under him and I put my foot on his neck. He mewed hideously, and even through my riding-boots I could feel that his flesh was not the flesh of a clean man.[1]

He struck at us with his hand and feet-stumps. We looped the lash of a dog-whip round him, under the arm-pits, and dragged him backwards into the hall and so into the dining-room where the beast lay. There we tied him with trunk-straps. He made no attempt to escape, but mewed.

When we confronted him with the beast the scene was beyond description. The beast doubled backwards into a bow as though he had been poisoned with strychnine, and moaned in the most pitiable fashion. Several other things happened also, but they cannot be put down here.

"I think I was right," said Strickland. "Now we will ask him to cure this case."

But the leper only mewed. Strickland wrapped a towel round his hand and took the gun-barrels out of the fire. I put the half of the broken walking stick through the loop of fishing-line and buckled the leper comfortably to Strickland's bedstead. I understood then how men and women and little children can endure to see a witch burnt alive; for the beast was moaning on the floor, and though the Silver Man had no face, you could see horrible feelings passing through the slab that took its place, exactly as waves of heat play across red-hot iron—gun-barrels for instance.

Strickland shaded his eyes with his hands for a moment and we got to work. This part is not to be printed.

★　★　★　★　★　★

The dawn was beginning to break when the leper spoke. His mewings had not been satisfactory up to that point. The beast had fainted from exhaustion and the house was very still. We

---

[1] Leprosy was considered a disease of the "unclean."

unstrapped the leper and told him to take away the evil spirit. He crawled to the beast and laid his hand upon the left breast. That was all. Then he fell face down and whined, drawing in his breath as he did so.

We watched the face of the beast, and saw the soul of Fleete coming back into the eyes. Then a sweat broke out on the forehead and the eyes—they were human eyes—closed. We waited for an hour but Fleete still slept. We carried him to his room and bade the leper go, giving him the bedstead, and the sheet on the bedstead to cover his nakedness, the gloves and the towels with which we had touched him, and the whip that had been hooked round his body. He put the sheet about him and went out into the early morning without speaking or mewing.

Strickland wiped his face and sat down. A night-gong, far away in the city, made seven o'clock.

"Exactly four-and-twenty hours!" said Strickland. "And I've done enough to ensure my dismissal from the service, besides permanent quarters in a lunatic asylum. Do you believe that we are awake?"

The red-hot gun-barrel had fallen on the floor and was singeing the carpet. The smell was entirely real.

That morning at eleven we two together went to wake up Fleete. We looked and saw that the black leopard-rosette on his chest had disappeared. He was very drowsy and tired, but as soon as he saw us, he said, "Oh! Confound you fellows. Happy New Year to you. Never mix your liquors. I'm nearly dead."

"Thanks for your kindness, but you're over time," said Strickland. "To-day is the morning of the second. You've slept the clock round with a vengeance."

The door opened, and little Dumoise put his head in. He had come on foot, and fancied that we were laying out Fleete.[1]

"I've brought a nurse," said Dumoise. "I suppose that she can come in for . . . what is necessary."

"By all means," said Fleete cheerily, sitting up in bed. "Bring on your nurses."

Dumoise was dumb. Strickland led him out and explained

---

1 Preparing him for burial.

that there must have been a mistake in the diagnosis. Dumoise remained dumb and left the house hastily. He considered that his professional reputation had been injured, and was inclined to make a personal matter of the recovery. Strickland went out too. When he came back, he said that he had been to call on the Temple of Hanuman to offer redress for the pollution of the god, and had been solemnly assured that no white man had ever touched the idol and that he was an incarnation of all the virtues labouring under a delusion. "What do you think?" said Strickland.

I said, "'There are more things . . .'"[1]

But Strickland hates that quotation. He says that I have worn it threadbare.

One other curious thing happened which frightened me as much as anything in all the night's work. When Fleete was dressed he came into the dining-room and sniffed. He had a quaint trick of moving his nose when he sniffed. "Horrid doggy smell, here," said he. "You should really keep those terriers of yours in better order. Try sulphur, Strick."

But Strickland did not answer. He caught hold of the back of a chair, and, without warning, went into an amazing fit of hysterics. It is terrible to see a strong man overtaken with hysteria. Then it struck me that we had fought for Fleete's soul with the Silver Man in that room, and had disgraced ourselves as Englishmen forever, and I laughed and gasped and gurgled just as shamefully as Strickland, while Fleete thought that we had both gone mad. We never told him what we had done.

Some years later, when Strickland had married and was a church-going member of society for his wife's sake, we reviewed the incident dispassionately, and Strickland suggested that I should put it before the public.

I cannot myself see that this step is likely to clear up the mystery; because, in the first place, no one will believe a rather unpleasant story, and, in the second, it is well known to every right-minded man that the gods of the heathen are stone and brass, and any attempt to deal with them otherwise is justly condemned.

---

1 See Shakespeare's *Hamlet*, 1.5.168-169.

The Were-Wolf

Clemence Housman

Clemence Housman (1861-1955) was born into a family dedicated to rigorous intellectual inquiry. She was educated at home by a governess along with her younger siblings, Laurence, Basil, Robert, and Kate. Her older brother Alfred would later become famous as the poet and scholar A. E. Housman. After her mother, Sara Jane Williams, died in 1871, Housman took responsibility for much of the household. Her father, Edward Housman, a solicitor at Bromsgrove, also relied heavily on his daughter to assist him in his business affairs.

In 1883, she received a small legacy and decided to leave Bromsgrove for an independent life in London. After settling in Kensington, Housman studied wood engraving and then supported herself and Laurence as an engraver for several well-established periodicals, including the Illustrated London News *and the* Graphic. *Housman found further employment as an engraver at private printing presses such as Peartree Press and C. R. Ashbee's Essex House Press.*

While living in Kensington, Housman became acquainted with artists and writers in the neighborhood such as William M. Thackeray, John Everett Millais, and Edward Burne-Jones. She was actively engaged in the art scene, becoming particularly enamored with the new school of British artists inspired by French Impressionism. During this time, Housman also devoted herself to the cause of women's suffrage, utilizing her skills as an engraver and embroiderer to produce banners for a number of women's suffrage organizations. Housman's home was often a hub of activity since the Suffrage Atelier, a feminist organization of writers, artists, and actors, used her studio as a work space. As a member of the Women's Social and Political Union, Housman played an active role in its meetings, demonstrations, and fundraisers. In 1909, she joined the Tax Resistance League and was arrested in 1911 when she refused to pay the Inhabited House Duty on a rental property in Dorset.

In addition to her political and artistic work, Housman was an author. She published short stories, including "The Drawn Arrow" (1923), which appeared in 31 Stories by Thirty and One Authors, *a collection featuring works by H. G. Wells, G. K. Chesterton, and Violet Hunt. Housman also published novels such as* The Unknown Sea *(1898) and* The Life of Sir Aglovale de Galis *(1905), inspired by Sir Thomas Malory's* Le Morte D'Arthur. *By 1924, Housman had retired from engraving and writing, choosing instead to focus on gardening at Longmeadow, the home in Somerset she shared with her brother Laurence.*

Clemence Housman's "The Were-Wolf" was originally published in the 1890 Christmas number of Atalanta, *a periodical for young women. The illustrations were created by Everard Hopkins, an artist best known for his cartoons in* Punch Magazine. *"The Were-wolf" was immensely popular. The issue of* Atalanta *featuring the story soon sold out, and in 1896, John Lane's Bodley Head press republished "The Were-Wolf" in book form with illustrations by Housman's brother, Laurence. These illustrations are included on pages 334-339 of the present edition.*

Bibliography

Born, Anne. "Clemence Housman's First Book." *Housman Society Journal* 3 (1977): 57-66.

Christie, Rechelle. "The Politics of Representation and Illustration in Clemence Housman's *The Were-Wolf*." *Housman Society Journal* 33 (2007): 54-67.

Crawford, Elizabeth. "Clemence Housman." *Oxford Dictionary of National Biography*. Oxford: Oxford University Press. http://www.oxforddnb.com.

Du Coudray, Chantal Bourgault. *The Curse of the Werewolf: Fantasy, Horror and the Beast Within*. New York: Tauris, 2006.

Hodge, Shari. "The Motif of the Double in Clemence Housman's *The Were-Wolf*." *Housman Society Journal* 17 (1991): 57-66.

Holton, Sandra Stanley. *Suffrage Days: Stories from the Women's Suffrage Movement*. London: Routledge, 1996.

Housman, Laurence. *The Unexpected Years*. New York: Bobbs-Merrill, 1936.

Housman, Clemence. "The Were-Wolf." *Atalanta* 4 (December 1890): 132-156.

Oakley, Elizabeth. *Inseparable Siblings: A Portrait of Clemence and Laurence Housman*. Studley, Warwickshire: Brewin, 2009.

Tickner, Lisa. *The Spectacle of Women: Imagery of the Suffrage Campaign, 1907-14*. Chicago: University of Chicago Press, 1988.

THE WERE-WOLF.

THE great farm hall[1] was ablaze with the firelight, and noisy with laughter and talk and many-sounding work. None could be idle but the very young and the very old—little Rol, who was hugging a puppy, and old Trella, whose palsied hand fumbled over her knitting. The early evening had closed in, and the farm-servants had come in from the out-door work and assembled in the ample hall, which had space for scores of workers. Several of the men were engaged in carving, and to these were yielded the best place and light; others made or repaired fishing tackle and harness, and a great seine net[2] occupied three pairs of hands. Of the women most were sorting and mixing eider feather and chopping straw[3] for the same. Looms were there, though not in present use, but three wheels whirred emulously,[4] and the finest and swiftest thread of the three ran between the fingers of the house-mistress. Near her were some children, busy too, plaiting wicks for candles and lamps. Each group of workers had a lamp in its centre, and those furthest from the fire had extra warmth from the two braziers[5] filled with glowing wood embers, replenished now and again from the generous hearth. But the flicker of the great fire was manifest to remotest corners, and prevailed beyond the limits of the lesser lights.

Little Rol grew tired of his puppy, dropped it incontinently, and made an onslaught on Tyr,[6] the old wolf-hound, who basked dozing, whimpering and twitching in his hunting dreams. Prone went

---

1 In medieval Scandinavia, many farms had rectangular longhouses that were partitioned into several rooms serving different functions. The farm hall had to be large enough to host an entire landholding family, which would likely include extended family and in-laws, as well as servants and farm workers.

2 A large fishing net.

3 Insulation for pillows and quilts.

4 Earnestly.

5 Containers filled with embers used as a heating source.

6 Tyr is the name of a god from Norse mythology who sacrificed his hand in order to tie up a monstrous wolf, Fenrir, and thus save the other gods.

Rol beside Tyr, his young arms round the shaggy neck, his curls against the black jowl. Tyr gave a perfunctory lick, and stretched with a sleepy sigh. Rol growled and rolled and shoved invitingly, but could gain nothing from the old dog but placid toleration and a half-observant blink. "Take that, then!" said Rol, indignant at this ignoring of his advances, and sent the puppy sprawling against the dignity that disdained him as playmate. The dog took no notice, and the child wandered off to find amusement elsewhere.

The baskets of white eider feathers caught his eye far off in a distant corner. He slipped under the table and crept along on all-fours, the ordinary commonplace custom of walking down a room upright not being to his fancy. When close to the women he lay still for a moment watching, with his elbows on the floor and his chin in his palms. One of the women seeing him nodded and smiled, and presently he crept out behind her skirts and passed, hardly noticed, from one to another, till he found opportunity to possess himself of a large handful of feathers. With these he traversed the length of the room, under the table again, and emerged near the spinners. At the feet of the youngest he curled himself round, sheltered by her knees from the observation of the others, and disarmed her of interference by secretly displaying his handful with a confiding smile. A dubious nod satisfied him, and presently he proceeded with the play he had planned. He took a tuft of the white down, and gently shook it free of his fingers close to the whirl of the wheel. The wind of the swift motion took it, spun it round and round in widening circles, till it floated above like a slow white moth. Little Rol's eyes danced, and the row of his small teeth shone in a silent laugh of delight. Another and another of the white tufts was sent whirling round like a winged thing in a spider's web, and floating clear at last. Presently the handful failed.

Rol sprawled forward to survey the room, and contemplate another journey under the table. His shoulder thrusting forward checked the wheel for an instant; he shifted hastily. The wheel flew on with a jerk and the thread snapped. "Naughty Rol!" said the girl. The swiftest wheel stopped also, and the house-mistress, Rol's aunt, leaned forward, and sighting the low curly head, gave a warning against mischief, and sent him off to old Trella's corner.

Rol obeyed, and after a discreet period of obedience, sidled out again down the length of the room furthest from his aunt's eye. As he slipped in among the men they looked up to see that their tools might be, as far as possible, out of reach of Rol's hands, and close to their own. Nevertheless, before long he managed to secure a fine chisel and take off its point on the leg of the table. The carver's strong objections to this disconcerted Rol, who for five minutes thereafter effaced himself under the table.

During this seclusion he contemplated the many pairs of legs that surrounded him, and almost shut out the light of the fire. How very odd some of the legs were: some were curved where they should be straight; some were straight where they should be curved; and as Rol said to himself, "they all seemed screwed on differently." Some were tucked away modestly under the benches, others were thrust far out under the table, encroaching on Rol's own particular domain. He stretched out his own short legs and regarded them critically and, after comparison, favourably. Why were not all legs made like his, or like *his?*

These legs approved by Rol were a little apart from the rest. He crawled opposite and again made comparison. His face grew quite solemn as he thought of the innumerable days to come before his legs could be as long and strong. He hoped they would be just like those, his models, as straight as to bone, as curved as to muscle.

A few moments later Sweyn[1] of the long legs felt a small hand caressing his foot, and looking down met the upturned eyes of his little cousin Rol. Lying on his back, still softly patting and stroking the young man's foot, the child was quite quiet and happy for a good while. He watched the movement of the strong, deft hands, and the shifting of the bright tools. Now and then minute chips of wood puffed off by Sweyn fell down upon his face. At last he raised himself, very gently, lest a jog should wake impatience in the carver, and crossing his own legs round Sweyn's ankle, clasping with his arms too, laid his head against the knee. Such act is evidence of a child's most wonderful hero worship. Quite content was Rol, and more than content when Sweyn paused a minute to joke, and pat his head and pull his curls. Quiet he remained, as long as quiescence is possible to limbs young as his. Sweyn forgot

---

[1] Sweyn's name might be a play on the word "swain," meaning a lover or a suitor.

he was near, hardly noticed when his leg was gently released, and never saw the stealthy abstraction of one of his tools.

Ten minutes thereafter was a lamentable wail from low on the floor, rising to the full pitch of Rol's healthy lungs, for his hand was gashed across, and the copious bleeding terrified him. Then there was soothing and comforting, washing and binding, and a modicum of scolding, till the loud outcry sank into occasional sobs, and the child, tear-stained and subdued, was returned to the chimney-corner settle, where Trella nodded.

In the reaction after pain and fright, Rol found that the quiet of that fire-lit corner was to his mind. Tyr, too, disdained him no longer, but, roused by his sobs, showed all the concern and sympathy that a dog can by licking and wistful watching. A little shame weighed also upon his spirits. He wished he had not cried quite so much. He remembered how once Sweyn had come home with his arm torn down from the shoulder, and a dead bear; and how he had never winced nor said a word, though his lips turned white with pain. Poor little Rol gave an extra sighing sob over his own faint-hearted shortcomings.

The light and motion of the great fire began to tell strange stories to the child, and the wind in the chimney roared a corroborative note now and then. The great black mouth of the chimney, impending high over the hearth, received the murky coils of smoke and brightness of aspiring sparks as into a mysterious gulf, and beyond, in the high darkness, were muttering and wailing and strange doings, so that sometimes the smoke rushed back in panic, and curled out and up to the roof, and condensed itself to invisibility among the rafters. And then the wind would rage after its lost prey, and rush around the house, rattling and shrieking at window and door.

In a lull, after one such loud gust, Rol lifted his head in surprise and listened. A lull had also come on the babble of talk, and thus could be heard with strange distinctness a sound without the door—the sound of a child's voice, a child's hands. "Open, open; let me in!" piped the little voice from low down, lower than the handle, and the latch rattled as though a tiptoe child reached up to it, and soft small knocks were struck. One near the door sprang up and opened it. "No one is here," he said. Tyr lifted his head and gave utterance to a howl, loud, prolonged, most dismal.

Sweyn, not able to believe that his ears had deceived him, got up and went to the door. It was a dark night; the clouds were heavy with snow that had fallen fitfully when the wind lulled. Untrodden snow lay up to the porch; there was no sight nor sound of any human being. Sweyn strained his eyes far and near, only to see dark sky, pure snow, and a line of black fir trees on a hill brow, bowing down before the wind. "It must have been the wind," he said, and closed the door.

Many faces looked scared. The sound of a child's voice had been so distinct—and the words, "Open, open; let me in!" The wind might creak the wood, or rattle the latch, but could not speak with a child's voice, nor knock with the soft plain blows that a plump fist gives. And the strange unusual howl of the wolf-hound was an omen to be feared, be the rest what it might. Strange things were said by one and another, till the rebuke of house-mistress quelled them into far off whispers. For a time after there was uneasiness, constraint, and silence; then the chill of fear thawed by degrees, and the babble of talk flowed on again.

Yet half-an-hour later a very slight noise outside the door sufficed to arrest every hand, every tongue. Every head was raised, every eye fixed in one direction. "It is Christian; he is late," said Sweyn.

No, no; this is a feeble shuffle, not a young man's tread. With the sound of uncertain feet came the hard tap tap of a stick against the door, and the high-pitched voice of eld[1] "Open, open; let me in!" Again Tyr flung up his head in a long, doleful howl.

Before the echo of the tapping stick and the high voice had fairly died way, Sweyn had sprung across to the door and flung it wide. "No one again," he said in a steady voice, though his eyes looked startled as he stared out. He saw the lonely expanse of snow, the clouds swagging low, and between the two the line of dark fir trees bowing in the wind. He closed the door without word of comment, and recrossed the room.

A score of blanched faces were turned to him as though he

---

1 Old.

were the solver of the enigma. He could not be unconscious of this mute eye-questioning, and it disturbed his resolute air of composure. He hesitated, glanced towards his mother, the house-mistress, then back at the frightened folk, and gravely, before them all, made the sign of the cross. There was a flutter of hands as the sign was repeated by all, and the dead silence was stirred as by a huge sigh, for the held breath of many was freed as though the sign gave magic relief.

Even the house-mistress was perturbed. She left her wheel and crossed the room to her son, and spoke with him for a moment in a low tone that none could overhear. But a moment later her voice was high-pitched and loud, so that all might benefit by her rebuke of the "heathen chatter" of one of the girls. Perhaps she essayed to silence thus her own misgivings and forebodings.

No other voice dared speak now with its natural fulness. Low tones made intermittent murmurs, and now and then silence drifted over the whole room. The handling of tools was as noiseless as might be, and suspended on the instant if the door rattled in a gust of wind. After a time Sweyn left his work, joined the group nearest the door, and loitered there on the pretence of giving advice and help to the unskilful.

A man's tread was heard outside in the porch. "Christian!" said Sweyn and his mother simultaneously, he confidently, she authoritatively, to set the checked wheels going again. But Tyr flung up his head with an appalling howl.

"Open, open; let me in!"

It was a man's voice, and the door shook and rattled as a man's strength beat against it. Sweyn could feel the planks quivering, as on the instant his hand was upon the door, flinging it open, to face the blank porch, and beyond only snow and sky, and firs aslant in the wind.

He stood for a long minute with the open door in his hand. The bitter wind swept in with its icy chill, but a deadlier chill of fear came swifter, and seemed to freeze the beating of hearts. Sweyn stepped back to snatch up a great bearskin cloak.

"Sweyn, where are you going?"

"No further than the porch, mother," and he stepped out and closed the door.

He wrapped himself in the heavy fur, and leaning against the most sheltered wall of the porch, steeled his nerves to face the devil and all his works. No sound of voices came from within; the most distinct sound was the crackle and roar of the fire.

It was bitterly cold. His feet grew numb, but he forbore stamping them into warmth lest the sound should strike panic within; nor would he leave the porch, nor print a footmark on the untrodden snow that testified conclusively to no human voices and hands having approached the door since snow fell two hours or more ago. "When the wind drops there will be more snow," thought Sweyn.

For the best part of an hour he kept his watch, and saw no living thing—heard no unwonted sound. "I will freeze here no longer," he muttered, and re-entered.

One woman gave a half-suppressed scream as his hand was laid on the latch, and then a gasp of relief as he came in. No one questioned him, only his mother said, in a tone of forced unconcern, "Could you not see Christian coming?" as though she were made anxious only by the absence of her younger son. Hardly had Sweyn stamped near to the fire than clear knocking was heard at the door. Tyr leaped from the hearth—his eyes red as fire—his fangs showing white in the black jowl—his neck ridged and bristling; and overleaping Rol, ramped at the door, barking furiously.

Outside the door a clear mellow voice was calling. Tyr's barking made the words undistinguishable.

No one offered to stir towards the door before Sweyn.

He stalked the room resolutely, lifted the latch, and swung back the door.

A white-robed woman glided in.

No wraith! Living—beautiful—young.

Tyr leapt upon her.

Lithely she baulked the sharp fangs with folds of her long fur robe, and snatching from her girdle a small two-edged axe, whirled it up for a blow of defence.

Sweyn caught the dog by the collar and dragged him off yelling and struggling.

The stranger stood in the doorway motionless, one foot set forward, one arm flung up, till the house-mistress hurried down the room; and Sweyn, relinquishing to others the furious Tyr, turned again to close the door, and offer excuse for so fierce a greeting. Then she lowered her arm, slung the axe in its place at her waist, loosened the furs about her face, and shook over her shoulders the long white robe—all, as it were, with the sway of one movement.

She was a maiden, tall and very fair. The fashion of her dress was strange—half masculine, yet not unwomanly. A fine fur tunic, reaching but little below the knee, was all the skirt she wore; below were the cross-bound shoes and leggings that a hunter wears. A white fur cap was set low upon the brows, and from its edge strips of fur fell lappet-wise[1] about her shoulders, two of which at her entrance had been drawn forward and crossed about her throat, but now, loosened and thrust back, left unhidden long plaits of fair hair that lay forward on shoulder and breast, down to the ivory-studded girdle where the axe gleamed.

Sweyn and his mother led the stranger to the hearth without question or sign of curiosity, till she voluntarily told her tale of a long journey to distant kindred, a promised guide unmet, and signals and landmarks mistaken.

"Alone!" exclaimed Sweyn in astonishment. "Have you journeyed thus far—a hundred leagues—alone?"

She answered "Yes" with a little smile.

"Over the hills and wastes! Why, the folk there are savage and wild as beasts!"

She dropped her hand upon her axe with a laugh of some scorn.

"I fear neither man nor beast; some few fear me;" and then she told strange tales of fierce attack and defence, and of the bold free huntress life she had led.

Her words came a little slowly and deliberately, as though she spoke in a scarce familiar tongue; now and then she hesitated, and stopped in a phrase, as though for lack of some word.

She became the centre of a group of listeners. The interest she excited dissipated, in some degree, the dread inspired by the

---

1 In flaps, like those on either side of a headdress or hat.

Everard Hopkins, illustration for *The Were-wolf*, by Clemence Housman,
Atalanta 4 (December 1890): 136.

mysterious voices. There was nothing ominous about this young, bright, fair reality, though her aspect was strange.

Little Rol crept near, staring at the stranger with all his might. Unnoticed, he softly stroked and patted a corner of her soft white robe that reached to the floor in ample folds. He laid his cheek against it caressingly, and then edged up close to her knees.

"What is your name?" he asked.

The stranger's smile and ready answer, as she looked down, saved Rol from the rebuke merited by his unmannerly question.

"My real name," she said, "would be uncouth to your ears and tongue. The folk of this country have given me another name, and from this"—she laid her hand on the fur robe—"they call me 'White Fell.'"

Little Rol repeated it to himself, stroking and patting as before. "White Fell, White Fell."

The fair face, and soft, beautiful dress pleased Rol. He knelt up, with his eyes on her face and an air of uncertain determination, like a robin's on a doorstep, and plumped his elbows into her lap with a little gasp at his own audacity.

"Rol!" exclaimed his aunt; but "Oh, let him!" said White Fell, smiling and stroking his head; and Rol stayed.

He advanced further, and panting at his own adventurousness in the face of his aunt's authority, climbed up on to her knees. Her welcoming arms hindered any protest. He nestled happily, fingering the axe head, the ivory studs in her girdle, the ivory clasp at her throat, the plaits of fair hair; rubbing his head against the softness of her fur-clad shoulder, with a child's confidence in the kindness of beauty.

White Fell had not uncovered her head, only knotted the pendant fur loosely behind her neck. Rol reached up his hand towards it, whispering her name to himself, "White Fell, White Fell," then slid his arms round her neck, and kissed her—once—twice. She laughed delightedly, and kissed him again.

"The child plagues you?" said Sweyn.

"No, indeed," she answered, with an earnestness so intense as to seem disproportionate to the occasion.

Rol settled himself again on her lap and began to unwind the bandage bound round his hand. He paused a little when he saw where the blood had soaked through, then went on till his hand was bare and the cut displayed, gaping and long, though only skin deep. He held it up towards White Fell, desirous of her pity and sympathy.

Everard Hopkins, illustration for *The Were-wolf*, by Clemence Housman, *Atalanta* 4 (December 1890): 141.

At sight of it, and the blood-stained linen, she drew in her breath suddenly, clasped Rol to her—hard, hard—till he began to struggle. Her face was hidden behind the boy, so that none could see its expression. It had lighted up with a most awful glee.

Afar, beyond the fir grove, beyond the low hill behind, the absent Christian was hastening his return. From day-break he had been afoot, carrying summons to a bear hunt to all the best hunters of the farms and hamlets that lay within a radius of twelve miles. Nevertheless, having been detained till a late hour, he now broke into a run, going with a long smooth stride of apparent ease that fast made the miles diminish.

He entered the midnight blackness of the fir grove with scarcely slackened pace, though the path was invisible; and passing through into the open again, sighted the farm lying a furlong off down the slope. Then he sprang out freely, and almost on the instant gave one great sideways leap, and stood still. There in the snow was the track of a great wolf.

His hand went to his knife, his only weapon. He stooped, knelt down, to bring his eyes to the level of a beast, and peered about; his teeth set, his heart beating—a little harder than the pace of his running had set it. A solitary wolf, nearly always savage and of large size, is a formidable beast that will not hesitate to attack a single man. This wolf track was the largest Christian had ever seen, and, as far as he could judge, recently made. It led from under the fir trees down the slope. Well for him, he thought, was the delay that had so vexed him before, well for him that he had not passed through the dark fir grove when that danger of jaws lurked there. Going warily, he followed the track.

It led down the slope, across a broad ice-bound stream, along the level beyond, leading towards the farm. A less sure knowledge than Christian's might have doubted of it being a wolf-track, and guessed it to be made by Tyr or some large dog; but he was sure, and knew better than to mistake between a wolf's and a dog's footmark.

Straight on—straight on towards the farm.

Christian grew surprised and anxious at a prowling wolf daring so near. He drew his knife and pressed on, more hastily, more keenly eyed. Oh that Tyr were with him!

Straight on, straight on, even to the very door, where the snow failed. His heart seemed to give a great leap and then stop. There the track *ended*.

Nothing lurked in the porch, and there was no sign of return. The firs stood straight against the sky, the clouds lay low; for the wind had fallen and a few snow flakes came drifting down. In a horror of surprise, Christian stood dazed a moment: then he lifted the latch and went in. His glance took in all the old familiar forms and faces, and with them that of the stranger, fur-clad and beautiful. The awful truth flashed upon him. He knew what she was.

Only a few were startled by the rattle of the latch as he entered. The room was filled with bustle and movement, for it was the supper hour, and all tools were being put aside, and trestles and tables shifted. Christian had no knowledge of what he said and did; he moved and spoke mechanically, half thinking that soon he must wake from this horrible dream. Sweyn and his mother supposed him to be cold and dead-tired, and spared all unnecessary questions. And he found himself seated beside the hearth, opposite that dreadful Thing that looked like a beautiful girl; watching her every movement, curdling with horror to see her fondle the child Rol.

Sweyn stood near them both, intent upon White Fell also; but how differently! She seemed unconscious of the gaze of both—neither aware of the chill dread in the eyes of Christian, nor of Sweyn's warm admiration.

These two brothers, who were twins, contrasted greatly, despite their striking likeness. They were alike in regular profile, fair brown hair, and deep blue eyes; but Sweyn's features were perfect as a young god's, while Christian's showed faulty details. Thus, the line of his mouth was set too straight, the eyes shelved too deeply back, and the contour of the face flowed in less generous curves than Sweyn's. Their height was the same, but Christian was too slender for perfect proportion, while Sweyn's well-knit frame, broad shoulders, and muscular arms made him pre-eminent for manly beauty as well as for strength. As a hunter Sweyn was without rival; as a fisher without rival. All the country side acknowledged him to be the best wrestler, rider, dancer, singer. Only in speed could he be surpassed, and in that only by his younger brother. All others

Sweyn could distance fairly; but Christian could outrun him easily. Ay, he could keep pace with Sweyn's most breathless burst, and laugh and talk the while. Christian took little pride in his fleetness of foot, counting a man's legs to be the least worthy of his limbs. He had no envy of his brother's athletic superiority, though to several feats he had made a moderate second. He loved as only a twin can love—proud of all that Sweyn did, content with all Sweyn was; humbly content also that his own great love should not be so exceedingly returned, since he knew himself to be so far less loveworthy.

Christian dared not, in the midst of women and children, launch the horror that he knew into words. He waited to consult his brother; but Sweyn did not, or would not, notice the signal he made, and kept his face always turned towards White Fell. Christian drew away from the hearth, unable to remain passive with that dread upon him.

"Where is Tyr?" he said suddenly. Then catching sight of the dog in a distant corner, "Why is he chained there?"

"He flew at the stranger," one answered.

Christian's eyes glowed. "Yes?" he said, interrogatively.

"He was within an ace of having his brain knocked out."

"Tyr?"

"Yes; she was nimbly up with that little axe she has at her waist. It was well for old Tyr that his master throttled him off."

Christian went without a word to the corner where Tyr was chained. The dog rose up to meet him, as piteous and indignant as a dumb beast can be. He stroked the black head. "Good Tyr! brave dog!"

They knew—they only—and the man and the dumb dog had comfort of each other.

Christian's eyes turned again towards White Fell. Tyr's also; and he strained against the length of the chain. Christian's hand lay on the dog's neck, and he felt it ridge and bristle with the quivering of impotent fury. Then he began to quiver in like manner, with a fury born of reason, not instinct; as impotent morally as was Tyr physically. Oh! the woman's form that he dare not touch! Anything but that, and he with Tyr would be free to kill or be killed.

Then he returned to ask fresh questions.

"How long has the stranger been here?"

"She came about half-an-hour before you."

"Who opened the door to her?"

"Sweyn. No one else dared."

The tone of the answer was mysterious.

"Why?" queried Christian. "Has anything strange happened? Tell me?"

For answer he was told in a low undertone of the summons at the door, thrice repeated, without human agency; and of Tyr's ominous howls; and of Sweyn's fruitless watch outside.

Christian turned towards his brother in a torment of impatience for a word apart. The board was spread and Sweyn was leading White Fell to the guest's place. This was more awful! She would break bread with them under the roof-tree.

He started forward, and touching Sweyn's arm, whispered an urgent entreaty. Sweyn stared, and shook his head in angry impatience.

Thereupon Christian would take no morsel of food.

His opportunity came at last. White Fell questioned the landmarks of the country, and of one Cairn Hill,[1] which was an appointed meeting place at which she was due that night. The house-mistress and Sweyn both exclaimed.

"It is three long miles away," said Sweyn; "with no place for shelter but a wretched hut. Stay with us this night and I will show you the way to-morrow."

White Fell seemed to hesitate. "Three miles," she said; "then I should be able to see or hear a signal."

"I will look out," said Sweyn; "then, if there be no signal, you must not leave us."

He went to the door. Christian rose silently, and followed him out.

"Sweyn, do you know what she is?"

Sweyn, surprised at the vehement grasp, and low hoarse voice, made answer:

"She? Who? White Fell?"

---

1 A hill used as a landmark for travelers, sometimes indicating that a site has a cache of provisions.

"Yes."

"She is the most beautiful girl I have ever seen."

"She is a Were-Wolf."

Sweyn burst out laughing. "Are you mad?" he asked.

"No; here, see for yourself."

Christian drew him out of the porch, pointing to the snow where the footmarks had been. Had been, for now they were not. Snow was falling fast, and every dint was blotted out.

"Well?" asked Sweyn.

"Had you come when I signed to you, you would have seen for yourself."

"Seen what?"

"The footprints of a wolf leading up to the door; none leading away."

It was impossible not to be startled by the tone alone, though it was hardly above a whisper. Sweyn eyed his brother anxiously, but in the darkness could make nothing of his face. Then he laid his hands kindly and reassuringly on Christian's shoulders and felt how he was quivering with excitement and horror.

"One sees strange things," he said, "when the cold has got into the brain behind the eyes; you came in cold and worn out."

"No," interrupted Christian. "I saw the track first on the brow of the slope, and followed it down right here to the door. This is no delusion."

Sweyn in his heart felt positive that it was. Christian was given to day-dreams and strange fancies, though never had he been possessed with so mad a notion before.

"Don't you believe me?" said Christian desperately. "You must. I swear it is sane truth. Are you blind? Why, even Tyr knows."

"You will be clearer headed to-morrow after a night's rest. Then come too, if you will, with White Fell, to the Hill Cairn, and if you have doubts still, watch and follow, and see what footprints she leaves."

Galled by Sweyn's evident contempt Christian turned abruptly to the door. Sweyn caught him back.

"What now, Christian? What are you going to do?"

"You do not believe me; my mother shall."

Sweyn's grasp tightened. "You shall not tell her," he said authoritatively.

Customarily Christian was so docile to his brother's mastery that it was now a surprising thing when he wrenched himself free vigorously, and said as determinedly as Sweyn, "She shall know;" but Sweyn was nearer the door and would not let him pass.

"There has been scare enough for one night already. If this notion of yours will keep, broach it to-morrow." Christian would not yield.

"Women are so easily scared," pursued Sweyn, "and are ready to believe any folly without shadow of proof. Be a man, Christian, and fight this notion of a Were-Wolf by yourself."

"If you would believe me," began Christian.

"I believe you to be a fool," said Sweyn, losing patience. "Another, who was not your brother, might believe you to be a knave, and guess that you had transformed White Fell into a Were-Wolf because she smiled more readily on me than on you."

The jest was not without foundation, for the grace of White Fell's bright looks had been bestowed on him—on Christian never a whit. Sweyn's coxcombery[1] was always frank, and most forgivable, and not without justifiableness.

"If you want an ally," continued Sweyn, "confide in old Trella. Out of her stores of wisdom—if her memory holds good—she can instruct you in the orthodox manner of tackling a Were-Wolf. If I remember aright, you should watch the suspected person till midnight, when the beast's form must be resumed, and retained ever after if a human eye sees the change; or better still, sprinkle hands and feet with holy water, which is certain death. Oh! never fear, but old Trella will be equal to the occasion."

Sweyn's contempt was no longer good humoured, for he began to feel excessively annoyed at this monstrous doubt of White Fell. But Christian was too deeply distressed to take offence.

"You speak of them as old wives' tales; but if you had seen the proof I have seen, you would be ready at least to wish them true, if not also to put them to the test."

"Well," said Sweyn with a laugh that had a little sneer in

---

1 Vanity.

it—"put them to the test—I will not object to that, if you will only keep your notions to yourself. Now, Christian, give me your word for silence, and we will freeze here no longer."

Christian remained silent.

Sweyn put his hands on his shoulders again and vainly tried to see his face in the darkness.

"We have never quarreled yet, Christian?"

"*I* have never quarreled," returned the other, aware for the first time that his dictatorial brother had sometimes offered occasion for quarrel, had he been ready to take it.

"Well," said Sweyn empathetically, "if you speak against White Fell to any other, as to-night you have spoken to me—*we shall.*"

He delivered the words like an ultimatum, turned sharp round, and re-entered the house. Christian, more fearful and wretched than before, followed.

"Snow is falling fast—not a single light is to be seen."

White Fell's eyes passed over Christian without apparent notice, and turned bright and shining upon Sweyn.

"Nor any signal to be heard?" she queried. "Did you not hear the sound of a sea-horn?"

"I saw nothing, and heard nothing, and signal or no signal, the heavy snow would keep you here perforce."

She smiled her thanks beautifully. And Christian's heart sank like lead with a deadly foreboding, as he noted what a light was kindled in Sweyn's eyes by her smile.

That night, when all others slept, Christian, the weariest of all, watched outside the guest chamber till midnight was past. No sound, not the faintest could be heard. Could the old tale be true of the midnight change? What was on the other side of the door—a woman or a beast—he would have given his right hand to know. Instinctively he laid his hand on the latch, and drew it softly, though believing that bolts fastened the inner side. The door yielded to his hand; he stood on the threshold; a keen gust of air cut at him; the window stood open; the room was empty.

So Christian could sleep with a somewhat lightened heart.

In the morning there was surprise and conjecture when White Fell's absence was discovered. Christian held his peace, not even to his brother did he say how he knew that she had fled before midnight; and Sweyn, though evidently greatly chagrined, seemed to disdain reference to the subject of Christian's fears.

The elder brother alone joined the bear hunt; Christian found pretext to stay behind. Sweyn, being out of humour, manifested his contempt by uttering not a single expostulation.

All that day, and for many a day after, Christian would never go out of sight of his home. Sweyn alone noticed how he manœuvered for this, and was clearly annoyed by it. White Fell's name was never mentioned between them, though not seldom was it heard in general talk. Hardly a day passed without little Rol asking when White Fell would come again; pretty White Fell, who kissed like a snowflake. And if Sweyn answered, Christian would be quite sure that the light in his eyes, kindled by White Fell's smile, had not yet died out.

Little Rol! Naughty, merry, fair-haired little Rol. A day came when his feet raced over the threshold never to return; when his chatter and laugh were heard no more; when tears of anguish were wept by eyes that never would see his bright head again—never again—living or dead.

He was seen at dusk for the last time, escaping from the house with his puppy, in freakish rebellion against old Trella. Later, when his absence had begun to cause anxiety, his puppy crept back to the farm, cowed, whimpering and yelping—a pitiful, dumb lump of terror—without intelligence or courage to guide the frightened search.

Rol was never found, nor any trace of him. Where he had perished was never known; how he had perished was known only by an awful guess—a wild beast had devoured him.

Christian heard the conjecture, "a wolf," and a horrible certainty flashed upon him that he knew what wolf it was. He tried to declare what he knew, but Sweyn saw him start at the words with white face and struggling lips, and, guessing his purpose, pulled him back and kept him silent, hardly, by his imperious grip and wrathful eyes, and one low whisper.

That Christian should retain his most irrational suspicion against beautiful White Fell was, to Sweyn, evidence of a weak obstinacy of mind that would but thrive upon expostulation and argument. But this evident intention to direct the passions of grief and anguish to a hatred and fear of the fair stranger, such as his own, was intolerable, and Sweyn set his will against it. Again Christian yielded to his brother's stronger words and will, and against his own judgment consented to silence.

Repentance came before the new moon—the first of the year—was old. White Fell came again, smiling as she entered as though assured of a glad and kindly welcome; and, in truth, there was only one who saw again her fair face and strange white garb without pleasure. Sweyn's face glowed with delight, while Christian's grew pale and rigid as death. He had given his word to keep silence; but he had not thought that she would dare to come again. Silence was impossible—face to face with that Thing—impossible. Irrepressibly he cried out—

"Where is Rol?"

Not a quiver disturbed White Fell's face; she heard yet remained bright and tranquil—Sweyn's eyes flashed round at his brother dangerously. Among the women some tears fell at the poor child's name, but none caught alarm from its sudden utterance, for the thought of Rol rose naturally. Where was Rol, who had nestled in the stranger's arms, kissing her; and watched for her since; and prattled of her daily?

Christian went out silently. One only thing there was that he could do, and he must not delay. His horror overmastered any curiosity to hear White Fell's glib excuses and smiling apologies for her strange and uncourteous departure; or her easy tale of the circumstances of her return; or to watch her bearing as she heard the sad tale of little Rol.

The swiftest runner of the country side had started on his hardest race. Little less than three leagues and back which he reckoned to accomplish in two hours, though the night was moonless and the way rugged. He rushed against the still cold air till it felt like a wind upon his face. The dim homestead sank below the ridges at his back, and fresh ridges of snowlands rose out of the obscure horizon level to drive past him as the stirless air drove, and sink away behind into obscure level again. He took no conscious heed of landmarks, not even when all sign of a path was gone under depths of snow. His will was set to reach his goal with unexampled speed, and thither by instinct his physical forces bore him, without one definite thought to guide.

And the idle brain lay passive, inert, receiving into its vacancy restless siftings of past sights and sounds: Rol, weeping, laughing, playing, coiled in the arms of that dreadful Thing; Tyr—oh, Tyr!—white fangs in the black jowl; the women who wept on the foolish puppy, precious for the child's last touch; footprints from pinewood to door; the smiling face among furs, of such womanly beauty—smiling—smiling; and Sweyn's face.

"Sweyn, Sweyn, oh Sweyn, my brother!"

Sweyn's angry laugh possessed his ear within the sound of the wind of his speed; Sweyn's scorn assailed more quick and keen than the biting cold at his throat. And yet he was unimpressed by any thought of how Sweyn's anger and scorn would rise if this errand were known.

Sweyn was a sceptic. His utter disbelief in Christian's testimony regarding the footprints was based upon positive scepticism. His reason refused to bend in accepting the possibility of the supernatural materialized. That a living beast could ever be other than palpably bestial—pawed, toothed, shagged, and eared as such, was to him incredible; far more that a human presence could be transformed from its godlike aspect, upright, free-handed, with brows, and speech, and laughter. The wild and fearful legends that he had known from childhood and then believed, he regarded now as built upon facts distorted, overlaid by imagination, and quickened by superstition. Even the strange summons at the threshold, that he himself had vainly answered, was, after the first shock of surprise, rationally explained by him as malicious foolery on the part of some clever trickster, who withheld the key to the enigma.

To the younger brother all life was a spiritual mystery, veiled from his clear knowledge by the density of flesh. Since he knew his own body to be linked to the complex and antagonistic forces that constitute one soul, it seemed to him not impossibly strange that one spiritual force should possess diverse forms for widely various manifestation. Nor, to him, was it great effort to believe that as pure water washes away all natural foulness, so, water holy by consecration must needs cleanse God's world from that supernatural evil Thing. Therefore, faster than ever man's foot had covered

those leagues, he sped under the dark still night, over the waste
trackless snow-ridges to the far-away church, where salvation lay
in the holy-water stoop at the door. His faith was as firm as any
that wrought miracles in days past, simple as a child's wish, strong
as a man's will.

He was hardly missed during these hours, every second of
which was by him fulfilled to its utmost extent by extremest
effort that sinews and nerves could attain. Within the homestead
the while[1] the easy moments went bright with words and looks
of unwonted animation, for the kindly hospitable instincts of the
inmates were roused into cordial expression of welcome and interest by the grace and beauty of the returned stranger.

But Sweyn was eager and earnest, with more than a host's
courteous warmth. The impression that at her first coming had
charmed him, that had lived since through memory, deepened now
in her actual presence. Sweyn, the matchless among men, acknowledged in this fair White Fell a spirit high and bold as his own, and
a frame so firm and capable that only bulk was lacking for equal
strength. Yet the white skin was moulded most smoothly, without
such muscular swelling as made his might evident. Such love as his
frank self-love could concede was called forth by an ardent admiration for this supreme stranger. More admiration than love was
in his passion, and therefore he was free from a lover's hesitancy,
and delicate reserve and doubts. Frankly and boldly he courted her
favour by looks and tones, and an address that was his by natural
ease, needless of skill by practice.

Nor was she a woman to be wooed otherwise. Tender whispers
and sighs would never gain her ear; but her eyes would brighten
and shine if she heard of a brave feat, and her prompt hand in sympathy fall swiftly on the axe-haft and clasp it hard. That movement
ever fired Sweyn's admiration anew; he watched for it, strove to
elicit it, and glowed when it came. Wonderful and beautiful was
that wrist, slender and steel-strong; also the smooth shapely hand,
that curved so fast and firm, ready to deal instant death.

Desiring to feel the pressure of these hands, this bold lover
schemed with palpable directness, proposing that she should hear
how their hunting songs were sung, with a chorus that signalled

---

1 Meanwhile.

hands to be clasped. So his splendid voice gave the verses, and, as the chorus was taken up, he claimed her hands, and, even through the easy grip, felt, as he desired, the strength that was latent, and the vigour that quickened the very finger tips, as the song fired her, and her voice was caught out of her by the rhythmic swell, and rang clear on the top of the closing surge.

Afterwards she sang alone. For contrast, or in the pride of swaying moods by her voice, she chose a mournful song that drifted along in a minor chant, sad as a wind that dirges:

> Oh, let me go!
> Around spin wreaths of snow;
> The dark earth sleeps below.
>
> Far up the plain
> Moans on a voice of pain:
> "Where shall my babe be lain?"
>
> In my white breast
> Lay the sweet life to rest!
> Lay, where it can be best!
>
> 'Hush! hush its cries!
> "Tense night is on the skies:
> Two stars are in thine eyes."
>
> Come, babe, away!
> But lie thou till dawn be grey,
> Who must be dead by day.
>
> This cannot last;
> But, e'er the sickening blast,
> All sorrow shall be past;
>
> And kings shall be
> Low bending at thy knee,
> Worshipping life from thee.
>
> For men long sore
> To hope of what's before,—
> To leave the things of yore.
>
> Mine, and not thine,
> How deep their jewels shine!
> Peace laps thy head, not mine!

Old Trella came tottering from her corner, shaken to additional palsy by an aroused memory. She strained her dim eyes towards the singer, and then bent her head that the one ear yet sensible to sound might avail of every note. At the close, groping forward, she murmured with the high pitched quaver of old age:

"So she sang, my Thora; my last and brightest. What is she like—she, whose voice is like my dead Thora's? Are her eyes blue?"

"Blue as the sky."

"So were my Thora's! Is her hair fair, and in plaits to the waist?"

"Even so," answered White Fell herself, and met the advancing hands with her own, and guided them to corroborate her words by touch.

"Like my dead Thora's," repeated the old woman; and then her trembling hands rested on the fur-clad shoulders, and she bent forward and kissed the smooth fair face that White Fell upturned, nothing loath, to receive and return the caress.

So Christian saw them as he entered.

He stood a moment. After the starless darkness and the icy night air, and the fierce silent two hours' race, his senses reeled on sudden entrance into warmth, and light, and the cheery hum of voices. A sudden unforeseen anguish assailed him, as now first he entertained the possibility of being overmatched by her wiles and her daring, if at the approach of pure death she should start up at bay transformed to a terrible beast, and achieve a savage glut at the last. He looked with horror and pity on the harmless helpless folk, so unwitting of outrage to their comfort and security. The dreadful Thing in their midst, that was veiled from their knowledge by womanly beauty, was a centre of pleasant interest. There, before him, signally impressive, was poor old Trella, weakest and feeblest of all, in fond nearness. And a moment might bring about the revelation of a monstrous horror—a ghastly, deadly danger, set loose and at bay, in a circle of girls and women and careless, defenceless men—so hideous and terrible a thing as might crack the brain, or curdle the heart stone dead.

And he alone of the throng prepared!

For one breathing space he faltered, no longer than that, while over him swept the agony of compunction that yet could not make him surrender his purpose.

He alone? Nay, but Tyr also; and he crossed to the dumb sole sharer of his knowledge.

So timeless is thought that a few seconds only lay between his lifting of the latch and his loosening of Tyr's collar; but in those few seconds succeeding his first glance, as lightning-swift had been the impulses of others, their motion as quick and sure. Sweyn's vigilant eye had darted upon him, and instantly his every fibre was alert with hostile instinct; and, half divining, half incredulous, of Christian's object in stooping to Tyr, he came hastily, wary, wrathful, resolute to oppose the malice of his wild-eyed brother.

But beyond Sweyn rose White Fell, blanching white as her furs, and with eyes grown fierce and wild. She leapt down the room to the door, whirling her long robe closely to her. "Hark!" she panted. "The signal horn! Hark, I must go!" as she snatched at the latch to be out and away.

For one precious moment Christian had hesitated on the half loosened collar; for, except the womanly form were exchanged for the bestial, Tyr's jaws would gnash to rags his honour of manhood. Then he heard her voice, and turned—too late.

As she tugged at the door, he sprang across grasping his flask, but Sweyn dashed between, and caught him back irresistibly, so that a most frantic effort only availed to wrench one arm free. With that, on the impulse of sheer despair, he cast at her with all his force. The door swung behind her, and the flask flew into fragments against it. Then, as Sweyn's grasp slackened, and he met the questioning astonishment of surrounding faces, with a hoarse inarticulate cry: "God help us all!" he said. "She is a Were-Wolf."

Sweyn turned upon him, "Liar, coward!" and his hands gripped his brother's throat with deadly force, as though the spoken word could be killed so; and as Christian struggled, lifted him clear off his feet and flung him crashing backward. So furious was he, that, as his brother lay motionless, he stirred him roughly with his foot, till their mother came between crying shame; and yet then he stood by, his teeth set, his brows knit, his hands clenched, ready to enforce silence again violently, as Christian rose staggering and bewildered.

But utter silence and submission was more than he expected, and turned his anger into contempt for one so easily cowed and held in subjection by mere force. "He is mad!" he said, turning on his heel as he spoke, so that he lost his mother's look of pained reproach at this sudden free utterance of what was a lurking dread within her.

Christian was too spent for the effort of speech. His hard-drawn breath laboured in great sobs; his limbs were powerless and unstrung in utter relax after hard service. His failure in this endeavour induced a stupor of misery and despair. In addition was the wretched humiliation of open violence and strife with his brother, and the distress of hearing misjudging contempt expressed without reserve; for he was aware that Sweyn had turned to allay the scared excitement half by imperious mastery, half by explanation and argument, that showed painful disregard of brotherly consideration. All this unkindness of his twin he charged upon the Fell Thing who had wrought this their first dissention, and, ah! most terrible thought, interposed between them so effectually, that Sweyn was wilfully blind and deaf on her account, restful of interference, arbitrary beyond reason.

Dread and perplexity unfathomable darkened upon him; unshared the burden was overwhelming: a foreboding of unspeakable calamity, based upon his ghastly discovery, bore down upon him, crushing out hope of power to withstand impending fate.

Sweyn the while was observant of his brother, despite the continual check of finding, turn and glance when he would, Christian's eyes always upon him, with a strange look of helpless distress, discomposing enough to the angry aggressor. "Like a beaten dog!" he said to himself, rallying contempt to withstand compunction. Observation set him wondering on Christian's exhausted condition. The heavy labouring breath and the slack inert fall of the limbs told surely of unusual and prolonged exertion. And then why had close upon two hours' absence been followed by manifestly hostile behaviour towards White Fell? Suddenly, the fragments of the flask giving a clue, he guessed all, and faced about to stare at his brother in amaze. He forgot that the motive scheme was against White Fell, demanding derision and resentment from him; that was swept out of remembrance by astonishment and admiration for the feat of speed and endurance. In eagerness to question he inclined to attempt a generous part and frankly offer to heal the breach; but Christian's depression and sad following gaze provoked him to self-justification by recalling the offence of that outrageous utterance against White Fell; and the impulse passed. Then other considerations counselled silence; and afterwards a humour possessed him to wait and see how Christian would find opportunity to proclaim his performance and establish the fact, without exciting ridicule on account of the absurdity of the errand.

This expectation remained unfulfilled. Christian never attempted the proud avowal that would have placed his feat on record to be told to the next generation.

That night Sweyn and his mother talked long and late together, shaping into certainty the suspicion that Christian's mind had lost its balance, and discussing the evident cause. For Sweyn, declaring his own love for White Fell, suggested that his unfortunate brother with a like passion—they being twins in loves as in birth—had through jealousy and despair turned from love to hate, until reason failed at the strain, and a craze developed, which the malice and treachery of madness made a serious and dangerous force.

So Sweyn theorized; convincing himself as he spoke; convincing afterwards others who advanced doubts against White Fell; fettering his judgment by his advocacy, and by his staunch defence of her hurried flight, silencing his own inner consciousness of the unaccountability of her action.

But a little time and Sweyn lost his vantage in the shock of a fresh horror at the homestead. Trella was no more, and her end a mystery. The poor old woman crawled out in a bright gleam to visit a bed-ridden gossip living beyond the fir grove. Under the trees she was last seen, halting for her companion, sent back for a forgotten present. Quick alarm sprang, calling every man to the search. Her stick was found among the brushwood only a few paces from the path, but no track or stain, for a gusty wind was sifting the snow from the branches and hid all sign of how she came by her death.

So panic-stricken were the farm folk that none dared go singly on the search. Known danger could be braced, but not this stealthy

Death that walked by day invisible, that cut off alike the child in his play, and the aged woman so near to her quiet grave.

"Rol she kissed; Trella she kissed!" So rang Christian's frantic cry again and again, till Sweyn dragged him away and strove to keep him apart, albeit in his agony of grief and remorse he accused himself wildly as answerable for the tragedy, and gave clear proof that the charge of the madness was well founded, if strange looks and desperate, incoherent words were evidence enough.

But thenceforward all Sweyn's reasoning and mastery could not uphold White Fell above suspicion. He was not called upon to defend her from accusation, when Christian had been brought to silence again; but he well knew the significance of this fact, that her name, formerly uttered freely and often, he never heard now— it was huddled away into whispers that he could not catch.

The passing of time did not sweep away the superstitious fears that Sweyn despised. He was angry and anxious; eager that White Fell should return, and, merely by her bright gracious presence, reinstate herself in favour; but doubtful if all his authority and example could keep from her notice an altered aspect of welcome; and he foresaw clearly that Christian would prove unmanageable, and might be capable of some dangerous outbreak.

For a time the twins' variance was marked, on Sweyn's part by an air of rigid indifference, on Christian's by heavy downcast silence, and a nervous apprehensive observation of his brother. Superadded to his remorse and foreboding, Sweyn's displeasure weighed upon him intolerably, and the remembrance of their violent rupture was a ceaseless misery. The elder brother, self-sufficient and insensitive, could little know how deeply his unkindness stabbed. A depth and force of affection such as Christian's was unknown to him. The loyal subservience that he could not appreciate, had encouraged him to domineer; this strenuous opposition to his reason and will was accounted as furious malice, if not sheer insanity.

Christian's ceaseless surveillance annoyed him greatly. He anticipated embarrassment and danger as the outcome. Therefore, that suspicion might be lulled, he judged it wise to make overtures for peace. Most easily done. A little kindliness, a few evidences of consideration, a slight return of the old brotherly imperiousness, and Christian replied by a gratefulness and relief that might have touched him had he understood all, but instead increased his secret contempt.

So successful was this finesse, that when, late on a day, a message summoning Christian to a distance was transmitted by Sweyn, no doubt of its genuineness occurred. When, his errand proved useless, he set out to return, mistake or misapprehension was all that he surmised. Not till he sighted the homestead, lying low between the night-grey snow ridges, did vivid recollection of the time when he had tracked that horror to the door rouse an intense dread, and with it a hardly defined suspicion.

His grasp tightened on the bear-spear that he carried as a staff; every sense was alert, every muscle strung; excitement urged him on, caution checked him, and the two governed his long stride, swiftly, noiselessly, to the climax he felt was at hand.

As he drew near to the outer gates, a light shadow stirred and went, as though the grey of the snow had taken detached motion. A darker shadow stayed and faced Christian, striking his life-blood chill with utmost despair.

Sweyn stood before him, and surely, the shadow that had went was White Fell.

They had been together—close. Had she not been in his arms, near enough for lips to meet?

There was no moon, but the stars gave light enough to show that Sweyn's face was flushed and elate. The flush remained, though the expression changed quickly at sight of his brother. How, if Christian had seen all, should one of his frenzied outbursts be met and managed—by resolution? by indifference? He halted between the two, and as a result, he swaggered.

"White Fell?" questioned Christian, hoarse and breathless.

"Yes?" Sweyn's answer was a query, with an intonation that implied he was clearing the ground for action.

From Christian came: "Have you kissed her?" like a bolt direct, staggering Sweyn by its sheer, prompt temerity.

He flushed yet darker, and yet half smiled over this earnest of success he had won. Had there been really between himself and Christian the rivalry that he imagined, his face had enough of the insolence of triumph to exasperate jealous rage.

"You dare ask this!"

"Sweyn, oh, Sweyn, I must know! You have!"

The ring of despair and anguish in his tone angered Sweyn, misconstruing it. Jealousy urging to such presumption was intolerable.

"Mad fool!" he said, constraining himself no longer. "Win for yourself a woman to kiss. Leave mine without question. Such an one as I should desire to kiss is such an one as shall never allow a kiss to you."

Then Christian fully understood his supposition.

"I—I!" he cried. "White Fell—that deadly Thing! Sweyn, are you blind, mad? I would save you from her—a Were-Wolf!"

Sweyn maddened again at the accusation—a dastardly way of revenge, as he conceived; and instantly, for the second time, the brothers were at strife violently.

But Christian was now too desperate to be scrupulous; for a dim glimpse had shot a possibility into his mind, and to be free to follow it the striking of his brother was a necessity. Thank God! he was armed, and so Sweyn's equal.

Facing his assailant with the bear-spear, he struck up his arms, and with the butt end hit hard so that he fell. Then the matchless runner leapt away on the instant, to follow a forlorn hope.

Sweyn, on regaining his feet, was as amazed as angry at this unaccountable flight. He knew in his heart that his brother was no coward, and that it was unlike him to shrink from an encounter because defeat was certain, and cruel humiliation from a vindictive victor probable. Of the uselessness of pursuit he was well aware: he must abide his chagrin, content to know that his time for advantage would come. Since White Fell had parted to the right, Christian to the left, the event of a sequent encounter did not occur to him.

And now Christian, acting on the dim glimpse he had had, just as Sweyn turned upon him, of something that moved against the sky along the ridge behind the homestead, was staking his only hope on a chance, and his own superlative speed. If what he saw was really White Fell, he guessed that she was bending her steps towards the open wastes; and there was just a possibility that, by a straight dash, and a desperate perilous leap over a sheer bluff, he might yet meet or head her. And then—he had no further thought.

It was past, the quick, fierce race, and the chance of death at the leap, and he halted in a hollow to fetch his breath and to look— did she come? Had she gone?

She came.

She came with a smooth, gliding, noiseless speed, that was neither walking nor running; her arms were folded in her furs that were drawn tight about her body; the white lappets from her head were wrapped and knotted closely beneath her face; her eyes were set on a far distance. So she went till the even sway of her going was startled to a pause by Christian.

"Fell!"

She drew a quick, sharp breath at the sound of her name thus mutilated, and faced Sweyn's brother. Her eyes glittered; her upper lip was lifted, and shewed the teeth. The half of her name, impressed with an ominous sense as uttered by him, warned her of the aspect of a deadly foe. Yet she cast loose her robes till they trailed ample, and spoke as a mild woman.

"What would you?"

Then Christian answered with his solemn dreadful accusation:

"You kissed Rol—and Rol is dead! You kissed Trella—she is dead! You have kissed Sweyn, my brother, but he shall not die!"

He added: "You may live till midnight."

The edge of the teeth and the glitter of the eyes stayed a moment, and her right hand also slid down to the axe haft. Then, without a word, she swerved from him, and sprang out and away swiftly over the snow.

And Christian sprang out and away, and followed her swiftly over the snow, keeping behind, but half-a-stride's length from her side.

So they went running together, silent, towards the vast wastes of snow, where no living thing but they two moved under the stars of night.

Never before had Christian so rejoiced in his powers. The gift of speed, and the training of use and endurance were priceless to him now. Though midnight was hours away he was confident that go where that Fell Thing would, hasten as she would, she could not outstrip him, nor escape from him. Then, when came the time for transformation, when the woman's form made no longer a shield against a man's hand, he could slay or be slain to save Sweyn. He had struck his dear brother in dire extremity, but he could not, though reason urged, strike a woman.

For one mile, for two miles they ran: White Fell ever foremost, Christian ever at an equal distance from her side, so near that, now and again, her out-flying furs touched him. She spoke no word; nor he. She never turned her head to look at him, nor swerved to evade him; but, with set face looking forward, sped straight on, over rough, over smooth, aware of his nearness by the regular beat of his feet, and the sound of his breath behind.

In a while she quickened her pace. From the first Christian had judged of her speed as admirable, yet with exulting security in his own excelling and enduring whatever her efforts. But, when the pace increased, he found himself put to the test as never had been done before in any race. Her feet indeed flew faster than his; it was only by his length of stride that he kept his place at her side. But his heart was high and resolute, and he did not fear failure yet.

So the desperate race flew on. Their feet struck up the powdery snow, their breath smoked into the sharp clear air, and they were gone before the air was cleared of snow and vapour. Now and then Christian glanced up to judge, by the rising of the stars, of the coming of midnight. So long—so long!

White Fell held on without slack. She, it was evident, with confidence in her speed proving matchless, as resolute to outrun her pursuer, as he to endure till midnight and fulfil his purpose. And Christian held on, still self-assured. He could not fail; he would not fail. To avenge Rol and Trella was motive enough for him to do what man could do; but for Sweyn more. She had kissed Sweyn, but he should not die too—with Sweyn to save he could not fail.

Never before was such a race as this; no, not when in old Greece man and maid raced together with two fates at stake,[1] for the hard running was sustained unabated, while star after star rose

---

[1] In Ovid's *Metamorphoses* (8 A.D.), Hippomenes races Atalanta. If he loses the race he will be put to death; if he wins, Atalanta must marry him. After receiving help from Venus, Hippomenes wins the race and Atalanta becomes his wife. Unwisely, Hippomenes forgets to thank Venus and so both he and Atalanta are transformed into lions.

and went wheeling up towards midnight—for one hour, for two hours.

Then Christian saw and heard what shot him through with fear. Where a fringe of trees hung round a slope he saw something dark moving, and heard a yelp, followed by a full horrid cry, and the dark spread out upon the snow—a pack of wolves in pursuit.

Of the beasts alone he had little cause for fear; at the pace he held he could distance them, four-footed though they were. But of White Fell's wiles he had infinite apprehension, for how might she not avail herself of the savage jaws of these wolves, akin as they were to half her nature. She vouchsafed to them nor look nor sign; but Christian, on an impulse, to assure himself that she should not escape him, caught and held the back-flung edge of her furs, running still.

She turned like a flash with a beastly snarl, teeth and eyes gleaming again. Her axe shone, on the upstroke, on the downstroke, as she hacked at his hand. She had lopped it off at the wrist, but that he parried with the bear-spear. Even then she shore through the shaft and shattered the bones of the hand at the same blow, so that he loosed perforce.

Then again they raced on as before, Christian not losing a pace, though his left hand swung useless, bleeding and broken.

The snarl, indubitable, though modified from a woman's organs; the vicious fury revealed in teeth and eyes; the sharp arrogant pain of her maiming blow, caught away Christian's heed of the beasts behind, by striking into him close vivid realization of the infinitely greater danger that ran before him in that deadly Thing.

When he bethought to look behind, lo! the pack had but reached their tracks, and instantly slunk aside, cowed; the yell of pursuit changing to yelps and whines. So abhorrent was that fell creature to beast as to man.

She had drawn her furs more closely to her, disposing them so, that instead of flying loose to her heels, no drapery hung lower than her knees, and this without a check to her wonderful speed, nor embarrassment by the cumbering[1] of the folds. She held her

---

1 Encumberment.

head as before; her lips were firmly set, only the tense nostrils gave her breath; not a sign of distress witnessed to the long sustaining of that terrible speed.

But on Christian by now the strain was telling palpably. His head weighed heavy, and his breath came labouring in great sobs; the bear-spear would have been a burden now. His heart was beating like a hammer, but such a dulness oppressed his brain, that it was only by degrees he could realize his helpless state; wounded and weaponless, chasing that Thing, that was a fierce, desperate, axe-armed woman, except she should assume the beast with fangs yet more formidable.

And still the far slow stars went lingering nearly an hour from midnight.

So far was his brain astray, that an impression took him that she was fleeing from the midnight stars, whose gain was by such slow degrees, that a time equalling days and days had gone in the race round the northern circle of the world, and days and days as long as might last before the end—except she slackened, or except he failed.

But he would not fail yet.

How long had he been praying so? He had started with a self-confidence and reliance that had felt no need for that aid; and now it seemed the only means by which to restrain his heart from swelling beyond the compass of his body; by which to cherish his brain from dwindling and shrivelling quite away. Some sharp-toothed creature kept tearing and dragging on his maimed left hand; he never could see it, he could not shake it off, but he prayed it off at times.

The clear stars before him took to shuddering and he knew why: they shuddered at sight of what was behind him. He had never divined before that strange Things hid themselves from men, under pretence of being snow-clad mounds or swaying trees; but now they came slipping out from their harmless covers to follow him, and mock at his impotence to make a kindred Thing resolve to truer form. He knew the air behind him was thronged; he heard the hum of innumerable murmurings together; but his eyes could never catch them—they were too swift and nimble; but he knew they were there, because, on a backward glance, he saw the snow mounds surge as they grovelled flatlings out of sight; he saw the trees reel as they screwed themselves rigid past recognition among the boughs.

And after such glance the stars for awhile returned to steadfastness, and an infinite stretch of silence froze upon the chill grey world, only deranged by the swift even beat of the flying feet, and his own—slower from the longer stride, and the sound of his breath. And for some clear moments he knew that his only concern was, to sustain his speed regardless of pain and distress, to deny with every nerve he had her power to outstrip him or to widen the space between them, till the stars crept up to midnight. Then out again would come that crowd invisible, humming and hustling behind, dense and dark enough, he knew, to blot out the stars at his back, yet ever skipping and jerking from his sight.

A hideous check came to the race. White Fell swirled about and leapt to the right, and Christian, unprepared for so prompt a lurch, found close at his feet a deep pit yawning, and his own impetus past control. But he snatched at her as he bore past, clasping her right arm with his one whole hand, and the two swung together upon the brink.

And her straining away in self preservation was vigorous enough to counterbalance his headlong impulse, and brought them reeling together to safety.

Then, before he was verily sure that they were not to perish so, crashing down, he saw her gnashing in wild pale fury, as she wrenched to be free; and since her right arm was in his grasp, used her axe left-handed, striking back at him.

The blow was effectual enough even so; his right arm dropped powerless, gashed and with the lesser bone broken that jarred with horrid pain when he let it swing, as he leaped out again, and ran to recover the few feet she had gained at his pause at the shock.

The near escape and this new quick pain made again every faculty alive and intense. He knew that what he followed was most surely Death animate: wounded and helpless, he was utterly at her mercy if so she should realize and take action. Hopeless to avenge, hopeless to save, his very despair for Sweyn swept him on to follow and follow and precede the kiss-doomed to death. Could he yet fail to hunt that Thing past midnight, out of the womanly form,

Everard Hopkins, illustration for *The Were-wolf*, by Clemence Housman,
Atalanta 4 (December 1890): 151.

alluring and treacherous, into lasting restraint of the bestial, which was the last shred of hope left from the confident purpose of the outset?

"Sweyn—Sweyn—oh, Sweyn!" He thought he was praying, though his heart wrung out nothing but this: "Sweyn—Sweyn—oh, Sweyn!"

The last hour from midnight had lost half its quarters, and the stars went lifting up the great minutes, and again his greatening heart, and his shrinking brain, and the sickening agony that swung at either side, conspired to appal the will that had only seeming empire over his feet.

Now White Fell's body was so closely enveloped that not a lap nor an edge flew free. She stretched forward strangely aslant, leaning from the upright poise of a runner. She cleared the ground at times by long bounds, gaining an increase of speed that Christian agonized to equal.

Because the stars pointed that the end was nearing, the black brood came behind again, and followed noising. Ah! if they could but be kept quiet and still, nor slip their usual harmless masks to encourage with their interest the last speed of the most deadly congener.[1] What shape had they? Should he ever know? If it were not that he was bound to compel the Fell Thing that ran before him into her truer form, he might face about and follow them. No—no—not so; if he might do anything but what he did—race, race, and racing bear this agony—he would just stand still and die, to be quit of the pain of breathing.

He grew bewildered, uncertain of his own identity, doubting of his own true form. He could not really be a man, no more than that running Thing was really a woman; his real form was only hidden under embodiment of a man, but what he was he did not know. And Sweyn's real form he did not know. Sweyn lay fallen at his feet, where he had struck him down—his own brother—he: he had stumbled over him and had to overleap him and race harder because she who had kissed Sweyn leapt so fast. "Sweyn—Sweyn—oh, Sweyn!"

Why did the stars stop to shudder? Midnight else had surely come!

---

1 Member of the pack.

The leaning, leaping Thing looked back at him a wild, fierce look, and laughed in a savage scorn and triumph. He saw in a flash why, for within a time measurable by seconds she would have escaped him utterly. As the land lay, a slope of ice sunk on the one hand; on the other hand a steep rose, shouldering forwards; between the two was space for a foot to be planted, but none for a body to stand; yet a juniper bough, thrusting out, gave a handhold secure enough for one with a resolute grasp to swing past the perilous place, and pass on safe.

Though the first seconds of the last moment were going, she dared to flash back a wicked look, and laugh at the pursuer who was impotent to grasp.

The crisis struck convulsive life into his last supreme effort; his will surged up indomitable, his speed proved matchless yet. He leapt with a rush, passed her before her laugh had time to go out, and turned short, barring the way, and braced to withstand her.

She came hurling desperate, with a feint to the right hand, and then launched herself upon him with a spring like a wild beast when it leaps to kill. And he, with one strong arm and a hand that could not hold, with one strong hand and an arm that could not guide and sustain, he caught and held her even so. And they fell together. And because he felt his whole arm slipping and his whole hand loosing, to slack the dreadful agony of the wrenched bone above, he caught and held with his teeth the tunic at her knee, as she struggled up and wrung off his hands to overleap him victorious.

Like lightning she snatched her axe, and struck him on the neck—deep—once—twice—his life-blood gushed out staining her feet.

The stars touched midnight.

The death scream he heard was not his, for his set teeth had hardly yet relaxed when it rang out. And the dreadful cry began with a woman's shriek, and changed and ended as the yell of a beast. And before the final blank overtook his dying eyes, he saw the She gave place to It; he saw more, that Life gave place to Death—causelessly—incomprehensibly.

For he did not dream that no holy-water could be more holy,

more potent to destroy an evil thing than the life-blood of a pure heart poured out for another in free willing devotion.

His own true hidden reality that he had desired to know grew palpable, recognisable. It seemed to him just this: a great glad abounding hope that he had saved his brother; too expansive to be contained by the limited form of a sole man, it yearned for a new embodiment infinite as the stars.

What did it matter to that true reality that the man's brain shrank, shrank, till it was nothing; that the man's body could not retain the huge pain of his heart, and heaved it out through the red exit riven at the neck; that the black noise came again hurtling from behind, reinforced by that dissolved shape, and blotted out for ever the man's sight, hearing, sense?

In the early grey of day Sweyn chanced upon the footprints of a man—of a runner, as he saw by the shifted snow; and the direction they had taken aroused curiosity, since a little further their line must be crossed by the edge of a sheer height. He turned to trace them. And so doing, the length of the stride struck his attention—a stride long as his own if he ran. He knew he was following Christian.

In his anger he had hardened himself to be indifferent to the night-long absence of his brother; but now, seeing where the footsteps went, he was seized with compunction and dread. He had failed to give thought and care to his poor frantic twin, who might—was it possible?—have rushed to a frantic death.

His heart stood still when he came to the place where the leap had been taken. A piled edge of snow had fallen too, and nothing but snow lay below when he peered. Along the upper edge he ran for a furlong,[1] till he came to a dip where he could slip and climb down, and then back again on the lower level to the pile of fallen snow. There he saw that the vigorous running had started afresh.

He stood pondering; vexed that any man should have taken that leap where he had not ventured to follow; vexed that he had been

---

1 220 yards.

beguiled to such painful emotions; guessing vainly at Christian's object in this mad freak. He began sauntering along, half-unconsciously following his brother's track; and so in a while he came to the place where the footprints were doubled.

Small prints were these others, small as a woman's, though the pace from one to another was longer than that which the skirts of women allow.

Did not White Fell tread so?

A dreadful guess appalled him—so dreadful that he recoiled from belief. Yet his face grew ashy white, and he gasped to fetch back motion to his checked heart. Unbelievable? Closer attention showed how the smaller footfall had altered for greater speed, striking into the snow with a deeper onset and a lighter pressure on the heels. Unbelievable? Could any woman but White Fell run so? Could any man but Christian run so? The guess became a certainty. He was following where alone in the dark night White Fell had fled from Christian pursuing.

Such villainy set heart and brain on fire with rage and indignation—such villainy in his own brother, till lately love-worthy, praiseworthy, though a fool for meekness. He would kill Christian; had he lives as many as the footprints he had trodden, vengeance should demand them all. In a tempest of murderous hate he followed on in haste, for the track was plain enough, starting with such a burst of speed as could not be maintained, but brought him back soon to a plod for the spent, sobbing breath to be regulated. He cursed Christian aloud and called White Fell's name on high in a frenzied expense of passion. His grief itself was a rage, being such an intolerable anguish of pity and shame at the thought of his love, White Fell, who had parted from his kiss free and radiant, to be hounded straightway by his brother, mad with jealousy, fleeing for more than life while her lover was housed at his ease. If he had but known, he raved, in impotent rebellion at the cruelty of events, if he had but known that his strength and love might have availed in her defence; now the only service to her that he could render was to kill Christian.

As a woman he knew she was matchless in speed, matchless in strength; but Christian was matchless in speed among men, nor easily to be matched in strength. Brave and swift and strong though she were, what chance had she against a man of his strength and inches, frantic too, and intent on horrid revenge against his brother, his successful rival?

Mile after mile he travelled with a bursting heart; more piteous, more tragic, seemed the case at this evidence of White Fell's splendid supremacy, holding her own so long against Christian's famous speed. So long, so long that his love and admiration grew more and more boundless, and his grief and indignation therewith also. Whenever the track lay clear he ran, with such reckless prodigality[1] of strength, that it was soon spent, and he dragged on heavily, till, sometimes on the ice of a mere,[2] sometimes on a windswept place, all signs were lost; but, so undeviating had been their line that a course straight on, and then a short questing to either hand, recovered them again.

Hour after hour had gone by through more than half that winter day, before ever he came to the place where the trampled snow showed that a scurry of feet had come—and gone! Wolves' feet—and gone most amazingly! Only a little beyond he came to the lopped point of Christian's bear-spear—further on he would see where the remnant of the useless shaft had been dropped. The snow here was dashed with blood, and the footsteps of the two had fallen closer together. Some hoarse sound of exultation came from him that might have been a laugh had breath sufficed. "Oh, White Fell, my poor brave love! Well struck!" he groaned, torn by his pity and great admiration, as he guessed surely how she had turned and dealt a blow.

The sight of the blood inflamed him as it might a beast that ravens. He grew mad with a desire to once again have Christian by the throat, not to loose this time till he had crushed out his life—or beat out his life—or stabbed out his life—or all these, and torn him piecemeal likewise—and ah! then, not till then, bleed his heart with weeping, like a child, like a girl, over the piteous fate of his poor lost love.

On—on—on—through the aching time, toiling and straining in the track of those two superb runners, aware of the marvel of

1 Waste.
2 Pond.

their endurance, but unaware of the marvel of their speed, that, in the three hours before midnight had overpassed all that vast distance that he could only traverse from twilight to twilight. For clear daylight was passing when he came to the edge of an old marlpit,[1] and saw how the two who had gone before had stamped and trampled together in desperate peril on the verge. And here fresh blood stains spoke to him of a valiant defence against his infamous brother; and he followed where the blood had dripped till the cold had staunched its flow, taking a savage gratification from this evidence that Christian had been gashed deeply, maddening afresh with desire to do likewise more excellently and so slake his murderous hate. And he began to know that through all his despair he had entertained a germ of hope, that grew apace, rained upon by his brother's blood.

He strove on as best he might, wrung now by an access of hope—now of despair, in agony to reach the end, however terrible, sick with the aching of the toiled miles that deferred it.

And the light went lingering out of the sky, giving place to uncertain stars.

He came to the finish.

Two bodies lay in a narrow place. Christian's was one, but the other beyond not White Fell's. There where the footsteps ended lay a great white wolf.

At the sight Sweyn's strength was blasted; body and soul he was struck down grovelling.

The stars had grown sure and intense before he stirred from where he had dropped prone. Very feebly he crawled to his dead brother, and laid his hands upon him, and crouched so, afraid to look or stir further.

Cold—stiff—hours dead. Yet the dead body was his only shelter and stay in that most dreadful hour. His soul, stripped bare of all sceptic comfort, cowered, shivering, naked, abject, and the living clung to the dead out of piteous need for grace from the soul that had passed away.

He rose to his knees, lifting the body. Christian had fallen face forward in the snow, with his arms flung up and wide, and so had

---

1 Clay pit.

Everard Hopkins, illustration for *The Were-wolf*, by Clemence Housman,
Atalanta 4 (December 1890): 155.

the frost made him rigid: strange, ghastly, unyielding to Sweyn lifting, so that he laid him down again and crouched above, with his arms fast round him and a low heart-wrung groan.

When at last he found force to raise his brother's body and gather it in his arms, tight clasped to his breast, he tried to face the Thing that lay beyond. The sight set his limbs in a palsy with horror and dread. His senses had failed and fainted in utter cowardice, but for the strength that came from holding dead Christian in his arms, enabling him to compel his eyes to endure the sight, and take into the brain the complete aspect of the Thing. No wound—only blood stains on the feet. The great grim jaws had a savage grin, though dead-stiff. And his kiss—he could bear it no longer, and turned away, nor ever looked again.

And the dead man in his arms, knowing the full horror, had followed and faced it for his sake; had suffered agony and death for his sake; in the neck was the deep death gash, one arm and both hands were dark with frozen blood, for his sake! Dead he knew him—as in life he had not known him—to give the right meed[1] of love and worship. Because the outward man lacked perfection and strength equal to his, he had taken the love and worship of that great pure heart as his due; he, so unworthy in the inner reality, so mean, so despicable, callous and contemptuous towards the brother who had laid down life to save him. He longed for utter annihilation, that so he might lose the agony of knowing himself so unworthy of such perfect love. The frozen calm of death on the face appalled him. He dared not touch it with lips that had cursed so lately; with lips fouled by kiss of the Horror that had been Death.

He struggled to his feet, still clasping Christian. The dead man stood upright within his arm, frozen rigid. The eyes were not quite closed; the head had stiffened, bowed slightly to one side; the arms stayed straight and wide. It was the figure of one crucified, the bloodstained hands also conforming.

So living and dead went back along the track, that one had passed in the deepest passion of love, and one in the deepest passion of hate. All that night Sweyn toiled through the snow, bearing the weight of dead Christian, treading back along the

---

1 Reward.

steps he before had trodden when he was wronging with vilest thoughts, and cursing with murderous hate, the brother who all the while lay dead for his sake.

Everard Hopkins, illustration for *The Were-wolf*, by Clemence Housman, *Atalanta* 4 (December 1890): 154.

Cold, silence, darkness encompassed the strong man bowed with the dolorous[1] burden; and yet he knew surely that that night he entered hell, and trod hell-fire along the homeward road, and endured through it only because Christian was with him. And he knew surely that to him Christian had been as Christ, and had suffered and died to save him from his sins.

---

1 Sorrowful.

Dracula's Guest

BRAM STOKER

Abraham "Bram" Stoker (1847-1912) was born in Dublin, the third of seven children in a middle-class Protestant family. His father, Abraham Stoker, was a civil servant, and his mother, Charlotte Stoker, was a social activist. He was bedridden as a child but later went on to enroll at Trinity College, Dublin, where he studied mathematics and was known for his skills as a debater and athlete. After graduating from Trinity in 1870, he followed his father into civil service, working as a clerk at Dublin Castle. The next year, Stoker began working in his spare time as an unpaid theater critic for the Daily Mail, *a position which brought him into contact with a number of writers and actors, including Henry Irving. His glowing reviews of Irving's performances planted a seed of friendship between the two men, and in 1878, Stoker became Irving's business manager, a position he held for twenty-seven years. In the same year, Stoker married Florence Balcombe, and the two welcomed a son, Noel, in 1879.*

Assuming the position as Irving's business manager required that Stoker move from his native Dublin to London, where he was responsible for running Irving's Lyceum Theatre. During the next few years, the two men, along with partner Ellen Terry, developed the theater into one of the most popular and esteemed West End venues. Stoker oversaw a number of international tours as well as the daily operations of the theater. The Lyceum came to be seen primarily as a vehicle for Irving's and Terry's work, especially their acclaimed performances of Shakespeare. In part due to Stoker's devoted management, Irving achieved the pinnacle of fame when he received the knighthood in 1895.

In 1872, Stoker published his first work of short fiction, "The Crystal Cup," in London Society *magazine, and in the 1880s and '90s, he published a number of books, including a collection of fairy tales titled* Under the Sunset *(1882) and an adventure novel titled* The Snake's

Pass (1890). *However, it wasn't until the publication of* Dracula *in 1897 that Stoker became a literary celebrity. Stoker went on to write ten more novels, including* The Jewel of Seven Stars *(1903) and* The Lair of the White Worm *(1911), but these works did not significantly advance his literary reputation. Indeed, by the early twentieth century, he was perhaps best known as the author of a celebrity memoir,* Personal Reminiscences of Henry Irving *(1906).*

"Dracula's Guest" was most likely[1] written in the early 1890s when Stoker was drafting Dracula. *At some point during the composing process, Stoker made the decision to omit the episode from his working draft. After Stoker's death, his widow, Florence Stoker, published "Dracula's Guest" in* Dracula's Guest and Other Weird Stories *(1914).*

Bibliography

Belford, Barbara. "Bram Stoker." *Oxford Dictionary of National Biography.* Oxford: Oxford University Press, 2004. http://www.oxforddnb.com.

—. *Bram Stoker: A Biography of the Author of* Dracula. New York: Knopf, 1996.

Eighteen-Bisang, Robert, and Elizabeth Miller, eds. *Bram Stoker's Notes for* Dracula. Jefferson, N.C.: McFarland, 2008.

Klinger, Leslie, ed. *The New Annotated* Dracula. New York: Norton, 2008.

Miller, Elizabeth, ed. *Bram Stoker's* Dracula: *A Documentary Volume. Dictionary of Literary Bibliography,* Vol. 304. Detroit: Thomson Gale, 2005.

Murray, Paul. *From the Shadow of* Dracula: *A Life of Bram Stoker.* London: Pimlico, 2005.

Stoker, Bram. *Dracula's Guest and Other Weird Stories.* London: Routledge, 1914.

DRACULA'S GUEST.

WHEN we started for our drive the sun was shining brightly on Munich, and the air was full of the joyousness of early summer.

---

[1] There has been a great deal of controversy over the dating of the story and its relationship to *Dracula.* See Elizabeth Miller, *Bram Stoker's* Dracula: *A Documentary Volume,* 226-235, for a concise overview of this scholarly debate.

Just as we were about to depart, Herr Delbrück (the maître d'hôtel of the Quatre Saisons, where I was staying) came down, bareheaded, to the carriage and, after wishing me a pleasant drive, said to the coachman, still holding his hand on the handle of the carriage door:

"Remember you are back by nightfall. The sky looks bright but there is a shiver in the north wind that says there may be a sudden storm. But I am sure you will not be late." Here he smiled, and added, "for you know what night it is."

Johann answered with an emphatic, "Ja, mein Herr,"[1] and, touching his hat, drove off quickly. When we had cleared the town, I said, after signalling to him to stop:

"Tell me, Johann, what is to-night?"

He crossed himself, as he answered laconically: "Walpurgis nacht."[2] Then he took out his watch, a great, old-fashioned German silver thing as big as a turnip, and looked at it, with his eyebrows gathered together and a little impatient shrug of his shoulders. I realized that this was his way of respectfully protesting against the unnecessary delay, and sank back in the carriage, merely motioning him to proceed. He started off rapidly, as if to make up for lost time. Every now and then the horses seemed to throw up their heads and sniffed the air suspiciously. On such occasions I often looked round in alarm. The road was pretty bleak, for we were traversing a sort of high, wind-swept plateau. As we drove, I saw a road that looked but little used, and which seemed to dip through a little, winding valley. It looked so inviting that, even at the risk of offending him, I called Johann to stop—and when he had pulled up, I told him I would like to drive down that road. He made all sorts of excuses, and frequently crossed himself as he spoke. This somewhat piqued my curiosity, so I asked him various questions. He answered fencingly, and repeatedly looked at his watch in protest. Finally I said:

"Well, Johann, I want to go down this road. I shall not ask you to come unless you like; but tell me why you do not like to go, that is all I ask." For answer he seemed to throw himself off the

---

1 Yes, sir.

2 In German folklore, a night of demonic revelry celebrated on April 30.

box, so quickly did he reach the ground. Then he stretched out his hands appealingly to me, and implored me not to go. There was just enough of English mixed with the German for me to understand the drift of his talk. He seemed always just about to tell me something—the very idea of which evidently frightened him; but each time he pulled himself up, saying, as he crossed himself: "Walpurgis-Nacht!"

I tried to argue with him, but it was difficult to argue with a man when I did not know his language. The advantage certainly rested with him, for although he began to speak in English, of a very crude and broken kind, he always got excited and broke into his native tongue—and every time he did so, he looked at his watch. Then the horses became restless and sniffed the air. At this he grew very pale, and, looking around in a frightened way, he suddenly jumped forward, took them by the bridles and led them on some twenty feet. I followed, and asked why he had done this. For answer he crossed himself, pointed to the spot we had left and drew his carriage in the direction of the other road, indicating a cross, and said, first in German, then in English: "Buried him—him what killed themselves."

I remembered the old custom of burying suicides at cross-roads: "Ah! I see, a suicide. How interesting!" But for the life of me I could not make out why the horses were frightened.

Whilst we were talking, we heard a sort of sound between a yelp and a bark. It was far away; but the horses got very restless, and it took Johann all his time to quiet them. He was pale, and said: "It sounds like a wolf—but yet there are no wolves here now."

"No?" I said, questioning him; "isn't it long since the wolves were so near the city?"

"Long, long," he answered, "in the spring and summer; but with the snow the wolves have been here not so long."

Whilst he was petting the horses and trying to quiet them, dark clouds drifted rapidly across the sky. The sunshine passed away, and a breath of cold wind seemed to drift past us. It was only a breath, however, and more in the nature of a warning than a fact, for the sun came out brightly again. Johann looked under his lifted hand at the horizon and said:

"The storm of snow, he comes before long time." Then he

looked at his watch again, and, straightway holding his reins firmly—for the horses were still pawing the ground restlessly and shaking their heads—he climbed to his box as though the time had come for proceeding on our journey.

I felt a little obstinate and did not at once get into the carriage.

"Tell me," I said, "about this place where the road leads," and I pointed down.

Again he crossed himself and mumbled a prayer, before he answered: "It is unholy."

"What is unholy?" I enquired.

"The village."

"Then there is a village?"

"No, no. No one lives there hundreds of years." My curiosity was piqued: "But you said there was a village."

"There was."

"Where is it now?"

Whereupon he burst out into a long story in German and English, so mixed up that I could not quite understand exactly what he said, but roughly I gathered that long ago, hundreds of years, men had died there and been buried in their graves; and sounds were heard under the clay, and when the graves were opened, men and women were found rosy with life, and their mouths red with blood. And so, in haste to save their lives (aye, and their souls!—and here he crossed himself) those who were left fled away to other places, where the living lived, and the dead were dead and not—not something. He was evidently afraid to speak the last words. As he proceeded with his narration, he grew more and more excited. It seemed as if his imagination had got hold of him, and he ended in a perfect paroxysm of fear—white-faced, perspiring, trembling and looking round him, as if expecting that some dreadful presence would manifest itself there in the bright sunshine on the open plain. Finally, in an agony of desperation, he cried:

"Walpurgis nacht!" and pointed to the carriage for me to get in. All my English blood rose at this, and, standing back, I said:

"You are afraid, Johann—you are afraid. Go home; I shall return alone; the walk will do me good." The carriage door was open. I took from the seat my oak walking-stick—which I always carry on my holiday excursions—and closed the door, pointing back to Munich, and said, "Go home, Johann—Walpurgis-Nacht doesn't concern Englishmen."

The horses were now more restive than ever, and Johann was trying to hold them in, while excitedly imploring me not to do anything so foolish. I pitied the poor fellow, he was deeply in earnest; but all the same I could not help laughing. His English was quite gone now. In his anxiety he had forgotten that his only means of making me understand was to talk my language, so he jabbered away in his native German. It began to be a little tedious. After giving the direction, "Home!" I turned to go down the cross-road into the valley.

With a despairing gesture, Johann turned his horses towards Munich. I leaned on my stick and looked after him. He went slowly along the road for a while: then there came over the crest of the hill a man tall and thin. I could see so much in the distance. When he drew near the horses, they began to jump and kick about, then to scream with terror. Johann could not hold them in; they bolted down the road, running away madly. I watched them out of sight, then looked for the stranger, but I found that he, too, was gone.

With a light heart I turned down the side road through the deepening valley to which Johann had objected. There was not the slightest reason, that I could see, for his objection; and I daresay I tramped for a couple of hours without thinking of time or distance, and certainly without seeing a person or a house. So far as the place was concerned, it was desolation itself. But I did not notice this particularly till, on turning a bend in the road, I came upon a scattered fringe of wood; then I recognised that I had been impressed unconsciously by the desolation of the region through which I had passed.

I sat down to rest myself, and began to look around. It struck me that it was considerably colder than it had been at the commencement of my walk—a sort of sighing sound seemed to be around me, with, now and then, high overhead, a sort of muffled roar. Looking upwards I noticed that great thick clouds were drifting rapidly across the sky from North to South at a great height. There were signs of coming storm in some lofty stratum of the air.

I was a little chilly, and, thinking that it was the sitting still after the exercise of walking, I resumed my journey.

The ground I passed over was now much more picturesque. There were no striking objects that the eye might single out; but in all there was a charm of beauty. I took little heed of time and it was only when the deepening twilight forced itself upon me that I began to think of how I should find my way home. The brightness of the day had gone. The air was cold, and the drifting of clouds high overhead was more marked. They were accompanied by a sort of far-away rushing sound, through which seemed to come at intervals that mysterious cry which the driver had said came from a wolf. For a while I hesitated. I had said I would see the deserted village, so on I went, and presently came on a wide stretch of open country, shut in by hills all around. Their sides were covered with trees which spread down to the plain, dotting, in clumps, the gentler slopes and hollows which showed here and there. I followed with my eye the winding of the road, and saw that it curved close to one of the densest of these clumps and was lost behind it.

As I looked there came a cold shiver in the air, and the snow began to fall. I thought of the miles and miles of bleak country I had passed, and then hurried on to seek the shelter of the wood in front. Darker and darker grew the sky, and faster and heavier fell the snow, till the earth before and around me was a glistening white carpet the further edge of which was lost in misty vagueness. The road was here but crude, and when on the level its boundaries were not so marked, as when it passed through the cuttings;[1] and in a little while I found that I must have strayed from it, for I missed underfoot the hard surface, and my feet sank deeper in the grass and moss. Then the wind grew stronger and blew with ever increasing force, till I was fain[2] to run before it. The air became icy-cold, and in spite of my exercise I began to suffer. The snow was now falling so thickly and whirling around me in such rapid eddies that I could hardly keep my eyes open. Every now and then the heavens were torn asunder by vivid lightning, and in the flashes I could see ahead of me a great mass of trees, chiefly yew and cypress all heavily coated with snow.

---

1 Trench-like roadbed.
2 Obliged.

I was soon amongst the shelter of the trees, and there, in comparative silence, I could hear the rush of the wind high overhead.
Presently the blackness of the storm had become merged in the
darkness of the night. By-and-by the storm seemed to be passing
away: it now only came in fierce puffs or blasts. At such moments
the weird sound of the wolf appeared to be echoed by many
similar sounds around me.

Now and again, through the black mass of drifting cloud, came
a straggling ray of moonlight, which lit up the expanse, and showed
me that I was at the edge of a dense mass of cypress and yew trees.
As the snow had ceased to fall, I walked out from the shelter and
began to investigate more closely. It appeared to me that, amongst
so many old foundations as I had passed, there might be still standing a house in which, though in ruins, I could find some sort of
shelter for a while. As I skirted the edge of the copse,[1] I found
that a low wall encircled it, and following this I presently found
an opening. Here the cypresses formed an alley leading up to a
square mass of some kind of building. Just as I caught sight of
this, however, the drifting clouds obscured the moon, and I passed
up the path in darkness. The wind must have grown colder, for I
felt myself shiver as I walked; but there was hope of shelter, and I
groped my way blindly on.

I stopped, for there was a sudden stillness. The storm had
passed; and, perhaps in sympathy with nature's silence, my heart
seemed to cease to beat. But this was only momentarily; for suddenly the moonlight broke through the clouds, showing me that
I was in a graveyard, and that the square object before me was a
great massive tomb of marble, as white as the snow that lay on
and all around it. With the moonlight there came a fierce sigh of
the storm, which appeared to resume its course with a long, low
howl, as of many dogs or wolves. I was awed and shocked, and felt
the cold perceptibly grow upon me till it seemed to grip me by the
heart. Then while the flood of moonlight still fell on the marble
tomb, the storm gave further evidence of renewing, as though it
was returning on its track. Impelled by some sort of fascination, I
approached the sepulchre to see what it was, and why such a thing

---

1 Thicket of trees.

stood alone in such a place. I walked around it, and read, over the Doric[1] door, in German—

COUNTESS DOLINGEN OF GRATZ
IN STYRIA
SOUGHT AND FOUND DEATH.
1801.

On the top of the tomb, seemingly driven through the solid marble—for the structure was composed of a few vast blocks of stone—was a great iron spike or stake. On going to the back I saw, graven in great Russian letters:

"The dead travel fast."

There was something so weird and uncanny about the whole thing that it gave me a turn and made me feel quite faint. I began to wish, for the first time, that I had taken Johann's advice. Here a thought struck me, which came under almost mysterious circum-stances and with a terrible shock. This was Walpurgis Night!

Walpurgis Night, when, according to the belief of millions of people, the devil was abroad—when the graves were opened and the dead came forth and walked. When all evil things of earth and air and water held revel. This very place the driver had spe-cially shunned. This was the depopulated village of centuries ago. This was where the suicide lay; and this was the place where I was alone—unmanned, shivering with cold in a shroud of snow with a wild storm gathering again upon me! It took all my philosophy, all the religion I had been taught, all my courage, not to collapse in a paroxysm of fright.

And now a perfect tornado burst upon me. The ground shook as though thousands of horses thundered across it; and this time the storm bore on its icy wings, not snow, but great hailstones which drove with such violence that they might have come from the thongs of Balearic slingers[2]—hailstones that beat down leaf and

---

1 Designed after the Doric style of Greek architecture.
2 Ancient warriors from the Balearic Islands who were famous for their use of deadly slingshots.

branch and made the shelter of the cypresses of no more avail than though their stems were standing-corn. At the first I had rushed to the nearest tree; but I was soon fain to leave it and seek the only spot that seemed to afford refuge, the deep Doric doorway of the marble tomb. There, crouching against the massive bronze-door, I gained a certain amount of protection from the beating of the hail-stones, for now they only drove against me as they ricochetted from the ground and the side of the marble.

As I leaned against the door, it moved slightly and opened inwards. The shelter of even a tomb was welcome in that pitiless tempest, and I was about to enter it when there came a flash of forked-lightning that lit up the whole expanse of the heavens. In the instant, as I am a living man, I saw, as my eyes were turned into the darkness of the tomb, a beautiful woman, with rounded cheeks and red lips, seemingly sleeping on a bier.[1] As the thunder broke overhead, I was grasped as by the hand of a giant and hurled out into the storm. The whole thing was so sudden that, before I could realize the shock, moral as well as physical, I found the hailstones beating me down. At the same time I had a strange, dominating feeling that I was not alone. I looked towards the tomb. Just then there came another blinding flash, which seemed to strike the iron stake that surmounted the tomb and to pour through to the earth, blasting and crumbling the marble, as in a burst of flame. The dead woman rose for a moment of agony, while she was lapped in the flame, and her bitter scream of pain was drowned in the thunder-crash. The last thing I heard was this mingling of dreadful sound, as again I was seized in the giant-grasp and dragged away, while the hailstones beat on me, and the air around seemed reverberant with the howling of wolves. The last sight that I remembered was a vague, white, moving mass, as if all the graves around me had sent out the phantoms of their sheeted-dead, and that they were closing in on me through the white cloudiness of the driving hail.

$$\star \quad \star \quad \star \quad \star \quad \star \quad \star$$

Gradually there came a sort of vague beginning of conscious-ness; then a sense of weariness that was dreadful. For a time I

---

1 A stand or stretcher used to carry a corpse or coffin to a burial site.

remembered nothing; but slowly my senses returned. My feet seemed positively racked with pain, yet I could not move them. They seemed to be numbed. There was an icy feeling at the back of my neck and all down my spine, and my ears, like my feet, were dead, yet in torment; but there was in my breast a sense of warmth which was, by comparison, delicious. It was as a nightmare—a physical nightmare, if one may use such an expression; for some heavy weight on my chest made it difficult for me to breathe.

This period of semi-lethargy seemed to remain a long time, and as it faded away I must have slept or swooned. Then came a sort of loathing, like the first stage of sea-sickness, and a wild desire to be free from something—I knew not what. A vast stillness enveloped me, as though all the world were asleep or dead— only broken by the low panting as of some animal close to me. I felt a warm rasping at my throat, then came a consciousness of the awful truth, which chilled me to the heart and sent the blood surging up through my brain. Some great animal was lying on me and now licking my throat. I feared to stir, for some instinct of prudence bade me lie still; but the brute seemed to realize that there was now some change in me, for it raised its head. Through my eyelashes I saw above me the two great flaming eyes of a gigantic wolf. Its sharp white teeth gleamed in the gaping red mouth, and I could feel its hot breath fierce and acrid upon me.

For another spell of time I remembered no more. Then I became conscious of a low growl, followed by a yelp, renewed again and again. Then, seemingly very far away, I heard a "Holloa! holloa!" as of many voices calling in unison. Cautiously I raised my head and looked in the direction whence the sound came; but the cemetery blocked my view. The wolf still continued to yelp in a strange way, and a red glare began to move round the grove of cypresses, as though following the sound. As the voices drew closer, the wolf yelped faster and louder. I feared to make either sound or motion. Nearer came the red glow, over the white pall which stretched into the darkness around me. Then all at once from beyond the trees there came at a trot a troop of horsemen bearing torches. The wolf rose from my breast and made for the cemetery. I saw one of the horsemen (soldiers by their caps and their long military cloaks) raise his carbine[1] and take aim. A companion knocked up his arm, and I heard the ball whizz over my head. He had evidently taken my body for that of the wolf. Another sighted the animal as it slunk away, and a shot followed. Then, at a gallop, the troop rode forward—some towards me, others following the wolf as it disappeared amongst the snow-clad cypresses.

As they drew nearer I tried to move, but was powerless, although I could see and hear all that went on around me. Two or three of the soldiers jumped from their horses and knelt beside me. One of them raised my head, and placed his hand over my heart.

"Good news, comrades!" he cried. "His heart still beats!"

Then some brandy was poured down my throat; it put vigour into me, and I was able to open my eyes fully and look around. Lights and shadows were moving among the trees, and I heard men call to one another. They drew together, uttering frightened exclamations; and the lights flashed as the others came pouring out of the cemetery pell-mell, like men possessed. When the further ones came close to us, those who were around me asked them eagerly:

"Well, have you found him?"

The reply rang out hurriedly:

"No! no! Come away quick—quick! This is no place to stay, and on this of all nights!"

"What was it?" was the question, asked in all manner of keys. The answer came variously and all indefinitely as though the men were moved by some common impulse to speak, yet were restrained by some common fear from giving their thoughts.

"It—it—indeed!" gibbered one, whose wits had plainly given out for the moment.

"A wolf—and yet not a wolf!" another put in shudderingly.

"No use trying for him without the sacred bullet," a third remarked in a more ordinary manner.

"Serve us right for coming out on this night! Truly we have earned our thousand marks!"[2] were the ejaculations of a fourth.

---

1 A firearm used by the cavalry or other military officers.
2 Unit of German currency.

"There was blood on the broken marble," another said after a pause—"the lightning never brought that there. And for him—is he safe? Look at his throat! See, comrades, the wolf has been lying on him and keeping his blood warm."

The officer looked at my throat and replied:

"He is all right; the skin is not pierced. What does it all mean? We should never have found him but for the yelping of the wolf."

"What became of it?" asked the man who was holding up my head, and who seemed the least panic-stricken of the party, for his hands were steady and without tremor. On his sleeve was the chevron of a petty officer.

"It went to its home," answered the man, whose long face was pallid, and who actually shook with terror as he glanced around him fearfully. "There are graves enough there in which it may lie. Come, comrades—come quickly! Let us leave this cursed spot."

The officer raised me to a sitting posture, as he uttered a word of command; then several men placed me upon a horse. He sprang to the saddle behind me, took me in his arms, gave the word to advance; and, turning our faces away from the cypresses, we rode away in swift, military order.

As yet my tongue refused its office, and I was perforce silent. I must have fallen asleep; for the next thing I remembered was finding myself standing up, supported by a soldier on each side of me. It was almost broad daylight, and to the north a red streak of sunlight was reflected, like a path of blood, over the waste of snow. The officer was telling the men to say nothing of what they had seen, except that they found an English stranger, guarded by a large dog.

"Dog! that was no dog," cut in the man who had exhibited such fear. "I think I know a wolf when I see one."

The young officer answered calmly: "I said a dog."

"Dog!" reiterated the other ironically. It was evident that his courage was rising with the sun; and, pointing to me, he said, "Look at his throat. Is that the work of a dog, master?"

Instinctively I raised my hand to my throat, and as I touched it I cried out in pain. The men crowded round to look, some stooping down from their saddles; and again there came the calm voice of the young officer:

"A dog, as I said. If aught else were said we should only be laughed at."

I was then mounted behind a trooper, and we rode on into the suburbs of Munich. Here we came across a stray carriage, into which I was lifted, and it was driven off to the Quatre Saisons—the young officer accompanying me, whilst a trooper followed with his horse, and the others rode off to their barracks.

When we arrived, Herr Delbrück rushed so quickly down the steps to meet me, that it was apparent he had been watching within. Taking me by both hands he solicitously led me in. The officer saluted me and was turning to withdraw, when I recognized his purpose, and insisted that he should come to my rooms. Over a glass of wine I warmly thanked him and his brave comrades for saving me. He replied simply that he was more than glad, and that Herr Delbrück had at the first taken steps to make all the searching party pleased; at which ambiguous utterance the maître d'hôtel smiled, while the officer pleaded duty and withdrew.

"But Herr Delbrück," I enquired, "how and why was it that the soldiers searched for me?"

He shrugged his shoulders, as if in depreciation of his own deed, as he replied:

"I was so fortunate as to obtain leave from the commander of the regiment in which I served, to ask for volunteers."

"But how did you know I was lost?" I asked.

"The driver came hither with the remains of his carriage, which had been upset when the horses ran away."

"But surely you would not send a search-party of soldiers merely on this account?"

"Oh, no!" he answered; "but even before the coachman arrived, I had this telegram from the Boyar[1] whose guest you are," and he took from his pocket a telegram which he handed to me, and I read:

BISTRITZ[2]

"Be careful of my guest—his safety is most precious to me.

---

1 Romanian lord.
2 Bistria, a city in Transylvania, Romania.

Should aught happen to him, or if he be missed, spare nothing to find him and ensure his safety. He is English and therefore adventurous. There are often dangers from snow and wolves and night. Lose not a moment if you suspect harm to him. I answer your zeal with my fortune.—Dracula."

As I held the telegram in my hand, the room seemed to whirl around me; and, if the attentive maître d'hôtel had not caught me, I think I should have fallen. There was something so strange in all this, something so weird and impossible to imagine, that there grew on me a sense of my being in some way the sport of opposite forces—the mere vague idea of which seemed in a way to paralyse me. I was certainly under some form of mysterious protection. From a distant country had come, in the very nick of time, a message that took me out of the danger of the snow-sleep and the jaws of the wolf.

The Other Side: A Breton Legend

Eric Stenbock

Count Stanislas Eric Stenbock (1860-1895) was born into an aristocratic family with roots in Estonia, Sweden, and Russia. He spent many years abroad as a young man and eventually studied at Balliol College, Oxford. In 1881, he published his first volume of poetry, Love, Sleep and Dreams, *and shortly thereafter privately published his second collection of verse,* Myrtle, Rue and Cypress *(1883). After inheriting a fortune from his grandfather in 1885, Stenbock relocated to his ancestral estate in Estonia, where he lived happily for nearly two years with his extended family.*

During this time, he developed eccentric habits that soon became legendary. Inspired by the Pre-Raphaelites and aesthetes, he created aesthetic chambers complete with peacock-blue walls, a statue of Eros, and a menagerie of exotic animals. He also developed addictions to opium and alcohol. Stenbock returned to Britain in 1887, where he became acquainted with More Adey, Ernest Rhys, Aubrey Beardsley, and W. B. Yeats. His London lodgings were just as eccentric as his aesthetic chambers in Estonia. Scented with incense and inhabited by parakeets, his rooms featured an eternally lit red lamp illuminating busts of Buddha and Shelley. Although like many other aesthetes Stenbock converted to Catholicism, his religious influences were eclectic, incorporating aspects of Buddhism and idolatry. In his religious practices, domestic habits, and literary works, he displayed an overarching obsession with death. For example, at one dinner party, he placed a coffin on the table that concealed a sumptuous meal. With one touch, the walls of the coffin fell away, leaving his guests gasping in amazement. In 1893, he published a third volume of verse, The Shadow of Death, *and a year later, he published a book of stories,* Studies of Death: Romantic Tales. *"The True Story of a Vampire," first published in* Studies of Death, *is a classic of the genre. He died in 1895 from cirrhosis of the liver.*

"The Other Side: A Breton Legend" was originally published in The Spirit Lamp *in June 1893. The Spirit Lamp (1892-93) was an undergraduate student publication at Oxford that came to be closely associated with Aestheticism and the followers of Oscar Wilde. Even though the story's subtitle suggests that it is set in Brittany, the setting was most likely inspired by the landscape of Estonia, which was known for its thick forests and howling wolves.*

Bibliography

Adlard, John. *Stenbock, Yeats and the Nineties*. London: Cecil and Amelia Woolf, 1969.

Beckson, Karl. "Eric Stenbock." *Oxford Dictionary of National Biography*. Oxford: Oxford University Press, 2004. http://www.oxforddnb.com.

Cevasco, G. A. *The Breviary of Decadence: J.-K. Huysmans's* A Rebours *and English Literature*. New York: AMS, 2001.

d'Arch Smith, Timothy. *Love in Earnest: Some Notes on the Lives and Writings of the English "Uranian" Poets from 1889 to 1930*. London: Routledge, 1970.

Reed, Jeremy. *A Hundred Years of Disappearance: Count Eric Stenbock*. Edinburgh: Tragara Press, 1995.

Reade, Brian. *Sexual Heretics: Male Homosexuality in English Literature from 1850 to 1900*. New York: Coward-McCann, 1970.

Stenbock, Eric. "The Other Side: A Breton Legend." *The Spirit Lamp* 4, no. 2 (June 6, 1893): 52-68.

THE OTHER SIDE.

A BRETON LEGEND.

A la joyouse Messe noire.[1]

"NOT that I like it, but one does feel so much better after it—oh, thank you, Mère Yvonne, yes just a little drop more." So the old crones fell to drinking their hot brandy and water (although of course they only took it medicinally, as a remedy for their

---

[1] Dedicated to the joyous black Mass.

rheumatics), all seated round the big fire and Mère Pinquèle continued her story.

"Oh, yes, then when they get to the top of the hill, there is
an altar with six candles quite black and a sort of something in
between, that nobody sees quite clearly, and the old black ram
with the man's face and long horns begins to say Mass in a sort of
gibberish nobody understands, and two black strange things like
monkeys glide about with the book and the cruets[1]—and there's
music too, such music. There are things the top half like black
cats, and the bottom part like men only their legs are all covered
with close black hair, and they play on the bag-pipes, and when
they come to the elevation, then——" Amid the old crones there
was lying on the hearth-rug, before the fire, a boy, whose large
lovely eyes dilated and whose limbs quivered in the very ecstacy of
terror.

"Is that all true, Mère Pinquèle?" he said.

"Oh, quite true, and not only that, the best part is yet to come;
for they take a child and——." Here Mère Pinquèle showed her
fang-like teeth.

"Oh! Mère Pinquèle, are you a witch too?"

"Silence, Gabriel," said Mère Yvonne, "how can you say anything so wicked? Why, bless me, the boy ought to have been in bed
ages ago."

Just then all shuddered, and all made the sign of the cross
except Mère Pinquèle, for they heard that most dreadful of dreadful sounds—the howl of a wolf, which begins with three sharp
barks and then lifts itself up in a long protracted wail of com-
mingled cruelty and despair, and at last subsides into a whispered
growl fraught with eternal malice.

There was a forest and a village and a brook, the village was
on one side of the brook, none had dared to cross to the other
side. Where the village was, all was green and glad and fertile and
fruitful; on the other side the trees never put forth green leaves,
and a dark shadow hung over it even at noon-day, and in the night-
time one could hear the wolves howling—the were-wolves and the

---

1 Small glass bottles filled with unconsecrated wine or water used in the Christian
Eucharist.

wolf-men and the men-wolves, and those very wicked men who for nine days in every year are turned into wolves; but on the green side no wolf was ever seen, and only one little running brook like a silver streak flowed between.

It was spring now and the old crones sat no longer by the fire but before their cottages sunning themselves, and everyone felt so happy that they ceased to tell stories of the "other side." But Gabriel wandered by the brook as he was wont to wander, drawn thither by some strange attraction mingled with intense horror.

His schoolfellows did not like Gabriel; all laughed and jeered at him, because he was less cruel and more gentle of nature than the rest, and even as a rare and beautiful bird escaped from a cage is hacked to death by the common sparrows, so was Gabriel among his fellows. Everyone wondered how Mère Yvonne, that buxom and worthy matron, could have produced a son like this, with strange dreamy eyes, who was as they said "pas comme les autres gamins."[1] His only friends were the Abbé[2] Félicien whose Mass he served each morning, and one little girl called Carmeille, who loved him, no one could make out why.

The sun had already set, Gabriel still wandered by the brook, filled with vague terror and irresistible fascination. The sun set and the moon rose, the full moon, very large and very clear, and the moonlight flooded the forest both this side and "the other side," and just on the "other side" of the brook, hanging over, Gabriel saw a large deep blue flower, whose strange intoxicating perfume reached him and fascinated him even where he stood.

"If I could only make one step across," he thought, "nothing could harm me if I only plucked that one flower, and nobody would know I had been over at all," for the villagers looked with hatred and suspicion on anyone who was said to have crossed to the "other side," so summing up courage he leapt lightly to the other side of the brook. Then the moon breaking from a cloud shone with unusual brilliance, and he saw, stretching before him, long reaches of the same strange blue flowers, each one lovelier than the last, till, not being able to make up his mind which one

---

1 Not like other children.
2 Abbot.

flower to take or whether to take several, he went on and on, and the moon shone very brightly, and a strange unseen bird, somewhat like a nightingale, but louder and lovelier, sang, and his heart was filled with longing for he knew not what, and the moon shone and the nightingale sang. But on a sudden a black cloud covered the moon entirely, and all was black, utter darkness, and through the darkness he heard wolves howling and shrieking in the hideous ardour of the chase, and there passed before him a horrible procession of wolves (black wolves with red fiery eyes), and with them men that had the heads of wolves and wolves that had the heads of men, and above them flew owls (black owls with red fiery eyes), and bats and long serpentine black things, and last of all seated on an enormous black ram with hideous human face the wolf-keeper on whose face was eternal shadow; but they continued their horrid chase and passed him by, and when they had passed the moon shone out more beautiful than ever, and the strange nightingale sang again, and the strange intense blue flowers were in long reaches in front to the right and to the left. But one thing was there which had not been before, among the deep blue flowers walked one with long gleaming golden hair, and she turned once round and her eyes were of the same colour as the strange blue flowers, and she walked on and Gabriel could not choose but follow. But when a cloud passed over the moon he saw no beautiful woman but a wolf, so in utter terror he turned and fled, plucking one of the strange blue flowers on the way, and leapt again over the brook and ran home.

When he got home Gabriel could not resist showing his treasure to his mother, though he knew she would not appreciate it; but when she saw the strange blue flower, Mère Yvonne turned pale and said, "Why child, where hast thou been? sure it is the witch flower"; and so saying she snatched it from him and cast it into the corner, and immediately all its beauty and strange fragrance faded from it and it looked charred as though it had been burnt. So Gabriel sat down silently and rather sulkily, and having eaten no supper went up to bed, but he did not sleep but waited and waited till all was quiet within the house. Then he crept downstairs in his long white night-shirt and bare feet on the square cold stones and picked hurriedly up the charred and faded flower and put it in his warm bosom next his heart, and immediately the flower bloomed again lovelier than ever, and he fell into a deep sleep, but through his sleep he seemed to hear a soft low voice singing underneath his window in a strange language (in which the subtle sounds melted into one another), but he could distinguish no word except his own name.

When he went forth in the morning to serve Mass, he still kept the flower with him next his heart. Now when the priest began Mass and said "Intriobo ad altare Dei," then said Gabriel "Qui nequiquam laetificavit juventutem meam."[1] And the Abbé Félicien turned round on hearing this strange response, and he saw the boy's face deadly pale, his eyes fixed and his limbs rigid, and as the priest looked on him Gabriel fell fainting to the floor, so the sacristan[2] had to carry him home and seek another acolyte[3] for the Abbé Félicien.

Now when the Abbé Félicien came to see after him, Gabriel felt strangely reluctant to say anything about the blue flower and for the first time he deceived the priest.

In the afternoon as sunset drew nigh he felt better and Carmeille came to see him and begged him to go out with her into the fresh air. So they went out hand in hand, the dark haired, gazelle-eyed boy, and the fair wavy haired girl, and something, he knew not what, led his steps (half knowingly and yet not so, for he could not but walk thither) to the brook, and they sat down together on the bank.

Gabriel thought at least he might tell his secret to Carmeille, so he took out the flower from his bosom and said, "Look here, Carmeille, hast thou seen ever so lovely a flower as this?" but Carmeille turned pale and faint and said, "Oh, Gabriel what is this flower? I but touched it and I felt something strange come over me. No, no, I don't like its perfume, no, there's something not quite right about it, oh, dear Gabriel, do let me throw it away," and

---

1 The correct passage from the Catholic Tridentine Mass reads, "I will go unto the altar of God, to God who gives joy to my youth." However, Gabriel changes the second half of the passage to read, "who in vain gave joy to my youth."

2 Religious officer responsible for sacred vestments and other ceremonial church property.

3 Altar server.

before he had time to answer, she cast it from her, and again all its beauty and fragrance went from it and it looked charred as though it had been burnt. But suddenly where the flower had been thrown on this side of the brook, there appeared a wolf, which stood and looked at the children.

Carmeille said, "What shall we do," and clung to Gabriel, but the wolf looked at them very steadfastly and Gabriel recognized in the eyes of the wolf the strange deep intense blue eyes of the wolf-woman he had seen on the "other side," so he said, "Stay here, dear Carmeille, see she is looking gently at us and will not hurt us."

"But it is a wolf," said Carmeille, and quivered all over with fear, but again Gabriel said languidly, "She will not hurt us." Then Carmeille seized Gabriel's hand in an agony of terror and dragged him along with her till they reached the village, where she gave the alarm and all the lads of the village gathered together. They had never seen a wolf on this side of the brook, so they excited themselves greatly and arranged a grand wolf hunt for the morrow, but Gabriel sat silently apart and said no word.

That night Gabriel could not sleep at all nor could he bring himself to say his prayers; but he sat in his little room by the window with his shirt open at the throat and the strange blue flower at his heart and again this night he heard a voice singing beneath his window in the same soft, subtle, liquid language as before—

Ma zála liràl va jé
Cwamûlo zhajéla je
Cárma urádi el javé
Járma, symai,—carmé—
Zhála javály thra je
al vú al vlaûle va azré
Safralje vairálje va já?
Cárma serâja
Lâja lâja
Luzhà![1]

---

[1] This spell appears to be written in a language of Stenbock's own creation.

and as he looked he could see the silvern shadows slide on the lim-mering[1] light of golden hair, and the strange eyes gleaming dark blue through the night and it seemed to him that he could not but follow; so he walked half clad and bare foot as he was with eyes fixed as in a dream silently down the stairs and out into the night.

And ever and again she turned to look on him with her strange blue eyes full of tenderness and passion and sadness beyond the sadness of things human—and as he foreknew his steps led him to the brink of the Brook. Then she, taking his hand, familiarly said, "Won't you help me over Gabriel?"

Then it seemed to him as though he had known her all his life—so he went with her to the "other side" but he saw no one by him; and looking again beside him there were *two wolves*. In a frenzy of terror, he (who had never thought to kill any living thing before) seized a log of wood lying by and smote one of the wolves on the head.

Immediately he saw the wolf-woman at his side with blood streaming from her forehead, staining her wonderful golden hair, and with eyes looking at him with infinite reproach, she said— "Who did this?"

Then she whispered a few words to the other wolf, which leapt over the brook and made its way towards the village, and turning again towards him she said, "Oh Gabriel, how could you strike me, who would have loved you so long and so well." Then it seemed to him again as though he had known her all his life but he felt dazed and said nothing—but she gathered a dark green strangely shaped leaf and holding it to her forehead, she said—"Gabriel, kiss the place all will be well again." So he kissed as she had bidden him and he felt the salt taste of blood in his mouth and then he knew no more.

* * * *

Again he saw the wolf-keeper with his horrible troupe around him, but this time not engaged in the chase but sitting in strange conclave in a circle and the black owls sat in the trees and the black

---

1 Glimmering.

bats hung downwards from the branches. Gabriel stood alone in the middle with a hundred wicked eyes fixed on him. They seemed to deliberate about what should be done with him, speaking in that same strange tongue which he had heard in the songs beneath his window. Suddenly he felt a hand pressing in his and saw the mysterious wolf-woman by his side. Then began what seemed a kind of incantation where human or half human creatures seemed to howl, and beasts to speak with human speech but in the unknown tongue. Then the wolf-keeper whose face was ever veiled in shadow spake some words in a voice that seemed to come from afar off, but all he could distinguish was his own name Gabriel and her name Lilith.[1] Then he felt arms enlacing him.—

Gabriel awoke—in his own room—so it was a dream after all—but what a dreadful dream. Yes, but was it his own room? Of course there was his coat hanging over the chair—yes but—the Crucifix—where was the Crucifix and the benetier[2] and the consecrated palm branch and the antique image of Our Lady perpetuae salutis,[3] with the little ever-burning lamp before it, before which he placed every day the flowers he had gathered, yet had not dared to place the blue flower.—

Every morning he lifted his still dream-laden eyes to it and said Ave Maria[4] and made the sign of the cross, which bringeth peace to the soul—but how horrible, how maddening, it was not there, not at all. No surely he could not be awake, at least not *quite* awake, he would make the benedictive sign and he would be freed from this fearful illusion—yes but the sign, he would make the sign—oh, but what was the sign? Had he forgotten? or was his arm paralyzed? No he could move. Then he had forgotten—and the prayer—he must remember that. A—vae—nunc—mortis—fructus.[5] No surely it did not run thus—but something like it surely—yes, he was awake he could move at any rate—he would reassure himself—he would get up—he would see the grey old church with the exquisitely pointed

---

1 In Jewish folklore, Lilith is known as a female demon or, alternatively, as Adam's first wife who refused to bend to his will.

2 Holy water font.

3 Of perpetual salvation.

4 Hail Mary.

5 Fragments of "Hail Mary," a Catholic prayer.

gables bathed in the light of dawn, and presently the deep solemn bell would toll and he would run down and don his red cassock and lace-worked cotta[1] and light the tall candles on the altar and wait reverently to vest the good and gracious Abbé Félicien, kissing each vestment as he lifted it with reverent hands.

But surely this was not the light of dawn; it was liker sunset! He leapt from his small white bed, and a vague terror came over him, he trembled and had to hold on to the chair before he reached the window. No, the solemn spires of the grey church were not to be seen—he was in the depths of the forest; but in a part he had never seen before—but surely he had explored every part, it must be the "other side." To terror succeeded a languor and lassitude not without charm—passivity, acquiescence, indulgence—he felt, as it were, the strong caress of another will flowing over him like water and clothing him with invisible hands in an impalpable garment; so he dressed himself almost mechanically and walked downstairs, the same stairs it seemed to him down which it was his wont to run and spring. The broad square stones seemed singularly beautiful and irridescent with many strange colours—how was it he had never noticed this before—but he was gradually losing the power of wondering—he entered the room below—the wonted coffee and bread-rolls were on the table.

"Why Gabriel, how late you are to-day." The voice was very sweet but the intonation strange—and there sat Lilith, the mysterious wolf-woman, her glittering gold hair tied loose in a loose knot and an embroidery whereon she was tracing strange serpentine patterns, lay over the lap of her maize coloured garment—and she looked at Gabriel steadfastly with her wonderful dark blue eyes and said, "Why, Gabriel, you are late to-day," and Gabriel answered, "I was tired yesterday, give me some coffee."

★　　★　　★　　★

A dream within a dream—yes, he had known her all his life, and they dwelt together; had they not always done so? And she would take him through the glades of the forest and gather for

---

1 A loose vestment worn by priests over a cassock.

him flowers, such as he had never seen before, and tell him stories in her strange, low deep voice, which seemed ever to be accompanied by the faint vibration of strings, looking at him fixedly the while with her marvellous blue eyes.

*   *   *   *

Little by little the flame of vitality which burned within him seemed to grow fainter and fainter, and his lithe lissom[1] limbs waxed languorous and luxurious—yet was he ever filled with a languid content and a will not his own perpetually overshadowed him.

One day in their wanderings he saw a strange dark blue flower like unto the eyes of Lilith, and a sudden half remembrance flashed through his mind.

"What is this blue flower?" he said, and Lilith shuddered and said nothing; but as they went a little further there was a brook—*the* brook he thought, and felt his fetters falling off him, and he prepared to spring over the brook; but Lilith seized him by the arm and held him back with all her strength, and trembling all over she said, "Promise me Gabriel that you will not cross over." But he said, "Tell me what is this blue flower, and why you will not tell me?" And she said, "Look Gabriel at the brook." And he looked and saw that though it was just like the brook of separation it was not the same, the waters did not flow.

As Gabriel looked steadfastly into the still waters it seemed to him as though he saw voices—some impression of the Vespers for the Dead.[2] "Hei mihi quia incolatus sum," and again "De profundis clamavi ad te"[3]—oh, that veil, that overshadowing veil! Why could he not hear properly and see, and why did he only remember as one looking through a threefold semi-transparent curtain. Yes they were praying for him—but who were they? He heard again the voice of Lilith in whispered anguish, "Come away!"

---

1 Agile.

2 Hymns sung the evening before a funeral mass.

3 The first exclamation—Woe is me, for I am sojourning here—is a passage from Psalm 119. The second—Out of the depths I have cried to thee—is a passage from Psalm 130.

Then he said, this time in monotone, "What is this blue flower, and what is its use?"

And the low thrilling voice answered, "It is called 'lûli uzhûri,'[1] two drops pressed upon the face of the sleeper and he will *sleep*."

He was as a child in her hand and suffered himself to be led from thence, nevertheless he plucked listlessly one of the blue flowers, holding it downwards in his hand. What did she mean? Would the sleeper wake? Would the blue flower leave any stain? Could that stain be wiped off?

But as he lay asleep at early dawn he heard voices from afar off praying for him—the Abbé Félicien, Carmeille, his mother too, then some familiar words struck his ear: "Libera mea porta inferi."[2] Mass was being said for the repose of his soul, he knew this. No, he could not stay, he would leap over the brook, he knew the way—he had forgotten that the brook did not flow. Ah, but Lilith would know—what should he do? The blue flower—there it lay close by his bedside—he understood now; so he crept very silently to where Lilith lay asleep, her long hair glistening gold, shining like a glory round about her. He pressed two drops on her forehead, she sighed once, and a shade of praeternatural anguish passed over her beautiful face. He fled—terror, remorse, and hope tearing his soul and making fleet his feet. He came to the brook— he did not see that the water did not flow—of course it was the brook of separation; one bound, he should be with things human again. He leapt over and ——

A change had come over him—what was it? He could not tell—did he walk on all fours? Yes surely. He looked into the brook, whose still waters were fixed as a mirror, and there, horror, he beheld himself; or was it himself? His head and face, yes; but his body transformed to that of a wolf. Even as he looked he heard a sound of hideous mocking laughter behind him. He turned round—there, in a gleam of red lurid light, he saw one whose body was human, but whose head was that of a wolf, with eyes of infinite malice; and, while this hideous being laughed with a loud human laugh, he, essaying to speak, could only utter the prolonged howl of a wolf.

---

1 This untranslatable phrase seems to have been invented by Stenbock.
2 Deliver me from the gate of hell.

*　　*　　*　　*

But we will transfer our thoughts from the alien things on the "other side" to the simple human village where Gabriel used to dwell. Mère Yvonne was not much surprised when Gabriel did not turn up to breakfast—he often did not, so absent minded was he; this time she said, "I suppose he has gone with the others to the wolf hunt." Not that Gabriel was given to hunting, but, as she sagely said, "there was no knowing what he might do next." The boys said, "Of course that muff[1] Gabriel is skulking and hiding himself, he's afraid to join the wolf hunt; why, he wouldn't even kill a cat," for their one notion of excellence was slaughter—so the greater the game the greater the glory. They were chiefly now confined to cats and sparrows, but they all hoped in after time to become generals of armies.

Yet these children had been taught all their life through with the gentle words of Christ—but alas, nearly all the seed falls by the wayside, where it could not bear flower or fruit; how little these know the suffering and bitter anguish or realize the full meaning of the words to those, of whom it is written "Some fell among thorns."[2]

The wolf hunt was so far a success that they did actually see a wolf, but not a success, as they did not kill it before it leapt over the brook to the "other side," where, of course, they were afraid to pursue it. No emotion is more inrooted and intense in the minds of common people than hatred and fear of anything "strange."

Days passed by, but Gabriel was nowhere seen—and Mère Yvonne began to see clearly at last how deeply she loved her only son, who was so unlike her that she had thought herself an object of pity to other mothers—the goose and the swan's egg. People searched and pretended to search, they even went to the length of dragging the ponds, which the boys thought very amusing, as it enabled them to kill a great number of water rats, and Carmeille sat in a corner and cried all day long. Mère Pinquèle also sat in a corner and chuckled and said that she had always said Gabriel

---

1 Fool.
2 See Mark 4:7.

would come to no good. The Abbé Félicien looked pale and anxious, but said very little, save to God and those that dwelt with God.

At last, as Gabriel was not there, they supposed he must be nowhere—that is *dead*. (Their knowledge of other localities being so limited, that it did not even occur to them to suppose he might be living elsewhere than in the village.) So it was agreed that an empty catafalque[1] should be put up in the church with tall candles round it, and Mère Yvonne said all the prayers that were in her prayer book, beginning at the beginning and ending at the end, regardless of their appropriateness—not even omitting the instructions of the rubrics.[2] And Carmeille sat in the corner of the little side chapel and cried, and cried. And the Abbé Félicien caused the boys to sing the Vespers for the Dead (this did not amuse them so much as dragging the pond), and on the following morning, in the silence of early dawn, said the Dirge and the Requiem—*and this Gabriel heard*.

Then the Abbé Félicien received a message to bring the Holy Viaticum[3] to one sick. So they set forth in solemn procession with great torches, and their way lay along the brook of separation.

*   *   *   *

Essaying to speak he could only utter the prolonged howl of a wolf—the most fearful of all beastial sounds. He howled and howled again—perhaps Lilith would hear him! Perhaps she could rescue him? Then he remembered the blue flower—the beginning and end of all his woe. His cries aroused all the denizens of the forest—the wolves, the wolf-men, and the men-wolves. He fled before them in an agony of terror—behind him, seated on the black ram with human face, was the wolf-keeper, whose face was veiled in eternal shadow. Only once he turned to look behind—for among the shrieks and howls of beastial chase he heard one thrilling voice moan with pain. And there among them he beheld Lilith, her body too was that of a wolf, almost hidden in the masses of

---

1 Platform for displaying a coffin in a church.
2 Directions for religious rituals.
3 Last rites before death.

her glittering golden hair, on her forehead was a stain of blue, like in colour to her mysterious eyes, now veiled with tears she could not shed.

★ ★ ★ ★

The way of the Most Holy Viaticum lay along the brook of separation. They heard the fearful howlings afar off, the torch bearers turned pale and trembled—but the Abbé Félicien, holding aloft the Ciborium,[1] said "They cannot harm us."

Suddenly the whole horrid chase came in sight. Gabriel sprang over the brook, the Abbé Félicien held the most Blessed Sacrament before him, and his shape was restored to him and he fell down prostrate in adoration. But the Abbé Félicien still held aloft the Sacred Ciborium, and the people fell on their knees in the agony of fear, but the face of the priest seemed to shine with divine effulgence. Then the wolf-keeper held up in his hands the shape of something horrible and inconceivable—a monstrance to the Sacrament of Hell, and three times he raised it, in mockery of the blessed rite of Benediction. And on the third time streams of fire went forth from his fingers, and all the "other side" of the forest took fire, and great darkness was over all.

All who were there and saw and heard it have kept the impress thereof for the rest of their lives—nor till in their death hour was the remembrance thereof absent from their minds. Shrieks, horrible beyond conception, were heard till nightfall—then the rain rained.

The "other side" is harmless now—charred ashes only; but none dares to cross but Gabriel alone—for once a year for nine days a strange madness comes over him.

---

1 A covered cup used to hold communion wafers or sacramental bread for the Christian Eucharist.

Morraha

JOSEPH JACOBS

Joseph Jacobs (1854-1916) was born in Sydney, Australia, and attended Sydney grammar school, excelling in mathematics, the physical sciences, and English. In 1872, he immigrated to Great Britain and soon began his studies at St. John's College, Cambridge, where he graduated with distinction, receiving both the highest score on his moral philosophy exam and the coveted Wright Prize.

In 1877, Jacobs published an article in Macmillan's *Magazine responding to anti-Semitic criticism of George Eliot's* Daniel Deronda *(1876). Moved by Jacobs's defense of her work, Eliot invited Jacobs to a reception hosted by herself and her partner, George Lewes, where he met William Morris, who would become another lifelong friend. Jacobs's interest in Judaism continued to grow and he spent a year in Berlin studying Jewish philosophy with renowned scholars, Moritz Lazarus and Moritz Steinschneider. As an activist, Jacobs published articles in the* Times *drawing attention to the pogroms and persecution of Jews in Russia that began in 1881. Jacobs's efforts resulted in the formation of the Mansion House Committee and Fund for which he served as secretary from 1882 to 1900. He also served as the secretary of the Society of Hebrew Literature from 1878 to 1884, and he was the president and founding member of the Jewish Historical Society of England.*

Jacobs continued his scholarly interests in 1888 when he traveled to Spain and returned to Britain with over 1,700 documents that he published as An Inquiry into the Sources of Spanish-Jewish History *(1893). In addition to his scholarly writing, he translated over twenty-nine books into English and edited classic novels, such as Jane Austen's* Emma, *as well as obituaries for prominent artists and intellectuals, including Robert Browning and Matthew Arnold.*

Sometime after 1890, Jacobs married Georgina Horne and the couple had two sons and a daughter. Jacobs's love for his family seemed to inspire an interest in fairy tales and folklore. In 1889, he joined the Folk-Lore Society and published The Fables of Aesop, followed by a series of collections: English Fairy Tales (1890), Celtic Fairy Tales (1892), Indian Fairy Tales (1892), More English Fairy Tales (1893), and More Celtic Fairy Tales (1894). He dedicated his collections to his children, reading each fairy tale aloud to them to determine which stories should be published. In 1916, he published his final collection, Europa's Fairy Book, which he dedicated to his granddaughters. Jacobs's fairy tale and folktale collections were extremely successful, and with the exception of Andrew Lang's fairy tales they were the most popular of the late Victorian era. "Morraha" appears in the collection More Celtic Tales. Jacobs credits his use of this tale to William Larminie, whose West Irish Folk-tales and Romances was published in 1893.

In 1896, Jacobs went on a lecturing tour of America, an experience that proved to be profound and life-altering. As a result, he decided to move his family to New York where he worked as editor of the Jewish Encyclopedia, contributing over four hundred articles. He was also editor of the American Hebrew as well as a professor at the Jewish Theological Seminary of America. Jacobs died in 1916 in Yonkers, New York, and his final work, Jewish Contribution to Civilisation, was published posthumously in 1919.

Bibliography

Fine, Gary Alan. "Joseph Jacobs: A Sociological Folklorist." Folklore 98, no. 2 (1987): 183-193.

Jacobs, Joseph. "Morraha." In More Celtic Fairy Tales, 80-96. London: David Nutt, 1894.

Kaplan, Mabel. "Presenter of Folk Tales and Children's Literature: Joseph Jacobs (1854-1916)." Australian Folklore: A Yearly Journal of Folklore Studies 18 (2003): 15-25.

Kershen, Anne J. "Joseph Jacobs." Oxford Dictionary of National Biography. Oxford: Oxford University Press. http://www.oxforddnb.com.

Rabinovitch, Simon. "Jews, Englishmen, and Folklorists: The Scholarship of Joseph Jacobs and Moses Gaster." In The Jew in Late-Victorian and Edwardian Culture: Between the East End and East Africa, edited by Eitan Bar-Yosef and Nadia Valman, 113-130. Basingstoke: Palgrave Macmillan, 2009.

Shaner, Mary E. "Joseph Jacobs." In British Children's Writers, 1880-1914.

Dictionary of Literary Biography, Vol. 141, edited by Laura M. Zaidman, 134-141. Detroit: Gale, 1994.

Stewig, John Warren. "Joseph Jacobs' English Fairy Tales: A Legacy for Today." In *Touchstones: Reflections on the Best in Children's Literature: Fairy Tales, Fables, Myths, Legends, and Poetry*, vol. 2, edited by Perry Nodelman, 128-139. West Lafayette, Ind.: Children's Literature Association, 1987.

FROM "MORRAHA."

WHEN I was growing up, my mother taught me the language of the birds; and when I got married, I used to be listening to their conversation; and I would be laughing; and my wife would be asking me what was the reason of my laughing, but I did not like to tell her, as women are always asking questions. We went out walking one fine morning, and the birds were arguing with one another. One of them said to another:

"Why should you be comparing yourself with me, when there is not a king nor knight that does not come to look at my tree?"

"What advantage has your tree over mine, on which there are three rods[1] of magic and mastery growing?"

When I heard them arguing, and knew that the rods were there, I began to laugh.

"Oh," asked my wife, "why are you always laughing? I believe it is at myself you are jesting, and I'll walk with you no more."

"Oh, it is not about you I am laughing. It is because I understand the language of the birds."

Then I had to tell her what the birds were saying to one another; and she was greatly delighted, and she asked me to go home, and she gave orders to the cook to have breakfast ready at six o'clock in the morning. I did not know why she was going out early, and breakfast was ready in the morning at the hour she appointed. She asked me to go out walking. I went with her. She went to the tree, and asked me to cut a rod for her.

"Oh, I will not cut it. Are we not better without it?"

---

1 Branches.

"I will not leave this until I get the rod, to see if there is any good in it."

I cut the rod and gave it to her. She turned from me and struck a blow on a stone, and changed it; and she struck a second blow on me, and made of me a black raven, and she went home and left me after her. I thought she would come back; she did not come, and I had to go into a tree till morning. In the morning, at six o'clock, there was a bellman out, proclaiming that every one who killed a raven would get a fourpenny-bit.[1] At last you would not find man or boy without a gun, nor, if you were to walk three miles, a raven that was not killed. I had to make a nest in the top of the parlour chimney, and hide myself all day till night came, and go out to pick up a bit to support me, till I spent a month. Here she is herself to say if it is a lie I am telling.

"It is not," said she.

John Batten, illustration from "Morraha," in *More Celtic Fairy Tales*, by Joseph Jacobs (London: Nutt, 1894), 87.

1 A silver coin valued at four pence.

Then I saw her out walking. I went up to her, and I thought she would turn me back to my own shape, and she struck me with the rod and made of me an old white horse, and she ordered me to be put to a cart with a man, to draw stones from morning till night. I was worse off then. She spread abroad a report that I had died suddenly in my bed, and prepared a coffin, and waked and buried me. Then she had no trouble. But when I got tired I began to kill every one who came near me, and I used to go into the haggard[1] every night and destroy the stacks of corn; and when a man came near me in the morning I would follow him till I broke his bones. Every one got afraid of me. When she saw I was doing mischief she came to meet me, and I thought she would change me. And she did change me, and made a fox of me. When I saw she was doing me every sort of damage I went away from her. I knew there was a badger's hole in the garden, and I went there till night came, and I made great slaughter among the geese and ducks. There she is herself to say if I am telling a lie.

"Oh! you are telling nothing but the truth, only less than the truth."

When she had enough of my killing the fowl she came out into the garden, for she knew I was in the badger's hole. She came to me and made me a wolf. I had to be off, and go to an island, where no one at all would see me, and now and then I used to be killing sheep, for there were not many of them, and I was afraid of being seen and hunted; and so I passed a year, till a shepherd saw me among the sheep and a pursuit was made after me. And when the dogs came near me there was no place for me to escape to from them; but I recognised the sign of the king among the men, and I made for him, and the king cried out to stop the hounds.[2] I took a leap upon the front of the king's saddle, and the woman behind cried out, "My king and my lord, kill him, or he will kill you!"

"Oh! he will not kill me. He knew me; he must be pardoned."

The king took me home with him, and gave orders I should be

1 Field of haystacks.
2 The supplication of the wolf to the king is a motif found in several medieval tales, including Marie de France's *Bisclavret*, the *Lai de Melion*, and *Guillaume de Palerne*.

well cared for. I was so wise, when I got food, I would not eat one morsel until I got a knife and fork. The man told the king, and the king came to see if it was true, and I got a knife and fork, and I took the knife in one paw and the fork in the other, and I bowed to the king. The king gave orders to bring him drink, and it came; and the king filled a glass of wine and gave it to me.

I took hold of it in my paw and drank it, and thanked the king.

"On my honour," said he, "it is some king or other has lost him, when he came on the island; and I will keep him, as he is trained; and perhaps he will serve us yet."

And this is the sort of king he was,—a king who had not a child living. Eight sons were born to him and three daughters, and they were stolen the same night they were born. No matter what guard was placed over them, the child would be gone in the morning. A twelfth child now came to the queen, and the king took me with him to watch the baby. The women were not satisfied with me.

"Oh," said the king, "what was all your watching ever good for? One that was born to me I have not; I will leave this one in the dog's care, and he will not let it go."

A coupling[1] was put between me and the cradle, and when every one went to sleep I was watching till the person woke who attended in the daytime; but I was there only two nights; when it was near the day, I saw a hand coming down through the chimney, and the hand was so big that it took round the child altogether, and thought to take him away. I caught hold of the hand above the wrist, and as I was fastened to the cradle, I did not let go my hold till I cut the hand from the wrist, and there was a howl from the person without. I laid the hand in the cradle with the child, and as I was tired I fell asleep; and when I awoke, I had neither child nor hand; and I began to howl, and the king heard me, and he cried out that something was wrong with me, and he sent servants to see what was the matter with me, and when the messenger came he saw me covered with blood, and he could not see the child; and he went to the king and told him the child was not to be got. The king came and saw the cradle coloured with the blood, and he cried out "where was the child gone?" and every one said it was the dog had eaten it.

---

1 Chain.

MORRAHA

John Batten, illustration from "Morraha," in *More Celtic Fairy Tales*, by Joseph Jacobs (London: Nutt, 1894), 90.

The king said: "It is not: loose him, and he will get the pursuit himself."

When I was loosed, I found the scent of the blood till I came to a door of the room in which the child was. I went back to the king and took hold of him, and went back again and began to tear at the door. The king followed me and asked for the key. The servant said it was in the room of the stranger woman. The king caused search to be made for her, and she was not to be found. "I will break the door," said the king, "as I can't get the key." The king broke the door, and I went in, and went to the trunk, and the king asked for a key to unlock it. He got no key, and he broke the lock. When he opened the trunk, the child and the hand were stretched side by side, and the child was asleep. The king took the hand and ordered a woman to come for the child, and he showed the hand to every one in the house. But the stranger woman was gone, and she did not see the king;—and here she is herself to say if I am telling lies of her.

"Oh, it's nothing but the truth you have!"

The king did not allow me to be tied any more. He said there was nothing so much to wonder at as that I cut the hand off, as I was tied.

The child was growing till he was a year old. He was beginning to walk, and no one cared for him more than I did. He was growing till he was three, and he was running out every minute; so the king ordered a silver chain to be put between me and the child, that he might not go away from me. I was out with him in the garden every day, and the king was as proud as the world of the child. He would be watching him everywhere we went, till the child grew so wise that he would loose the chain and get off. But one day that he loosed it I failed to find him; and I ran into the house and searched the house, but there was no getting him for me. The king cried to go out and find the child, that had got loose from the dog. They went searching for him, but could not find him. When they failed altogether to find him, there remained no more favour with the king towards me, and everyone disliked me, and I grew weak, for I did not get a morsel to eat half the time. When summer came, I said I would try and go home to my own country. I went away one fine morning, and I went swimming, and God helped me till

I came home. I went into the garden, for I knew there was a place in the garden where I could hide myself, for fear my wife should see me. In the morning I saw her out walking, and the child with her, held by the hand. I pushed out to see the child, and as he was looking about him everywhere, he saw me and called out, "I see my shaggy papa. Oh!" said he; "oh, my heart's love, my shaggy papa, come here till I see you!"

John Batten, illustration from "Morraha," in *More Celtic Fairy Tales*, by Joseph Jacobs (London: Nutt, 1894), 92.

I was afraid the woman would see me, as she was asking the child where he saw me, and he said I was up in a tree; and the more the child called me, the more I hid myself. The woman took the child home with her, but I knew he would be up early in the morning.

I went to the parlour-window, and the child was within, and he was playing. When he saw me he cried out, "Oh! my heart's love, come here till I see you, shaggy papa." I broke the window and went in, and he began to kiss me. I saw the rod in front of the chimney, and I jumped up at the rod and knocked it down. "Oh! my heart's love, no one would give me the pretty rod," said he. I hoped he would strike me with the rod, but he did not. When I saw the time was short I raised my paw, and I gave him a scratch below the knee. "Oh! you naughty, dirty, shaggy papa, you have hurt me so much, I'll give you a blow of the rod." He struck me a light blow, and so I came back to my own shape again. When he saw a man standing before him he gave a cry, and I took him up in my arms. The servants heard the child. A maid came in to see what was the matter with him. When she saw me she gave a cry out of her, and she said, "Oh, if the master isn't come to life again!"

Another came in, and said it was he really. When the mistress heard of it, she came to see with her own eyes, for she would not believe I was there; and when she saw me she said she'd drown herself. But I said to her, "If you yourself will keep the secret, no living man will ever get the story from me until I lose my head." Here she is herself to say if I am telling the truth. "Oh, it's nothing but truth you are telling."

When I saw I was in a man's shape, I said I would take the child back to his father and mother, as I knew the grief they were in after him. I got a ship, and took the child with me; and as I journeyed I came to land on an island, and I saw not a living soul on it, only a castle dark and gloomy. I went in to see was there any one in it. There was no one but an old hag, tall and frightful, and she asked me, "What sort of person are you?" I heard some one groaning in another room, and I said I was a doctor, and I asked her what ailed the person who was groaning.

"Oh," said she, "it is my son, whose hand has been bitten from his wrist by a dog."

I knew then that it was he who had taken the child from me, and I said I would cure him if I got a good reward.

"I have nothing; but there are eight young lads and three young women, as handsome as any one ever laid eyes on, and if you cure him I will give you them."

"Tell me first in what place his hand was cut from him?"

"Oh, it was out in another country, twelve years ago."

"Show me the way, that I may see him."

She brought me into a room, so that I saw him, and his arm was swelled up to the shoulder. He asked me if I would cure him;

and I said I would cure him if he would give me the reward his mother promised.

"Oh, I will give it; but cure me."

"Well, bring them out to me."

The hag brought them out of the room. I said I should burn the flesh that was on his arm. When I looked on him he was howling with pain. I said that I would not leave him in pain long. The wretch had only one eye in his forehead. I took a bar of iron, and put it in the fire till it was red, and I said to the hag, "He will be howling at first, but will fall asleep presently, and do not wake him till he has slept as much as he wants. I will close the door when I am going out." I took the bar with me, and I stood over him, and I turned it across through his eye as far as I could. He began to bellow, and tried to catch me, but I was out and away, having closed the door. The hag asked me, "Why is he bellowing?"

"Oh, he will be quiet presently, and will sleep for a good while, and I'll come again to have a look at him; but bring me out the young men and the young women."

I took them with me, and I said to her, "Tell me where you got them."

"My son brought them with him, and they are all the children of one king."

I was well satisfied, and I had no wish for delay to get myself free from the hag, so I took them on board the ship, and the child I had myself. I thought the king might leave me the child I nursed myself; but when I came to land, and all those young people with me, the king and queen were out walking. The king was very aged, and the queen aged likewise. When I came to converse with them, and the twelve with me, the king and queen began to cry. I asked, "Why are you crying?"

"It is for good cause I am crying. As many children as these I should have, and now I am withered, grey, at the end of my life, and I have not one at all."

I told him all I went through, and I gave him the child in his hand, and "These are your other children who were stolen from you, whom I am giving to you safe. They are gently reared."

When the king heard who they were he smothered them with kisses and drowned them with tears, and dried them with fine cloths silken and the hair of his own head, and so also did their mother, and great was his welcome for me, as it was I who found them all. The king said to me, "I will give you the last child, as it is you who have earned him best; but you must come to my court every year, and the child with you, and I will share with you my possessions."

"I have enough of my own, and after my death I will leave it to the child."

I spent a time, till my visit was over, and I told the king all the troubles I went through, only I said nothing about my wife. And now you have the story.

Ⓦhere There Is Ⓝothing, There Is Ⓖod

WILLIAM BUTLER YEATS

*William Butler Yeats (1865-1939) was born in Dublin, Ireland, but lived
in London for much of his childhood. After completing high school in
Dublin, he was at first attracted to a career in the visual arts but soon
turned to poetry. When his family returned to London in 1887, Yeats
began writing prolifically, and in 1889, he published his first collection,*
The Wanderings of Oisin and Other Poems. *One year later, Yeats co-
founded the Rhymers' Club in London, a bohemian literary society that
included many of the best young poets of the period, including Lionel
Johnson and Ernest Dowson. During the 1890s, Yeats developed an interest in the occult, which led to his induction into the Golden Dawn, a
secret society focused on mysticism and magic. He simultaneously became
deeply involved in the Irish nationalist movement, and consequently, his
work became more distinctly Irish in its themes and motifs.*

*As an expression of his nationalist fervor, in 1899 Yeats co-founded
the Irish National Theatre, an effort which led to the founding of the
Abbey Theatre five years later. During the first decade of the twentieth
century, Yeats co-managed the Abbey Theatre while at the same time
writing and producing his own plays, including* Deirdre *(1906) and* The
Golden Helmet *(1908). After the Irish War of Independence ended in
1922, Yeats served as a senator in the Irish Free State, a position he held
until 1928. Today Yeats is best known as a visionary poet whose work
embodied the modernist spirit of the age, as epitomized by his later collections,* The Tower *(1928) and* The Winding Stair *(1933). He was
awarded the Nobel Prize for Literature in 1923.*

*Yeats's reputation rests largely on the brilliance of his poetry, and
as a result his fiction has received significantly less critical attention. Yet
between 1887 and 1905, Yeats was a prolific fiction writer. He published
twenty-three short stories in popular periodicals, including the* Savoy,
National Observer, Sketch, *and* Speaker. *In addition, he published a*

novel, John Sherman (1891), *and drafted another long work of prose fiction,* The Speckled Bird. *During this period, Yeats also edited anthologies of traditional Irish folklore, including* The Celtic Twilight (1893). *Yeats adapted motifs from the folkloric tradition when writing original short fiction for a popular audience.*

"Where There Is Nothing, There Is God" (1896) was originally published in a popular illustrated weekly magazine, Sketch, *as part of its "A Novel in a Nutshell" series. It was subsequently anthologized in* The Secret Rose (1897). *Yeats began drafting* The Secret Rose *stories in 1894 when visiting his uncle in Sligo, a rural setting that informed the imagery and subject matter of his work. In a dedication to the published collection, Yeats notes that the stories "have but one subject, the war of spiritual with natural order."*[1]

Bibliography

Foster, R. F. "William Butler Yeats." *Oxford Dictionary of National Biography.* Oxford University Press, 2004. http://www.oxforddnb.com.

Gould, Warwick, Phillip Marcus, and Michael Sidnell, eds. *The Secret Rose, Stories by W. B. Yeats: A Variorum Edition.* 2nd ed. London: Macmillan, 1992.

Hirsch, Edward. "A War between the Orders: Yeats's Fiction and the Transcendental Moment." *Novel: A Forum on Fiction* 17, no. 1 (1983): 52-66.

Myers, Stephen. *Yeats's Book of the Nineties: Poetry, Politics, and Rhetoric.* New York: Peter Lang, 1993.

O'Donnell, William. "William Butler Yeats." In *British Short Fiction Writers, 1880-1914: The Romantic Tradition. Dictionary of Literary Biography,* Vol. 156, edited by William Naufftus. Detroit: Gale, 1995. *Literature Resource Center,* http://gogalegroup.com.

—. "Yeats as Adept and Artist: *The Speckled Bird, The Secret Rose,* and *The Wind among the Reeds.*" In *Yeats and the Occult,* edited by George Mills Harper, 55-79. Toronto: Macmillan, 1975.

Putzel, Steven. *Reconstructing Yeats: The Secret Rose and The Wind Among the Reeds.* Totowa, N.J.: Barnes and Noble, 1986.

Yeats, William Butler. Dedication to *The Secret Rose,* vii. London: Lawrence and Bullen, 1897.

—. "Where There Is Nothing, There Is God." *Sketch,* Oct. 21, 1896, 548.

---

[1] William Butler Yeats, dedication to *The Secret Rose,* vii. The dedication was written to "A. E.," Yeats's friend and fellow writer, George William Russell.

WHERE THERE IS NOTHING, THERE IS GOD.

THE little wicker houses[1] where the Brothers of Tullagh[2] were accustomed to pray or bend over many handicrafts when twilight had driven them from the fields, were empty, for the severity of the winter had brought the brotherhood together in the square wooden house under the shadow of the wooden chapel; and Coarb[3] Malathgeneus, Brother Moal Columb, Brother Maol Melruan, Brother Peter, Brother Patrick, Brother Fintain, and many too young to have won names in the great battle, sat about the fire with ruddy faces, one mending lines to lay in the river for eels, one fashioning a snare for birds, one mending the broken handle of a spade, one writing in a large book, and one shaping a jewelled box to hold the book; and among the rushes at their feet lay the scholars, brothers to be, whose school-house it was, and for the succour of whose tender years the great fire was supposed to leap and flicker. One of these, a child of eight or nine years, called Aodh, lay upon his back gazing up through the hole in the roof, through which the smoke poured, watching the stars appearing and disappearing in the smoke with mild eyes, like the eyes of a beast of the field. He turned presently to the Brother who wrote in the big book, and whose duty was to teach the children, and said, "Brother Maol Columb, to what are the stars fastened?" The Brother, rejoicing to see so much curiosity in the stupidest of his scholars, laid down the style[4] and said, "There are nine crystalline spheres, and on the first the moon is fastened, on the second the planet Mercury, on the third the planet Venus, on the fourth the sun, on the fifth the planet Mars, on the sixth the planet Jupiter, on the seventh the planet Saturn (these are the wandering stars), and

---

1 Cylindrical dwellings made of woven branches or twigs and crowned with a rustic thatched roof.

2 Probably the medieval Monastery of Tallaght, an ascetic brotherhood founded by Saint Maelruain in the eighth century near the site of present-day Dublin.

3 Abbot in the medieval Irish church.

4 Pen.

on the eighth are fastened the fixed stars; but the ninth sphere is a sphere of the substance on which the breath of God moved in the beginning."

"What is beyond that sphere?" said the child.

"There is nothing beyond that; there is God."

And then the child's eyes strayed to the jewelled box, where one great ruby was gleaming in the light of the fire, and he said, "Why has Brother Peter put a great ruby on the side of the box?"

"The ruby is a symbol of the love of God."

"Why is the ruby a symbol of the love of God?"

"Because it is red, like fire, and fire burns up everything, and where there is nothing, there is God."

The child sank into silence, but presently sat up and said, "There is somebody outside."

"No," replied the Brother. "It is only the wolves; I have heard them moving about in the snow for some time. They are growing very wild, now that the winter drives them from the mountains. They broke into a fold last night and carried off many sheep, and if we are not careful they will devour everything."

"No, it is the footstep of a man, for it is heavy; but I can hear the footsteps of the wolves also."

He had no sooner done speaking than somebody rapped three times, but with no great loudness.

"I will go and open, for he must be very cold."

"Do not open, for it may be a man-wolf, and he may devour us all."

But the boy had already shot back the heavy wooden bolt, and all faces, the most a little pale, turned towards the slowly opening door.

"He has beads and a cross, and cannot be a man-wolf," said the child, as a man with the snow heavy on his long, ragged beard, and on the matted hair, that fell over his shoulders and nearly to his waist, and dropping from the tattered cloak that but half-covered his withered brown body, came in and looked from face to face with mild, ecstatic eyes. Standing some way from the fire, and with eyes that had rested at last upon the Coarb Malathgeneus, he cried out, "O blessed Coarb, let me come to the fire and warm myself and dry the snow from my beard and my hair and my cloak; that I may not die of the cold of the mountains and anger the Lord with a wilful martyrdom."

"Come to the fire," said the Coarb, "and warm yourself, and eat the food the boy Aodh will bring you. It is sad indeed that any for whom Christ has died should be as poor as you."

The man sat over the fire, and Aodh took away his now dripping cloak and laid meat and bread and wine before him; but he would only eat of the bread, and he put away the wine, asking for water in its stead. When his beard and hair had begun to dry a little and his limbs had ceased to shiver with the cold, he spoke again.

"O blessed Coarb, have pity on the poor, have pity on a beggar who has trodden the bare world this many a year, and give me some labour to do, the hardest there is, for I am the poorest of God's poor."

Then the brethren discussed together what work they could put him to, and at first to little purpose, for there was no labour that had not found its labourer in that busy community; but at last one remembered that Brother Melruan, whose business it was to turn the great quern[1] in the quern-house, for he was too stupid for aught else, was getting old for so heavy a labour; and so the beggar was bid labour at the quern from the morrow.

The cold passed away, and the spring grew to summer, and the quern was never idle, nor was it turned with grudging labour, for when any passed the beggar was heard singing as he drove the handle round. The last gloom, too, had passed from that happy community, for Aodh,who had always been stupid and unteachable, grew clever and alert, and this was the more miraculous because it had come of a sudden. One day he had been even duller than usual, and was beaten and bid know his lesson the better on the morrow or be sent into a lower class among little boys who would make a jeer of him. He had gone out in tears, and when he came the next day, although his stupidity, born of a mind that would listen to every wandering sound and brood upon every wandering light, had so long been the byword of the school, he knew it with such perfection that he passed to the head of the class, and from that day was the best of scholars. At first Brother

---

1 A hand-operated mill used for grinding grain.

Maol Columb thought the change an answer to his own prayers to the Virgin, and took it for a great proof of the love she bore him; but when many far more fervid prayers had failed to add a single wheat-sheaf to the harvest, he began to think that the child was trafficking with bards,[1] or druids, or witches, and resolved to follow and watch. He had told his thought to the Coarb, who bid him come to him the moment he hit the truth; and the next day, which was a Sunday, he stood in the path when the Coarb and the brethren were coming from vespers, with their white habits upon them, and took the Coarb by the habit and said, "The beggar is of the greatest of saints and of the workers of miracle. I followed Aodh but now, and by his slow steps and his bent head I saw that the weariness of his stupidity was over him, and when we came to the little wood by the quern-house I knew by the path broken in the underwood and by the foot-marks in the muddy places that he had gone that way many times. I hid behind a bush where the path doubled upon itself at a sloping place, and understood by the tears in his eyes that his stupidity was too old and his wisdom too new to bring him peace unshaken by terror of the rod. When he was in the quern-house I went to the window and looked in, and the birds came down and perched upon my head and my shoulders, for they are not timid in that holy place; and a wolf passed by, his right side shaking my habit, his left the leaves of a bush. Aodh opened his book and turned to the page I had bid him learn, and began to cry, and the beggar sat beside him and comforted him until he fell asleep. When his sleep was of the deepest the beggar knelt down and prayed aloud, and said, "O Thou Who dwellest beyond the stars, show forth Thy power as at the beginning, and let knowledge sent from Thee awaken in this mind, wherein is nothing from the world, that the nine orders of angels may glorify Thy name"; and then a light broke out of the air and wrapped Aodh, and I smelt the breath of roses. I stirred a little in my wonder, and the beggar turned and saw me, and, bending low, said, "O Brother Maol Columb, if I have done wrong, forgive me, and I will do penance. It was my pity moved me"; but terror had taken hold of me, and I fled, and did not stop running until I came hither."

---

1 Pagan minstrels.

Then all the brothers began talking together, one saying it was such and such a saint, and one that it was not he, but another; and one that it was none of these, for they were still in their brotherhoods, but that it was such and such a one; and the talk was as near to quarrelling as might be in that gentle community, for each would claim so great a saint for his native province. At last the Coarb said, "He is none that you have named, for at Easter I had greeting from all, and each was in his brotherhood; but he is Angus[1] the Lover of God, and the first of those who have gone to live in the wild places and among the wild beasts. Ten years ago he felt the burden of many labours in a brotherhood under the Croagh of Patrick[2] and went into the forest that he might labour only with song to the Lord; but the fame of his holiness brought many thousands to his cell, so that a little pride clung to a soul from which all else had been driven. Nine years ago he dressed himself in rags, and from that day none has seen him, unless, indeed, it be true that he has been seen living among the wolves on the mountains and eating the grass of the fields. Let us go to him and bow down before him; for at last, after long seeking, he has found the nothing that is God; and bid him lead us in the pathway he has trodden." They passed in their white habits along the beaten path in the wood, the acolytes swinging their censers[3] before them, and the Coarb, with his crozier[4] studded with precious stones, in the midst of the incense; and came before the quern-house and knelt down and began to pray, awaiting the moment when the child would wake, and the Saint cease from his watch and come forth and look at the sun going down into the unknown darkness, as his way was.

---

1 Probably the ninth-century Irish saint Óengus of Tallaght (or Óengus the Culdee, here anglicized as Angus), who lived part of his life as a hermit in the wilderness. Disguised as a lay brother, he entered the Monastery of Tallaght, but his true identity was ultimately revealed by the presiding abbot, Saint Maelruain. Yeats may also be alluding to Óengus, the god of youth, beauty, and poetry in ancient Irish mythology.

2 Sacred mountain dedicated to St. Patrick located in County Mayo, Ireland.

3 Vessels used for burning incense.

4 An abbot's crook or staff.

ℭolf-ℭhildren[1]

Chambers's Edinburgh Journal was a cheap weekly magazine first published in 1832. By the 1850s, it had a circulation of about 23,000, which primarily included readers from lower-class and middle-class backgrounds. Articles were short and published anonymously. The magazine was designed to provide entertainment, instruction, and moral guidance. Like many other Victorian periodicals, Chambers's was steeped in the rhetoric of imperialism and thus often expressed racist attitudes about non-British cultures. In these contexts, India was interpreted as a backward, exotic land full of danger and adventure. Such representations supported the nation's broader colonial ambitions on the Indian sub-continent. Queen Victoria was crowned Empress of India in 1876 after many years of British military, cultural, economic colonization. India did not achieve independence from Britain until 1947.

IT is a pity that the present age is so completely absorbed in materialities, at a time when the facilities are so singularly great for a philosophy which would inquire into the constitution of our moral nature. In the North Pacific, we are in contact with tribes of savages ripening, sensibly to the eye, into civilised communities; and we are able to watch the change as dispassionately as if we were in our studies examining the wonders of the minute creation through a microscope. In America, we have before us a living model, blind, mute, deaf, and without the sense of smell; communicating with the external world by the sense of touch alone; yet endowed with a rare intelligence, which permits us to see, through the fourfold veil that shrouds her, the original germs of the human character.[2] Nearer home, we have been from time

---

1 *Chambers' Edinburgh Journal* 446 (July 17, 1852): 33-36.
2 See "The Rudimental," in No. 391. [Author's note.]

to time attracted and astonished by the spectacle of children, born of European parents, emerging from forests where they had been lost for a series of years, fallen back, not into the moral condition of savages, but of wild beasts, with the sentiments and even the instincts of their kind obliterated for ever. And now we have several cases before us, occurring in India, of the same lapses from humanity, involving circumstances curious in themselves, but more important than curious, as throwing a strange light upon what before was an impenetrable mystery. It is to these we mean to direct our attention on the present occasion; but before doing so, it will be well just to glance at the natural history of the wild children of Europe.[1]

The most remarkable specimen, and the best type of the class, was found in the year 1725, in a wood in Hanover.[2] With the appearance of a human being—of a boy about thirteen years of age—he was in every respect a wild animal, walking on all-fours, feeding on grass and moss, and lodging in trees. When captured, he exhibited a strong repugnance to clothing; he could not be induced to lie on a bed, frequently tearing the clothes to express his indignation; and in the absence of his customary lair among the boughs of a tree, he crouched in a corner of the room to sleep. Raw food he devoured with relish, more especially cabbage-leaves and other vegetables, but turned away from the sophistications of cookery. He had no articulate language, expressing his emotions only by the sounds emitted by various animals. Although only five feet three inches, he was remarkably strong; he never exhibited any interest in the female sex; and even in his old age—for he was supposed to be seventy-three when he died—it was only in external manners he had advanced from the character of a wild beast to that of a good-tempered savage, for he was still without consciousness of the Great Spirit.

In other children that were caught subsequently to Peter, for that was the name they gave him, the same character was observable, although with considerable modifications. One of them, a

---

1 A paper on this subject will be found in *Chambers's Miscellany of Useful and Entertaining Tracts*, vol. v., No. 48. [Author's note.]

2 Probably the city of Hanover, the capital of Lower Saxony located in north-central Germany.

young girl of twelve or thirteen, was not merely without sympathy for persons of the male sex, but she held them all her life in great abhorrence. Her temper was ungovernable; she was fond of blood, which she sucked from the living animal; and was something more than suspected of the cannibal propensity. On one occasion, she was seen to dive as naturally as an otter in a lake, catch a fish, and devour it on the spot. Yet this girl eventually acquired language; was even able to give some indistinct account of her early career in the woods; and towards the close of her life, when subdued by long illness, exhibited few traces of having once been a wild animal. Another, a boy of eleven or twelve, was caught in the woods of Canne, in France. He was impatient, capricious, violent; rushing even through crowded streets like an ill-trained dog; slovenly and disgusting in his manners; affected with spasmodic motions of the head and limbs; biting and scratching all who displeased him; and always, when at comparative rest, balancing his body like a wild animal in a menagerie. His senses were incapable of being affected by anything not appealing to his personal feelings: a pistol fired close to his head excited little or no emotion, yet he heard distinctly the cracking of a walnut, or the touch of a hand upon the key which kept him captive. The most delicious perfumes, or the most fetid exhalations, were the same thing to his sense of smell, because these did not affect, one way or other, his relish for his food, which was of a disgusting nature, and which he dragged about the floor like a dog, eating it when besmeared with filth. Like almost all the lower animals, he was affected by the changes of the weather; but on some of these occasions, his feelings approached to the human in their manifestations. When he saw the sun break suddenly from a cloud, he expressed his joy by bursting into convulsive peals of laughter; and one morning, when he awoke, on seeing the ground covered with snow, he leaped out of bed, rushed naked into the garden, rolled himself over and over in the snow, and, stuffing handfuls of it into his mouth, devoured it eagerly. Sometimes he showed signs of a true madness, wringing his hands, gnashing his teeth, and becoming formidable to those about him. But in other moods, the phenomena of nature seemed to tranquillise and sadden him. When the severity of the season, as we are informed by the French physician who had charge of him, had driven every other person out of the garden, he still delighted to walk there; and, after taking many turns, would seat himself beside a pond of water. Here his convulsive motions, and the continual balancing of his whole body, diminished, and gave way to a more tranquil attitude; his face gradually assumed the character of sorrow or melancholy reverie, while his eyes were steadfastly fixed on the surface of the water, and he threw into it, from time to time, some withered leaves. In like manner, on a moonlight night, when the rays of the moon entered his room, he seldom failed to awake, and to place himself at the window. Here he would remain for a considerable time, motionless, with his neck extended, and his eyes fixed on the moonlight landscape, and wrapped in a kind of contemplative ecstasy, the silence of which was interrupted only by profound inspirations, accompanied by a slight plaintive noise.

We have only to add, that by the anxious care of the physician, and a thousand ingenious contrivances, the senses of this human animal, with the exception of his hearing, which always remained dull and impassive, were gradually stimulated, and he was even able at length to pronounce two or three words. Here his history breaks off.

The scene of these extraordinary narratives has hitherto been confined to Europe; but we have now to draw attention to the wild children of India. It happens, fortunately, that in this case the character of the testimony is unimpeachable; for although brought forward in a brief, rough pamphlet, published in a provincial town, and merely said to be "by an Indian Official," we recognise both in the manner and matter the pen of Colonel Sleeman, the British Resident at the court of Lucknow,[1] whose invaluable services in putting down thuggee and dacoitee[2] in India we have already described to our readers.[3]

The district of Sultanpoor, in the kingdom of Oude, a portion of the great plain of the Ganges, is watered by the Goomtee River,

---

[1] A city in northern India.

[2] Robberies.

[3] See "Gang-Robbers of India," in Nos. 360 and 361 of this Journal. The title of the pamphlet alluded to is, *An Account of Wolves nurturing Children in their Dens.* By an Indian Official. Plymouth: Jenkin Thomas, printer. 1852. [Author's note.]

a navigable stream, about 140 yards broad, the banks of which are much infested by wolves. These animals are protected by the superstition of the Hindoos, and to such an extent, that a village community within whose boundaries a single drop of their blood has been shed, is believed to be doomed to destruction. The wolf is safe—but from a very different reason—even from those vagrant tribes who have no permanent abiding-place, but bivouac[1] in the jungle, and feed upon jackals, reptiles—anything, and who make a trade of catching and selling such wild animals as they consider too valuable to eat. The reason why the vulpine[2] ravager is spared by these wretches is—*that wolves devour children!* Not, however, that the wanderers have any dislike to children, but they are tempted by the jewels with which they are adorned; and knowing the dens of the animals, they make this fearful gold-seeking a part of their business. The adornment of their persons with jewelry is a passion with the Hindoos which nothing can overcome. Vast numbers of women—even those of the most infamous class—are murdered for the sake of their ornaments, yet the lesson is lost upon the survivors. Vast numbers of children, too, fall victims in the same way, and from the same cause, or are permitted, by those who shrink from murder, to be carried off and devoured by the wolves; yet no Indian mother can withstand the temptation to bedizen[3] her child, whenever it is in her power, with bracelets, necklaces, and other ornaments of gold and silver. So much is necessary as an introduction to the incidents that follow.

One day, a trooper, like Spenser's gentle knight, "was pricking on the plain,"[4] near the banks of the Goomtee. He was within a short distance of Chandour, a village about ten miles from Sultanpoor, the capital of the district, when he halted to observe a large female wolf and her whelps come out of a wood near the roadside, and go down to the river to drink. There were four whelps. Four!—surely not more than three; for the fourth of the juvenile company was as little like a wolf as possible. The horseman stared; for in fact it was a boy, going on all-fours like his comrades, evidently on excel-

---

1 Camp.
2 Cunning (literally, fox-like).
3 Decorate.
4 From Canto I of Edmund Spenser's *The Faerie Queen* (1590).

lent terms with them all, and guarded, as well as the rest, by the dam[1] with the same jealous care which that exemplary mother, but unpleasant neighbour, bestows upon her progeny. The trooper sat still in his saddle watching this curious company till they had satisfied their thirst; but as soon as they commenced their return, he put spurs to his horse, to intercept the boy. Off ran the wolves, and off ran the boy helter-skelter—the latter keeping close up with the dam; and the horseman, owing to the unevenness of the ground, found it impossible to overtake them before they had all entered their den. He was determined, nevertheless, to attain his object, and assembling some people from the neighboring village with pickaxes, they began to dig in the usual way into the hole. Having made an excavation of six or eight feet, the garrison evacuated the place—the wolf, the three whelps, and the boy, leaping suddenly out and taking to flight. The trooper instantly threw himself upon his horse, and set off in pursuit, followed by the fleetest of the party; and the ground over which they had to fly being this time more even, he at length headed the chase, and turned the whole back upon the men on foot. These secured the boy, and, according to prescriptive rule, allowed the wolf and her three whelps to go on their way.

"They took the boy to the village," says Colonel Sleeman, "but had to tie him, for he was very restive, and struggled hard to rush into every hole or den they came near. They tried to make him speak, but could get nothing from him but an angry growl or snarl. He was kept for several days at the village, and a large crowd assembled every day to see him. When a grown-up person came near him, he became alarmed, and tried to steal away; but when a child came near him, he rushed at it with a fierce snarl, like that of a dog, and tried to bite it. When any cooked meat was put near him, he rejected it in disgust; but when raw meat was offered, he seized it with avidity, put it upon the ground, under his hands, like a dog, and ate it with evident pleasure. He would not let anyone come near while he was eating, but he made no objection to a dog's coming and sharing his food with him."

This wild boy was sent to Captain Nicholetts, the European

---

1 Female wolf.

officer commanding the 1st regiment of Oude Local Infantry, stationed at Sultanpoor. He lived only three years after his capture, and died in August 1850. According to Captain Nicholetts' account of him, he was very inoffensive except when teased, and would then growl and snarl. He came to eat anything that was thrown to him, although much preferring raw flesh. He was very fond of uncooked bones, masticating them apparently with as much ease as meat; and he had likewise a still more curious partiality for small stones and earth. So great was his appetite, that he has been known to eat half a lamb at one meal; and buttermilk he would drink by the pitcher full without seeming to draw breath. He would never submit to wear any article of dress even in the coldest weather; and when a quilt stuffed with cotton was given to him, "he tore it to pieces, and ate a portion of it—cotton and all—with his bread every day." The countenance of the boy was repulsive, and his habits filthy in the extreme. He was never known to smile; and, although fond of dogs and jackals, formed no attachment for any human being. Even when a favorite pariah dog, which used to feed with him, was shot for having fallen under suspicion of taking the lion's share of the meal, he appeared to be quite indifferent. He sometimes walked erect; but generally ran on all-fours—more especially to his food when it was placed at a distance from him.

Another of these wolf-children was carried off from his parents at Chupra (twenty miles from Sultanpoor), when he was three years of age. They were at work in the field, the man cutting his crop of wheat and pulse,[1] and the woman gleaning after him, with the child sitting on the grass. Suddenly, there rushed into the family party, from behind a bush, a gaunt wolf, and seizing the boy by the loins, ran off with him to a neighbouring ravine. The mother followed with loud screams, which brought the whole village to her assistance; but they soon lost sight of the wolf and his prey, and the boy was heard no more of for six years. At the end of that time, he was found by two sipahis[2] associating, as in the former case, with wolves, and caught by the leg when he had got half-way into the den. He was very ferocious when drawn out, biting at

---

1 Beans or other legumes.
2 Ottoman calvary officers.

his deliverers, and seizing hold of the barrel of one of their guns with his teeth. They secured him, however, and carried him home, when they fed him on raw flesh, hares, and birds, till they found the charge too onerous, and gave him up to the public charity of the village till he should be recognised by his parents. This actually came to pass. His mother, by that time a widow, hearing a report of the strange boy at Koeleapoor, hastened to the place from her own village of Chupra, and by means of indubitable marks upon his person, recognised her child, transformed into a wild animal. She carried him home with her; but finding him destitute of natural affection, and in other respects wholly irreclaimable, at the end of two months she left him to the common charity of the village.

When this boy drank, he dipped his face in the water, and sucked. The front of his elbows and knees had become hardened from going on all-fours with the wolves. The village boys amused themselves by throwing frogs to him, which he caught and devoured; and when a bullock died and was skinned, he resorted to the carcass like the dogs of the place, and fed upon the carrion. His body smelled offensively. He remained in the village during the day, for the sake of what he could get to eat, but always went off to the jungle at night. In other particulars, his habits resembled those already described. We have only to add respecting him, that, in November 1850, he was sent from Sultanpoor, under the charge of his mother, to Colonel Sleeman—then probably at Lucknow—but something alarming him on the way, he ran into a jungle, and had not been recovered at the date of the last dispatch.

We pass over three other narratives of a similar kind, that present nothing peculiar, and shall conclude with one more specimen of the Indian wolf-boy. This human animal was captured, like the first we have described, by a trooper, with the assistance of another person on foot. When placed on the pommel of the saddle, he tore the horseman's clothes, and, although his hands were tied, contrived to bite him severely in several places. He was taken to Bondee, where the rajah[1] took charge of him till he was carried off by Janoo, a lad who was khidmutgar (table-attendant) to a traveling Cashmere merchant. The boy was then apparently

---

1 Indian prince.

about twelve years of age, and went upon all-fours, although he could stand, and go awkwardly on his legs when threatened. Under Janoo's attention, however, in beating and rubbing his legs with oil, he learned to walk like other human beings. But the vulpine smell continued to be very offensive, although his body was rubbed for some months with mustard-seed soaked in water, and he was compelled during the discipline to live on rice, pulse, and bread. He slept under the mango tree, where Janoo himself lodged, but was always tied to a tent-pin.

One night, when the wild boy was lying asleep under his tree, Janoo saw two wolves come up stealthily, and smell at him. They touched him, and he awoke; and rising from his reclining posture, he put his hands upon the heads of his visitors, and they licked his face. They capered[1] round him, and he threw straw and leaves at them. The khidmutgar gave up his protégé for lost; but presently he became convinced that they were only at play, and he kept quiet. He at length gained confidence enough to drive the wolves away; but they soon came back, and resumed their sport for a time. The next night, three playfellows made their appearance, and in a few nights after, four. They came four or five times, till Janoo lost all his fear of them. When the Cashmere merchant returned to Lucknow, where his establishment was, Janoo still carried his pet with him, tied by a string to his own arm; and, to make him useful according to his capacity, with a bundle on his head. At every jungle they passed, however, the boy would throw down the bundle, and attempt to dart into the thicket; repeating the insubordination, though repeatedly beaten for it, till he was fairly subdued, and became docile by degrees. The greatest difficulty was to get him to wear clothes, which to the last he often injured or destroyed, by rubbing them against posts like a beast, when some part of his body itched. Some months after their arrival at Lucknow, Janoo was sent away from the place for a day or two on some business, and on his return he found that the wild boy had escaped. He was never more seen.

It is a curious circumstance, that the wild children, whether of Europe or Asia, have never been found above a certain age. They

---

1 Pranced.

do not grow into adults in the woods. Colonel Sleeman thinks their lives may be cut short by their living exclusively on animal food; but to some of them, as we have seen, a vegetable diet has been habitual. The probability seems to be, that with increasing years, their added boldness and consciousness of strength may lead them into fatal adventures with their brethren of the forest. As for the protection of the animal by which they were originally nurtured becoming powerless from age, which is another hypothesis, that supposes too romantic a system of patronage and dependence. The head of the family must have several successive series of descendants to care for after the arrival of the stranger, and it is far more probable that the wild boy is obliged to turn out with his playmates, when they are ordered to shift for themselves, than that he alone remains a fixture at home. That protection of some kind at first is a necessary condition of his surviving at all, there can be no manner of doubt, although it does not follow that a wolf is always the patron. The different habits of some of the European children we have mentioned, show a totally different course of education. If, for instance, they had been nurtured by wolves, they would no more have learned to climb trees than to fly in the air. As for the female specimen we have mentioned, hers was obviously an exceptional case. She was lost, as appeared from her own statement, when old enough to work at some employment, and a club she used as a weapon was one of her earliest recollections.

The wild children of India, however, were obviously indebted to wolves for their miserable lives; and it is not so difficult as at first sight might be supposed, to imagine the possibility of such an occurrence. The parent wolves are so careful of their progeny, that they feed them for some time with half-digested food, disgorged by themselves; and after that—if we may believe Buffon,[1] who seems as familiar with the interior of a den as if he had boarded and lodged in the family—they bring home to them live animals, such as hares and rabbits. These the young wolves play with, and when at length they are hungry, kill: the mother then for the first time interfering, to divide the prey in equal portions. But in the case of a child being brought to the den—a child accustomed, in all

---

1 French naturalist Georges-Louis Leclerc, Comte de Buffon (1707-1788).

probability, to tyrannise over the whelps of pariah dogs and other young animals, they would find it far easier to play than to kill; and if we only suppose the whole family going to sleep together, and the parents bringing home fresh food in the morning—contingencies not highly improbable—the mystery is solved, although the marvel remains. It may be added, that such wolves as we have an opportunity of observing in menageries, are always gentle and playful when young, and it is only time that develops the latent ferocity of a character the most detestable, perhaps, in the whole animal kingdom. Cowardly and cruel in equal proportion, the wolf has no defenders. "In short," says Goldsmith—probably translating Buffon, for we have not the latter at hand to ascertain— "every way offensive, a savage aspect, a frightful howl, an insupportable odour, a perverse disposition, fierce habits, he is hateful while living, and useless when dead."

But what, then, is man, whom mere accidental association for a few years can strip of the faculties inherent in his race and convert into a wolf? The lower animals retain their instincts in all circumstances. The kitten, brought up from birth on its mistress's lap, imbibes none of her tastes in food or anything else. It rejects vegetables, sweets, fruits, all drinks but water or milk, and although content to satisfy its hunger with dressed meat, darts with an eager growl upon raw flesh. Man alone is the creature of imitation in good or in bad. His faculties and instincts, although containing the *germ* of everything noble, are not independent and self-existing like those of the brutes. This fact accounts for the difference observable, in an almost stereotyped form, in the different classes of society; it affords a hint to legislators touching their obligation to use the power they possess in elevating, by means of education, the character of the more degraded portions of the community; and it brings home to us all the great lesson of sympathy for the bad as well as the afflicted—both victims alike of *circumstances*, over which they in many cases have nearly as little control as the wild children of the desert.

Wolf Lore[1]

Once a Week (1859-80) was a monthly illustrated magazine that published articles, poetry, and serialized fiction intended for a middle-class family audience. Many of the articles in Once a Week *were published anonymously, including "Wolf Lore."*

It is curious how few subjects can be chosen which will not afford a fund of amusing legends and strange learning to those who take the trouble to search in old books. Let us take, for example, such an unpromising creature as the wolf, and trace out a few of his associations; premising that tales and incidents connected with wolves are so abundant, we shall only extract a few as samples. Everyone is familiar with the wolf from zoological gardens and menageries, and knows that he is much like a large shepherd-dog; from which he is, however, scientifically marked off by the fact of his tail being straight, whereas it is curved in the canine families. They are almost universally distributed through the temperate regions (where they have not been exterminated), shading off into jackals, hyenas, &c., towards the tropics, and giving way to their warmer-clad brethren, the foxes, in the Arctic regions. As their bones have been found in the great fossil cave of Aurignac in France, they can assert a high antiquity; for the relics of seventeen human skeletons were also found there, which are the oldest specimens of humanity known to geologists. With their regal memories of rearing the founders of Rome,[2] it is humiliating to be obliged to confess that, like Eastern ghouls, they condescend to tear up and devour the dead, when hard pressed by hunger. There are even stories extant

---

1 From *Once a Week* 9 (October 1863): 501-502.
2 Romulus and Remus, the legendary founders of Rome, were said to have been suckled by a she-wolf.

of their eating earth when in such straits, but their friends explain away this unpleasant fact by cleverly turning it into a virtue. They wisely lay up food in times of abundance, it is said, and then dig it up when starving; and hence the calumny has sprung.

In English poetry wolves serve as examples of cunning and ferocity. One modern poet makes Iphigenia[1] just before her sacrifice by the Grecian chiefs say:

> Dimly I could descry
> The stern, black-bearded kings, with wolfish eyes,
> Waiting to see me die.[2]

They are more important in the domain of fable. We all remember how wisely one discourses of the joys of perfect liberty to the pampered house-dog, whose neck is yet somewhat grazed by the chain; and how another picked a quarrel with the lamb, and reproached the crane for asking payment for its surgical assistance when it had had the good fortune to escape from his very jaws.[3] Their character is here looked at in its shrewd worldly-wise aspect: something like Ulysses[4] himself, they have seen much and learnt much, and are always equal to the occasion. They do not fare quite so well perhaps in popular estimation, if we judge from proverbs. "Talk of a wolf and you will see him," was the Roman proverb we translate "Talk of the devil, &c," or, as the present more delicate century paraphrases it, "Speak of the angels, and you may hear the rustling of their wings." The same people expressively spoke of "having a wolf by the ears," to signify that they were in great straits and could neither advance nor retire. Similarly, to "be between the dog and the wolf," was to be between two fires, to interfere between husband and wife; and to "take a lamb from the wolf," was to snatch meat from a dog's mouth. Dean Trench[5] justly stigmatises "One must howl with the wolves," as being the

---

1 Daughter of Clytemnestra and Agamemnon from Greek mythology.

2 From Alfred Tennyson's poem, "A Dream of Fair Women" (1833).

3 From *Aesop's Fables*.

4 Roman name of Odysseus, legendary hero of Greek epic poetry (e.g., Homer's *The Odyssey*).

5 Rev. Richard Trench (1807-1886), Dean of Westminster Abbey and Archbishop of Dublin.

most dastardly of all proverbs. You must join in running down, that is, every object of popular detestation, lest you should be supposed guilty of sympathising with it. The Greeks with their lively fancy took a humorous view of the animal, speaking of "a wolf's wings," as we do of pigeon's milk or pig's wool.

As for wolves in England, everyone knows from his schoolbooks in whose reign they were exterminated by making taxes payable in their heads.[1] Quite recently, however, a few have been killed at different places in England, the theory for their discovery being that when fox-cubs are imported (as often happens) from France, one or two wolf-cubs have come accidentally amongst them. As late as Queen Elizabeth's reign[2] they are said to have been seen in Dean Forest and Dartmoor,[3] and in 1281 a commission was appointed to destroy wolves in the midland counties. We may gather the rigour with which wolves used to be hunted down in earlier times from a collection of Edward the Confessor's Laws, ratified by the Conqueror.[4] If anyone violently infringe the Church's protection, it is there laid down, on contempt of its sentence, he is to be outlawed by the king, and then, "from the day of the outlawry his head is a wolf's head." In Ireland wolves used to swarm and the Irish wolf-dog is a breed as distinct and as celebrated as the Scottish deer-hound. In this latter country the last two wolves were killed between 1690 and 1700. An amusing writer, who traveled through Sutherlandshire about 1650, says of it, after enumerating divers animals, "specially here never lack wolves more than are expedient."[5] Even now, in a severe winter, wolves leave the forests and press up to the very outskirts of a place no further from us than Rouen,[6] attacking the sheep and alarming the inhabitants.

But it is in superstition and magical ceremonies that the wolf's

---

1 King Edgar the Peaceful (943-975) allowed men to pay their taxes in wolf heads.

2 Queen Elizabeth I ruled England from 1558 to 1603.

3 The Forest of Dean is an ancient woodland in Gloucestershire, England, and Dartmoor is a moorland in Devon, England.

4 Edward the Confessor ruled England from 1044-66 and was succeeded briefly by Harold II (1066) before William the Conqueror took the throne (1066-87).

5 From William Blaeu's *Atlas* (1665).

6 A city in Normandy, northern France.

fame stands highest. All the ancient nations associated it with the world of darkness. It is represented on the painted walls of the Egyptian catacombs and temples, and is probably connected there with some esoteric doctrine of the transmigration of souls. In all the descriptions of Roman magical practices which have come down to us, the commonest feasts ascribed to Moeris or Canidia[1] (those wizards of world-wide renown), are to draw the moon down from the sky, and to become wolves at pleasure and hide themselves in the woods. If the unfortunate wryneck[2] was the bird sacred to the softer impulses of love, and when bound to a wheel and slowly turned round was believed to bring a recreant[3] lover to his languishing admirer's feet, the wolf was universally conse-crated to darker deeds of blood and vengeance. Nothing escaped Shakespeare, and the "tooth of wolf" is of course an ingredient in the hell-broth brewed by the witches in Macbeth. That most credulous of old naturalists, Pliny,[4] has some wonderful stories of the potent effects of this animal's influence. Horses are rendered torpid if they do but tread on its tracks. With some glimmering, we suppose, of the mediæval doctrine of signatures,[5] he goes on to tell us its liver is shaped like a horse's hoof. If any one wished for an infallible receipt[6] to keep wolves off his premises, he had only to cut off a wolf's feet, sprinkle the blood round his grounds, and take care to bury the animal itself at the place where the operation commenced. This has a wonderful smack of Mrs. Glasse's[7] cele-brated roast-hare, which it is first necessary to catch. Just as peas-ants nail up horseshoes at the present day to keep away witches, so the snout of a wolf used at Rome to be considered a sure charm against witchcraft, and was frequently fastened over house-doors.

---

1 Moeris was a legendary Egyptian king who created Lake Moeris and other ancient engineering marvels. Canidia is a sorceress figure in the *Epodes* of Horace (65-68 B.C.), a Roman lyric poet.

2 Small migratory bird.

3 Unfaithful.

4 Roman naturalist Pliny the Elder (23-79 A.D.)

5 The belief that God created the shapes of medicinal plants to mimic the parts of the human body they were intended to heal.

6 Recipe.

7 Hannah Glasse (1708-1770), eighteenth-century cookbook author.

Superstitions, like children's games, often linger in the world longer than arts and kingdoms and schemes of government.

From very old times there has been a current belief that some men by the aid of magic and demons could become wolves, and return at will to their real nature. The author we have just quoted (than whom Herodotus[1] himself was not fonder of marvels) tells us of an Arcadian[2] who lived nine years with wolves and then returned to mankind just as "Bonny Kilmeny" spent her time with the fairies and came back,—

> When seven long years had come and fled;
> When grief was calm, and hope was dead.[3]

And another Arcadian priest,[4] while offering human sacrifices, chanced to taste "the boy he was offering up," and forthwith became a wolf for ten years; a story which must be true, for did not this very man after his restoration win a victory at the Olympic games? These "wolf-men," as they were called, curiously enough reappear under the name of were-wolves in Gothic superstition: that gloomy people told of strange men meeting you and forthwith bounding off like wolves. In this state they used to prey on sheep and men with unusual ferocity, and were objects of great dread to all. Our word "turncoats" springs from this belief. It was also said that if a wolf once looked behind it while feeding, a sudden forgetfulness came upon it and it departed. This story can easily be traced to the indiscriminate rapacity of the animal, which forbade its ever leaving off while anything remained to eat. Let us conclude these legends with one of special interest to the ladies. For the peace and quietness' sake of the poor wolves in the Zoological Gardens, we have half a mind to forbear; but remembering the fate of Orpheus,[5] and having once aroused a woman's

---

1 Ancient Greek historian (c.484-425 B.C.)

2 A citizen of Arcadia, a region of ancient Greece.

3 From James Hogg's poem, "Kilmeny," *The Queen's Wake* (1813).

4 Lycaon, King of Arcadia. See Ovid's *Metamorphoses*.

5 A renowned singer and poet in Greek mythology who travels to the underworld in order to reclaim his dead wife, Eurydice. Moved by Orpheus' grief, the gods of the underworld permit him to retrieve her from the underworld on the condition that he not look back at her when returning to the living world. He cannot resist looking back at her and consequently loses her forever.

curiosity, perhaps the safer plan will be to go on. Well, then, there is a love-charm of peculiar virtue resident in one hair of a wolf's tail. It is even more potent than the fabled hippomanes,[1] more quick than the drug the "caitiff wretch" of an apothecary sold Romeo in his need.[2] Alas, that we should throw any obstacles in a lady's way! but—it must be plucked from the tail of the animal while it is alive!

Wolves have left their traces on our flowery banks. The lycopodiums or puff-balls are so called from their resemblance to the dark circular cushion-like foot of a wolf. Its upper surface, again, was seen by the fanciful botanists of old in the cut leaves of the gipsy-wort or *lycopus*, which means wolf's-foot. The gaping mouth of the wolf has also its supposed analogue in the bugloss or *lycopsis* (wolf's-face).

How far the huge bits used by our horse-breakers answer to the "wolfish teeth-bits" with which the Roman horses were ridden, we must leave to those of our "horsey" friends who are also classical scholars.

Not unnecessarily to remind readers of the boy in the fable who cried "wolf, wolf!" untruly, we will now really conclude this paper with one more instance of wolf lore. It speaks with peculiar propriety to travellers in lands where wolves may reasonably be expected to appear. Be sure, then, that you keep a sharp look-out for the animal, and contrive if you possibly can to see him before he sets eyes on you; otherwise you will infallibly be struck dumb.

Lupi Mœrin videre priores.[3]

---

1 A black substance supposedly found on a foal's forehead at birth and believed to be an aphrodisiac.

2 See Shakespeare's *Romeo and Juliet* 5.1.

3 The line reads, "Wolves have seen Moerin first," suggesting that he will be struck dumb. Virgil, *Bucolics*, Eclogue ix.

FROM

The Book of Were-Wolves:

Being an Account of a Terrible Superstition[1]

SABINE BARING-GOULD

Sabine Baring-Gould (1834-1924) was an Anglican clergyman and prolific man of letters. Early on in his clerical career, he wrote hymns, including the famous "Onward Christian Soldiers" (1864) as well as a novel, Through Flood and Flame (1868). *He went on to publish over forty novels and a variety of other devotional, travel, and general interest books. He also developed an interest in folklore, which led him to publish* The Book of Were-wolves (1865) *and* Curious Myths of the Middle Ages (1866, 1868). *He envisioned his role as providing entertaining stories while at the same time debunking common superstitions. As he notes in his preface to* The Book of Were-wolves, *"The subject . . . [is] full of interest and importance as elucidating a very obscure and mysterious chapter in the history of the Human Mind. When a form of superstition is prevalent everywhere, and in all ages, it must rest upon foundation of fact."[2] Later in his career, Baring-Gould became an avid collector of folksongs from the region near his home in Devonshire.*

CHAPTER I.

INTRODUCTORY.

I SHALL never forget the walk I took one night in Vienne,[3] after having accomplished the examination of an unknown Druidical

---

1 London: Smith, Elder, 1865.
2 Baring-Gould, Preface to *The Book of Were-wolves*, xii.
3 A town near Lyon, France.

relic, the Pierre labie, at La Rondelle, near Champigni. I had learned of the existence of this cromlech[1] only on my arrival at Champigni in the afternoon, and I had started to visit the curiosity without calculating the time it would take me to reach it and to return. Suffice it to say that I discovered the venerable pile of grey stones as the sun set, and that I expended the last lights of evening in planning and sketching. I then turned my face homeward. My walk of about ten miles had wearied me, coming at the end of a long day's posting, and I had lamed myself in scrambling over some stones to the Gaulish relic.

A small hamlet was at no great distance, and I betook myself thither, in the hopes of hiring a trap[2] to convey me to the posthouse,[3] but I was disappointed. Few in the place could speak French, and the priest, when I applied to him, assured me that he believed there was no better conveyance in the place than a common charrue[4] with its solid wooden wheels; nor was a riding horse to be procured. The good man offered to house me for the night; but I was obliged to decline, as my family intended starting early on the following morning.

Out spake then the mayor—"Monsieur can never go back to-night across the flats, because of the—the—" and his voice dropped; "the loups-garoux."[5]

"He says that he must return!" replied the priest in patois. "But who will go with him?"

"Ah, ha! M. le Curé. It is all very well for one of us to accompany him, but think of the coming back alone!"

"Then two must go with him," said the priest, and you can take care of each other as you return."

"Picou tells me that he saw the were-wolf only this day se'nnight," said a peasant; "he was down by the hedge of his buckwheat field, and the sun had set, and he was thinking of coming home, when he heard a rustle on the far side of the hedge. He looked over, and there stood the wolf as big as a calf against the

---

1 Ancient stone structure.
2 Small horse-drawn carriage.
3 Inn.
4 Cart or plow.
5 Werewolves.

horizon, its tongue out, and its eyes glaring like marsh-fires. Mon Dieu! catch me going over the marais[1] to-night. Why, what could two men do if they were attacked by that wolf-fiend?"

"It is tempting Providence," said one of the elders of the village; "no man must expect the help of God if he throws himself wilfully in the way of danger. Is it not so, M. le Curé? I heard you say as much from the pulpit on the first Sunday in Lent, preaching from the Gospel."

"That is true," observed several, shaking their heads.

"His tongue hanging out, and his eyes glaring like marsh-fires!" said the confidant of Picou.

"Mon Dieu! if I met the monster, I should run," quoth another.

"I quite believe you, Cortrez; I can answer for it that you would," said the mayor.

"As big as a calf," threw in Picou's friend.

"If the loup-garou were *only* a natural wolf, why then, you see"—the mayor cleared his throat—"you see we should think nothing of it; *but*, M. le Curé, it is a fiend, a worse than fiend, a man-fiend,—a worse than man-fiend, a man-wolf-fiend."

"But what is the young monsieur to do?" asked the priest, looking from one to another.

"Never mind," said I, who had been quietly listening to their patois, which I understood. "Never mind; I will walk back by myself, and if I meet the loup-garou I will crop his ears and tail, and send them to M. le Maire with my compliments."

A sigh of relief from the assembly, as they found themselves clear of the difficulty.

"Il est Anglais,"[2] said the mayor, shaking his head, as though he meant that an Englishman might face the devil with impunity.

A melancholy flat was the marais, looking desolate enough by day, but now, in the gloaming, tenfold as desolate. The sky was perfectly clear, and of a soft, blue-grey tinge; illumined by the new moon, a curve of light approaching its western bed. To the horizon reached a fen,[3] blacked with pools of stagnant water, from which the frogs kept up an incessant trill through the summer

---

1 Swamp or marsh.
2 He is English.
3 Swamp or marsh.

night. Heath and fern covered the ground, but near the water grew dense masses of flag and bulrush,[1] amongst which the light wind sighed wearily. Here and there stood a sandy knoll, capped with firs, looking like black splashes against the grey sky; not a sign of habitation anywhere; the only trace of men being the white, straight road extending for miles across the fen.

That this district harboured wolves is not improbable, and I confess that I armed myself with a strong stick at the first clump of trees through which the road dived.

This was my first introduction to were-wolves, and the circumstance of finding the superstition still so prevalent, first gave me the idea of investigating the history and the habits of these mythical creatures.

I must acknowledge that I have been quite unsuccessful in obtaining a specimen of the animal, but I have found its traces in all directions. And just as the palæontologist has constructed the labyrinthodon[2] out of its footprints in marl,[3] and one splinter of bone, so may this monograph be complete and accurate, although I have no chained were-wolf before me which I may sketch and describe from the life.

The traces left are indeed numerous enough, and though perhaps like the dodo or the dinormis,[4] the were-wolf may have become extinct in our age, yet he has left his stamp on classic antiquity, he has trodden deep in Northern snows, has ridden rough-shod over the mediævals, and has howled amongst Oriental sepulchres. He belonged to a bad breed, and we are quite content to be freed from him and his kindred, the vampire and the ghoul. Yet who knows! We may be a little too hasty in concluding that he is extinct. He may still prowl in Abyssinian forests, range still over Asiatic steppes, and be found howling dismally in some padded room of a Hanwell or a Bedlam.[5]

In the following pages I design to investigate the notices of were-wolves to be found in the ancient writers of classic antiquity,

---

1 Wetland plants.
2 Amphibian dinosaur.
3 Mud found on the bottom of a lake or river.
4 Extinct species of bird.
5 Insane asylums.

those contained in the Northern Sagas, and, lastly, the numerous details afforded by the mediæval authors. In connection with this I shall give a sketch of modern folklore relating to Lycanthropy.

It will then be seen that under the veil of mythology lies a solid reality, that a floating superstition holds in solution a positive truth.

This I shall show to be an innate craving for blood implanted in certain natures, restrained under ordinary circumstances, but breaking forth occasionally, accompanied with hallucination, leading in most cases to cannibalism. I shall then give instances of persons thus afflicted, who were believed by others, and who believed themselves, to be transformed into beasts, and who, in the paroxysms of their madness, committed numerous murders, and devoured their victims.

I shall next give instances of persons suffering from the same passion for blood, who murdered for the mere gratification of their natural cruelty, but who were not subject to hallucinations, nor were addicted to cannibalism.

I shall also give instances of persons filled with the same propensities who murdered and ate their victims, but who were perfectly free from hallucination.

FROM CHAPTER IX.

NATURAL CAUSES OF LYCANTHROPY.

WHAT I have related from the chronicles of antiquity, or from the traditional lore of the people, is veiled under the form of myth or legend; and it is only from Scandinavian descriptions of those afflicted with the wolf-madness, and from the trials of those charged with the crime of lycanthropy in the later Middle Ages, that we can arrive at the truth respecting that form of madness which was invested by the superstitious with so much mystery.

It was not till the close of the Middle Ages that lycanthropy was recognized as a disease; but it is one which has so much that is ghastly and revolting in its form, and it is so remote from all our ordinary experience, that it is not surprising that the casual observer should leave the consideration of it, as a subject isolated

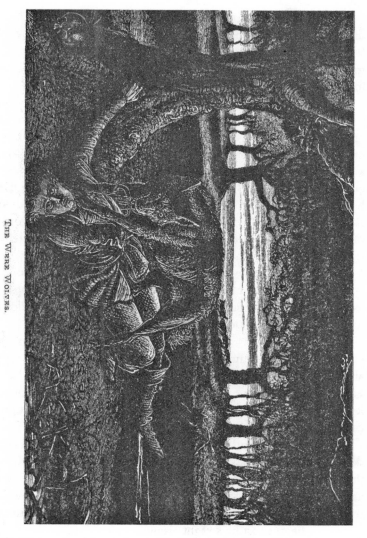

THE WERE WOLVES.

"The Were-wolves," frontispiece to *The Book of Were-Wolves: Being an Account of a Terrible Superstition*, by Sabine Baring-Gould (London: Smith, Elder, 1865).

and perplexing, and be disposed to regard as a myth that which the feared investigation might prove a reality.

In this chapter I purpose briefly examining the conditions under which men have been regarded as were-wolves.

Startling though the assertion may be, it is a matter of fact, that man, naturally, in common with other carnivora, is actuated by an impulse to kill, and by a love of destroying life.

It is positively true that there are many to whom the sight of suffering causes genuine pleasure, and in whom the passion to kill or torture is as strong as any other passion. Witness the number of boys who assemble around a sheep or pig when it is about to be killed, and who watch the struggle of the dying brute with hearts beating fast with pleasure, and eyes sparkling with delight. Often have I seen an eager crowd of children assembled around the slaughterhouses of French towns, absorbed in the expiring agonies of the sheep and cattle, and hushed into silence as they watched the flow of blood.

The propensity, however, exists in different degrees. In some it is manifest simply as indifference to suffering, in others it appears as simple pleasure in seeing killed, and in others again it is dominant as an irresistible desire to torture and destroy.

This propensity is widely diffused; it exists in children and adults, in the gross-minded and the refined, in the well-educated and the ignorant, in those who have never had the opportunity of gratifying it, and those who gratify it habitually, in spite of morality, religion, laws, so that it can only depend on constitutional causes.

The sportsman and the fisherman follow a natural instinct to destroy, when they make war on bird, beast, and fish: the pretence that the spoil is sought for the table cannot be made with justice, as the sportsman cares little for the game he has obtained, when once it is consigned to his pouch. The motive for his eager pursuit of bird or beast must be sought elsewhere; it will be found in the natural craving to extinguish life, which exists in his soul. Why does a child impulsively strike at a butterfly as it flits past him? He cares nothing for the insect when once it is beaten down at his feet, unless it be quivering in its agony, when he will watch it with interest. The child strikes at the fluttering creature because it has *life* in it, and he has an instinct within him impelling him to destroy life wherever he finds it.

Parents and nurses know well that children by nature are cruel, and that humanity has to be acquired by education. A child will gloat over the sufferings of a wounded animal till his mother bids him "put it out of its misery." An unsophisticated child would not dream of terminating the poor creature's agonies abruptly, any more than he would swallow whole a bon-bon till he had well sucked it. Inherent cruelty may be obscured by after impressions, or may be kept under moral restraint; the person who is constitutionally a Nero,[1] may scarcely know his own nature, till by some accident the master passion becomes dominant, and sweeps all before it. A relaxation of the moral check, a shock to the controlling intellect, an abnormal condition of body, are sufficient to allow the passion to assert itself.

As I have already observed, this passion exists in different persons in different degrees.

In some it is exhibited in simple want of feeling for other people's sufferings. This temperament may lead to crime, for the individual who is regardless of pain in another, will be ready to destroy that other, if it suit his own purposes. Such an one was the pauper Dumollard, who was the murderer of at least six poor girls, and who attempted to kill several others. He seems not to have felt much gratification in murdering them, but to have been so utterly indifferent to their sufferings, that he killed them solely for the sake of their clothes, which were of the poorest description. He was sentenced to the guillotine, and executed in 1862.[2]

In others, the passion for blood is developed alongside with indifference to suffering.

Thus Andreas Bichel enticed young women into his house, under the pretence that he was possessed of a magic mirror, in which he would show them their future husbands; when he had them in his power he bound their hands behind their backs, and stunned them with a blow. He then stabbed them and despoiled them of their clothes, for the sake of which he committed the

---

1 Tyrannical Roman emperor who ruled 54-68 A.D.
2 A full account of this man's trial is given by one who was present, in *All the Year Round*, No. 162. [Baring-Gould's note.]

murders; but as he killed the young women the passion of cruelty took possession of him, and he hacked the poor girls to pieces whilst they were still alive, in his anxiety to examine their insides. Catherine Seidel he opened with a hammer and a wedge, from her breast downwards, whilst still breathing. "I may say," he remarked at his trial, "that during the operation I was so eager, that I trembled all over, and I longed to rive off a piece and eat it."

Andreas Bichel was executed in 1809.[1]

Again, a third class of persons are cruel and bloodthirsty, because in them bloodthirstiness is a raging insatiable passion. In a civilized country those possessed by this passion are forced to control it through fear of the consequences, or to gratify it upon the brute creation. But in earlier days, when feudal lords were supreme in their domains, there have been frightful instances of their excesses, and the extent to which some of the Roman emperors indulged their passion for blood is matter of history.

Gall gives several authentic instances of bloodthirstiness.[2] A Dutch priest had such a desire to kill and to see killed, that he became chaplain to a regiment that he might have the satisfaction of seeing deaths occurring wholesale in engagements. The same man kept a large collection of various kinds of domestic animals, that he might be able to torture their young. He killed the animals for his kitchen, and was acquainted with all the hangmen in the country, who sent him notice of executions, and he would walk for days that he might have the gratification of seeing a man executed.

In the field of battle the passion is variously developed; some feel positive delight in slaying, others are indifferent. An old soldier, who had been in Waterloo, informed me that to his mind there was no pleasure equal to running a man through the body, and that he could lie awake at night musing on the pleasurable sensations afforded him by that act.

Highwaymen are frequently not content with robbery, but manifest a bloody inclination to torment and kill. John Rosbeck, for instance, is well known to have invented and exercised the most atrocious cruelties, merely that he might witness the sufferings of

---

1 The case of Andreas Bichel is given in Lady Duff Gordon's *Remarkable Criminal Trials*. [Baring-Gould's note.]

2 GALL: *Sur les Fonctions du Cerveau*, tom. iv. [Baring-Gould's note.]

his victims, who were especially women and children. Neither fear nor torture could break him of the dreadful passion till he was executed.

Gall tells of a violin-player, who, being arrested, confessed to thirty-four murders, all of which he had committed, not from enmity or intent to rob, but solely because it afforded him an intense pleasure to kill.

Spurzheim[1] tells of a priest at Strasbourg, who, though rich, and uninfluenced by envy or revenge, from exactly the same motive, killed three persons.

Gall relates the case of a brother of the Duke of Bourbon, Condé, Count of Charlois, who, from infancy, had an inveterate pleasure in torturing animals: growing older, he lived to shed the blood of human beings, and to exercise various kinds of cruelty. He also murdered many from no other motive, and shot at slaters[2] for the pleasure of seeing them fall from the roofs of houses.

Louis XI of France[3] caused the death of 4,000 people during his reign; he used to watch their executions from a neighbouring lattice. He had gibbets placed outside his own palace, and himself conducted the executions.

It must not be supposed that cruelty exists merely in the coarse and rude; it is quite as frequently observed in the refined and educated. Among the former it is manifest chiefly in insensibility to the sufferings of others; in the latter it appears as a passion, the indulgence of which causes intense pleasure.

* * * * * *

The cases in which bloodthirstiness and cannibalism are united with insanity are those which properly fall under the head of Lycanthropy. The instances recorded in the preceding chapter point unmistakably to hallucination accompanying the lust for blood. Jean Grenier, Roulet,[4] and others, were firmly convinced that they had undergone transformation. A disordered condition of mind or body may produce hallucination in a form depending

---

1 *Doctrine of the Mind*, p. 158. [Baring-Gould's note.]
2 Laborer who specializes in building and repairing slate roofs.
3 King of France who reigned 1461-1483.
4 French serial killers who claimed to be werewolves.

on the character and instincts of the individual. Thus, an ambitious man labouring under monomania will imagine himself to be a king; a covetous man will be plunged in despair, believing himself to be penniless, or exult at the vastness of the treasure which he imagines that he has discovered. The old man suffering from rheumatism or gout conceives himself to be formed of china or glass, and the foxhunter tallyhos! at each new moon, as though he were following a pack. In like manner, the naturally cruel man, if the least affected in his brain, will suppose himself to be transformed into the most cruel and bloodthirsty animal with which he is acquainted.

The hallucinations under which lycanthropists suffered may have arisen from various causes. The older writers, as Forestus and Burton,[1] regard the were-wolf mania as a species of melancholy madness, and some do not deem it necessary for the patient to believe in his transformation for them to regard him as a lycanthropist.

In the present state of medical knowledge, we know that very different conditions may give rise to hallucinations.

In fever cases the sensibility is so disturbed that the patient is often deceived as to the space occupied by his limbs, and he supposes them to be preternaturally distended or contracted. In the case of typhus,[2] it is not uncommon for the sick person, with deranged nervous system, to believe himself to be double in the bed, or to be severed in half, or to have lost his limbs. He may regard his members as composed of foreign and often fragile materials, as glass, or he may so lose his personality as to suppose himself to have become a woman.

A monomaniac who believes himself to be some one else, seeks to enter into the feelings, thoughts, and habits of the assumed personality, and from the facility with which this is effected, he draws an argument, conclusive to himself, of the reality of the change. He thenceforth speaks of himself under the assumed character, and experiences all its needs, wishes, passions, and the like. The closer the identification becomes, the more confirmed

---

1 Robert Burton, *Anatomy of Melancholy* (1621). For more on Forestus, see Burton and Baring-Gould's chapter 5.

2 Severe infectious disease marked by a high fever.

is the monomaniac in his madness, the character of which varies with the temperament of the individual. If the person's mind be weak, or rude and uncultivated, the tenacity with which he clings to his metamorphosis is feebler, and it becomes more difficult to draw the line between his lucid and insane utterances. Thus Jean Grenier, who laboured under this form of mania, said in his trial much that was true, but it was mixed with the ramblings of insanity.

* * * * * *

Whatever may have been the cause of the hallucination, it is not surprising that the lycanthropist should have imagined himself transformed into a beast. The cases I have instanced are those of shepherds, who were by nature of their employment, brought into collision with wolves; and it is not surprising that these persons, in a condition liable to hallucinations, should imagine themselves to be transformed into wild beasts, and that their minds revert-ing to the injuries sustained from these animals, they should, in their state of temporary insanity, accuse themselves of the acts of rapacity committed by the beasts into which they believed them-selves to be transformed. It is a well-known fact that men, whose minds are unhinged, will deliver themselves up to justice, accus-ing themselves of having committed crimes which have actually taken place, and it is only on investigation that their self-accusation proves to be false; and yet they will describe the circumstances with the greatest minuteness, and be thoroughly convinced of their own criminality.

A Ballad of the Were-Wolf[1]

Rosamund Marriott Watson

*Rosamund Marriott Watson (1860-1911) published six books of poetry,
including* The Bird-Bride: A Volume of Ballads and Sonnets *(1889),*
A Summer Night, and Other Poems *(1891), and* Vespertilia, and
Other Verses *(1895). Watson was also a prolific journalist. She edited*
Sylvia's Journal *from 1893 to 1894 and contributed to several periodicals,
including the* Yellow Book, *the* Pall Mall Gazette, *and the* Athenæum.
*Watson's private life was unconventional for a Victorian woman. She was
twice divorced and gave birth to a child out of wedlock. Over the course
of her writing life, Watson published under a variety of names, including R. Armytage, Graham R. Tomson, and Rosamund Marriott Watson.
As a poet and journalist, Watson was closely associated with writers of
the Aesthetic movement, including Oscar Wilde, Richard Le Gallienne,
and Vernon Lee. Dialect poems were popular among writers at the fin de
siècle. Watson contributed to this body of work by editing a collection
of border ballads in 1888. In "A Ballad of the Were-Wolf," Watson uses
Scots dialect in order to recreate the mysterious tone, supernatural motifs,
and antique language associated with folklore.*

The gudewife sits i' the chimney-neuk,
   An' looks on the louping[2] flame;
The rain fa's chill, and the win' ca's shrill,
   Ere the auld gudeman comes hame.

"Oh, why is your cheek sae wan, gudewife?
   An' why do ye glower on me?
Sae dour ye luik i' the chimney-neuk,
   Wi' the red licht in your e'e!

---

1 From *A Summer Night, and Other Poems.* London: Methuen, 1891.
2 Leaping. *Loup* is also the French word for *wolf.*

330

"Yet this nicht should ye welcome me,
　This ae nicht mair than a',
For I hae scotched yon great grey wolf
　That took our bairnies twa.[1]

"'Twas a sair, sair[2] strife for my very life,
　As I warstled there my lane;[3]
But I'll hae her heart or e'er we part,
　Gin ever we meet again.

"An' 'twas ae sharp stroke o' my bonny knife
　That gar'd her haud awa';
Fu' fast she went out owre the bent[4]
　Wi'outen her right fore-paw.

"Gae tak' the foot o' the drumlie[5] brute,
　And hang it upo' the wa';
An' the next time that we meet, gudewife,
　The tane[6] of us shall fa'."

He's flung his pouch on the gudewife's lap,
　I' the firelicht shinin' fair,
Yet naught they saw o' the grey wolf's paw,
　For a bluidy hand lay there.

O hooly, hooly[7] rose she up,
　Wi' the red licht in her e'e,
Till she stude but a span frae the auld gudeman
　Whiles never a word spak' she.

But she stripped the claiths frae her lang richt arm,
　That were wrappit roun' and roun',
The first was white, an' the last was red;
　And the fresh bluid dreeped adown.

---

1 Two children.
2 Sore.
3 Wrestled alone.
4 Field.
5 Gloomy.
6 One.
7 Gently.

She stretchit him out her lang right arm,
 An' cauld as the deid stude he.
The flames louped bricht i' the gloamin' licht—
 There was nae hand there to see!

Illustrations for Clemence Housman's The Were-Wolf[1]

Laurence Housman

Laurence Housman (1865-1959) was a prolific writer and artist. He published two volumes of poetry, Green Arras *(1896) and* Spikenard *(1898); a series of plays, including* Pains and Penalties *(1910) and* Alice in Ganderland *(1911); as well as novels, including* John of Jingalo *(1912),* Trimblerigg *(1924), and* The Life of HRH the Duke of Flamborough *(1928). In addition to his literary accomplishments, Housman was also a talented artist. After moving to London with his sister, Clemence Housman, he studied at the Arts and Crafts School and at Miller's Lane City and Guilds Art School. In addition to exhibiting his work at the New English Art Club, the Baillie Gallery, and the Fine Art Society, Housman worked extensively as a book illustrator in the 1890s. He wrote and illustrated* The Green Gaffer *(1890), a fairy tale published in* Universal Review *that was praised by Oscar Wilde. He also provided illustrations for George Meredith's* Jump to Glory Jane *(1892) and Christina Rossetti's* Goblin Market *(1893). For his own collection of fairy tales,* The House of Joy *(1895), Housman collaborated with his sister Clemence, who created engravings based on his illustrations. They also collaborated on* All Fellows *(1896) and* The Field of Clover *(1898). In 1896, Clemence and Laurence completed their most significant collaborative project:* The Were-Wolf. *This richly illustrated volume was produced by John Lane at the Bodley Head, a press known for publishing aesthete writers such as Richard Le Gallienne and Oscar Wilde as well as a groundbreaking periodical,* The Yellow Book. *Laurence created illustrations based on Clemence's story, which was originally published in* Atalanta *(included in this volume). Clemence then created engravings based on Laurence's illustrations which were used to produce the published volume.*

---

1 London: John Lane, 1896.

Laurence Housman, frontispiece to *The Were-wolf*, by Clemence
Housman (London: John Lane, 1896).

Laurence Housman, "Rol's Worship," illustration from *The Were-wolf*, by Clemence Housman (London: John Lane, 1896), 10.

Laurence Housman, "White Fell's Escape," illustration from *The Were-wolf,* by Clemence Housman (London: John Lane, 1896), 62.

Laurence Housman, "The Race," illustration from *The Were-wolf*,
by Clemence Housman (London: John Lane, 1896), 82.

Laurence Housman, "The Finish," illustration from *The Were-wolf*, by Clemence Housman (London: John Lane, 1896), 102.

Laurence Housman, "Sweyn's Finding," illustration from *The Were-wolf*, by Clemence Housman (London: John Lane, 1896), 118.

Wolf-Madness (Lycanthropy)[1]

A. M. JUDD

A. M. Judd was a prolific novelist and journalist who wrote articles for a variety of periodicals, including London Society *and* Belgravia Magazine. *Judd's work demonstrates sustained interest in folklore and the occult, including articles on werewolves, mummies, and witchcraft, and novels such as* A Daughter of Lilith *(1899),* Pharaoh's Turquoise *(1906),* Lot's Wife *(1913), and* The White Vampire *(1914).*

PART I.

BY Wolf-madness is meant, not hydrophobia, which occasionally attacks wolves as well as other animals, but that far more terrible malady, which, in almost all nations, and in all ages, afflicted men and made them fancy themselves wolves, and act as such.

Half the world believed that certain persons had the power of changing themselves into beasts, and indeed the superstition is not wholly extinct in the present day. In parts of France the peasants still firmly believe in the *loups-garoux*, and will not pass their haunts after nightfall.

Wehr-wolves were called by different names in different places. The French called them *loups-garoux;* the Bretons,[2] *Bisclaveret;* in Normandy they were designated garwolves, and they were known in the Perigord[3] as *louléerous.* With regard to these latter, bastards were supposed to be obliged at each full moon to transform themselves into these beasts, and in the form of *louléerous* to pass the

---

1 *London Society* 72 (September 1897): 242-258.
2 Inhabitants of Brittany in northwestern France.
3 A region in southwestern France.

night ranging over the country, biting and devouring any animals, but more especially dogs, they might meet. Sometimes they were made ill in consequence of having eaten tough old hounds, and vomited up their undigested paws.

The belief in wehr-wolves has come down from the earliest times, from ancient mythology and classic fable. Ovid tells the story of Lycaon, king of Arcadia, who, to test the omniscience of Jupiter, served up for him a dish of human flesh, and was promptly punished by the god for his insolence, by being transformed into a wolf.

That there was a wide-spread superstition of lycanthropy, or wolf-madness, is undoubted, and the belief in a creature combining human intelligence with wolfish ferocity and demoniac strength, was especially strong and prevalent in the middle ages. To this day the idea is still cherished by peasants in remote and secluded parts of Europe.

There was a basis of truth on which the wehr-wolf superstition rested. The old Norse freebooters[1] were celebrated for the murderous frenzy, "Berseker[2] rage," which possessed them at times. The craving for blood and rapine, stimulated by their ravages in summer climes, was developed at home into a strange homicidal madness. When the fit was on them, they would go forth at night, dressed in the skins of wolves and bears, and crush the skulls, or cleave the backbones of any unfortunate belated traveller they might meet, whose blood they sometimes drank. In their frenzied excitement, they acquired superhuman strength and insensibility to pain, and, as they rushed about with glaring eyeballs, gnashing their teeth, foaming at the mouth, and howling like wild beasts, it is not strange that the terrified peasantry should have regarded them as veritable wehr-wolves. Great exhaustion and nervous depression followed these attacks. According to the Norse historians this "Berseker rage" was extinguished by baptism.

The belief in these transformations in the middle ages derived a new and terrible significance from its connection with witchcraft. The ancients regarded the subjects of metamorphoses with

---

1 Pirates.

2 Bearskin in Old Norse. The berserkers were warriors who worshipped Odin and wore wolf pelts or bearskins into battle.

superstitious reverence. Divine natures were believed to assume earthly forms, and human beings were supposed to assume, after death, the shapes of those animals their natures most resembled, but these mythological conceptions were degraded by the mediæval christians, into diabolical influences. The Church, jealous of miraculous powers exercised beyond its pale, denounced the wehr-wolf as a devil. Thus a person suspected of beast metamorphosis ran the double risk of losing both his soul and his life, of being anathematized[1] by the clergy, and then burnt at the stake. Ignorance of the phenomena of mental disease led to a belief that its victims were ministers of the Evil One, and even mere eccentricity was often fatal to its unfortunate possessor. These ideas were strengthened by some terrible instances of homicidal insanity, occasionally accompanied by cannibalism and lycanthropic hallucinations which were often ascribed to demoniac agency.

The saints were believed to have a power similar to that of the demons. Vereticus, king of Wales, was said to have been transformed into a wolf by St. Patrick, and another saint[2] doomed the members of an illustrious family in Ireland to become wolves for seven years, prowling among the bogs and forests, uttering mournful howls, and devouring the peasants' sheep to allay their hunger.

Though imprisoned in a lupine form, the unfortunate victims were believed to retain their human consciousness, and in some cases their voices, and to yearn for an alleviation of their condition.

The superstitious belief in lycanthropy is of very remote antiquity and its origin is involved in much obscurity. It pervaded Greece, Rome, Germany and other nations; even in England it was prevalent in the middle ages, and was supposed to have come down from the Chaldeans[3] and other nomadic people, who had unceasingly to defend their flocks from the attacks of wolves. The terror that those ferocious beasts spread by prowling at night round the folds proved favourable to malefactors, who, assuming the guise of furious wolves, were the better enabled to perpetrate acts of theft or vengeance.

This lycanthropy was a disease, and a very terrible one. The

---

1 Cursed.
2 Saint Natalis (447-563).
3 Babylonians.

victims of the hallucination that they were wehr-wolves were undoubted madmen who fully believed they were able to transform themselves into wolves. At the present day some of the inmates of lunatic asylums fancy they can turn themselves at will into beasts, and howl and gnash their teeth in decided wolfish fashion.

Sometimes the wehr-wolves were satisfied with rending and tearing sheep and drinking their blood, but in others this insane appetite took the still more horrible form of cannibalism. Animal flesh would not satisfy their dreadful cravings; human beings, generally children, falling victims to this frightfully depraved taste.

There is another revolting phase that this madness took. Occasionally persons were transformed into human hyenas. Their craving was not, as was that of lycanthropists, for fresh, warm human flesh, they preferred their tit-bits to have been kept some time, as game is hung in order to make it tender; in other words these hyena victims of the terrible malady preferred to dig the corpses out of the graveyards. They were seized with an irresistible desire to enter cemeteries and rifle the newly-made graves so that they might enjoy their gruesome repast.

Strangely enough, these human ghouls were sometimes found in the ranks of the upper classes, unlike the majority of those who killed their victims; these latter being, for the greater part, composed of the most poverty-stricken, ignorant and degraded, of a very low type of intellectual and moral development.

So lately as 1849, one of these ghouls was discovered in Paris. He was a French officer named Bertrand. Delicate and refined in appearance, he was beloved by his comrades for his generous and cheerful qualities. He was, however, of retiring habits, and occasionally subject to fits of depression; but no one had any idea of his ghoulish propensities till they were brought to light.

In the autumn of 1848 several of the cemeteries in the neighbourhood of Paris were found to have been entered during the night, and some of the graves rifled.

It was at first supposed that wild beasts were the perpetrators of these outrages; but footprints in the soft earth showed that it was a man.

Close watch was kept in Père la Chaise,[1] and the outrages there ceased. But in the following winter other cemeteries were ravaged.

It was not until the March of 1849 that the depredator[2] was discovered by means of a spring gun, which had been set in the cemetery of St. Parnasse. One night it went off, and the watchers rushed to the spot, just in time to see a dark figure in a military cloak leap over the wall and disappear in the darkness, but not without leaving traces behind; there were marks of blood and a fragment of blue cloth, and these were the means of bringing the guilt home to Bertrand.

He was an officer in the 1st Infantry regiment; and when he was cured of his wound, he was tried by court-martial, and sentenced to a year's imprisonment. He said that the madness suddenly came upon him one day when, walking in a cemetery, he saw a grave not yet filled in, and a spade near at hand. He soon dragged the corpse out and hacked it about with the spade. After this he visited the cemeteries at night, and dug up various corpses, principally women and little girls, and mutilated them in a horrible manner, some he chopped up with the spade, others he ripped and tore with his teeth and nails, rending the flesh from the bones. Sometimes he tore the mouth open, and rent the face back to the ears; he opened the stomachs, pulled off the limbs, and scattering the pieces around, rolled among the fragments. He used to dig up the bodies of men also, but never felt any inclination to mutilate them; it was female corpses he used to delight in rending.

It was excess in drinking that first brought on this horrible madness, and after these accesses of diabolical ghoulishness he would fall into fits of utter exhaustion and helplessness, when, after crawling to some place of concealment he would lie prone on the ground for hours, no matter what the weather might be, unable to stir or rise. It is not stated whether he went on with his ghoul's work after he was liberated from the year's imprisonment to which he was sentenced.

Bertrand's case shows how the brute still underlies the polish

---

1 A cemetery in Paris.
2 Plunderer.

of civilization. He was not accounted mad, yet these fits of cannibalism must have been due to some form of insanity, and he seemed totally unable to control his dreadful appetite.

Somehow, much more horrible interest appears to centre on these nineteenth-century miscreants, such as Bertrand and Swiatek, than on those of former and remoter ages. There might have been exaggeration and misstatements about the ancient men-beasts, but there could be none about their modern prototypes.

Ghouls and vampires have some connection with lycanthropists, for they were supposed in the daytime to be able to turn themselves into wolves or hyenas, while on moonlight nights they would steal among the tombs, and burrowing into them with their long nails, they disinterred the bodies of the dead ere the first streak of dawn compelled them to retire from their unhallowed feast.

To such an extent did the fear of ghouls extend in Brittany, that it was customary to keep lamps burning during the night in churchyards, so that the witches might be deterred from venturing, under cover of darkness, to violate the graves. It was supposed that troops of female ghouls used to appear upon battlefields unearthing the hastily buried bodies of the soldiers and devouring the flesh off their bones.

That the belief in vampires is not extinct in the present day, the following, which appeared in the *Standard* of May 11th, 1893, will show. "Eleven peasants in the Polish village of Muszina, in Galicia, actuated by a superstition that the recent frosts were the work of a vampire which had entered into an old man who had lately been buried, opened the grave, beheaded the body, and pierced the heart with a stake. They were all arrested."

There was a very ghastly idea in Normandy, that the *loup-garou* was sometimes a metamorphosis forced upon the body of a damned person, who, after being tormented in his grave, worked his way out of it. It was supposed that he first devoured the cere-cloth[1] which enveloped his face, then his moans and muffled howls rang from the tomb through the gloom of night, the earth of the grave began to heave, and at last, having torn his way up, with

---

1 Cloth wrapped around a corpse before burial.

a scream, surrounded by a phosphorescent glare, and exhaling a fœtid odour, he burst away as a wolf.

Sometimes the transformed was supposed to be a white dog that haunted churchyards. With regard to this latter superstition, at this day in some country places in England, the farmers hold white animals to be unlucky, and will not choose white horses, cats or dogs, and consider it an omen of misfortune if they come across a white hare or rabbit. Some two or three years ago the writer was in Devonshire, and near the place where he took up his temporary abode was a very picturesque-looking churchyard. One moonlight evening, all unconscious of there being anything unusual in it, he announced his intention of sitting there for an hour or so before turning in, there being a magnificent view over a long stretch of sea, the church being built on the edge of the cliff. The landlady, a prosaic enough looking old woman, one would think, threw up her hands in protestation.

"You surely wouldn't do anything so rash, sir," she said.

"Why not?"

"Because," and she lowered her voice to an awed whisper, "it's haunted."

"Indeed?"

"Yes, sir; it's haunted by the ghost of——"

Oh! shades of wehr-wolves, *loups-garoux*, bear-men or other ferocious creatures, shiver in your graves and hide your diminished heads before the terrible monster the landlady's imagination conjured up. This evil thing that had the power to work untold harm was nothing more nor less than the ghost of a "white rabbit."

This was too much for the writer's risible[1] nerves, and he disgusted the landlady, not only by a peal of laughter, but also by making a point of going every night during the remainder of his stay to the haunted churchyard. It is needless to add that the formidable ghost never gratified him by making its appearance.

The earliest mention of wehr-wolves is to be found among the traditions and in the mythology of the Scandinavians. The wolf is frequently mentioned in the Edda.[2] There is Fenris, the offspring

---

1 Laughter-producing.

2 The *Prose Edda* by Snorri Sturluson (1179-1241).

of Loki, the Evil Principle, an enormous and appalling wolf. The ancient Scandinavians believed that he will continue to cause great mischief to humanity until the Last Day, when, after a fearful combat, he will devour Odin;[1] not content with this, he will devour the sun, but will in his turn, be killed by Vidar.

There are also two wolves, one of which pursues the sun, and the other the moon, and one day both these orbs will be caught and devoured by them; probably one of these is confounded with Fenris, for two wolves would scarcely devour one sun, unless they divided it in halves.

Of the origin of these wolves the Edda tells that "a hag dwells in a wood to the east of Midgard,[2] this is called J'arnvid, or the Iron Wood, and is the abode of a race of witches called J'arnvidjur."

This old hag is the mother of many gigantic sons, who are all of them wolf-shaped. The most formidable of these is named Mánagarm; he will be filled with the life-blood of men who draw near their end, and will swallow up the moon, and stain the heavens and the earth with blood. Then shall the sun grow dim (preparatory to being devoured) and the winds howl tumultuously to and fro. The snow will fall from the four corners of the world. The stars will vanish from the heavens. The tottering mountains will crumble to pieces; the sea will rush upon the land; and the great serpent, advancing to the shore will inundate the air and water with floods of venom. Then will follow "the twilight of the Gods"—the end of the world.

It may not be out of place here to mention that that apocryphal monster, the dragon, was by many affirmed to be the offspring of an eagle and a she-wolf. An old writer[3] declared that "the dragon had the beake and wings of an eagle, a serpente's taile, the feete of a wolfe, and a skin speckled and partie-coloured like a serpente." He adds the following extraordinary statement, "Neither can it *open the eyelids*, and it liveth in caves."

Olaus Magnus,[4] Archbishop of Upsal, and Metropolitan of Sweden in the sixteenth century, wrote a great deal on the subject

1 Old Norse god, father of Thor.
2 According to Norse mythology, the part of the world inhabited by humans.
3 Leo Africanus, *The History and Description of Africa* (1550).
4 Swedish historian and ecclesiastic who lived from 1490 to 1558.

of wehr-wolves. He relates, that in the northern parts, at Christmas, there is a great gathering of these men-wolves, who, during the night, rage with such fierceness against mankind, for they are much more savage than natural wolves, that the inhabitants suffer infinite miseries. They attack houses, break open doors, destroy the inmates, and going to the cellars, drink amazing quantities of ale and mead, leaving the empty barrels heaped one on another. Somewhere in those wild northern regions, there was once a wall, belonging to a castle which had been destroyed; and here the wehr-wolves were wont to assemble at a given time and exercise themselves in trying to leap over the wall. The fat ones that could not succeed were flogged by their captains. Olaus asserts that great men and members of the chief nobility of the land belonged to this singular confraternity. The change was effected by mumbling certain words and drinking a cup of ale to a man-wolf. It was necessary that the transformation should take place in some secret cellar or private wood, and the wehr-wolves could change to and fro as often as they pleased. It was not always, however, that the man-wolf could change his shape in time to save his life.

There is a story told of a Russian Archduke, who seized a sorcerer, named Lycaon (perhaps a descendant of the Arcadian king), and commanded him to change himself into a wolf. The enchanter obeyed; not thinking of treachery, he crouched down, muttering incantations, and straightway became a wolf, with glaring eyes, grinning jaws, and raging so fearfully that the keepers could scarcely hold him. By way of having a little sport, the Archduke set two ferocious hounds upon him, and the unfortunate Lycaon was torn to pieces before he could resume his human form.

Some of the lycanthropists felt no uneasiness during the change, but others were afflicted with great pain and horror, while the hair was breaking out of their skin even before they were thoroughly changed.

Some could change themselves whenever they wished, others were transformed twice a year, at Christmas and Midsummer, at which times they grew savage, and were seized with a desire to converse with wolves in the woods. Many of these wehr-wolves bore marks of wounds and scars on their faces and bodies which had been inflicted on them by dogs or men when in their lupine form.

Wehr-wolves were distinguished from natural wolves by having no tails, and by their eyes; for these latter never changed, they were always human. The salve, which in some places was supposed to work the change, was composed of gruesome ingredients, in which the fat of newly-born strangled infants, the marrow of malefactors collected at the foot of the gibbet,[1] the blood of bats, toads and owls, the grease of sows, wolves and weasels, mixed with belladonna,[2] aconite,[3] parsley, poppy, hemlock, combined with various other noxious ingredients, and must have formed a delectable compound.

That lycanthropy was known as a disease is evident, from some of the old writers speaking of it: "The infected," says one of them, "imitate wolves, and think themselves such, leaping out of their beds and running wild about the fields at night, worrying the flocks, and snarling like a dog. They lurk about the sepulchres by day with pale looks, hollow eyes, thirsty tongues, and exulcerated[4] bodies. They have a black, ugly and fearful look."

It is supposed that Nebuchadnezzar[5] was attacked with this kind of madness when he groveled about on all fours and ate grass like the beasts.

So late as the reign of James the First,[6] an Englishman, Bishop Hall, traveling in Germany, related that he went through a certain wood that was haunted, not only by freebooters, but by wolves and witches (although these last are oft-times but one). He saw there a boy, half of whose face had been devoured by a witch-wolf, yet so as that the ear was rather cut than bitten off.

At Limburgh[7] the Bishop saw one of these creatures executed; the wretched woman was put on the wheel, and confessed in her tortures that she had devoured two-and-forty children in her wolf-form.

Other authorities state that wehr-wolves were always at enmity

---

1 Gallows.
2 Deadly nightshade, a poisonous flower.
3 Monkshood, a poisonous flower.
4 Blistered.
5 Ancient Babylonian king.
6 King of England (1566-1625).
7 A region located on the border of Belgium and the Netherlands.

with witches. There is a tale told of a countryman who put up at the house of a jovial bailiff, drank too much, and was left to have his sleep out on the floor. The next morning, a horse was found dead in the paddock,[1] cut in two with a scythe.[2] In answer to questions, the guest admitted that he was a wehr-wolf, and that he had hunted a witch about the field. She had taken refuge under the horse, and in aiming at her he had unintentionally divided the animal in halves.

PART II.

Many are the stories related of wehr-wolves; but they differ somewhat according to the locality from which they come. Thus, there are many versions of the following.

A nobleman was traveling with his retainers; and one night they found themselves in a thick wood, far from all human habitations. They were hungry, for they had no provisions with them and did not know what to do. One of the servants, however, told them not to be surprised at anything that might happen. He then went into a dark part of the forest, and presently a wolf was seen to run past, and soon came back with a sheep it had slain, which the company were very grateful for. Then the wolf went to the dark spot, and the servant emerged from there in his proper shape. He was a wehr-wolf.

Another account says that it was a slave who turned himself into a wolf, but unfortunately the dogs set upon him and tore out one of his eyes, so that afterwards he was blind of one eye.

Again, a tale says it was a gentleman who transformed himself because a lady wished to see the change, and lost his eye in consequence.

There are numerous instances of wolves having been wounded, and the next day human beings being found wounded in exactly the same place, thus clearly demonstrating the fact that they were wehr-wolves.

In one case a nobleman had a beautiful wife; whether he had

---

1 Pasture.

2 A hand tool used to mow grass.

tired of her is not stated, but the sequel looks like it, and that he took this means of getting rid of her. A friend came to stay at the castle, who went out hunting. On his return he informed the nobleman that a huge wolf had attacked him, but that he had succeeded in cutting off one of its forepaws which he brought home with him. On taking it out of the cloth in which he had wrapped it, he was horrified to see, not a wolf's paw, but a delicate white hand, having jewels on the fingers. The nobleman instantly recognised the rings as his wife's. Going to her room he found her looking very ill and carefully keeping her right hand covered up. Insisting on seeing it, he soon discovered the bleeding wrist, and knew for certain that his wife was a wehr-wolf. This unfortunate lady was tried and executed, falling a victim to her husband's dislike.

In one version, a man going home in the dark was attacked by a wolf, but managed to cut off a paw, which, on reaching his house, he found was a human hand. In a day or two he discovered that a young man of his acquaintance had lost his right hand that very night, which was proof-positive that he was the wehr-wolf who had attacked him.

There is a story related that a nobleman traveling with his servants in some part of France came upon an old beggar-man who was toiling along under a heavy wallet.[1] One of the servants good naturedly offered to carry it, an offer which was accepted. The man felt curious to know what was in the bag, and opening it saw a wolf skin. A desire to put it on came over him, and doing so, he was instantly transformed into a wolf, and rushed about snarling and howling, and trying to attack everyone near him. The dogs had to be set on him, and he only succeeded in getting out of the wolf skin with his life, having received several wounds from the dogs. This man averred that the nature of a wolf seemed to come upon him with its skin, and he had a desire to rend anyone he could seize. Of course they looked at once for the original owner of the skin, the beggar, but the old *loup-garou* had disappeared and never came to claim his property.

In different countries these metamorphoses were effected by different means. A Swedish tradition relates that a cottager named

---

1 Knapsack.

Lasse, having gone into the forest to fell a tree, neglected to cross himself and say his Paternoster.[1] By this neglect a troll was enabled to change him into a wolf. His wife, who mourned his loss for many years, was told by a beggar-woman, to whom she had been kind, that she would see her husband again as he was not dead, but roaming the forest as a wolf. That very evening, as she was in her pantry putting away a joint of meat, a wolf put its paws on the window-sill, and looked sorrowfully at her. "Ah!" said she, "if I knew that thou wert my husband, I would give thee this meat." At that instant the wolf skin fell off, and her husband stood before her in the same old clothes which he had on on the day of his disappearance.

In parts of Germany, those who wished to become wehr-wolves, obtained the power by drinking a nauseous draught from the hands of one already initiated.

In France, usually, the change was made by rubbing with some unguent,[2] generally of demoniacal origin. Others asserted that wolf skins given them by devils, had the quality of transforming those who put them on into ferocious animals themselves.

Mostly the *loup-garou* was able to re-transform himself back into his human shape at his own will by such expedients as plunging into water, rolling over and over in the dew, or resuming his clothes, which were usually hidden in some thicket while the wehr-wolves were on their runs; but there were cases where the victims were unable to escape from their lupine form for periods ranging from a month to seven years. These were generally victims of the hatred of relatives who took this method of punishing those who were obnoxious to them.

It was said that jilted mistresses and deserted wives used to bribe witches to turn their faithless swains or husbands into wolves for the term of seven years. These wolves, however, were not credited with a taste for human flesh.

Some of those who were executed as lycanthropists, declared in their confessions, that no sooner had they put on the wolf-skin received from a demon, than their whole nature seemed to change.

---

1 The Lord's prayer.
2 Ointment.

Their teeth felt on edge to bite and rend, the bloodthirst awoke in them, and they would dart forth from hut or brake[1] or thicket, wherever, in fact, the metamorphoses had taken place, and traverse meadows, forests, plains and marshes, howling in a frightful manner until they met a victim, when they would rend him with teeth and claws, preparatory to making a meal of him. In great fear were these wehr-wolves held, and terrible tales were told of them and the bloody scenes and unhallowed deeds that were supposed to be enacted in their nocturnal haunts.

Real wolves in severe winters have been known to come into villages and kill children, and cases have been heard of, when terribly pressed by hunger, their invading burial grounds, and disinterring the dead, and occasionally, perhaps, their depredations have been put down wrongfully to some unfortunate being suspected of being a *loup-garou*; but unfortunately there was only too much truth in the stories told of some of these human wolves and their propensities for cannibalism.

These insane creatures actually believed that they turned into wolves, though no trustworthy person had ever seen the transformation. Some of them ran about on all-fours, and devoured with eagerness any offal[2] that came in their way.

As with witchcraft, so with lycanthropy.

When the persecution against wehr-wolves was disconnected and fitful, isolated cases only were heard of; but when, towards the end of the sixteenth century, something like a crusade was preached, and priestly anathemas were hurled against it, lycanthropy alarmingly increased. Nothing else being talked about, hundreds of weak heads were turned, silly persons accused themselves of the crime and attempted to play wolf, though somehow or other they could never manage the transformation to the satisfaction of their neighbours. Not to be done however, some of them got over this difficulty by asserting that they *wore their bristles inside their skin.*

The folly and ignorance of our ancestors in those days must have been prodigious. Look at the scientific treatises they wrote to

---

1 Brush.
2 Entrails or other waste products.

prove witchcraft true, and now this palpable lie took in these same learned persons, and a very animated discussion ensued upon the why and the wherefore of this extraordinary fact. The *savants*,[1] with their usual discernment propounded a great many ingenious theories to account for so remarkable a circumstance, theories which satisfied everybody, except those who had counter-theories of their own. It must have been an edifying sight, these grave and reverend *seignors*,[2] explaining to their own and everybody else's satisfaction how it was that the bristles of the invisible wolf-pelts could be worn under the human skin.

In 1598, a tailor of Chalons[3] was sentenced to be burned alive for lycanthropy. He used to decoy children into his shop, or waylay them in the woods at dusk. After tearing them with his teeth and killing them, he dressed their flesh like ordinary meat, and devoured it with great relish. A cask full of bones was found in his house, but the number of his victims is unknown.

Peter Bourgot, a shepherd of Besançon,[4] having lost his sheep in a storm, recovered them by the aid of the devil, whom he agreed to serve, and was transformed into a wolf by being smeared with a salve. He confessed that he had often killed and eaten children and even grown persons. On one of his raids, a boy whom he attacked screamed so loudly that he was obliged to return to his clothes, and smear himself again in order to escape detection.

One Roulet was a wretched beggar, whose idiotic mind was completely mastered by his cannibal appetite. The first knowledge of his depraved taste was obtained by some countrymen, who, while passing a wild and lonely spot near Caude,[5] found the mutilated corpse of a boy of fifteen. On their approach, two wolves which had been rending the body ran off. Following their tracks, the men came upon a half-naked man crouching in the bushes. His hair and beard were long and straggling, and his nails, which were the length of claws, were clotted with blood and shreds of human flesh. Roulet acknowledged that he had killed the boy, and would

---

1 Wise men.
2 Lords.
3 Châlons-en-Champagne, a city in northeastern France.
4 A city in eastern France.
5 A city in southern France.

have devoured the body completely had it not been for the arrival of the men. He said, at his trial, that he transformed himself into a wolf by using an ointment his parents had given him; and added, that the wolves that had been seen leaving the corpse were his brother and cousin. There is no doubt this man killed and ate several children, under the belief that he was a wolf. He was sentenced to death, but afterwards placed in a madhouse.

Another lycanthropist, Jacques Raollet, was a native of Maumusson, near Nantes.[1] His hair floated over his shoulders like a mane, his eyes were buried in his head, his brows knit, his nails excessively long, and he smelt so strong that nobody cared to go near him. This wehr-wolf had a propensity for which a good many persons, instead of finding fault with him, would applaud him in the present day; he confessed that it was a frequent custom of his to devour lawyers, bailiffs and others of the same sort, though he avowed that their flesh was so tough that he could never digest it.

Raollet was captured by the aid of dogs. During his examination he asked a gentleman who was present if he did not remember once to have discharged his arquebuss[2] at three wolves.

The gentleman, a noted sportsman, admitted that he had done so, upon which Raollet declared that he was one of those wolves, and if they had not been put to flight by the peppering they had received on that occasion they would have devoured a woman who was working in a field close by. He was condemned to death by the Parliament of Angers[3] and was burned at the stake.

Though wolves were the principal animals into which men were supposed to be transformed, there were stories of other metamorphoses into bears, cats and hares. According to one tale a man was cleaving wood in his courtyard, when he was suddenly attacked by three very large and ferocious cats. He defended himself by his prayers and his axe, and finally drove off the animals, who were considerably the worse for the combat. What was the man's astonishment shortly afterwards to be hauled before a magistrate on the charge of grievously wounding three honourable matrons. The ferocious cats were ladies of high rank, the affair was hushed

---

1 A city in northwestern France.
2 Portable gun.
3 A city in northwestern France.

up, and the man was dismissed under a strict injunction to secrecy on forfeit of his life.

In 1661, in Poland, in the forest of Lithuania, some huntsmen perceived a great many bears together, and in the midst of them two of small size, which exhibited some affinity to the human shape. Their curiosity excited, the men with considerable difficulty, for the creature defended itself with its teeth and claws, managed to capture one of these small bears. It ran about on all fours, the skin and hair were white, the limbs well proportioned and strong, the visage fair and the eyes blue, but the creature could not speak, and its inclinations were altogether brutish. It appeared to be about nine years old. This bear-child was shown to the king and queen. It was christened by an archbishop in the name of Joseph Ursin, the Queen of Poland standing godmother, and the French Ambassador, godfather. Attempts were made to tame Joseph, but with not much success. He could not be taught to speak, though there was no apparent defect in his tongue; nor could he be induced to throw aside his fierceness, or to wear clothes or shoes, or anything on his head; however, he learned to walk upright on his feet and go where he was bidden. He liked raw flesh. Sometimes he would steal to the woods and there suck the sap from the trees after he had torn off the bark with his nails.

One day it was observed that he being in a wood when a bear had killed two men, that ferocious beast came to him, and instead of harming him, fondled him and licked his face and body.

Whether this creature was really a human child stolen by bears in its infancy, is not stated, nor what eventually became of him.

There have been accounts too, but whether trustworthy or not, it is impossible to say, of baboons carrying off children and bringing them up with their own young, and these children grew up with all the characteristics of their baboon foster parents save that their skins were not hairy. When found and taken back to their rightful place among men, they pined, were miserable, and seized the first opportunity of returning to the haunts of the wild men of the woods whose natures seemed to be in affinity with their own.

It is also said that Romulus and Remus[1] have had modern

---

1 Twin brothers, mythological founders of Rome, who were said to have been suckled by a she-wolf.

counterparts. A case occurred in Oude[1] not many years ago.

This story is vouched for as being absolutely true. It was some-where about 1840 that a child of eighteen months old was missed by its parents. It was supposed that wolves had devoured it. About seven years after a man shooting in the jungle saw a she-wolf with several cubs, one of these had the appearance of a boy running about on all fours. With considerable difficulty he captured it, for the she-wolf showed fight. The animal snarled and growled like a wolf, and tried to bite its captor. It was exhibited at Lucknow[2] and caused considerable sensation. It was eventually handed over to one of the authorities (an English officer) who had a cage made for it, as it was dangerous to let it loose. None doubted that it was a human being, though it never stood erect, or uttered any sound save a growl or hoarse bark. It would only eat raw flesh, and when clothes were made for it, it tore them to pieces. A rank wolfish smell issued from the pores of its skin, which was covered with thin short hair. Among the crowds who came to see the monster was the woman who had lost the child seven years before. To her horror she discovered by certain marks upon it that it was her own missing offspring. Every effort was made to tame him but without effect. He pined away and died in about a year after his capture.

In 1849 at the little hamlet of Polomyja, in Austrian Galicia,[3] a white-bearded venerable man might have been seen sitting at the porch of a church asking alms of the poor woodcutters who made up the population. This beggar, whose name was Swiatek, eked out his subsistence by the charity of the villagers and the sale of small pinchbeck[4] ornaments and beads. Several children disappeared about this time, but nobody connected their disappearance with the venerable looking Swiatek, and as the wolves happened to be particularly ravenous that winter, it was supposed they had eaten them, and the exasperated villagers killed several. But a horrible discovery was made in the following May. An innkeeper lost two ducks and suspected Swiatek of being the thief. To satisfy himself he went to the beggar's cottage. The smell of roasted meat which

---

1 Belgian city.
2 A city in northern India.
3 A village which is today located in southern Poland.
4 Cheap, non-precious.

greeted his nostrils when he entered confirmed his suspicions. As he threw open the door he saw the beggar hide something under his long robe. The innkeeper at once seized Swiatek by the throat and charged him with the theft, when, to his horror, he saw the head of a girl of fourteen drop from beneath the pauper's clothes.

He called the neighbours, and the old beggar, his wife, his daughter aged sixteen, and his son, aged five, were locked up. The hut was then thoroughly examined, and the mutilated remains of the poor girl were discovered, part being cooked. At his trial Swiatek stated that he and his family had eaten six persons. His children, however, declared that the number was much larger, and this testimony was confirmed by the discovery in the hut of four-teen different suits of clothes. For three years Swiatek had been indulging in this horrible propensity, which had suddenly sprung into existence by the following circumstance:—In 1846 he found amid the charred ruins of a Jewish tavern, the half-roasted corpse of its proprietor, who had perished in the flames. The half-starved beggar could not resist the desire to taste it, and having done so, the unnatural craving impelled him to gratify his depraved appetite by murder. The indignation against him was so great that he would have been torn in pieces by the populace only he anticipated their vengeance by hanging himself the first night of his confinement from the bars of the prison-window.

There is a romantic Breton story of a nobleman who used to transform himself.[1]

His wife discovered his secret, and possessed herself of his clothes while he was in the lupine state, thus preventing him from returning to his proper form. She then married a lover, and Bisclavaret lurked miserably in woods, longing in vain to shake off the brutish semblance that imprisoned him.

The king hunting one day pursued the man-wolf, and at last ran him down. He was about to kill the animal, when it seized his stirrup and appeared to implore his protection.

The king, greatly astonished, had him taken to court, where he became a great favourite, his manners were so gentle and dog-like.

But one day his faithless wife's husband came to court, when

---

1 "Bisclavret" by French poet Marie de France, written in the twelfth century.

Bisclavaret jumped savagely upon him and nearly killed him before he could be rescued by the attendants. Again the same thing happened, but on the faithless dame herself appearing Bisclavaret seized upon her and tore her nose from her face.

This incensed the king greatly, and he would have put the wolf to death, when an aged counselor perceiving some mystery, advised that the lady and the knight should be imprisoned until the truth should be extorted from them.

This was done and Bisclavaret's clothes being restored to him, he became a comely gentleman, who was taken into high favour. The wicked wife and her companion were banished from the land.

Instances might be multiplied by the score, but enough has been said to show that while wehr-wolves were a myth built up by superstition, Lycanthropy, or wolf-madness was no myth, but a dread and appalling reality.